Serendipity

Serendipity

FERN MICHAELS

BALLANTINE BOOKS • New York

Copyright © 1994 by Fern Michaels, Inc.

All rights reserved under International
and Pan-American Copyright Conventions.
Published in the United States by Ballantine Books, a division of Random
House, Inc., New York, and simultaneously in Canada by Random
House of Canada Limited, Toronto.

Library of Congress Cataloging-in-Publication Data
Michaels, Fern.
Serendipity / Fern Michaels.
p.   cm.
ISBN 0-345-39271-X
1. Women in business—Pennsylvania—Philadelphia—Fiction.   2. Married
women—Pennsylvania—Philadelphia—Fiction.   3. Divorce—Pennsylvania—
Philadelphia—Fiction.   4. Philadelphia (Pa.)—Fiction.   I. Title.
PS3563.I27S47   1994
813'.54—dc20   94-19693
                                                                    CIP

Text design by Debby Jay

Manufactured in the United States of America
First Edition: August 1994
10 9 8 7 6 5 4 3 2 1

Serendipity

Chapter 1

Jory Ryan—that's how she thought of herself now—finally gave into the tremors she'd been holding in check during the past hour, but still fought her tears back. The front she'd managed to put up for Ross when he'd asked for a divorce was the hardest thing she'd ever done, harder than going through the miscarriage, harder than going off alone, harder than living alone, working and going to night school. Harder than getting through her estranged father's funeral. But she'd done it, she thought. She'd not only persevered, but had prevailed, even when he'd tried to ease his own conscience by buying her off.

A day didn't go by that she didn't think of Ross Landers and the mistakes she'd made back in the beginning. Would she really have cried rape? Back then, she'd threatened Ross with it, but to this day she couldn't say yes or no with certainty. Back then she'd been a wild, incorrigible teenager, without a mother, whose father was away from home so much, she'd had all the latitude and freedom she wanted.

How badly she'd needed a mother; but her mother died giving birth to a baby brother, who also died—one year later, when she was seven. Since then, it seemed, she'd gotten into one scrape after another.

As a teenager she'd been a tease and a flirt. But she'd only gone all the way with one other boy, and only once, before she'd done it with Ross Landers, a dozen times. She would never forget the look on Ross's face when she told him she was pregnant. He'd said something so hateful, so vitriolic, she'd run from him, wanting to hide her shame. Afterward, Woo, Ross's best friend, had tried to console her, saying she should be patient, that Ross would do the right thing.

For three months she waited for Ross to do the right thing. She'd called Woo again, but he'd gone back to Lancaster; so instead she showed up on Ross's doorstep and told him she intended to have the baby, and if anyone asked why she wasn't married, she'd say he'd raped her. She'd gone back to her father's house then, and sat on the swing on the front porch, freezing. Ross arrived an hour later and, without emotion, told her to get in the car. They drove to Maryland and were married by a justice of the peace at eleven o'clock at night.

The following months, when she and Ross lived in a small house, were the most miserable of Jory's life. One night in particular stood out. She'd been three months pregnant, and feeling sick and out of sorts all day. She hadn't gone down to dinner, and at ten o'clock, when she was almost asleep, Ross came to her room and tried to make love to her. She'd done her best to help him, but he was incapable of sustaining an erection. He'd stared down at her, said she repulsed him, that she was nothing but a slut he'd had the misfortune to marry. He stormed from the room, and returned only after she'd miscarried.

Sick with humiliation, Jory packed her bags in the sixth month of her marriage and left. She hadn't said good-bye to Ross, and saw him only three times afterward. The last time was at her father's funeral, eighteen months ago. He'd been among the city employees who turned out to pay their final respects. He hadn't tried to speak to her then, nor had she tried to speak to him. Jory couldn't help but wonder what people thought about her and Ross. Did they think they were divorced, separated, strangers? She came to the conclusion they simply didn't care. She didn't care either.

"Driver, I changed my mind," Jory said now. "Turn around. I

want to go to Chestnut Hill. Gravers Lane, number sixteen." Going back to the house she'd grown up in couldn't be any more traumatic than what she'd just gone through with Ross.

Forty minutes later Jory paid the driver and got out of the taxi. The house was a Tudor, the yard overgrown, the trim on the windows in need of paint. She'd painted the front door a bright red as an act of defiance when she was sixteen, but she couldn't remember why now. She did recall her father telling her to strip off the paint and varnish the door. She told him to do it himself, and took his slap high on her cheekbone. She still carried the scar his college ring made with the fierce blow. Her hand moved to her cheek to touch the thin line her skillfully applied makeup covered.

Maybe it wasn't an act of defiance after all. Maybe she'd painted the door to bring some color into her life. At Christmastime the red door always seemed particularly festive. Now it was simply a red door with peeling paint. She felt like crying as she fit her old house key into the lock.

It was cool inside, the blinds drawn, the furniture covered with dusty white sheets. The rugs were rolled up against the wall, the floors gritty and dusty.

Tears rolled down Jory's cheeks as she walked from room to room, peeking under the dust covers. If there had just been one person in the whole world to love her, to care about her, she wouldn't be here right now.

She should sell the house, she thought, take the money and invest it in something that would give her a small income. The ten thousand dollars she'd received from her father's insurance was still sitting in the Mellon Bank, along with the three thousand he had always kept in his checking account. The same perverse streak that wouldn't allow her to spend Ross's money wouldn't allow her to spend her father's money either. She knew her father's car was in the garage. When she sold the house, she'd sell the car too.

She could live here if she wanted to, Jory thought. The two hundred dollars rent she was paying in Florida could go toward the taxes on this house. She could ask her boss to help her get a job at the *Philadelphia Democrat*. If she wanted to, that is. She could do a lot of things if she wanted to. But did she want to risk running into Ross and his family? She might have guts, but did she have enough to put herself through more heartache?

Jory was in her old room now, staring at the four-poster with the draped sheets. She thought of harems, jewels, and silk veils. This room should have been a sanctuary, but it wasn't. She'd really only slept and changed her clothes here. She couldn't remember what she did in this room when she was little. Did she play with blocks, have a rocking horse, dolls? She couldn't remember. She lifted the dust sheet on the bed. The mattress was pale blue and quilted, the tag at the bottom wilted and wrinkled. She smiled at the slight dip in the middle. She still slept in the middle of the bed. She let the sheet fall back. It was just a bed she used to sleep in.

Tears burned Jory's eyes when she opened dresser drawers, looked in the two closets. There should be treasures here, things she left behind. But there had been no treasures—except one. Damn, where was it? She yanked and pulled at the drawers, distinctly remembered thumb-tacking it to the back of one of them. God, let it be here, she prayed. Please, let it be here. And it was, a length of satin tied in knots, the binding from her childhood blanket. She literally swooned with feeling when she brought it up to her cheek. The one and only thing in the world that had ever given her comfort. So many times it had been drenched with tears. She couldn't count the times she woke up in the morning with the treasure pressed into her cheek. Now, her fingers worked the knots the way a nun would her rosary. How good it felt, how wonderfully comforting. She remembered each knot, big and small. She thought of each knot as a milestone in her life. Her eyes dry, her mouth grim, Jory added a last knot to the end of the satin.

"For my pending divorce," she said sadly.

Jory removed the dust cover from an oak rocking chair with a faded orange cushion and sat down.

If she did come back, she thought, and lived here in Chestnut Hill, she might be able to avoid Ross. Financially the move made sense. She would have a car, once she replaced the tires and got it tuned up. She could make the house into the home she never really had. She could probably take off from now till the end of the year and get the place cleaned up. She could take a sewing class and make new covers for the furniture; there was a night class for *everything*. There was an old treadle sewing machine somewhere in the house. She could make bright cushions, valances instead of drapes—those poofy kind she'd seen in magazines, which allowed for a lot of sunlight. She could shampoo the carpets herself, wax the floors, clean the windows. And if she decided to leave Florida, she would get severance pay, and maybe she could even collect unemployment insurance. She had eight hundred dollars in a savings account, and would get back her rental deposit and the deposits on her utilities. A thousand dollars might see her through the worst of things. And if she absolutely had to, she could dip into her father's insurance money.

Outside in the afternoon sunshine, Jory looked around. "I'm coming back," she said aloud, saluting the bright red door before she started down the hill to Germantown Avenue to catch a cab.

Three weeks later she moved into the house in Chestnut Hill.

Chapter 2

"There is no way in hell I will allow you to turn this magazine into a *sewer* publication. I absolutely forbid it, Justine!"

Justine Landers's lips curled into a sneer, and when she replied, her voice was as contemptuous as her gaze. "Do I need to remind you that *I* am the publisher of this magazine? I even have a contract to prove it. It was my wedding present. Remember, Jasper dear?"

"You might be the publisher, but I own this magazine, just as my father and his father before him owned it. One day Ross will own it. Until this moment it has been a publication to be proud of. The answer is no, Justine, an unequivocal no!"

Ross Landers, watching his parents argue about *TIF*, appeared impassive, as if he were a spectator at a tennis match.

"We've lost money six years in a row," Justine said. "We are in the red up to our necks, Jasper. We publish a magazine no one wants to buy or read. People train their dogs or line their trash cans with our expensive magazine. Even I don't read it, and I publish it. When was the last time *you* read it? When was the last time you even bothered to come down here to see how things were going? I can tell you—three years ago. Three years, Jasper. The employees of this magazine are almost as old as God. None of them has had an original idea in the last twenty years. Even this building is archaic.

Everything looks like it came over on the ark." To make her point, Justine grabbed a glass paperweight from a desk and threw it onto the cushion of a Morris chair. Dust spiraled upward. Her facial muscles stretched into a grimace.

"The answer, Justine, is still no."

His wife threw her elegantly manicured hands in the air. "What do you think I'm going to do to this magazine, Jasper? *TIF,* Truth in Fiction . . . People will believe what we print, but it has to be interesting. I can make it interesting. Then, I thought I'd do a feature story on Judge Halvorsen, for instance. I'm sure all of Philadelphia will rush to buy next month's issue if they can read about 'Hizhonor' and his charming wife Helen.

"I can have this magazine in the black inside of six months," Justine said. "*In the black,* Jasper. Give me a year, that's all I ask. Ross will head the legal department. You trust your own son, don't you?"

Worms of fear skittered around inside Jasper's stomach.

Ross was Justine's big gun; Justine knew it, and so did Ross. Should he hold out? Jasper wondered. He knew his wife was right, because she never dealt from anything but a position of strength. He also knew that *TIF* was the laughingstock of the publishing industry, but he hated change of any kind. He wondered, then, as he did every day, why he'd ever married Justine. And the answer was always the same: Justine had opened her legs for him three times a day. Until the day she found out she was pregnant with Ross and closed them.

Justine's eyes narrowed. She had him, she could feel it. She pressed again, saying, "Deed *TIF* over to me. Ross will draw up the necessary papers. Surely you have no objection to that."

He had a thousand objections, but he said, "Eight months with eight hundred thousand in the black, then we'll talk about ownership. Take it or leave it, Justine." The expression on his son's face changed then. To admiration? Jasper wondered. For him?

"That's blackmail!" Justine shrieked. "You're blackmailing me, your own wife? Ross, do something."

"Not on your life," Ross said quietly. "This is between you and Father."

"My wife?" Jasper's laugh was so bitter, Ross cringed. "Do you want me to recite chapter and verse here in front of our son? Don't ever refer to yourself as my wife again. You live in my house, live off my generosity, and you feed off your son. You're a disgrace to this family, Justine."

"How dare you speak to me like that!" Justine sputtered.

The look of approval was still on his son's face. Jasper felt giddy. He didn't ever want that look to go away. "I just did, Justine. Don't even think about pushing me one inch further." His voice turned thoughtful: "I see you sitting on an orange plastic chair. I can actually see it." Obviously Ross could see it too, because he was grinning.

"What does that mean?" Justine demanded.

"What that means, Justine, is you're no lady. You wear a lady's clothes, you wear makeup like a lady, and at times you can converse like a lady, but don't ever forget for a minute where I found you. You belong on an orange plastic chair. You're a mongrel."

Abruptly, Jasper turned away from her and toward his son. "Ross, it was nice to see you. Perhaps we can have dinner at the club one of these days."

"I'd like that," Ross said quietly.

"Good. I'll call you."

Justine watched her husband leave the room. She bit down on her lower lip. She'd just been put in her place by a master. Who would have thought such a thing could come out of Jasper's mouth? Certainly not Ross, whose mouth was hanging open. Her heart was pumping furiously and she knew her face was a mask of shame.

She pulled herself together before turning to face her son. "Don't take any of this to heart, Ross," she said. "Your father has never paid any attention to finances. It's nice to have unlimited resources," she added sardonically. "He just clips coupons and cashes checks. That's your father's life. Besides playing golf and dining at the club. But this magazine *is* losing money."

Ross stared at his mother. She was dressed to the nines, her heavy makeup garish. His father had to clip at least three coupons to pay for the designer outfit she was wearing. Crocodile shoes were expensive. He should know, he had a pair.

She wasn't pretty or even attractive, this woman he called Mother. More than once he'd heard his father call her a mongrel, and at times it showed, like today. Justine was cold, callous, and manipulative, and he didn't like her at all. However, he did respect her keen business sense. The opposite was true of his father. He liked Jasper, but didn't respect him.

"Eight months and eight hundred thousand in the black is pretty stiff, Mother," he said. "Are you sure you want to go ahead with this?"

"I'm damn well sure, Ross. Draw up the papers. I'll make your father eat those words. I have a few little . . . insertions I want you to add."

"Just a minute, Mother. What kind of *little* insertions? This has to be a cut and dried professional contract. I won't be a party to trying to put something over on Father."

"Get off it, Ross. Don't get sanctimonious on me. You'll do as I say or you'll be disinherited. Let's not forget all those little scrapes I got you out of, all the strings I pulled. To be blunt, *son*, you'd be in jail if it wasn't for me. The first rule of business is, you fuck them before they fuck you. Now, I suggest you go to your office and get to work on that contract," she said coldly.

Anger, hot and scorching, flared in Ross's eyes. Standing, he towered over his mother. He wanted to tell her how much he disliked her, how his earlier rebellion was because of her; wanted to tell her she wasn't and never had been parent material, and yes, she bailed him out of scrapes because he had no role model growing up. He also wanted to tell her to go home and wash the heavy pancake off her face, and to take off the artificial eyelashes that made her small eyes feral-looking. The urge to yank at her upswept hairdo was so strong, he clenched his fists. What the hell would she look like without all the trappings? Like a *real* mother?

"Don't threaten me, Mother," he said coolly. "I'm a good attorney, I can get a job anywhere. In fact, I was asked last week if I had any interest in going back to work in the prosecutor's office. What that means is I have other options."

"My, we're uppity today, aren't we?"

"Is this where you give me that tired old line about changing my shitty diapers when I was born? Forget it, Mother, and don't ever dismiss me again."

"Ross, you are an ungrateful snot. I will not tolerate such talk from my son. Not now, not ever."

Ross threw his hands in the air. "Are you firing me?" Jesus, how hopeful his voice sounded.

Justine heard it too. "Of course not. One doesn't fire one's son. We are merely having a business discussion. Clearing the air, so to speak. I will not apologize for my drive, for my business sense. Remember this, Ross, you do what you have to do. Business comes first."

"Well, I can certainly relate to that," Ross said bitterly. "First-hand of course."

"Why don't we have dinner this evening?" Justine said.

Ross's stomach heaved. Dinner with either one of his parents was, in his opinion, like dining out with vipers, each of the vipers trying to find ways to do the other in, with him always in the middle. "I have other plans, Mother. Didn't we just have dinner, let's see, wasn't it three years, two months, and sixteen days ago?"

"That will be enough, Ross. *Enough!*"

The moment the door closed behind Ross, Justine clapped her hands. She'd won both rounds. So what if Jasper held her down with restrictions? She could keep him in line by simply mentioning Judge Halvorsen and his wife Helen, who was cuckolding the judge with Jasper.

Justine sat back in her swivel chair, long legs stretched out in front of her. She had nice legs. Nice high breasts too. All in all, she was perfectly proportioned. Back then—meaning back when she'd married Jasper thirty years ago—she'd been good in bed. Jasper had said so.

Orange plastic chairs. She winced. She would have ordered them too. For the reception area. Her thoughts whirled as she tried to come up with suitable justification. Mongrels versus pedigrees. She wasn't actually going to sit on them herself. They were for other people to sit on. She would never, under any circumstance, sit on any kind of plastic chair. Never.

Jasper Landers settled his pudgy body in one of the three club chairs in his office. It was his office by right of succession. His leg twitched and then his entire body started to tremble. He hated confrontations of any kind. In the past he would go out of his way, lie, evade, disappear, anything to avoid a face-to-face meeting with his wife. He didn't know how it was possible for Justine to intimidate him, but she did.

A drink. A stiff shot of Irish whiskey would help get his emotions under control. Somewhere in this office there was a liquor cabinet complete with liquor, unless Justine had tossed it out. He looked around, his eyes vague and slightly disoriented. How could Justine do this to him? Why did he allow her to reduce him to this . . . old fart? And he wasn't an old fart. He was a decent, caring human being, who loved Helen Halvorsen.

He hadn't meant it to happen. In fact he'd had months of sleepless nights over his attraction for Helen. And he probably would never have acted on that attraction if Ross hadn't been rushed to the hospital with a ruptured appendix. He'd been only four at the time. Helen had been a volunteer in the pediatric ward that day; Justine hadn't been around. Helen had held Ross's hand, smoothed back his dark curls, crooned soft words of comfort to his son, and then to him. She'd stayed on after her shift was over, to sit with him, and when the doctor assured them both that Ross would sleep through the night, they left to have coffee in an all-night diner. God, he could still taste that wonderful coffee and smell the sticky Danish neither of them had eaten. He could still smell Helen's perfume, a scent she still used.

Once, they'd had a long discussion about Justine and the judge, and Helen told him that Matthew married her for her position and background. He refused to have children, saying they would clutter up their lives.

Today, their affair was in its twenty-first year.

What they were doing wasn't right, but Helen was a Catholic, and said divorce was out of the question. Jasper didn't understand how adultery could be better than divorce. His own reasons for not divorcing Justine were far less noble. The stipulations of his father's will, as they applied to him—though, oddly, not to his descendants—forbade divorce. For him, divorce would mean giving up everything, which he wasn't prepared to do, his love for Helen notwithstanding.

Jasper gulped at the fiery liquid in his glass. That wasn't quite true. He would have given it up if a guardian could have been appointed to monitor the Landers holdings, but his attorneys had said Justine, as the boy's mother, would control everything.

Life wasn't all that bad for Jasper. Helen made it all bearable. Right now he wanted to call her, to run to her, to wrap her in his arms and tell her what had just transpired. It was late now, though, and he couldn't call her house because Matthew would be home. Matthew answered the phone after four o'clock. Unless . . . unless he called and invited both Helen and the judge to dinner at the club. No, tomorrow would be soon enough.

Jasper sighed wearily. All he wanted was to be happy, and for Ross to be happy. He wished he was stronger, more forceful. He gazed then at the pictures of his ancestors lining the walls of his office. Once they'd hung in the reception room, but Justine had moved them in here. He should have paid more attention, demanded they be returned to the entry walls.

His father, his grandfather, and his great-grandfather were tall men, imposing figures; hale and hearty, whereas he was short, pudgy, and simple-looking, with his horn-rimmed glasses. He didn't have their strength, their business acumen. "I can, however, cut straight lines when I clip coupons, and I sign my name legibly when I cash my checks," he muttered. It was a hell of a thing to be good at nothing. "I love, I'm human, I care. I care about everything and everyone. I love my son as much as I love Helen," he whispered to the pictures on the wall.

He did have one bit of spunk though. He'd put his foot down and insisted this office remain the way it was the day his father died. It had the same old furniture, dusty now, the same carpet, which was even dustier, the same lamps, the same drapes. The only thing different was the recent addition of Justine's picture on the wall. As publisher, she was entitled to be here with the three past publishers of *TIF*.

God, how he hated Justine. She was going to wreak havoc on *TIF*, and they both knew he was powerless to stop her. Maybe Ross could keep her in line. "I'm sorry," he apologized to his ancestors, "but I can't let her destroy Matthew and Helen."

It was the easy way out. Don't fight it. Accept the situation and move on.

"Die, Justine, just goddamn die already," Jasper said. "I'll dance at your funeral. I swear to God I'll strip naked and dance on your coffin."

He whimpered then, the way Helen did when things got out of control.

When Jasper left the office a long time later, he was carrying the empty liquor bottle in one hand and Justine's portrait in the other. He tossed both in the Dumpster in the parking lot.

He stood for a moment looking at the Landers Building. He would never come back here, because he'd failed. He had no one to blame but himself. Hopefully, Ross would do what he hadn't been able to do all these years—take control. He realized what a stupid thought it was. No one controlled Justine.

"Just die, Justine."

Chapter 3

It was early, not yet dawn, but Justine Landers was made-up, dressed, and ready for breakfast. Her own private motto was, early to rise, be ready for a prize. The prize was almost in her grasp. Being publisher, turning the Landers magazine *TIF* around, was only half the prize. *Ownership* was the prize. Ross would handle the details.

Justine rang the breakfast bell. Rosa the cook appeared at her elbow with a huge silver coffeepot. "Two eggs, three slices of bacon, toast, strawberry jelly, orange juice, and five small pancakes," Justine said as she poured cream from a cut-glass pitcher into her cup. "Remember what I told you, Rosa, don't turn your back to me."

"Yes, Ma'am," Rosa said respectfully. "How would you like your eggs this morning, Mrs. Landers?"

"Three and three-quarter minutes, not a second longer."

"Three and three-quarter minutes, not a second longer. Will there be anything else, ma'am?"

"As a matter of fact there is something else. Why is my food bill two dollars higher this week? Have you been feeding that fool gardener again?"

"Mr. Landers asked for fresh melon. He was leaving the house on Thursday morning when the produce man arrived. He picked out the melon himself, ma'am."

"From now on serve Mr. Landers canned peaches. You do not buy anything that is not on my list. If Mr. Landers wants something that is not on my list, have him give you money."

The moment the dining room door closed, Justine withdrew the last issue of *Confidential* from her briefcase. Her greedy eyes devoured the sleazy headlines, the cheap paper, the large print. She could do this and do it better. She could hardly wait to find out which starlet cavorted in which pool with which star in his skivvies.

Justine closed the magazine and sipped at her coffee. For the past year she'd read every single sleazy published tabloid. In her room, in her cedar chest, she had every copy of *Confidential*, with notes on how to publish it better than Robert Harrison did. If anyone could give him a run for his money, Justine thought, she could. With the new, young, and greedy reporters she was hiring, she would pull it off. She knew it. Her only regret was that she hadn't done it earlier.

Today was a bright new day. The sun would shine just for her. Even if it rained, it wouldn't dampen her spirits. She finally had what she wanted. Today was going to be the best day of her life, the day when she fired everyone in the office and started new. The day the payback started.

Today people would start to take her seriously; she would begin her reign as publisher of the new *TIF.* After today, she wouldn't be Jasper Landers's wrong-side-of-the-tracks wife who had never been really accepted by the old Main Line Philadelphia families. One by one the old pompous farts would come to her when she started to dig into the skeletons in their closets. They'd beg her not to print their sordid little secrets, and she would damn well turn a deaf ear. All the slights, all the slurs, all the raised eyebrows, would be a thing of the past.

Power was the name of the game.

Justine attacked her breakfast the way she did everything: with force. She ate every single thing and could have eaten more. She debated asking for another stack of pancakes, but negated the idea almost immediately. Women ate daintily at the club and usually left half their meals on their plates. She did too, when she dined out, but when she was home she ate like a stevedore.

Living on the wrong side of the tracks, with a drunken father and a mother who took in wash, didn't allow for a lot of food on the table. Growing up, she'd always been hungry. The oldest of seven children, she'd had to give up her portions to the little ones more times than she could remember. The day she walked out of the mean little shanty, she'd vowed she would never go back and never be hungry again.

She was seventeen years old when she left to work in the dime store. She'd lived in a boardinghouse until she met Jasper Landers. Her first thought when she met him: meal ticket. And all Jasper wanted in return was sex. But then she found herself falling in love with him. So she decided to marry him.

She talked to the girls at the dime store, who gladly shared their bedroom secrets, before she gave in to his desires. She, in turn, embroidered and improvised, until Jasper howled at the moon, at which point she cut him off completely, demanding marriage. He hadn't balked at all. In fact he'd slipped the ring on her finger so fast he made her head spin. She'd looked him straight in the eye and, meaning every word, said, "I will be Mrs. Jasper Landers for the rest of my life."

At that point she didn't know much about the old family and how worried they were about scandal. Nor did she know about the stipulation in Jasper's father's will, that his son, if married, could not divorce and still retain the family fortune. She knew now, of course, and relished the position in which it placed her.

She hadn't known a thing about Main Line living. She made all the classical mistakes, dressed wrong, said the wrong things, wore too much makeup, used the wrong fork, messed up the food on her plate, and of course her speech was all wrong. Jasper hadn't helped her either, preferring to spend his time on the golf course, when he wasn't fucking her brains out three times a day. She'd tried to teach herself, and often the results were totally disastrous. Eventually she'd conquered most of her more outrageous social faults, but it had taken her fifteen years. She constantly read the dictionary, not that it did her any good. It made her feel better, though.

Once, after Jasper officially made her the publisher of *TIF*, she'd been in one of the bathroom stalls at the club and overheard several women talking about her. What they said was so cruel, so hateful, she'd stayed in the stall for an hour, her face burning with shame. When she finally got up the nerve to leave, she'd had to slink from the club like a beaten, weary alley cat. She cried to Jasper afterward and tried to explain how she felt. His response was to tell her it was her imagination, to take long walks and drink plenty of water.

"And all good things come to those who wait," Justine murmured as she patted her lips.

It was a lovely room, a far cry from the three-room shanty she'd grown up in. Here everything was old and real. Not necessarily beautiful. She'd learned the hard way that expensive didn't mean beautiful. During the second year of her marriage, she insisted on redecorating the entire first floor. All the antiques, all the rare carpets, were put in storage. When she thought of the results, she cringed, for in the end all the rooms looked like Sears Roebuck pictures. Jasper had gasped and then turned purple. For the first time in her life she experienced fear. She'd run upstairs and cried for hours. When she came downstairs for dinner, all the furniture was gone. It took a week before the Landerses' furniture could be taken out of storage and the rooms restored to their former appearance. That story had gotten around the club too.

She blamed Jasper for everything, and he accepted the blame, which only convinced Justine she was right.

Everyone knew about Jasper and Helen except Matthew Halvorsen. But then, Matthew was stupid and didn't know night from day. She'd been tempted to send him an anonymous letter informing him of his wife's infidelity, but was deathly afraid it would be traced back to her somehow. She did hate to be shamed, and of late it was getting harder for her to hold her head up in public. All that was going to change now. Now her head would be higher and the others would slink around. "And you all deserve it," she muttered.

"Rosa!"

"Yes, ma'am."

"Replace this tablecloth for dinner. Order fresh flowers, and is that dust I see on the sideboard? If it is, it better be gone when I get home this evening. And this coffeepot needs to be polished."

"Today, ma'am?"

"Yesterday is gone, tomorrow isn't here yet, so that leaves today. Yes, Rosa, today," Justine said coldly.

Justine took a last look around the dining room. Wainscotting was so depressing. So was the wallpaper. She remembered her devastating decorating endeavor. "I like it, I like it," she muttered.

What the hell was he doing here? He didn't want to be here, had no intention of ever working here, but here he was, with no desk. What the hell kind of lawyer was he if he didn't have a damn desk? He felt like bellowing, until he remembered that Nigel Sandor, *TIF*'s attorney, would be unemployed by noon, at which point he would take over the battered old desk that was so dusty he couldn't see what kind of wood it was. He couldn't help but wonder when the last time any legal business was conducted in this office.

Ross shook his head in disgust. Damn, what was he doing here? Why was he here? He hated to think he was so shallow he would compromise his ideals to work here. Was there anything wrong with getting hands-on experience in ye olde family business? A matter of opinion, he decided.

Office hours were eight to five. It was already nine o'clock, and Nigel was conspicuously absent. It didn't surprise him. The other employees weren't in their offices either, with the exception of his mother, who always arrived by 6:45 to do God only knew what behind closed doors.

Ross's eyes fell on a memo slip clipped to a worn-out lampshade. "Contractors will arrive at noon. Business will be conducted on the first floor in the conference room." It was his mother's handwriting.

The big meeting was scheduled for ten o'clock. At eleven o'clock a second meeting was scheduled with the new employees. Ross grimaced. Out with the old, in with the new, and don't give the bodies a chance to cool off.

Because he couldn't yet take possession of Nigel's chair and desk, Ross had no choice but to go downstairs to the conference room and work on the publicity release his mother wanted sent to the

Philadelphia Democrat for tomorrow morning's edition. Plus, he had to compile a severance-pay list. The list was his own idea, one his mother would have a hairy conniption over. One week's severance pay for every year's employment. It was fair and just. His father would approve, and he had to make sure it was done before Jasper signed over *TIF* in its entirety to his mother.

Careful not to touch anything, Ross left the office to take the back stairs to the first floor. He winced when the door to the conference room creaked open. The room was long, narrow, and dismal-looking. He opened the venetian blinds, and in an instant his navy-blue jacket was covered with gray dust. He shook himself like a dog, cursing at the same time. Jesus, how had things gotten to this point? His mother had taken an active role in the magazine only fifteen years ago, even though his father had appointed her publisher as a wedding gift. If Hillary Blumgarten hadn't died at the age of ninety-two, Justine would never have taken an active role. Ross remembered his father's words to his mother on her first day at the magazine: "Don't do anything, just sit there and let the magazine run itself. Hillary has a well-oiled machine that works." Ross snorted. How had his mother lasted all these years? Why was his father so damn stubborn?

God, how he dreaded this meeting. How did you fire fifteen people who worked for you for thirty years? That was 450 years between them all. It was a shitful thing his mother was doing. He upped the severance pay in his head to two weeks for every year of employment.

Smack in the middle of the long oak table was a stack of magazines. The last twelve issues of *TIF.* The only other thing in the room aside from the conference table were twelve cane chairs and a Tiffany lamp minus a light bulb. Let someone else raise the venetian blinds, he thought; he'd opened them.

Ross scanned the magazines, yawning as he did so. It was hard to believe *anyone* bought the damn things. He slammed the issue he was holding back on the table. Dirt and grit moved around. He'd be better off going out to the parking lot and working in his car. His watch said he had almost twenty minutes. Time to go around the corner for a bagel and some coffee. The hell with the lists, the hell with this conference room. The fucking hell with his parents.

On the short walk to the corner deli, Ross thought about his parents, wished he could love them, wished they were a close family, wished for kind words he could return.

He saw her then, the prettiest girl he'd ever seen. She looked familiar. God, where had he seen her? The theater, the movies, on the street? He forgot his intention to buy coffee and a bagel. When he'd seen her before, she'd also been wearing blue. How could he not remember her? Every hair was in place, the blue-checkered sundress crisply ironed, her leather sandals polished. Bare legs, he liked that. No ring on her fingers, no jewelry.

"Villanova!" he blurted.

She smiled, her blue eyes dancing. "Are you speaking to me?"

"Yes, yes I am. I've seen you before, but I can't remember where. Was it Villanova? I went to law school there."

The girl studied him. He crossed his fingers that she would remember him. He bit down on his lower lip when she apologized and said, "I'm sorry, I don't remember meeting you."

"Oh, we never met. What I mean is, we weren't introduced or anything like that. I saw you. I remember seeing you. You were wearing something blue, maybe it was this same dress. Do you have two blue dresses?" Jesus, he didn't just say that, did he? His neck grew warm.

"As a matter of fact I do have two blue dresses, this one and another one. I went to Villanova for two years but had to drop out to save money. I'll go back when I can afford it. Perhaps you saw me in the library."

"Yes, that's probably it. I spent a lot of time there. Listen, would you like some coffee, a bagel, some Danish?"

The girl held up her muffin and then pointed to her coffee. "Do you want to share?"

Did he want to share? Did he want to keep on breathing? "Absolutely. That's yes. One bite though, okay?" He leaned down to take a bite and looked into the clearest, warmest eyes he'd ever seen. "Your eyes kind of have a purplish tinge to them," he blurted.

"I know. Not much I can do about it, though," she said, finishing off the muffin. "You have to live with what you're given."

"I didn't mean that in a negative way," Ross said quickly.

"I know you didn't. I was just teasing. It isn't every day a handsome man tells me he remembers me. Thank you for the compliment. Lena Davis," she said, holding out her hand.

He was about to introduce himself when a voice behind him roared, "I've been looking for you all over. Come on, get a move on, Lena, or we'll be late. First impressions are important."

"I lost track of time." She laughed. To Ross, she smiled and said, "I really didn't touch the coffee, so if you want it, it's yours." A moment later she was gone, with a giant of a man whose voice was a mixture of gravel and molasses.

Ross ran then, around the corner, cutting through the alley to the parking lot in back of the Landers Building. He took the back stairs two steps at a time, until he realized he was supposed to be in the conference room on the first floor. He ran back down, winded. He took a moment to smooth his hair and adjust his tie. Lena Davis. Nice name. Pretty as its owner. He closed his eyes for a moment to remember her warm smile. Her curls looked soft and feathery, and fit just right around her head. She was wearing little pearl earrings. Everything about her was pretty, her eyes, her smile, her hair, even her white teeth. He'd almost asked her if she used Pepsodent or Ipana. Jesus. One hundred ten pounds, maybe 108. Perfectly proportioned. Her toenails were painted. He'd noticed that too. "Shit!" The story of his thirty-one-year-old life. He always was the last one out of the gate.

His breathing under control, he opened the door. Maybe she was in the phone book. A sea of white heads greeted him. He felt laughter bubble in his throat when he noticed his mother standing at the head of the conference table. For the first time in her life, she looked frazzled. He quietly took a seat in the corner. No one seemed to notice his arrival. Half of the assembly appeared to be asleep.

"Devon, wake up or else turn your hearing aid up," Justine shouted. "Nigel, wake them up, for God's sake. I don't believe this!" she sputtered. "Ross, do something!"

Grinning, Ross stood. Surely these kindly *old* men weren't his peers. He brought his fingers to his lips and whistled shrilly.

"Fire drill!" Justine screeched. "Ah, good, I have your attention now. Thank you, Ross."

"Gentleman, you're fired!"

"Sacked?" Devon said peevishly.

"Unemployed?" Nigel fretted.

"Think of it as retirement and resting on your laurels," Justine said loudly. "You're seventy-seven, Devon, and you, Nigel, are seventy-five. It's time to sit back and do what you always wanted to do."

"Why?" Arnold Baker grumbled.

"I knew you were going to say that," Justine sputtered. "I'm going to tell you why. Ross, give each of them a copy of *TIF*."

Her son passed out copies of the last issue.

"Now, look at the cover, look at the articles, look at *everything*," Justine said. "What you are looking at is a costly magazine no one wants to read. No one buys it. We are operating in the red. What's in this magazine are rehashes of articles printed in newspapers. Anniversary articles. I do not want anniversary articles. Who cares what happend ten years ago? Not me, not the reader. The reader wants to know what's going on *now*. I don't see anything on the Olympics or the mechanical heart used on that Pennsylvania man. Not one word about the King of England dying last year, nothing on the Rocky Marciano–Joe Walcott fight. People want to know when there's a new boxing champion and a new king or queen. I fail to understand why nothing was written concerning Albert Schweitzer winning the Nobel Peace Prize. *TIF* is probably the only magazine in the world that didn't have at least one paragraph. And for God's sake, the world needs to know that General Motors is going to have air-conditioning in its 1953 models. And last but certainly not least, why wasn't something written about the sex operation on Christine Jorgenson? That's something else the world wants to know. That, gentlemen, is why you're all being fired!"

"Did Jasper tell you to fire us, Justine?" an elderly man in the back of the room demanded.

"No, he did not. I'm firing you. Don't you understand, this magazine is changing course. It's mine now. If any of you were still capable of doing the job, I'd keep you on, but you aren't. You must all retire. You will be given severance pay. My son Ross will be handling the details. When this meeting breaks, you will leave the building because renovations are to begin. You could choke on the dust," she said defensively.

"What will we do, Justine?" Devon dithered.

"Take life easy. Enjoy your life. Walk in the park, dine out, play checkers, play cards, meet with friends. Whatever you want."

"You're casting us aside after we gave our lives to this magazine," Saul Wimple grumbled.

"May I make a suggestion?" Ross said quietly.

"Absolutely," Justine said, relieved at his intercession.

"When the renovations are completed, there will be a large room off the first-floor corridor. I suggest we make it into a club room for all of you. You'll be free to come and go as you please. My mother will be more than happy to appoint all of you honorary officers of the magazine. Your name will appear in the credits column. Two weeks severance pay for every year's employment is not shabby, gentlemen. The club room will be stocked with your favorite wines and liquors. *Updated* magazines and newspapers will be available, along with several chessboards for your convenience. Will that be satisfactory?"

"That sounds like a Jasper Landers solution," Nigel cracked. "Am I right, boy?" Ross shrugged. His mother glared.

The moment the door closed behind the *TIF* employees, Justine said, "That was uncalled for, Ross. You're awfully generous with my money. You had no right."

"Every right, Mother. Father would be like a bull if you didn't give severance pay. *It is* his money, after all, and if you really want him to turn this paper over to you, you have to start out fair. What I just did was fair, for you and for father. Everyone is happy. The men will have someplace to go everyday. *TIF* has been their lives. You can't just throw them out. The papers will pick up on it, and for a new venture like the one you're contemplating, it doesn't pay to get bad press. Those men are entitled to their dignity, and it isn't their fault they grew old. You, Mother, will be old one day. Think about *that*."

An ugly look crossed Justine's face. "They better not get in the way, is all I can say to you, Ross. I am personally going to hold you responsible for the good old boys club. Their names on the credits. No!"

"Yes."

"I refuse."

"Then I'm out of here. Decide now, Mother."

Justine seethed. "Very well," she said grudgingly. "But only for six months."

"At which point we will renegotiate the terms," Ross said affably.

"You better drive the same hard bargains when I need you."

"I wouldn't have it any other way, Mother. Now what?"

"Now we go to the second floor and meet all our new employees and lay down the rules. I expect the renovations to take thirty days. We can go to press in forty days. Everyone will have a job, working out of the basement, and if need be, the parking lot. I'm having lunch catered by the corner deli. When it arrives, we'll open the meeting. Feel free to interject at any point. You do that well, Ross," Justine said coolly.

"I had a good teacher," Ross replied wearily.

"You don't like me, do you, Ross?" Justine said. "Why is that?"

"Because I'm afraid I might turn out like you. I *am* your son."

Justine didn't flinch, her eyes didn't waver. "Is that another way of telling me you'd rather be like your father?"

"No, I don't want to be like him either. I just want to be myself. Being your son has never helped me. You were never there for me when I needed you. I'm here now because . . ." Jesus, why was he here? "Because I consider myself a worthwhile person. I guess because I feel I owe you something for bringing me into the world and getting me to this place in time." How stupid, Ross groaned to himself. Was that the best he could come up with? He knew the only thing his mother heard were the words "owe you something." The bottom line, for now, was hands-on experience. The time would come when he'd wake up some morning and realize his debt was paid. Then he'd make his next decision about hanging out his shingle. On the other hand, he might head out to the Fiji Islands and strum a guitar under a palm tree. He had enough money to do that right now if he wanted to, thanks to generous grandparents and an equally generous father.

By any standard, he was wealthy, his accounts totaling so many zeros, he'd lost count at the age of eighteen. Aside from his Buick Skylark, he'd made no excessive purchases. He wore fine clothes, yes, but only because they wore well, lasted longer, and he detested shopping. He was not one to pick up tabs for his roommates, because they wouldn't allow it back in college and law school. He'd wanted to be one of *them*, so he'd lived the way they all did, pooling money, going Dutch, loaning and borrowing and keeping strict records.

"Are you going to be able to handle this, Ross?"

Ross fought the laughter bubbling in his throat at his mother's worried expression. He'd graduated in the top three percent of his class. His favorite law professor had told him he was a natural for the law. On top of that, Dr. Peters said, "You have compassion, something most lawyers lack." Plus he had five years as an assistant district attorney. "As a matter of fact, Mother, I've been meaning to talk to you about an associate. I have just the person in mind. He's almost as good as I am, maybe better. Yes, he's better," he said generously. "We tied for second place in law school. We work well together. Between the two of us, we can handle things here."

"Hiring a second lawyer isn't in my business plan," Justine said sourly. "How much of a salary would he demand?"

"The same as mine. I really don't know how I can get along without someone like Woo. Maybe you should think about it right now, Mother, before we head down to the next meeting."

"This is the eleventh hour, Ross. You're doing this deliberately, aren't you? You're pushing my back to the wall to get what you want. I don't like this Ross, not one little bit."

"I knew you were going to say that, Mother, but if you stop and think about it, isn't that exactly what you're doing to Father? What makes me any different?" Ross shrugged. "Like mother, like son."

"Woo? You mean that . . . that Polish person you roomed with at school? His ears stick out and he always needs a haircut?"

"You only saw him once, and the reason he didn't have a haircut was because it wasn't in his budget that week. If I remember correctly, he needed new heels on his shoes that week, and he needed to eat. He's my best friend, Mother."

"Is he the one you always spent holidays with?" Justine asked quietly.

"Ah, you remember that, do you? Yes, Woo is the one. The Woojaleskys always invited me, and treated me like one of their own. Mrs. Woojalesky makes the best meat loaf in Lancaster, Pennsylvania."

"Meat loaf?" Justine said stupidly.

Ross was enjoying this. Woo was in the bag. "Yeah, she puts all kinds of little green things in it, and the gravy is so good I always have thirds. She makes pies and cake, sews, and she loves all nine of her kids. Well, Mother?"

Justine's eyes narrowed. "You're blackmailing me, Ross. Half what I'm paying you."

"The same," Ross said coldly.

"Three-quarters," Justine snapped.

"The same, Mother," Ross said, picking up his briefcase.

Justine patted her pompadour. "You drive a hard bargain, Ross. I like that. I was testing you," she said sweetly.

Ross knew it was a lie. He grimaced.

"It's time to greet our new employees," Justine said smoothly.

"I'll be down in a minute. I have to call Woo."

"Why? You already told him he has the job. You wouldn't have haggled so hard if you hadn't," Justine called over her shoulder.

"Touché, Mother," Ross said under his breath.

A moment later he was talking to his best friend. "Woo, it's in the bag. Show up at eight tomorrow, and you're on the payroll. You'll be making the same salary as me. Eighteen months, Woo, and we can leave and start up our own business, just the way we planned." He listened to the rapid-fire questions on the other end of the wire. "It was no problem. Of course you'll have a contract.

I'll draw it up myself. Guaranteed salary. A raise every six months. Christmas bonus."

He listened again. "I'll drive up and get you late this afternoon. What's your mother making for dinner?" he asked wistfully. "No kidding? And those little white potatoes and skinny carrots? . . . I'll be there. Strawberry rhubarb pie? . . . Three of them? Jesus. . . . Of course you're staying with me. We discussed all of this, Woo. We're a team . . . Okay, I'll see you around six. Maybe sooner if my stomach starts to growl."

God, he felt good. Ross looked at his watch. Shit, he was almost fifteen minutes late. His mother was going to hiss like a snake. He laughed. Now he finally had his answer as to why he'd agreed to come here to work. It was for Woo. His way of paying back the big guy and his family for all they'd done for him over the past years. Woo had confided to him, "Who's going to hire someone that looks like a big, shaggy bear with big ears, and has hands so big you can't see his pencil when he's holding it?" Indeed, on one of his depressed days, Woo was as homely as a mud fence. He'd known Woo so well, he knew in his gut that if the big guy was rejected more than once, he'd pack it in and go to work at the lumber mill where his father and three brothers worked. Which is what happened six months after Woo passed the bar.

Five minutes later Ross let himself into the meeting room by the rear door. He quietly took a seat in back of the room and listened to his mother tell the eighteen people in the room what she expected from them.

"The reporter who has the best feature story for the month will receive a bonus. At the end of the year, at the Christmas party, the reporter with the most feature stories will receive another bonus. An exclusive scoop will receive a *substantial* bonus. Pictures will be paid for with a different bonus system. You all have the potential to make a large sum of money if you desire. I want this new format I've designed to outsell *Confidential.* Each of you will develop your own style, gather your own sources, and keep accurate expense accounts. If we have to pay for an exclusive, money is no object as long as the story sells. Now, do any of you have any questions?"

Ross listened with one ear, his thoughts on a girl named Lena, and on Woo. His eyebrows shot upward when he heard his mother say, "I'm not against opening a small West Coast office if need be."

He saw the blue-checkered dress with the white collar. He sat bolt upright, craning his neck for a better look. She was sitting next to the large man who'd whisked her from the deli. A reporter, or was she going to work in the office? Perhaps both, if she was saving money to return to school. The bonus system his mother was out-lining sounded good, and to a girl trying to save money, it probably seemed the answer to all her worries.

Ross watched her, his eyes intense, willing her to turn and look at him. This must be some kind of divine providence. Seeing her twice in one day had to mean something. He thought about Jory and the divorce. He switched his thoughts to Woo and his mother. If he closed his eyes, he could feel the plump woman's thank-you hug. He felt good all over.

"My son, Ross, who you'll meet in a moment, will head our legal department with Peter Woojalesky," Justine said quietly. "Both men will be in charge of payroll and the bonus plans I've outlined for you. All your stories and articles will be checked by both attorneys for accuracy and libel." Justine motioned for Ross to come forward.

Ross straightened his tie and buttoned his jacket before he skirted the folding chairs set up in small aisles. He heard a gasp from the girl in the blue-checkered dress. At least he thought it was a gasp. Surprise? Happiness? Dismay? He felt self-conscious, and re-sented his mother's arm around his shoulder. This kind of intimacy was reserved for Woo's mother. He shrugged off her arm as he stepped forward to shake hands with the new employees.

"Peter Davis," the tall man next to the blue-checkered dress said. "I'm a photographer." His handshake was hard and firm. Ross ex-erted pressure and thought he saw approval in the photographer's eyes. Davis. Lena Davis, she'd said. No ring on her finger. Brother and sister? Thank you, God.

She was smiling again, amusement shining in her eyes. She held out her hand. "Lena Davis. My friends call me Lena. Yes, this is my big brother." She was grinning now, enjoying the relief she saw on Ross's face.

"Thank God," he said in a confidential voice. "For a minute there I thought he might be your husband. Or something. Have dinner with me tomorrow?"

Lena smiled. "I'd love to."

"Ross, is there a problem here?" Justine demanded, stepping over.

"No. I just recognized an old friend and was renewing our friendship." He moved on, shaking hands, saying a word here, a word there, until he met everyone in the room.

"I guess that takes care of everything," Justine announced. "We're going to be working in the basement, as I told you, for the time being. It will take us at the very least a full month to get organized. You can all use that time to make your own schedules, develop your sources. I want all of you to read your competition from cover to cover so you'll know what you're up against. I've purchased our competitor's magazines, and they're stacked up by the front door. Each of you take a copy. If there are no further questions, we can break up now." A second later she was gone, the door slamming behind her.

"Is she as tough as she looks?" Peter Davis asked brashly.

"Tougher," Ross said, his eyes on Lena. Her eyes were like bluebells, the summer sky, the old blue blanket he'd lugged to camp when he was six.

"I guess it'll do until the *New York Times* knocks on my door." Ross liked Peter Davis immediately. "So, what are your credentials?" Peter asked, grinning. "Seeing as how you appear to be interested in my sister."

"I'm thirty-one," Ross replied. "I own and drive my own car. I have a job. I take a shower once a day and know how to treat a young lady. I'm Ross Landers. I like to think I'm fair-minded and honest. I have good friends. Oh, yeah, I polish my own shoes once a week. I was born wealthy but I do not now nor have I ever had a silver spoon in my mouth. Anything else you want to know?"

"That should do it. I like the part about polishing your own shoes." Peter laughed uproariously, to Lena's embarrassment.

"So, can your sister have dinner with me tomorrow night?" Ross asked quietly.

"In by eleven."

"Twelve."

"Eleven-thirty."

Ross grinned. "Agreed."

Ross copied down the Davises' address in his small address book.

But he was thinking about Jory when he made his way down to where he knew his mother was waiting for him. I'll tell her now, he decided, about the divorce, and get it out of the way. Ross stopped in midstride. He wasn't a kid anymore, and he sure as hell didn't need parental approval for what he was doing. And so, when he did tell his mother, a few minutes later, his tone said that this was his decision, and she would have to live with it.

To his surprise, Justine merely said, "All right, Ross, whatever you want."

A few minutes later, Ross swung the Buick onto the Pennsylvania Turnpike, his thoughts on everything but his driving. How the hell had he gotten to this point in time? Things were moving too fast, he thought irritably. He was thirty-one years old, a man. It was time to start thinking about a family and Sunday dinners, pets and kids, washing the car on Saturday afternoon. Woo's mother, according to Woo, always made hot dogs and baked beans on Thursdays. Christ, when was the last time he'd had a hot dog?

For the life of him, he couldn't remember half of what he'd done in the prosecutor's office for the past five years. Tried cases, winning some and losing some. Five years was long enough to work at anything. If he'd stayed on, he knew someday he'd be the district attorney, just the way Jake Ryan had been, but he didn't want that. He didn't want to be married to his career, he wanted to be married to a flesh and blood woman who shared his life, who cared if he worked late, who cared if he was overworked and got sick.

Jake Ryan, Jory's father, was married to his office. Once over a drink at Mortimer's, Ryan had looked at him and said, "You look familiar." Of course, he'd had three double shots of Irish whiskey in him at the time. He'd kept staring at him, and then he'd said, "I know you work in the office, but I know you from somewhere else, don't I?" At best, a feeble joke.

"Yeah," Ross had replied, "I'm married to Marjory."

Jake hadn't said another word. But from that day on, he'd gotten every single shit detail there was to be had. He literally worked around the clock, and lost more cases than he won. Twice he was called into his superior's office to defend himself and his caseload. He'd been put on probation, and it didn't matter if his name was Landers or John Doe. He'd worked his ass off on the Farber case, and would have won it and sent Farber to prison for life if a surprise witness hadn't shown up at the eleventh hour to give Farber an alibi. His gut told him it was a manufactured witness, that he'd been set up somehow. He'd written out his resignation the day he was summoned to Ryan's office for a three o'clock appointment. At noon, on his way to lunch, Jake Ryan suffered a massive coronary, and died five hours later. He'd torn up his resignation and stuck it out for eighteen more months. He'd probably still be there, but his mother's offer to head up the legal department at *TIF* and the chance to finally work with Woo won out.

There was every possibility he was making a mistake by going to work for his mother, but he wouldn't know that unless he tried. At night, when he hadn't been able to sleep, he'd thought about what he was contemplating, and always came to the same conclusion: his mother, and it didn't matter if he liked her or not, was headed for trouble with what she was planning. He would be able to divert some of that trouble. If and when the things started to run smoothly, he would turn it over to the other attorneys and go into business with Woo.

"And that, ladies and gentlemen of the jury, is the story of Ross Landers. Amen," he said fervently.

Ross rolled down the window. He liked this stretch of the turnpike, with fields and the grazing cows. Farm and milk country. He wondered how he'd do as a farmer. He laughed, a genuine sound of mirth. Jesus, when was the last time he'd erupted in laughter? So long ago he couldn't remember. He sniffed appreciatively as the scent of clover and buckwheat wafted through the open car windows. He probably would make a good farmer. Providing he could commandeer exactly the right amount of rainfall, exactly the right process for his crops, the right grass for the cows, so they gave off rich creamy milk.

On the other hand, he mused, I like all my creature comforts, my house, my car, good friends, fine restaurants, trips into New York, ball games. In short, the good life. He wondered what kind of life his soon to-be-ex-wife had growing up. He should know, but he didn't. Jake Ryan, his subordinates had said, was hell on wheels. He ate, slept, and drank his job. Two weeks out of every month, when Ross worked night court, Ryan was still in his office when he left at midnight.

What really boggled Ross's mind was that no one seemed to know he was married to Jake Ryan's daughter. Or, if they knew, they didn't care, which was fine with him. His private life wasn't anyone's business but his own.

He had to think about Jory, get it all clear in his mind before he met with Woo.

"What I *should* do," Ross muttered, "is go away on some retreat in the woods run by monks and do nothing but think and try to come up with workable solutions to life's problems, specifically my own."

Ross was saved from further introspection when the large green sign came into view. He turned on his signal light and moved to the right lane. In less than twenty minutes he'd be at Woo's house, where the family would meet him with hugs and smiles.

Twenty-seven minutes later the Buick coasted to a stop behind a blue Ford pickup truck. On the side of the single-car driveway, two other vehicles, both Fords, rested in the shade of a huge maple tree. The Woojaleskys were a Ford family. They were also staunch Democrats and union members.

The house was white clapboard and recently painted, with a huge front porch that held a swing and three wicker chairs. Stella and Stan, Woo's parents, sat on the porch on summer evenings drinking lemonade. Neighbors dropped by on their way to or from their evening stroll. The lemonade pitcher was usually filled at least three times in the course of an evening.

The house was small, the first floor consisting of a living room, dining room where the family ate on Sunday, a huge kitchen, and an over-large pantry. There was a back porch filled with crocks of bright red geraniums. Stella said she liked to look out her kitchen window and see flowers. Three of the bedrooms held two sets of bunk beds each. Dormitories, Woo called them, but they were chock full of life, laughter, tears, and love.

Ross knew there was going to be a hole in the front screen door before he saw it. Stella said, "Someone always puts their fingers through it as soon as Stan puts it up in the spring." And there it was, right by the handle. Ross stuck his pinkie in the hole just as Woo said, "I saw that!"

"Yeah, and I bet you're the one who punched it out, right?"

Woo grinned sheepishly. "It's a game we play. This year I was the first because I hung the damn door. Childish, I admit, but I love it when Ma gets riled up. We waited dinner, you made good time," Woo said, clapping his friend on the back. Ross advanced three steps with the friendly blow.

"You gotta stop doing that, Woo. One of these days you're going to lift me right off the ground or else I'm going to deck you."

Woo snorted. "You and what army?"

It was a wonderful meal, with easy conversation and lots of good-natured ribbing and laughter.

Ross loosened his belt. "It was a wonderful dinner, Mrs. W. I haven't eaten this much since the last time I was here. You must be the best cook in Pennsylvania."

"I am," Stella said proudly. "Stan says so."

Woo grinned. "She's so modest."

And beautiful, Ross thought. She was round like a basketball, possibly five feet tall from the tip of her topknot to the tip of her toes. Her face was round, her wide blue eyes just as round. Round circles of pink dotted her cheeks, and not from any cosmetic. She just had naturally pink cheeks. On one of his earlier visits, Ross had brashly demanded she prove it. She'd giggled like a schoolgirl and let him rub the rosy circles. She smiled continually and always sang lusty songs while she was at work in the kitchen. He'd never seen her in anything but a cotton dress with a wrap apron. Woo said she only got gussied up for church on Sundays and for weddings and funerals, when she wore a violet dress with a lace "dickey," whatever the hell a lace dickey was.

"Ma, you and Pop sit on the porch, and Ross and I will clean up," Woo said, pulling the chair from the table so his mother could join his father. "Bang on the screen door when you're ready for the lemonade."

"It's not right to make our guest do the dishes," Stella fretted.

"And why not? He ate more than I did," Woo said in mock outrage.

Ross winked at Stella. "I'll make sure he does a good job." He really loved this part of dinner, the cleaning up, putting everything away, getting to look in the cupboards, shaking out the tablecloth and then making the lemonade. If he could just belong here, he'd be the happiest man alive. He said so.

Woo reached for the salt and pepper shaker. "See these?" he said, holding them aloft. "They're a matched set, they belong together. We've had them since I was a kid. Salt and pepper go together the way Ma and Pop go together. Sometimes you get lucky and it works out that way, and sometimes it goes the other way. I guess that's a way of saying you deal with the hand you're dealt. You've done all right, Ross, and things will get better, you'll see."

"The eternal optimist, the one who thinks billable hours are dirty words," Ross said quietly.

"They are. Hey, I understand you have to bill for services rendered, but that isn't why I busted my ass to get through law school. I went so I could help people like my family and all these neighbors. They don't want to hear I have to bill so many hours every week or my ass is on the sidewalk. Oh, no, that's not for me."

"So you're working in the lumber mill and letting all that fine education you busted your ass for go down the tubes."

"Don't be a smart-ass, Ross. I haven't given up my profession. I handle the legal affairs of the lumber mill. I'm doing two jobs, and by doing this, my old man doesn't have to work so hard. He's getting old, in case you haven't noticed."

"I noticed," Ross said quietly.

Ross stared at his old roommate. He was six-four, two inches taller than Ross, and weighed in at two-seventy. He had, in Ross's opinion, the most endearing, homely face God ever created. He'd only read about eyes that sparkled and twinkled and infectious laughter until he met Woo. Peter Woojalesky took everything life had to offer in stride, his huge, graceful bulk at odds with that same life. His arms were like tree limbs, his hands twice the size of his own, but gentler. A huge, lovable grizzly bear of a man, with ears too big for his head. He wiggled them now, to Ross's amusement.

"You're trying to figure me out again, aren't you?"

"Hell no," Ross sputtered. "You just think you know me better than I know myself. Well, spit it out, what do you see written in my eyes, in the set of my shoulders? Come on, Woo, don't be shy."

"Guess someone stepped on your toes, huh? Want to talk about it? You washing or drying?"

"Washing, you use too much soap. I called Jory yesterday and told her I wanted to talk to her. She took the morning flight and got to the house around eleven-thirty. At ten I told my lawyer to file for divorce. This afternoon I met . . . I saw this girl in the deli. . . . My mother is—"

"Whoa. Let's take it one step at a time. I thought you said you couldn't . . . that there couldn't be a divorce in the Landers family."

"Yeah, that's what I said. I don't care about it anymore. It's not fair to tie Jory to me because of some cockamamy will set up by my great-great-grandfather. Shit like that went out with the Dark Ages. I want a life with someone who loves me, who I love. I want to try for what your parents have. Jory . . . you should see her, Woo. I couldn't believe it was her. I saw her at her father's funeral, but she was wearing one of those dark veils. I don't even know if she saw me. I didn't even get to talk to her, for Christ's sake. One minute she was there, and the next she was gone. She's a knockout. She has a job and an apartment in Florida, and she gave me back all the money I've sent her these past four and a half years. She said she didn't want *anything*, and she would sign whatever papers needed to be signed. That means she won't contest the divorce I said I was never going to get. I was speechless. She apologized for all the misery she caused me, wished me happiness, and left."

"Jesus."

"The lawyer told me she'd be entitled to take my skin. I thought so too, but she doesn't want anything."

"And you think it's some kind of trick," Woo said sourly.

"I thought so at first, but if you'd seen her, you'd know she meant what she said. This was not the Jory we used to know."

"How'd she look?" Woo asked.

"Good enough to be on a magazine cover. She got a college degree too, by going to night school. She graduated last month. You want to hear something crazy, Woo? I felt like cheering."

"Did you?" the big man asked carefully.

"No. No, I didn't. I wish I had, though. She turned out nice. Why does that sound so . . . so patronizing?"

"Because it is," Woo said, settling the meat-loaf platter in its proper place in the cupboard.

"That's exactly the way you sound right now, Woo," Ross said testily, slapping a dinner plate in his friend's hands. "You always liked Jory."

"Is that a question?" Woo said, just as testily.

"Yeah. Yeah, it's a question."

"Yes, I did like her. I felt sorry for her. I saw beneath that facade she presented to all of us college boys. I thought she was vulnerable. I never asked her any questions, I made my own observations."

"You never told me that," Ross accused.

"You never took the time to ask," Woo accused in return.

Ross snorted. "She told me she was going to accuse me of rape, me, a guy who worked for her father, for God's sake, and you say she was vulnerable. I did the honorable thing, I married her. If she'd had the baby, it would have carried my name."

"Is this the same baby you said wasn't yours?" Woo muttered.

Ross clenched his fists in the soapy water. "Say it, Woo. Let's get it all out now. A little late, though, isn't it?"

"About five years," Woo drawled.

"Are you trying to say it was all my fault?"

"In a manner of speaking. You called the shots, Ross. She was a kid, and you swept her off her feet. She loved you. She belongs to the same school my mother, sisters, and myself included, belong to. You fuck them, you marry them. And then you stay fucking married for the rest of your life." This last was said so coldly that Ross wanted the floor to rise up and swallow him.

"You've felt like this all along, and you never said a word. Why?" Ross asked, dumbfounded.

"It wasn't my business. You're running a little behind here, let's get a move on, I hear neighbors on the porch, so it's time to make lemonade."

"Fuck you, Woo. Don't give me that shit that it was none of your business. You always managed to yank me from something if it wasn't going to be good for me. Why'd you switch up back there?"

"Because that was personal, something that was going to affect the rest of your life, and it was none of my business. Hey, the girl did what you wanted, she withdrew from your life, didn't make any waves, didn't spend your money. She swallowed it all and made a life for herself. If I had the money, I'd send her a dozen red roses. I swear to God I would."

Ross wiped the strawberry-patterned oilcloth. "I have to change the water to do the pans. You can fill the pitcher, and I'll squeeze the lemons. Two or three?"

"Three. The lemons are washed, Ma always does that when she brings them home from the market."

They worked quietly, side by side, each busy with his own thoughts. This was the first time they'd had such a discussion, and each was wary of what was to come next. Woo took the initiative. "Tell me about the girl you met, and don't leave anything out. Just give me a minute to take this tray out to the porch."

Ross washed the leftover dish suds down the drain before he refilled the sink. He was scouring the meat-loaf pan when Woo opened the drawer for a clean dish towel. "She's pretty. I met her by accident at the deli. She's going to work at the magazine. She's a journalism major and is taking off a year to earn next year's tuition. Her brother is a photographer. I guess they're going to work as a team. Both of them seem to have a lot of savvy. I'm having dinner with her tomorrow night. Her eyes are kind of bluish-purple. Very different. She's a blonde. You'll probably get to meet her tomorrow. By the way, are you packed and ready to go? How'd it go when you told them at the mill you were leaving? Are your parents happy with this move? What about your father?"

"I'm packed. I'm ready. They were very nice at the mill. They said it was okay about no notice, and they wouldn't stand in my way. I can still do their legal work one day a month if I want to make the trip back here. I said I'd let them know. Ma's real happy for me. Pop was dependent on me, but Ivan and Steve will take up the slack. He's going to retire in nine months. Everything is going to work out just fine. We're all trying to save enough money to send them on a trip. Maybe Florida or California, when Pop retires. Hell, I don't even know if they'll go. They've never been out of Lancaster. They'll probably use the money for a new roof or something like that. Ma wants a new stove, and the washing machine is on the way out. Don't even think about saying it, Ross," Woo said tightly.

Ross clamped his lips shut. So many times in the past he'd offered to help, but Woo refused. Right now his face looked murderous.

"Okay, that's it," Ross said, looking around. "Almost as good as your mother does it. You got a lot of stuff?"

"No. That's a stupid question, Ross. I don't have any more than I had when I was at school. One good suit, three pairs of slacks, two sport coats, and the rest is knockabout clothes. Is that going to be a problem?"

"Hell no. You are testy tonight, and don't tell me otherwise."

"Then let's get this show on the road. Say good-bye to the folks while I get my bags."

The good-byes took half an hour. It was 10:45 when Ross steered the Buick onto the turnpike, and another two hours before he garaged the car. They parted in the upper hallway of Ross's house in Society Hill twenty minutes later.

Ross's last conscious thought before drifting into sleep was, he had to figure out what the wary look in Woo's eyes meant.

Chapter 4

Jory Ryan paid the driver and said she would carry her own bags into the house. It was August 1953, the month Burt Lancaster appeared in the movie *From Here to Eternity*.

Everything looked the same, the yard a little more overgrown, the gutters brimming with leaves, the moss thicker between the flagstones on the front walkway. The paint was still peeling on the front door. For some crazy reason, she thought it would look different, that she'd be disappointed when she saw it again.

There would be water and electricity now, because she'd called ahead to have them turned on. She'd called a garage and had them work on her father's Rambler station wagon too. She was assured by mail that the car was now serviceable, with a complete tune-up plus four new tires. Ready to be operated, the greasy bill had read. She'd sent a check for $160.

As soon as she carried her bags to the second floor, she was heading to the nearest grocery store for cleaning supplies and food. No, that was the second thing she was going to do. First she was going to get out of her traveling clothes and get into something more comfortable.

Jory was winded by the time she struggled up the stairs with the last of her suitcases. Thank God she didn't have a lot of clothes.

Thank God she'd had the good sense to join a group of tenants in her housing complex this last week when they had a yard sale. They were moving too. She'd netted over a hundred dollars from apartment accessories, and another hundred fifty from her secondhand furniture. That plus her severance pay and her personal savings accounted for the $1300 in her purse. She also had a letter from her boss that said she was laid off, so she could collect unemployment out of state. He'd given her a second letter for the personnel director at the *Democrat*. If she was frugal and collected unemployment, she could get by till the first of the year. Right now she was open to anything and everything. If the paper offered her a job, she'd snatch at it. In the meantime, while she was cleaning, repairing, and collecting insurance, she could send out résumés. She might even have a little extra time to write some articles for *Redbook* or the *Ladies' Home Journal.* If there was any way at all for her to squeeze even a few hours a week out of her busy schedule, she wanted to donate some time to the pediatric ward at the hospital.

Jory opened the smaller of the three suitcases and withdrew a playsuit and matching sandals she'd had the foresight to place on top of her clothes. Later, when the closet and dressers were cleaned, she'd transfer the clothes from the suitcases. For now she'd live out of her luggage. She'd just made her first decision. She smiled at her reflection in the dusty mirror. If the smile didn't reach her eyes, who was there to notice?

She moved quickly, wanted the shopping trip to the A&P out of the way so she could get started on making the place habitable. Besides, she was itching to try out the Rambler.

Fifteen minutes later Marjory steered the station wagon between two parked cars in the lot. She sat a moment, feeling rather like a queen. Only queens didn't shop at the A&P. She giggled.

An hour later she was back in the grimy, dirty kitchen unloading her purchases. She had two grocery bags full of cleaning supplies, a new broom, a dust mop, a wet mop, a galvanized pail, and three scrub brushes. There were cleaning rags in a pillowcase tacked to the back of the laundry room door. She had everything she needed. The food she'd purchased went into the refrigerator, which looked clean. When she tackled the kitchen, she'd clean it just to make sure.

Jory changed her clothes again. This time she donned a pair of shorts and a shirt-tail blouse. Her hair was covered with a plaid bandanna. She attacked the house the way she did everything in her life, with energy and confidence. She worked from sunup till sundown, scouring, scrubbing, polishing, and vacuuming. The washing machine ran constantly, the pile of scrub rags mounting by the hour.

On the fifth day, Jory opened her paint cans and proceeded to give the house on Gravers Lane a new, bright, white beginning. Her painting took another five days. Three additional days were used up by cleaning windows and hanging curtains and drapes from the attic. She found the treadle sewing machine the same time she found the boxes of curtains, drapes, and blankets, but there was no way she could get it down the steep attic stairs on her own. She sighed with relief, not really wanting to take the time to attend sewing classes. The canopy valances and new slipcovers would have to wait. If she managed to get a good-paying job, she could buy them at some point in the future.

She called a chimney sweep to clean the fireplaces, her one outside expense. He asked her if she had any odd jobs she needed done. For a reasonable fee he said he would scrape the paint on the doors and window frames. For a fee that was slightly less reasonable, he said he would paint the porch in the back and the garage doors. She agreed.

Her stomach in knots at what she would be spending, she'd casually asked how much he would charge to paint and fix the carriage house. She debated for an hour before she gave him the go-ahead to start work on the building, knowing she would have little trouble renting it. The hard part was how much to charge. As far as she knew, it had never been rented, and even now she couldn't remember why her father had renovated and furnished it. The furniture was old-fashioned, the windows bare, the utilities turned off. She didn't even know if there was water. The drawback to renting, the chimney sweep said, was the lack of central heat, but maybe, if he cleaned out the fireplaces and she provided the wood—and he knew just the person who could deliver cords of wood at a reasonable price—it wouldn't be a major concern. She agreed.

The Labor Day weekend dawned clear and beautiful. Her abode was finished to her satisfaction. Tomorrow she'd go into town, place her ad to rent the carriage house, and stop by the personnel office of the *Democrat*.

To celebrate the holiday, Jory prepared dinner on the outdoor grill: hot dogs, corn on the cob she wrapped in foil, and a potato that steamed along with the corn. For dessert she ate a whole melon and drank two bottles of soda pop. She smoked two cigarettes on the back porch, her eyes trying to see everything at once, the pretty yard, the rows and rows of colorful chrysanthemums, the patchy green lawn that would revive in the spring with the aid of lots of water and fertilizer, something that wasn't a top priority right now. It was enough that all the underbrush was cleared away, that the shrubs she pruned so meticulously were being shown to their advantage. In another few weeks she was going to have a major leaf problem, when the magnificent old chestnut trees started to shed. Hopefully she could rent the carriage house to someone who would help with the maintenance for a small rental discount. She told herself lots of people liked yard work, gardening, people who would care about maintaining the grounds around the carriage house. She hoped she wasn't wrong.

Now, though, she had to do something she'd been postponing since the day she arrived a month ago. She had to write to Ross and tell him she'd moved back here, that she was once again a Pennsylvania resident. She thought it was strange that no mail was forwarded from Florida. Obviously Ross's attorney was in no hurry to speed up the divorce process, or maybe things were moving normally and she was the impatient one.

"Be done with it already," she muttered. It would never be done, at least for her; some small part of her would always love Ross Landers. It was one thing to say the words aloud, another thing to accept it in her heart. Every time she thought about her brief marriage, she was consumed with shame and guilt. The years should have lessened her feelings, but they hadn't. Maybe the divorce would alleviate some of the shame, make her life a little more bearable. New beginnings were something she'd only read about in novels and magazines. Maybe now she could apply to her own life all those principles they wrote about in magazines.

The first rule was learn from your mistakes, don't live in the past. The second was to find someplace in your home and designate it as "the place" to pack up all your emotional baggage. In her case it was the downstairs linen closet. The emotional baggage consisted of her marriage license, one photograph of her and Ross at a football game, a small bouquet of violets she'd bought herself for the brief marriage ceremony at city hall. She'd centered her baggage carefully on the pristine white shelf before she closed the door. She would only open the door one more time to add her divorce papers to the envelope.

Some people, one of the articles went on to say, didn't get a second chance. Those who do should act on that good fortune, and it was exactly what she was doing. If she faltered and cried out in her sleep, there was no one to see or hear. If her eyes filled when a song was heard, or if her hands started to shake when she saw bouquets of violets in a florist's window, so be it. Each day it would get better. Childishly, she crossed her fingers.

The kitchen was neat and tidy. It looked like someone lived here now. Red-and-white-checkered place mats were on the round oak table. New red corduroy cushions were on the chairs, and ivy cuttings in clear glass pickle jars lined the wide windowsill. The curtains were white and ruffled with red string tieback tassels. Cheerful, homey. On the wall next to the refrigerator was a calendar she'd brought with her of Key West sunsets.

The electric percolator gleamed, the glasses on the shelves sparkled, and the copper-bottom pots were so shiny she could see her reflection in them in the morning when the sun came through the kitchen window. "I would have made a wonderful mother and wife," she said in a choked voice. "I know I would have."

Jory locked the back door and turned on the small night-light over the kitchen sink. She was done in the kitchen for the night, but later she might want a soda pop or a dish of ice cream. Often she came downstairs in the middle of the night for a sweet of some kind when she couldn't sleep. One of her favorite things in the kitchen was the bright red ceramic strawberry-shaped cookie jar that was filled almost daily with Fig Newtons. She'd bought it for half price at the hardware store because there were two chips around the rim. Nail polish corrected it perfectly.

"This is mine, and no one can take it from me. So, I'm a little late getting on with my life, but I'm doing it." It was something she said to herself every day since she'd returned to Chestnut Hill. She thought it helped.

Jory's second favorite room in the house was her father's study. She loved the floor-to-ceiling bookshelves, the smell of rich Corinthian leather–bound books. The shelves covered one entire wall, half devoted to a legal library, the other full of old classics and modern-day novels. She'd dusted each book, replacing it exactly where she found it, often reading a line or two.

The desk was solid mahogany with a layer of glass on top. She hadn't thrown anything away, preferring to clean, dust, and preserve everything. It was all she had now. Things. Stuff. There was a phone, a brass lamp, and a leather cup full of pencils and pens. A twelve-inch ruler stuck out of the cup and looked out of place, but she didn't care. The drawers were full of dozens of legal pads, memo pads, folders with partial case histories, some of her father's personal papers, letters from friends, some from criminals. A recording machine was in the bottom drawer. She had no idea how it worked. One of the drawers had been locked. Certain there was something of importance in it, she'd pried it open with the tip of her nail file. Inside was a loaded gun. It had taken her fifteen minutes to figure out how to take the bullets out. The gun was still there, the bullets in a coffee can in the garage. She shivered the way she had the day she found the gun.

She moved on, loving the smell of the lemon wax, the faint scent of the pine cleaner she'd used on the area carpets, the even fainter scent of the vinegar she'd used to clean the windows. The cover on the Underwood typewriter was real leather, and she'd oiled that too.

Jory sat down on her father's chair and leaned back. She had to think about what she was going to say in the note to Ross. All week

she'd been playing variations back and forth in her mind. She didn't
feel comfortable with anything she'd come up with. All of them
seemed to her to hold some kind of hidden meaning, a faint hope
that he would change his mind about the divorce. Hope springs
eternal, said the poet. She clucked her tongue at the thought.

The cover came off the typewriter with a flourish. From the second drawer of the desk she withdrew a sheet of her father's legal
stationery. She crossed out his name and added her own above the
address. She dropped down six spaces, dated the letter, added Ross's
address, and then dropped down another six spaces.

Dear Ross,
    As you can see by the address at the top of this letter, I have
moved back to Chestnut Hill. Please send any correspondence here.
    Before I left Florida I changed my name back to Ryan. I hope
this doesn't present a problem for you.

                                                    Sincerely,
                                                    Marjory Ryan

"That pretty much says it all," Jory muttered as she typed out
Ross's address on the stiff, crackly white envelope. "Done!" She covered the typewriter, pushed the swivel chair back into place, added
a stamp to the envelope, and carried it to the front hallway, where
she laid it on the table that had always held mail. She'd mail it
tomorrow.

Jory felt anxious, at odds with herself. She wished for a friend,
a pet, someone to talk to. Maybe she should think about getting a
cat or a dog. In Florida she'd had a fish tank, but she'd sold that
before she left. Fish weren't pets, they were something to look at
and feed. Never a pet. She'd need to get involved in something,
something besides a job. She needed to meet people, to do things.
She needed to be so busy, she told herself, that she didn't have time
to think.

Jory reached for a cable-stitched sweater hanging on the hat rack
next to the mail table. A walk might ease the tension building between her shoulder blades.

She walked aimlessly down Gravers Lane, nodding to other
strollers, her hands jammed into the pockets of her slacks. It

smelled like autumn already, her favorite time of the year. She'd missed the seasons in Florida. When she was a child, she'd played in the leaves, been breathless when the first pumpkins ripened. One year when she was thirteen she'd fashioned a scarecrow with corn stalks she purchased from the outdoor market with her allowance. She'd propped it up on the milk box by the front door. Her father threw it in the trash that same night, saying she was too big for such nonsense. He hadn't gone into the kitchen, so he didn't see the pumpkin. He did see it the following day, though, and hadn't touched it. She never understood what the difference was between a scarecrow and a pumpkin. If she was too old for scarecrows, it meant she was grown-up. That weekend she'd taken all of her allowance and rushed to the nearest dime store, where she spent it all on Maybelline cosmetics. For a while, until she learned how to apply the makeup, she alternated between looking like a raccoon and a real scarecrow.

She laughed when she remembered the greasy red lipstick and Billy Stevens telling her she had kissable lips. Boys noticed her, really noticed her, juniors and seniors, because the makeup made her look older than she was. When she met Ross and his college friends, she looked like she was twenty-five instead of seventeen going on eighteen. She'd lied to them and said she was twenty-two, had just graduated from Villanova, and was going to go for her master's in September. No one had questioned her age, not Ross, not Woo, none of his friends. Her face still burned with shame when she thought of all the things she'd done to snag Ross.

Now, she ran, her feet slapping on the pavement, until she was winded. She had to stop thinking about the past. She couldn't undo it, couldn't make it right. All she could do was move forward and not look back. Damn, the lace on one of her sneakers was untied. She bent down to tie it. She saw him then, he was caught in the low growth of a rosebush. He was fat, and all stomach and mewling softly. Poor thing, how long had he been caught like this? She pricked herself a dozen times until she got him untangled. How fast his little heart was beating. A small pink tongue licked at her face.

"Yoo hoo," Jory called as she walked around to the back of the house, where she could see a light. She could hear children squabbling, the sound of a radio playing and dogs yipping. Over all the din she could hear a masculine voice say, "I told you to find the dog. Do you want it to get hit by a car?"

"We looked and looked," a chorus of voices whined. "Someone stole him."

Jory called again as she walked up the steps of the back porch. She could see four children, a frazzled-looking man who must be the father, and what looked like a dozen dogs scampering around the kitchen floor. She saw two of them pee, the others sniffing the wet spots. One of the children stepped in the puddles while another child kicked the dog's food dish across the floor. The puppies beelined for the spilled food. The father said, "Oh Jesus, I really need this!" Where, Jory wondered, was the mother who she knew would have the situation under control in minutes. A moment later she had her answer. "Your mother said she had things under control when she left for her canasta game."

"She did, she did, Mickey tipped the box over," a cherub with a high-pitched voice said. During that one moment of silence while the father debated his answer Jory knocked on the door.

"Is this puppy yours?" she asked when she saw him. "I found him stuck in the rosebush."

"See, Dad, here he is," the cherub said. "Now Mom won't be mad when we tell her what happened. They're all boy dogs," he said to Jory.

"I can see that. What a lucky little boy you are to have so many puppies."

"Do you want some?"

Some. Not one. Did she? She handed over the puppy to the man, whose hair was standing on end. She smiled. "I think you need a bigger box."

"I think what we need is to get rid of these puppies. Who wants eight puppies? Four are promised. We think. Thanks for bringing this little guy back. Which one is he?" he asked the four kids.

"Clancy." Jory giggled as the kids ran off the roll call.

"So, miss, are you interested? They go to the pound tomorrow. We can't handle them. I've a mind to send these kids right along with them."

"Aw, Dad," the oldest said.

"Don't 'Aw Dad' me. We said if you couldn't find homes for them, they had to go. We had a family meeting, we all agreed."

"Which ones aren't taken?" Jory asked. She wasn't taking one of these dogs. Not till her life was settled.

The cherub pointed. "Clancy, Murphy, Sam, and Bernie."

"What kind of dogs are they?" Jory asked. It didn't hurt to ask. She'd always been a curious person.

"Part Yorkshire, part something else. Actually, the other half is a mystery. They won't shed. At least I don't think they will."

"They poop a lot," the cherub said. Jory thought she saw an evil glint in his eye.

"You have to put lots of paper down," one of the kids said.

A three-year-old with half his supper on his T-shirt mumbled something that sounded like, "They slop when they eat and you have to wash their heinie because poop sticks on it."

"Guess that killed this offer," the father said, holding out his hand. "Tom Reynolds."

"Jory Ryan, I live on Gravers Lane."

"Are you Jake Ryan's daughter?"

"Yes I am. Did you know my father?"

"Only by reputation and to nod when we passed one another. I heard someone was living in the house, but didn't know if it was sold or not. You got a lot of property out there. Might be a good idea to have a dog."

"Yes, but which one?" She didn't just say that, did she?

"They all have good dispositions. Why don't you take the four of them and make your decision tomorrow? You can bring the others back when you decide. They've had their shots, and I'll give you enough food for the morning. Great little guys, they love people. Come on, don't you feel sorry for us?" Reynolds wheedled. "The kids will help you with them."

Before she knew what she was doing, she had Clancy in her

arms, the boy with the evil glint in his eye had either Murphy or Sam, and the oldest boy had Bernie and one other.

"If I decide I don't want any of them, can I bring them all back?" Jory asked in a feeble voice.

"Absolutely," Reynolds said.

"You're sure you'll be here tomorrow?"

"My wife will be here, I'll be at work during the day. The kids are going back to school."

The walk to Gravers Lane was an experience Jory didn't think she'd ever forget. The fat, frisky puppies struggled until the boys, giggling happily, allowed them to trot alongside them. The kids shrieked with laughter when the fattest of the puppies squatted in the middle of the road. "Murphy has the splats," one of the boys said, smirking. "You need lots of papers." His business done, Murphy and the other puppies leapfrogged ahead, tumbling end over end. Jory no longer knew which one was Murphy.

Inside Jory's kitchen the kids dumped the puppies on the tile floor and backed out the door. The oldest looked wistful when he said, "They don't poop in their box. They don't like the box. They like to see what's going on. They . . ." He struggled for the right word. ". . . whimper at night. Sally doesn't want to be bothered with them anymore, and Mom said she's tired." Jory deduced that Sally was the dog's mother. The boy, seven at the most, advanced a step and said, "You'll take care of them, woncha? My friend says when you take dogs to the pound, they make them go to sleep and they don't wake up." Suddenly he dropped to his knees and fondled all the pups who rushed to him. Jory felt a lump in the middle of her throat.

"I'll take care of them. Have a nice day at school tomorrow. Do you want me to walk you home?"

The little boy looked disgusted. "I'm not afraid of the dark. I know my way. 'Sides, you can't leave *them* alone. Bernie likes to chew stuff. You gotta watch them. Can I come over and see them after school?"

"Well, yeah, but listen, I didn't say I was going to . . . your dad said . . ."

"I know what he said, he's taking them to the pound if no one wants them. It's not Sally's fault. Some dog smelled her and dug a hole under the fence and Sally got puppies. It's not Sally's fault," he said, running out the door, where his brothers waited for him.

They *were* adorable, Jory thought. They'd be company in the evenings. But how would they fare if she got a job working eight to five? They would have each other for company. Lord, she was making it sound like she was really going to keep them. No one in their right mind took on four dogs. Grown, they'd be a handful; as puppies, she'd go out of her mind. She didn't even know which one was which. She supposed she could wait for Murphy, or was it Bernie, to have the splats, and then she'd know at least one. As if the puppies read her mind, one squatted. Brown stuff splattered all over the kitchen floor. She reached for the paper towels and then burst out laughing as the four puppies sat back on their pudgy haunches to observe the cleaning-up process.

"This is a mistake," she said aloud. "You don't make mistakes any-more. You don't do impulsive things the way you used to. You think things through." Four sets of eyes watched her every move. She looked at them. "This is temporary. Tomorrow you are going . . . I will take you . . . damn it, don't look at me like that! I'm a nice per-son. I don't know anything about dogs. You'll drive me crazy. I don't have time for you. You belong with children who will run and play with you. I'm *old*. I just know one of you is going to be a chewer. I don't have a box for you. You need beds. You're going to miss your mother. Just tonight. God, you smell. Listen, I had . . . have my life all planned. It does not include any of you. You're sweet, lovable and . . . you're going to be so much trouble, and I don't know if the good can outweigh all the mischief I know you will . . . maybe if I had a book on dogs, knew the rules . . . but I don't. I just know you're going to yip all night long. I'm not going to get any sleep, and tomorrow I have to go into town and see about getting a job. How's it going to look when I have dark circles under my eyes? I can see that you are all really worried about my well-being," Jory said sourly. "Okay, here's the game plan. I'm giving each of you a bath. Then I'm going to bed, and so are you."

Ninety minutes later Jory was soaked to the skin, the floor of the laundry room a disaster. Wet dog fur smelled almost as bad as dry dog fur. She couldn't make up her mind if Prell shampoo was worse or better than the dog smell. In spite of herself, Jory broke out in a fit of giggles when the puppies squirmed together into a ball. They looked like a giant fur muff. They looked exhausted, their eyes closing wearily. From her knitting bag in the laundry room, Jory cut lengths of colored yarn. Red was Clancy, blue was Murphy, yellow was Bernie, and green was Sam. She wrote the dogs' names and their string colors on the notepad by the kitchen phone. It didn't mean she was going to keep them. All it meant was she was going to return them clean and by name.

Jory bent over to fondle their ears and to say good night. They were shivering, huddling together for warmth. "Okay, okay, this doesn't mean anything," she said, wrapping the four shaking puppies in a fluffy pink bath towel. She thought she heard a collective sigh of relief when she carried them upstairs and placed them on the end of her bed. "Don't move," she warned as she stripped off her wet clothes and put on her pajamas. She looked at them again when she pulled down the bedspread and fluffed her pillows. They were sound asleep, one fat ball of fur. She found herself inching her way to the center of the bed, paying careful attention to her legs so she wouldn't wake her roommates. She slept peacefully and dreamlessly until four o'clock, when she felt four tiny pink tongues lick at her face. She woke instantly, a smile on her face. She tussled with the dogs until she remembered what came next. She leaped from the bed, grabbed the towel and wrapped the squirming puppies together. She raced down the stairs and out to the yard. "Now, go!" she ordered. As one, the pups performed. Jory clapped her hands in approval as she praised them. "Now what do we do, it's not even light out yet?" she demanded, padding her way back into the kitchen.

"Breakfast is good. Always start the day with a good breakfast and you can handle anything," she muttered. In desperation, the dogs under her feet, Jory reached for the wax paper and ripped off four pieces, scrunching them into tight balls. She tossed them on the floor. The furry streaks of movement made her dizzy as she measured out coffee and added bacon to the frying pan. She added four extra slices. While the bacon sizzled, she whipped eggs in a bright yellow bowl. "At least I'm going to give you a send-off complete with a good breakfast." She eyed the small bowl of hard green pellets. "This," she said, "would give anyone the splats." She made toast for herself and two extra pieces, which she soaked in milk.

Jory forgot her own breakfast as she set the four plates side by side on the floor. It was fun, almost like having four babies, she thought, as she watched the puppies sample each other's dishes before they settled on their own. She laughed aloud when Sam stuck one of his paws in Clancy's dish, upending it. Eggs and bacon were all over the floor. A moment later the floor was licked clean. Before she started on her own breakfast, she set a water bowl on the floor. Four pink tongues lapped happily. Her breakfast was cold, but she didn't care. She chewed contentedly as she watched the dogs tumble over one another as they played with the wax paper. Jory relaxed with a cigarette. As a rule she didn't smoke except after meals or when she was under stress. Sometimes she had a cigarette before going to bed. Now, though, she smoked three, one after the other, to kill time. She also finished the coffee in the pot. She kept one eye on the puppies tumbling over one another as they played happily. She liked the idea of the colored strings. Should she take them back before she went to town or when she got back? Common sense said Mrs. Reynolds would be busy getting the children off to school, packing lunches, and perhaps shedding a tear or two. Mr. Reynolds would need his breakfast and his own send-off by the front door. The afternoon would be soon enough, she decided as she filled the sink with soapy water.

It was a simple matter to barricade the kitchen with the dining room chairs while she showered and dressed. The radio, tuned to relaxing music, would keep the dogs company. Four tails swished furiously when Jory stepped over the chair. She dropped to her knees and wagged a playful finger under their noses. "You behave now, you hear?" Four sets of tails and ears protested these strange goings-on. The dogs yipped, scrambling and pawing the barricade, their stubby tails fanning the air. "Be good." Jory smiled. "I'll take you outside as soon as I come down."

Did she dare leave them alone down there? She wondered as she showered. She had, so what was the point in thinking about it? Should she keep one of them? But which one? None, she said to

herself over and over. You'll be working, and it isn't fair to leave a
dog alone all day. Take them back. Later, when you're really settled,
you can think about getting a pet.

She was still arguing with herself as she dressed and applied a
light coat of powder and eye shadow. Her lipstick was coral, high-
lighting what was left of her summer tan. She pulled her hair back
into a skintight bun. The severe white porcelain earrings nestling
on her lobes again called attention to her honeyed tan. The beige-
and-white striped seersucker suit with the pencil-slim skirt was both
attractive and professional-looking. The beige heels added two
inches to her five-foot-eight. She felt successful when she descended
the stairs with her beige shoulder bag. She checked to make sure
she had the recommendation letter from her former boss, Aaron
Stephens. Maybe, just maybe, it would help. She crossed her fingers
and made a silent wish.

In the kitchen, Jory removed the barricade and let the pups out
the back door. As one they tumbled down the four steps to the
lawn, yipping and howling as they did so. They were like a minia-
ture herd, brushing against one another as they romped and chewed
at one another's ears and tails. As one they sat down and stared at
her, perfect little statues waiting for what was to come next.

"Pee," Jory said sternly. "Come on now," she said, motioning
with her hand, "do it." The pup with the red string yipped as he
turned a somersault. The pup with the green string sat on top of
him, while the one with the yellow string industriously chewed at
his left ear. She waited a full five minutes, and then five more minutes. Exhausted, the dogs lay down and went to sleep. Jory carried
them back to the house. The barricade went back up and a thick
layer of newspapers went down all over the kitchen floor. She
checked to make sure the water bowl was full before she left. The
word "disaster" stayed in her mind on the drive to town.

The pups were still on her mind when Jory filled out the newspaper's employment application at eight-fifteen. She handed the letter of recommendation to the middle-aged personnel director, who
read it immediately. The woman's voice was regretful when she said,
"You're overqualified for the one available opening. I can keep your
application, and if anything opens up I'll call you."

Why had she thought this was going to be a snap? She felt like crying. "I'd appreciate that," Jory said.

"Are you related to Jake Ryan? The resemblance is there," the woman said.

"He was my father. Well, thank you for your time."

"Wait. I don't know if this will interest you, but we're . . . this is going to sound peculiar, but hear me out. We're interviewing for Auntie Ann. It's an advice column. What we're doing is giving out five sample letter problems and asking our interviewees to respond. It's a job that can be done at home or here in the office. So far we've had three other applicants, all of them men. The identity of Auntie Ann will remain secret, and the name belongs to the paper. We're going to run the column one day a week. If it's successful, we'll go to three times a week, and if it goes over with a bang, it will be daily. Would you be interested in giving it a try?"

"Oh, yes. Yes, I would." A job was a job.

"Here's the packet," the woman said, holding out a manila envelope. "The guidelines are clear. We've done a mock-up of how we want the column to look. The space requirements are set up, but that's all subject to change with the popularity of the column. I'll need your response a week from today. I've attached a copy of the pay scale along with some background on the paper. It will take us several days, perhaps as long as a week, to make our decision once you've turned in your column. Good luck."

"Thank you. Thank you very much," Jory said breathlessly.

Outside in the hall, Jory literally swooned. An advice columnist. She could work at home if she wanted to. Providing she got the job. That meant she could keep one of the puppies. "Thank you, Lord," she sighed happily.

It took Jory fifteen minutes to find the classified office, where she placed her ad to rent the carriage house. She paid three dollars and told them to run the ad for a full week. She was told the ad would run in the next day's paper. While she waited for her change, Jory watched two young girls at back-to-back desks leaf through a tabloid. Even from this distance she could read the headlines. NAME THE STARLET WITH ROUND HEELS. She dropped the two one-dollar bills on the floor when she saw the banner at the top of the paper.

TIF. Surely this wasn't her in-laws' magazine. She craned her neck for a better look. Jory stumbled over her own feet in her hurry to leave the building. She had to buy a copy and see for herself. If what she saw was the Landerses' publication, it mean her soon-to-be-ex-father-in-law allowed . . . Not Jasper, not warm, wonderful Jasper. He wouldn't allow his family's magazine to take such a turn. And Ross . . . was he part of this? She felt sick as she hurried down the street in search of a newsstand.

Jory's eyes searched the rows of sleazy magazines for the one she was looking for. Her throat constricted when she saw what was once a respectable magazine. She handed the man behind the counter a dollar bill and bought five magazines. She folded them in a bunch and stuck them under her arm. Why she was buying them, she didn't know.

Was it possible the Landers family had fallen on hard times? Sleazy, steamy, sewer journalism sold. On the plane from Florida she saw both men and women reading the cheap-looking papers. When she herself had picked up a copy of the *Sun Sentinel,* she'd seen harried mothers, men dressed in three-piece business suits, and young giggly girls buying the papers, and not just one, but every paper on the rack. At the time she'd been mystified. Her old boss had told her it was a craze the public went through from time to time. He said it was an insatiable thirst for back-alley gossip, and no reputable publisher or journalist would work for such a publication. She'd figured that out on her own after their discussion. The only people who benefited from this type of publication were the owners, who probably laughed their way to the bank.

Jory retraced her steps to the parking lot. The Rambler purred to life, and she was back home at ten-fifteen. Total, absolute chaos greeted her. The moment the busy pups heard her steps on the back porch, they clustered into a tight ball. Jory thought they looked guilty. A sea of shredded newspaper was everywhere. Obviously, all four of them had the splats, and a second bath was called for. There was no way she could walk through the mess in the kitchen in her good clothes. She forgot about her new assignment and her in-laws' magazine as she raced around to the front of the house to enter by the red door. She was back in the kitchen ten minutes later trying to untangle the four dogs from their colored strings. "Not a good idea," she muttered as she took them into the laundry room, one by one, and scrubbed them down. While they dried, she cleaned the kitchen. At one o'clock she had new strings around their necks. They were going home clean and they were going to walk.

Halfway to the Reynolds house it occurred to Jory that if she didn't get the job, she'd have to return the dog. Better not get attached, she told herself.

As one, the puppies balked when she tried to lead them up the Reynolds driveway. Frustrated, Jory looped the four lengths of yarn into one string and tied it to a forsythia branch. "Wait here and don't get into trouble," she said sternly. She wagged her finger for emphasis.

The kids saw her first and whooped with delight, demanding to know how the dogs were. Mrs. Reynolds, a baby on her hip, was warming a bottle on the stove. The baby was screeching, his small fists tugging at his mother's hair. Four of the remaining puppies were racing back and forth across the kitchen floor, their mother barking shrilly. The kids, ages probably three and four, had peanut butter and jelly smeared all over their faces. The dogs yipped and cavorted as they too tried to lick one another. The baby continued to shriek.

"Mrs. Reynolds, I'm Marjory Ryan," Jory said, shouting to be heard over the din. "I brought the puppies back."

"You did *what?*" the woman said, collapsing into the kitchen chair. The pups tried to crawl up her leg. She jammed the bottle into the screaming baby's mouth. Jory thought she'd never seen a more frazzled person in her life.

"I brought the dogs back. I told your husband I didn't think I could keep them."

"Then why did you take them? You can't bring them back. My God, you just can't," the woman said, tears filling her eyes. The baby yanked the bottle from its mouth and sent it sailing across the room. The four pups pounced on it immediately. The baby wailed, the mother cried, the kids threw the last of their sandwiches at the dogs. The screen door banged. The three-year-old caught his foot in the door and started to howl. "I can't take any more of this," the woman sobbed.

"I can't either," Jory said. She thought about her nice clean house, the peace and quiet. She threw her hands in the air. "I guess I can put them in the garage. Will that be all right?"

"No, it's not all right. You shouldn't have taken them if you didn't want them. You'll have to take them to the pound yourself. I don't have the time and I . . . I can't be responsible for . . . putting them to sleep," the woman sobbed.

"But I told your husband—"

"I don't care. Do you see my husband here? No. He works. I stay home and take care of this . . . this menagerie. This child is sick, he should be seen by a doctor. I'm waiting for him to make a house call. I have to pick up the kids from school. I have to think about making dinner. The dogs smell, they should be given a bath. I'm tired, I was up all night with this child. I have diapers to wash." She cried again. The baby shrieked louder. "I think he has an ear infection, and I'm on the verge of a nervous breakdown."

"Can I do something?" Jory asked weakly.

"That's what my husband said last night when he told me to go out and play canasta with my friends. I fell asleep at the card table. That's not help. I'm sorry I got married, sorry I'm not the woman my mother was. I just want to run away and never come back."

"You don't mean that," Jory said, fidgeting with her hands.

"Right now, this very second I do. I can't help you, Miss . . . what did you say your name was?"

"Jory. Jory Ryan."

"Well, Jory Ryan, you are just going to have to cope like the rest of us. Now if you'll excuse me, I have to change this child, sterilize his bottles, and wash his diapers. Do the best you can. That's what my husband tells me when he comes home from work."

"But . . . the dogs—"

"Possession is nine-tenths of the law. Do whatever you have to do, just don't tell me what that is, because I can't . . . I don't . . ."

"All right, Mrs. Reynolds. I hope the baby feels better."

"He won't, not for four days," the woman said miserably.

Jory closed the screen door. One of the pups nipped at her heels while a second one pushed his head through the screen. In the front of the house the four-year-old was cracking eggs on the concrete driveway. "Do they really fry?" she asked curiously.

"Yeah. Want some?"

"No thanks." The pups were right where she left them, lined up like four fat little soldiers. She untied the string and marched them home.

On the back steps, Jory cuddled them, marveling at the fast beat of their little hearts. Tiny pink tongues licked at her face. Such warm little bodies, such energy. She couldn't be the one to snuff that out. Not now, not ever. Life was too wonderful, too precious. How hard could it be to take care of four puppies? She had an edge on Mrs. Reynolds, she had no children to contend with. Nothing could be harder than what she'd gone through five years ago when she left here. She'd had no one, she was sore and wounded, unloved and unhappy. She'd survived all of that. Maybe she was meant to be here, meant to take on these four warm little dogs, meant to keep them, to preserve their lives. "I believe in things like that, I really do," she crooned to the animals, who were now asleep in her arms. "Nobody ever trusted me before," she whispered. "No one has ever had to depend on me for their livelihood. You do your part and I'll do mine," she continued to whisper. The dog with the green string burrowed deeper into the crook of her arm. She smiled.

Marjory Ryan's world was almost right-side up.

Jory woke from her doze when the four pups began to squirm. They leaped from her arms, tumbled to the ground. They looked at one another, squatted, and then eyed one another again before they raced across the lawn. Jory whistled. They stopped, looked back at her as though undecided what course to follow. The dog with the red string trotted toward her. She whistled again, and the other three fell into line. She praised them, laughter in her voice. The dogs reacted happily as they struggled with the steps.

The hours passed quickly once Jory made a call to the local veterinarian. She flushed with the vet's warm praise for the awesome task she'd undertaken. She copied down his instructions and listened to his helpful hints. She sighed with relief when he promised to give her a discount for the dogs' checkups. When she hung up the phone, she knew about designated sleep areas, designated food areas, designated "duty" areas, rolled-up newspapers, about tones of voice for displeasure and pleasure. She was ahead of the game, according to the vet, because the dogs had each other for company and wouldn't depend on her to play and amuse them twenty-four hours a day. At nine o'clock when she sat down to read the material from the personnel director, she felt confident she'd established a routine. Of sorts.

Curled on the couch, she read the make-believe letters she was to respond to as Auntie Ann. An in-law problem, a cheating husband, a child out of wedlock, wife's cooking versus mother's cooking, and a man attracted to his next door neighbor's wife. Jory's eyebrows shot upward. "Like I really know about such things," she muttered.

Common sense should do it. A lifetime of experience wouldn't make a darn bit of difference. Each case was different, and what was best for her wouldn't necessarily be best for someone else. She could be impartial. She had to be impartial.

She counted lines, inches of space, words, as she tried to visualize her answers in print. She wondered how many people would write to someone named Auntie Ann for advice. Would someone like Mrs. Reynolds write about her frazzled existence, and if she did, how should Auntie Ann respond? Now that, she decided, was one of her better ideas. If she really wanted this job, she could type up a sixth letter from a real person and write her response. Maybe that kind of initiative would land her the job. Sitting on the back steps with the dogs asleep in her lap convinced her of that. And if it got into print, she might be helping Mrs. Reynolds without her knowing it. She'd make it her business to see that Mrs. Reynolds received a copy of the paper.

Ah, life was looking better and better. If she could just stop dreaming about Ross Landers, she might have a chance at the brass ring.

"The past is prologue," she said, struggling up from her cocoon. The pups hopped to attention, their tails swishing happily. Yipping and growling, they raced to the back door, where they skidded to a stop. Jory reached for the rolled-up newspaper. She gave the table a whack. Four pairs of eyes studied her. "I don't expect instant obedience, but I do expect obedience. One at a time gentlemen. Go!" She burst out laughing at the mad scramble through the open door.

Twenty minutes later Jory snapped off the lamp next to her bed, her roommates cuddled at the foot of her bed. " 'Night, guys." My God, she thought, when did I ever say that to anyone?

She had a routine now. She had a life, and she damn well had a purpose.

Jory felt at cross purposes with herself the following day as she worked and reworked her practice column. Auntie Ann was not going to be easy to please. Her wastebasket was testimony to the fact that it was indeed hard to be impartial, harder to write lean succinct sentences and still come across as having a heart full of advice.

She'd been at it since seven A.M., with brief breaks for lunch and to take the dogs out to play. Now it was time for the dogs' dinner as well as her own. Before she started work, she'd cooked up a batch of chicken gizzards and livers for the dogs, which she mixed with puppy chow. The house reeked of the smell, and the dogs had been sniffing everything in sight for hours. She had to get the dogs on a better morning schedule. Four-fifteen was too early for her. She felt ready for bed, and it was only six o'clock.

Jory brushed a stray tendril of hair that worked its way free of the tight bun she'd started out with earlier in the day. Sticking pencils in her hair didn't allow for the sleek look. Tousled, she thought, staring at her reflection in the chrome stove top. She threw her head back before she emptied the contents of the warming pan into a large yellow bowl. She was measuring the food into equal portions when the front doorbell ding-donged through the house. She almost jumped out of her sneakers. The dogs scurried between her legs. "A caller," she said to the dogs. "Or someone to rent the carriage house. A real neighbor if that's the case. Wait here," she said, knowing it was probably the stupidest thing she would ever say to four bouncing puppies.

"A gentleman," she whispered to the dogs. She smoothed back

her hair, tugged at her blouse, and took a deep breath before she opened the door.

Jory recognized him instantly. He seemed to be having difficulty speaking. "I came about the . . . Jesus," he said, trying to shake loose the four fur balls attacking both his legs.

"I'm sorry. I just . . . inherited them, and as yet they don't have any manners." He didn't recognize her. But then why should he? What in the world was he doing here? He wanted to rent the carriage house. "We have to catch them. If we get them in the house, I can show you the carriage house. I assume you're here about the ad." The big man nodded as he tried to rescue one of the pups from the iron rail where he was stuck. The one with the green string was busy untying his shoelace. The two Jory was holding leaped from her arms, tumbling down the walkway. "You watch them, I'll be right back," Jory said, running into the house. She was back a moment later with the four dishes in her hands. "This *might* do it," she sighed. "I really am sorry."

The big man grunted. "I'm taking the shoelaces off the rent," he said.

The pups returned to the steps like homing pigeons. "Okay, you grab two and I'll take two and come back for the food. Move fast now," Jory warned. The dogs yipped and yelped all the way to the kitchen. They shut up long enough for Jory to get the key to the carriage house and sneak out the door, the big man right behind her.

"Have I changed so much that you don't recognize me, Pete? Or should I call you Woo?" Jory asked quietly with a catch in her voice.

"My God, is that you Jory?" Woo asked in stunned surprise. Both her hands were suddenly in his and he was kissing first one cheek and then the other. "Woo is fine, Pete is fine too. Ross didn't tell me you were back here. Are you living here? Of course you are, you answered the door. Jory, it's good to see you. It really is."

She believed him. She looked up at him, felt like a midget next to his six-foot-four stature. He also seemed to be having trouble with what he probably perceived as her new persona. She wanted to say, It was always there, but no one allowed me to present it, but then that wasn't exactly true either.

"It's nice to see you again . . . Pete. Woo seems rather . . . what I mean is, it doesn't fit you anymore. Are you working in town? I seem to recall you saying you were going back to Lancaster."

"I did go back, but I didn't do well in the office politics department. I resented all those billable hours I was asked to inflate. I went to work at the lumber mill and handled the company's legal business on the weekends. I would probably still be there if Ross hadn't called and offered me a position at his parents' magazine. I've been staying with Ross for about a month now, but it's time I found my own place. I plan to get a car, so this would be ideal, if we can come to terms."

Terms. Did she really want Woo living here right next to her? He would be a constant reminder of her past. As nice as he was, and as much as she'd liked him in the past, she didn't think it would work. Ross and Woo were friends, nothing would ever change that. He would talk about her to Ross; he certainly was going to mention the four dogs. What should she do? Harp on the lack of central heat. Hike the rent. Damn, she couldn't do that, the price was in the paper. Obviously he could afford the two hundred dollars or he wouldn't be here.

"This is nice, Jory," Woo said as he walked around the spacious rooms of the carriage house. "Very nice. I think I could be very comfortable here. Are utilities included in the rent?"

"No. There's no central heat, just the fireplaces. You have to light that . . . that thing behind the pantry for hot water. It takes twenty minutes till it gets hot. It's gas. It's very old-fashioned."

"You sound like you aren't anxious to rent, or is it me you don't want to rent to?" Woo asked quietly.

"I . . . It probably isn't a good idea, Pete. Ross and I are getting a divorce. It was his idea," she added hastily. "I'm trying to make a new life for myself, and I would always wonder if you were . . . what I mean is . . ."

"I'd carry tales, is that it? That's not what I'm all about, Jory. Your life is yours, mine is mine. This is a very large piece of property. I can help maintain it on weekends. Autumn is coming up, there will be lots of leaves to rake. Those dogs, now, they're going to take some care. I like animals. Snow has to be shoveled. I can do that. I can see by the chimneys you have several fireplaces. I'm a whiz at chopping wood. I couldn't help but notice those two downed trees at the back of the lot. If you get the saw, I'll do the work. I'd like to rent this house, if you have no objections."

"Ross?"

"This has nothing to do with Ross. You're the landlord and I'm the tenant. I'll sign a lease."

"When do you want to move in?" No, this wasn't a good idea. This was a bad idea. She had to say so. Instead she said, "I'll rent the carriage house to you if you don't tell Ross you're living here."

"Jory, I can't do that. It won't make a difference. I have my own life and Ross has his. I promise not to talk about you with Ross, though. By the way, does he know you're back? He didn't say anything to me. All he said was he was getting divorced. I need an answer, Jory, otherwise I have to keep looking, and it's going to be dark soon. I like to see what I'm getting in daylight."

"There's no furnace. It's going to be cold in the winter."

"You already said that, and I said I didn't mind. I was a Boy Scout, so I know how to make a fire that will burn all day. It's not a problem Jory."

"All right, a six-month lease. A month's security in advance. Is that okay?"

"That's fine, Jory. Thanks, I really appreciate this. You won't be sorry."

"I hope not, Pete. If you break your word to me, you're out. I want that written into the lease." Woo nodded. "I guess we should get to it, then."

Jory locked the door and started across the lawn to the house. She could hear the dogs yipping and yelping. She wondered what kind of mess they'd made. To her surprise, the dogs were fine; the water dish was overturned, but that was it. She cleaned up the water spill and set down a full bowl. "They like to stick their feet in it," she muttered.

"That's . . . cute." Woo laughed.

"Not when you have to keep cleaning it up. I'll type this up and be back in a minute."

"Take your time. Me and the guys here will get acquainted."

Jory felt like there was a lead weight in her stomach when she sat down to write out a short lease. "This is a mistake, I know this is a mistake," she said through clenched teeth. Then why was she doing this? Because Woo was nice to her way back when, she recalled.

She typed furiously, one paragraph, then two. This was her lease, with no input from Woo. She thought about the last paragraph before she typed it: "This lease shall be terminated within twenty-four hours if the lessor deems the actions of the lessee are detrimental to her private life." The last line read: "Six-month lease to be renewed at lessor's discretion." Jory read the document three times to be sure she hadn't left anything out. It probably wasn't legal in some respects, and would not hold up in the court of law, but she didn't care. If Woo signed it in the presence of a notary, she would be satisfied. She'd meet him tomorrow at the Mellon Bank at lunchtime to sign the lease.

Woo was sitting on a kitchen chair when she returned, all four pups cradled in his lap. His busy hands rubbed bellies and scratched ears. The dogs were ecstatic. Woo looked so contented. "Making yourself at home," she said, annoyed for some reason.

"As a matter of fact, yes. I haven't felt this relaxed since I started to work for . . . in a long time. There's something very relaxing about an animal. We always had a dog when I was growing up. They love unconditionally," Woo said quietly.

She handed over the paper. "I am not amenable to *any* changes, Pete, so either you sign it or you don't rent the carriage house."

"It looks fine to me," he replied, scanning it. "I would prefer a year's lease, but this is fine. I hope I'll prove a good enough tenant that you won't have to think twice about renewing."

"I hope so too. I'll meet you tomorrow at the Mellon Bank. There's a notary there. You don't object, do you?"

"No, not at all. I'll see you tomorrow." Jory pretended not to see the wistful look he cast in the direction of the stove. She also ig-nored the way he sniffed the air. "What smells so good?"

"My dinner. Stuffed peppers."

Jory walked out to the road with Woo, who shook her hand good-bye.

"Thanks, Jory. I really appreciate this. I like to pay my own way. I know Ross would let me stay in his house forever if I wanted to, but I just can't freeload. I need to know something before I move in." He frowned when he sensed her tension. "Jory, what exactly are the ground rules in regard to Ross? Shouldn't I mention his name to you?"

"Pete, you and I are not going to be . . . bosom buddies. I'm your landlady, and you're my tenant. We're not going to socialize, but you're correct about Ross. I'd appreciate it if you didn't mention him or the pending divorce," Jory said flatly.

"Agreed. I'll be back on Saturday with my things. Early in the morning. If you like, I can mow the lawn and trim some of the hedges."

"Fine. You'll have to call to have the gas and phone turned on and put in your name."

"I'll do that tomorrow. Do I have to be here for the hookups?"

"I'll be here, that's no problem."

"I guess that's it, Jory, you now have a tenant."

"Good night, Pete."

She's already regretting renting to me, Woo thought as he walked down the hill to catch the bus. Ross was right, she was beautiful. And she was nice too. But then, she'd been nice when he met her years ago. She'd been mixed-up, vulnerable, and out of her depth with Ross. She'd made a hell of a recovery. Hands in his pockets, he whistled as he loped down the hill, remembering how attracted he'd been to her back then, but she was his buddy's girl. And he'd been a big lummox without a graceful bone in his body. She'd al-ways been nice to him, and he'd seen through the vulnerability. Oh yes, he'd had a crush on her, one that never quite went away.

Chapter 5

Woo let himself into Ross's house with the key Ross had given him, and pulled up short at the sight of his friend in the sun room, going over his mail. The strange look on his face made him say, "So, what's new?"

"Read this," Ross said, handing over the letter in his hand. "What do you make of it, Woo?"

Woo cleared his throat. "That your wife has moved back here to her father's house. Does that bother you, Ross?"

"Sure it bothers me. Why now? Why not before? This is kind of sudden. A month ago when she was here, she didn't say anything about moving back."

"I'm not following you, Ross. Why should it make a difference? It says you're to send any and all papers to her here, and she'll sign them. What difference does it make if she lives in Florida or here in Pennsylvania? Are you afraid of running into her? Or do you have some feelings for her that you haven't resolved? If so, this might be the time to come to terms with everything."

"I just feel uneasy, I can't explain it. Come on, let's eat. The cook made your favorite, roast beef."

"Does she ever make stuffed peppers?"

"Hell, I don't know. Ask her. She'll make whatever you want."

"Ross, I'll be moving out on Saturday."

Ross tossed Jory's letter onto the glass-topped table. The frown on his face was ferocious. "Moving? Not back to Lancaster? Why? Don't you like it here? I thought you wanted to get some money ahead."

"Three questions and one statement. You're getting better, Ross," Woo said quietly. "Look, we both knew this was temporary. I've been here a month. I don't deal well with charity. Hold your horses, Ross, I know this wasn't charity on your part, but it will be if I stay on. You're paying me more than I'm worth as it is. I want to be able to walk around in my underwear if I want to, I want to mess up the kitchen and not worry about dishes in the sink, and wad up wet towels and stuff like that."

They were at the dinner table now, and Ross was shaking out his napkin. Woo blinked as he always did at the array of crystal and silverware. What the hell was wrong with one fork, one knife, one glass? He absolutely refused to use the finger bowls. He thought of his hardworking mother and father, who never had anything half this fine. The tablecloth alone probably cost more than his father earned in three months. Ever since he'd arrived, he'd been mortally afraid of spilling something on the exquisite linen. He hadn't truly enjoyed one meal, even though the food was perfect. "I like to eat chicken with my fingers, chew on the bones, and then lick my fingers," Woo blurted out.

"So do it," Ross said tightly. "Hell, we can eat off paper plates if that makes you happy. Or we can eat in the sun room. You never said anything, so how was I supposed to know this . . . offended you?"

"It doesn't offend me. I'm simply not comfortable with things here. I don't ever expect to live like this, so there's no sense in me getting used to it. I'm trying to be truthful with you, Ross, and I hope we're good enough friends that you aren't going to take this personally."

"Hell yes, I'm taking this personally. I've been knocking myself out for you, and now you tell me you don't like . . . my style."

"There was no reason for you to knock yourself out for me. You know who I am and what I come from. I don't care for this lifestyle. For you it's fine, but not me. How about a little understanding?" Woo said, laying two emerald-colored asparagus stalks on his plate.

"If that's what you want, it's okay with me. Did you find a place? Why did you wait till the last minute to tell me about this?"

"I just found it today. I've been looking, but the rents were always more than I could afford. I can afford this. It's a converted carriage house, and I agreed to do some lawn work on weekends. For me it's perfect. If you play your cards right, I might even invite you over for some of my cabbage and noodles."

"So, where is this wonderful abode?" Ross said, forking a chunk of prime rib into his mouth.

Damn, here it was, the question he'd been dreading. "Chestnut Hill," he said quietly.

"What's the street? I know the Chestnut Hill area pretty well. It's nice out there," Ross said, buttering a flaky dinner roll that he stuffed whole into his mouth.

"Gravers Lane. The carriage house is set back into the grounds, away from the main house and garage. It has its own driveway. It's very comfortable. No central heat, though, but it has two fireplaces."

"Are you nuts, Woo? It gets cold as hell here in the winter. You'll freeze your ass off." Ross buttered another roll, but didn't eat it. He shoved his plate into the middle of the table. Gravy slopped over the side onto the linen cloth. He threw his napkin in the general direction of the spill.

"No, I won't. There's a decent woodpile, I can get a few cords more, if I have to. I can chop up logs and split wood. Actually, that's part of the deal. I'm going to be very comfortable," Woo said airily.

"I'm sorry, Woo. I'm edgy and out of sorts. I guess the letter from Jory . . . Jory lives on Gravers Lane. You'll probably run into her." This last was said so coldly, Woo blinked.

"I already did," Woo said, laying his knife and fork across his dinner plate. "I'm renting her carriage house. I'm sorry if this upsets you, Ross."

"You're *what*?"

"I answered an ad in the paper, and it turned out to be Jory. She's got four dogs," Woo said, a stupid look on his face. "She didn't mention you at all until I brought up your name. If it's any consolation to you, she didn't want to rent to me, I had to talk her into it. This young woman isn't the girl I remember. I hope, Ross, that you aren't going to make an issue out of this or have it change our friendship."

That's exactly what he *was* thinking. Woo renting from Jory. Goddamnit. "I don't like it," Ross said coldly, "but it is your business. I just find it a little strange that in this entire city, hers was the only place you could afford. I also find it very strange that she decided to move back here just as I filed for divorce. Maybe it's a good idea for you to move there, after all. You can pump her and tell me what's going on. I'd hate to be blindsided at some point down the road."

Woo was off his chair in a second. "No, I won't do that, Ross. Jory is my landlady and that's all. I'm not turning into a snoop for you, and I can't believe you'd ask me to . . . get off it, Ross. Don't involve me. I mean that. If you're so damn worried, then why don't you go out there and talk to her so you can put your mind at ease?"

Ross snorted. "That's probably exactly what she wants me to do, but I'm not going to do it. I know she's up to something."

"I certainly didn't get that feeling. She seems to have her life in order. She's a hell of a looker, Ross. Those dogs . . . they're puppies. They kind of . . . swirl, move together all at once, like a mini herd. She has a nice laugh. She looked real happy to me. I think you're paranoid where she's concerned. It has occurred to me that you're a little put out that Jory agreed to the divorce and didn't come out swinging the way you thought she would. Cut it out and get on with your life. That's what she seems to be doing. Obviously she doesn't need you, and you've said over and over that you don't need her."

"The Jory I knew wouldn't . . . this isn't like her. I'm telling you, she's up to something," Ross blustered.

Woo threw his hands in the air. "What, for God's sake? She agreed to what you want. She's given back all the money you sent. She grew up into a responsible adult and is taking charge of her life. Maybe you ought to do the same," Woo added as he walked away from the table.

"Just a goddamn minute, Woo. What the hell is *that* supposed to mean? Jesus, you can't blame me for being a little surprised and just a tad suspicious."

Woo stopped in the doorway and turned around. "Ross, I have never interfered in your personal life. I've never asked any questions about you and Jory. I listened if you wanted to talk, because that's what friends are for. Based on what little you've shared with me, I have to say you're the one who's acting immaturely. I have the impression Jory doesn't want to have anything to do with you, which is why she's taken back her maiden name. You're trying to build a case out of nothing, something no good lawyer ever does."

"And of course you don't approve," Ross said coolly.

The two men eyed one another. "No, Ross, I never approved. None of it was any of my business, and if your next question is did you do Jory dirty, my answer is yes. I believe you know what you did was wrong, and for five years you didn't have the guts to make it right. You're doing that now, and you're looking, in my opinion, for a way to justify it all. Now, if you plan to ask me for my advice, I'd advise you, as a friend and as an attorney, to go to Jory and talk it all out. Get your divorce and move on with your life."

"Wait a minute, Woo. You're right about one thing, I didn't unload on you because I . . . Jesus, what did I know about women? I mean, what did I *really* know? They flirted, we advanced, they retreated, and we closed in for the kill. Did you know Jory was only seventeen? Hell no you didn't, and neither did I. She looked and sounded a lot older, and you damn well know it. She was a tease, a flirt, and she knew the score. At least I thought she did. She wasn't a virgin, you know. She goddamn well knew more than me, so when she said she'd accuse me of rape if I didn't marry her . . . well, that turned my feelings toward her sour.

"But you play, you pay. She was seventeen, Woo. A minor. She was pregnant. I had no choice, I had to marry her. I didn't want to go to jail. Her father, as my father pointed out, was the district attorney.

"It was a disaster, something that never should have happened.

Both of us were too immature to deal with it. I blustered my way through, and she cried and whined her way through it. The miscarriage, as much as I hated to say this, was for the best. I didn't know what to do for her after that. And like I said, and I'll admit it, I didn't feel so good about Jory by that time, so it was hard for me to feel compassion. She was so lost, so woebegone, and all she did was cry. I never loved her, Woo. She knew that. She said she loved me, but she was in love with love. Seventeen-year-old girls don't know what love is all about," Ross said defensively.

"I think you're wrong about that. Jory loved you heart and soul." The wistfulness in Woo's voice was lost on Ross. "Go see her."

"In court will be soon enough. With this newfound independence of hers, she's liable to accuse me of harassing her. I'll just wait it out."

"Suit yourself." Woo's right hand shot out. "No hard feelings, Ross."

"Nah. You always tell it like it is, Woo, so how can I harbor any hard feelings? This will work out. I just wish I wasn't so damn suspicious of everything."

"So, how're things going with Lena?" Woo asked. In his eyes, there was something suspicious about Lena Davis.

"We're dating. I told her about Jory. As a matter of fact, Lena's older sister went to school with Jory. Lena's been turning in some pretty good pieces, don't you think? And she's managed to get us some additional advertising. Dumb luck on that score, but she did it. My mother was pleased."

"She's angling for the L.A. assignment," Woo blurted. Ross was so damn gullible.

Ross's shoulders stiffened. "Because she said she'd love to spend the winter in California. I say that every day from December first through March first." He added, "I thought, between you and me, that I was the suspicious one."

"I never said *I* wasn't suspicious at times," Woo replied, but what he really wanted to say was: Lena is after your money, she's a gold digger, and she's kissing up to your mother big-time and using you while she's doing it. Instead he said, "She's aggressive, and I guess that's the main trait a reporter needs to get ahead in this business."

"Initiative is what she has. She's been sending out letters to Hollywood and starting her own personal grapevine. Mother gave her some seed money to get started. She's got a couple of near scoops," Ross said proudly.

"Are you seriously interested in her?" Woo asked curiously.

"I could be," Ross said carefully.

"Uh-huh." Woo grinned. "See you in the morning. I'm going to get a head start on my packing, and I want to look over that last story Lena turned in. There's something that isn't sitting right. Parts of it are pure smut. Digging up one fact and embroidering it to two thousand words is one thing, smut is something else."

"Come on, Woo. Who's going to sue over a fact? The fact is true, the embroidery is embroidery. You're taking this too seriously. All we're doing is creating an illusion and giving the public what they perceive to be the 'real lowdown' on celebrities. The second issue sold out completely. I think I was the only one who was surprised. We're upping this next issue ten thousand copies. Mother is delirious. Personally speaking, I feel we should raise it fifty thousand if we decide to go ahead with the lead story on Johnnie Ray being seen in drag at the Copa. We've got a few words on that metal plate he's supposed to have in his head too. Of course he denies it. Jesus, this guy is something else. Hey, we have two psychiatrists willing to expound on Ray's outbursts of 'feminine nature.' "

Woo did his best to disguise what he was feeling. He knew Ross well enough to know he felt almost the same way, but because he was Ross Landers, son of publisher Justine Landers, he had to act as if he believed and was interested in what *TIF* was doing. "I need to check every source, Ross. Don't send anything out until we're one hundred percent sure we aren't going to be sued for libel. I also promised your mother I'd look over several other pieces. Guess I'll say good night. I think I'll take a walk."

" 'Night, Woo," Ross said as his friend headed for the front door. "Sorry about being so edgy this evening. I'm going to miss you."

"Get a dog and a couple of cats," Woo called over his shoulder. "You won't even know I'm gone."

"I'll know," Ross muttered. A few minutes later Ross looped the arms of his fisherman's sweater around his neck and left the house too, his destination uncertain. He needed to walk off his restlessness. A brisk walk and the cool night air usually worked wonders.

Thirty minutes later he became aware of his surroundings. He was a few blocks from Lena's apartment.

In the beginning he'd wanted to see Lena often, more often once she agreed to have sex with him, but she'd placed restrictions on their relationship. One date during the week and in by ten-thirty. A late Friday night date, sometimes the whole night if her brother was out of town. Saturday was a midnight date and Sunday was brunch. Teasingly she'd told him not to be greedy, that she had a job and didn't want to jeopardize it with a heavy romance and being groggy in the morning. He was extremely attracted to Lena, but he was the first to admit he wasn't sure if he'd be willing to remarry anytime soon.

At first he'd thought she was the kind of girl who would hold out for a wedding ring. He'd been stunned when she tumbled into bed with him. He'd been even more stunned when she said, I like *this* and *this* and ohhhh, do *that*. He thought about the *this* and the *that* for a moment before he walked up the five brick steps to ring the doorbell of the small apartment building. Lena lived on the second floor in a three-bedroom, front-view apartment. It was ideal, she said; her brother had one bedroom, she had one, and the third was used by both of them as an office. Ideal and not far from the Landers Building. Within walking distance.

Ross rang the doorbell. He rang it a second and then a third time before the buzzer sounded. Maybe she was busy, maybe she didn't want to see him. Maybe a lot of things. He took the steps two at a time and was barely winded when he reached the top.

"Ross! What are you doing here?"

"I was restless this evening. I thought a walk over to my parents' place would be nice. It's a beautiful evening, want to join me? If not, I apologize for intruding."

"Don't be silly, Ross. I'm delighted you stopped by. How about a cup of tea? I could use a break."

Ross looked down at his watch: eight-thirty. "You're working?"

Lord, she was pretty. Right now she looked sixteen, in her pink-striped pedal pushers and matching blouse. She was barefoot and her hair was done in a long, fat pigtail. He said, "You look cute."

Lena made a face and then laughed as she chucked him playfully under the chin. "Your mother was really excited about the information I gathered up on the Duke and Duchess of Windsor. She didn't quibble about the price of the pictures either. She's more or less agreed to use it as the cover story if I can back up all my facts. It's so juicy, Ross, my mouth waters just thinking about it." She winked at him. Ross almost drooled when she linked her arm though his and led him into the living room. "So, how about that tea?"

"No thanks," he said, sitting down on the sofa. "I had a late dinner and I'm trying to walk it off. I can't stay."

"You're welcome to stay if you like. I should call it a night, my eyes are starting to ache. Did your mother say anything about the duke and duchess?"

"Not to me. Woo didn't say anything, so I have to assume she's still in what she calls her thinking mode. You're really excited about this, aren't you?"

"Absolutely," she said, plopping down next to Ross. "You look tense, Ross, is something wrong?" Her fingers began kneading his arm.

"Do I?" He wanted to ask why she looked so intense, but thought better of it. "Well, maybe I am a little. Woo told me this evening he's moving out over the weekend. He found a carriage house to rent in Chestnut Hill."

"Isn't that where Jory lives?" Ross nodded. "I see," Lena said quietly. "Woo is going to rent the carriage house, is that it?"

Ross frowned. "How did you know?"

"I told you, my older sister went to school with Jory. The Ryans and the Belmonts are the only two people who have carriage houses. At least to my knowledge. Don't forget I grew up in Chestnut Hill. And," she grinned, tweaking his ear, "I'm a reporter." There was a slight chill in her voice when she said, "Are you jealous of Woo, Ross?"

"Hell no."

Lena tweaked his ear again and then bent over to nibble on it. She was being playful now, a prelude to what she called happy participating sex. Suddenly he wasn't in the mood. All he wanted was to be outside in the cool night air and walking aimlessly with no destination in mind.

"I can't stay, Lena. I have to meet my father," he lied. "Are we still on for tomorrow evening?"

"Of course," she said flatly. "Look, Ross, I'd really appreciate it if you'd kind of snoop around and see what you can find out about my royalty piece. You can tell me tomorrow over dinner, and by the way, my brother won't be here tomorrow." There it was, the bait she always threw out when she wanted something. "I think Justine really likes me. Your mother told me to call her Justine," she added hastily at the look of surprise on Ross's face. "She didn't like Marjory, did she?"

"I really don't want to discuss this, Lena, and there's one thing you should know about my mother. She doesn't like someone, meaning me, running interference. I'll see you tomorrow," he said, pecking her on the cheek.

"Now, Ross, what kind of kiss is that?" Lena said, throwing her arms around his neck. "I like to be kissed this way," she said, opening her mouth so her tongue could slide easily into his mouth. For one wild erratic moment Ross thought he was going to strangle with her tongue halfway down his throat. Maybe that was what she liked, but not what he liked.

His parents' house was not far away. Ross let himself in by the kitchen door. He patted Rosa on the shoulder and asked for his father.

"He's in the game room, Mr. Ross. I was just going to take this coffee to him. Would you like some?"

Ross nodded. "I'll take it in. Where's my mother?"

"She hasn't come home yet, Mr. Ross."

"Good. Don't tell her I'm here."

"Very well, Mr. Ross," Rosa said, adding a cup and saucer to the silver tray.

Ross stood in the doorway watching his father, whose back was to him. He was playing billiards by himself. How very lonely he must be, Ross thought. He wanted to say, Hey, Dad, how's it going? Instead he said. "Father, would you mind if I joined you for coffee?"

Jasper whirled around at his son's voice. "Ross, it's good to see you. What brings you here this hour of the night?" He's delighted, Ross thought, genuinely delighted that I'm here.

"I decided to go for a walk and ended up here. It's a nice night. I'm up for a little Eight Ball if you are."

"No, no, I'd rather sit here and talk. Is anything wrong, Ross?"

"No . . . yes. Oh, Father, I'm not sure. I'm just kind of jumpy, and I don't know why. Maybe it's the divorce, maybe it's Woo or Lena, or maybe it's all of the above."

Jasper felt his chest puff out. This was the first time Ross had ever come to him to *talk*. "Why don't we take it one thing at a time and see if we can relieve some of that jumpiness you're feeling? I'd like to start off by saying, Ross, I feel you made a mistake by going to work for your mother. The sad part is, I know you regret it too. Now, what's the problem with the divorce? I like Jory, always did. I've been thinking of calling her to set up lunch. She's kept in touch all these years."

"I didn't know that," Ross said tightly.

"When it came to Jory, son, you didn't *want* to know. You said I was to let sleeping dogs lie, and I would have if the girl hadn't called from time to time. She just needed to grow up, Ross. She told me she was coming back here to her father's house. She didn't make the decision until you told her you were divorcing her— about which, by the way, I wasn't too happy. But you have to live your own life, don't you? Anyway, Jory was relieved her self-imposed exile was over. She hated Florida."

"I didn't know that either. Look, I didn't send her there. It was her decision to leave Pennsylvania. For God's sake, I thought she was still in Florida. She gave me back all the money. I felt like King Shit. Why'd she do that, Father?"

Jasper shrugged. "If I had to take a guess, I'd say she's no different from most people. No one likes to be bought and paid for. She's her own person now. The bottom line is, Jory grew up, and I for

one am proud of her. If Jake was alive he'd be proud of his daughter too. Have you seen her?"

"Once when she gave me the bankbook. Not since she's been
back. Woo is going to rent her carriage house. He's moving out this
weekend."

"So that's it," Jasper said thoughtfully. "Your best friend and your
soon-to-be-ex-wife living in close proximity. Wasn't Woo Jory's
champion back in the early days of your marriage?"

"More or less," Ross said tightly. "Jory has taken her maiden
name back."

"That doesn't surprise me, Ross. When you cut something off,
you cut it off all the way. She's going to make a new life for herself.
The Landers name will only confuse her life. Why don't you make
an appointment to talk with her? This girl is not going to cause
you one iota of trouble, Ross."

"How do you know that, Father?"

"Because, like Woo, I took the time to get to know her. She was
hurting so badly when she left here, there was no reason for her to
make up stories and lie. I truly believe, Ross, you owe her an apology. Not that she expects one, but it would be the decent thing to
do."

"I've thought about it," Ross muttered.

"Do more than think," Jasper said sharply.

Ross poured a second cup of coffee. "The divorce will be final by
the end of the year."

"That's just a few months away," Jasper said, holding out his cup
for a refill. "Does that mean you and what's-her-name, Lena, will
get serious?"

"No, it doesn't mean Lena and I will get serious," Ross muttered.

"I should hope not. She's cut from the same bolt of cloth as your
mother. Surely you've seen it. I only met the young woman twice,
and she hit me right between the eyes. Guess she's good between
the sheets, eh?" Jasper mumbled, his eyes on a Monet across the
room.

The ring of heat around Ross's neck moved up to his face. "She's
aggressive. She's motivated. She works very hard, and yes, she more

or less idolizes Mother." He ignored the comment concerning the sheets.

"Birds of a feather flock together," Jasper said callously. "Be careful, boy, or you could end up with more than you bargain for. I signed the papers today giving Justine the magazine. I dropped them off at your office on my way home from the club. I do not in any way want to be responsible for that trash your mother is publishing. I took out full-page ads in every paper within a fifty-mile radius stating that Justine is sole publisher and owner of *TIF*."

Ross snorted. "Father, as long as you and mother are married, you are just as responsible as she is. If she gets sued, you get sued. You get tainted with the same brush. You said you wanted to wait until the magazine was in the black. I don't understand."

"You're not dim-witted, Ross. I hate Justine and she hates me. We stayed together because of that crazy will. I filed today for a legal separation. That gets me off the hook. I should have done it twenty years ago.

"Ross, don't make a similar mistake. I know you don't want to hear this, but I'm going to say it anyway. Leave the magazine. Your mother will ruin you, and Woo too. Get him out of there, Ross. Cut your losses and go on from there."

"Aren't you being melodramatic, Father? Just a little."

"Perhaps, but does it really matter?"

"Father, I'm an attorney, Woo is an attorney. We'll make sure Mother stays on the straight and narrow."

"Baloney! I've looked at the first two issues. I've never seen such trash in my life. Each issue is going to get worse as circulation increases, and it will increase. The public thirsts for this kind of garbage. What happens when there is no more trash to print? What happens when all those stars in Hollywood start to fight back? They will, you know," Jasper said passionately. "And the rumor at the club is your mother is thinking about a second publication she's going to run out of the basement. What do you know about that, Ross?"

"As much as you do, Father. She's mentioned it." Ross wanted to tell his father the new publication, if it came into being, would be three or four steps below *TIF.* She even had a name for the embryo: *Keyhole.* "Mother never lets grass grow under her feet. As far as I can determine, it's just a thought. She's pretty busy with *TIF* right now."

Ross stared into his empty coffee cup. It was time to go. But where was he going to go? Back to the big, empty house? And do what? Go to bed to wait for his nightmares. *Bullshit.* He stood up to shake the crease back into his trousers. He looked around. The room was so empty. Furniture, dark and massive, took up space, and the pool table covered the center of the floor, but it was empty. He hated the thick drapes, the sheer curtains underneath, detested the thick dark brown carpet, the huge chandelier with its winking bulbs. This room was his father's, and it had always intimidated him, as had the rest of the house. His taste ran to light, airy colors and green plants. There wasn't a green plant in the entire house. Growing up here had been a chore.

Jasper touched Ross's shoulder tentatively. There was so much he wanted to say to this young man who was his son, but he was afraid of saying the wrong thing. He didn't want to disturb the newfound empathy they'd developed in the past few months. "I enjoyed this little unexpected visit, Ross. I wish we could do it more often. Any time, drop by any time. I'm here most evenings. Don't bother to call, just come in." He was babbling, almost begging his son for companionship.

They were by the front door. In another second Ross would be outside. Jasper clapped him on the back and stage-whispered, "Son, tread lightly where Lena is concerned. I'm not trying to be fatherly, but there is something about that young woman . . . Sex isn't everything, even though it seems like it at times."

Suddenly Ross turned and wrapped his arms around his father, something he'd never done before in his life. He thought about the calculating look in Lena's eyes. "You're absolutely right, Father," he said lightly.

Outside, the air was cool, almost crisp, the night star spangled. The end of summer was fast approaching. He slipped his arms into the heavy knit sweater. It felt good. He jammed his hands in his pockets and started to walk. On a whim, he stepped on a bus and took a seat. He didn't even know where it was going. It didn't matter, he'd ride to the end of the line and then head back.

Thirty-five minutes later he stepped off the bus. The huge chestnut trees told him where he was. In ten minutes, if he walked fast,
he could be on Gravers Lane. Why the hell not? It was familiar and
yet unfamiliar. What was the harm in walking past Jory's house? He
wanted to see the carriage house Woo was moving into. That was
the reason for his being here. He didn't have to tell anyone about
his little evening stroll. He wasn't spying. He didn't know the bus
was coming here. This was legal reasoning at its worst, he told himself as he started up Hartwell Lane. He walked one block to Shaw-
nee Street, crossed Southhampton, and a block farther on turned
right onto Gravers Lane.

The house had a red door, that much he remembered. He
vaguely remembered a building in the back behind the garage.

Ross ambled along, his eyes taking in the cozy-looking houses
with light spilling outward. Lamp posts glowed warmly, front doors
were closed, windows opened slightly. It was quiet.

Families lived here. People with children and dogs and cats. The
yards had sandboxes, swing sets, and wading pools. He could hear
the crickets and frogs. It was a home sound, a belonging sound.
Ross ached with longing.

He heard her before he saw her. He moved quickly to step into
the deep shadows created by a low-limbed chestnut tree. And then
he saw her and the four dogs Woo mentioned. In the dim glow of
the streetlight he could distinguish the colored strings she was holding. She was laughing and giggling as the pups frisked about her
ankles. She stopped three times to untangle the strings from her ankles. He dug his heels into the ground to keep himself from stepping out into the road to help untangle the dogs.

She was still his wife.

Did he dare invade her privacy?

He bit down on his lower lip so hard he drew blood.

She was calling them by name now, her voice full of laughter.
Jesus, when was the last time he'd laughed like that? When did
he ever hear Jory laugh like that? Had Jory laughed like that
during their short marriage? No, she'd cried. And whined. And
cursed.

Jory was under the streetlight now, oblivious to anything other than the pups at her feet.

"This is very ungentlemenly of you," Jory gurgled. "You know the drill. If you walk nice, if you behave, you get a *cookie*. You get two *cookies* if you do what you're supposed to do. Clancy, you stop that! Now! Murphy, get your nose out of his butt. Bernie, stop chewing on Sam's ear. It's sore enough as it is. Enough!"

Ross whipped his hand to his mouth to stifle his laughter when the pup with the green string leaped into Jory's arms.

He could clearly see her hair, in a ponytail and tied with a red ribbon. She had on sneakers with a hole in the toe, khaki slacks, and a gray Villanova sweatshirt with holes in the arms. It looked like one of his. Had she taken it with her? He wanted to run out from his hiding place and ask her. His feet dug deeper into the grass. She looked *cute.* She looked healthy, happy, and so goddamn *normal.* She looked the way Woo looked. At peace. And he was churning like a fucking windmill.

Ross almost clapped his hands when the pups squatted one at a time and pooped. Jory did clap her hands. "*Good boys!* Two cookies! Fig Newtons. Okay, troops, let's head back to the ranch." She ran then, the dogs leapfrogging ahead of her.

Ross stepped from his hiding place in the shadows and watched until Jory and the dogs were dark shadows in the starlit night. When he was certain they were in the house at the end of the block, he meandered down the street, searching for the red door. He vaguely remembered Jory saying she was the one who painted the door red, but he couldn't remember why. He couldn't remember why the old Jory did any of the things she'd done back then. He hadn't cared, hadn't wanted to know anything about the girl he'd consented to marry against his will.

Now he wanted to know. Now, when it was too late.

There were lights on all over the house. Upstairs as well as down. Obviously Jory didn't like the dark. He was by the driveway, wondering if he dared walk around the back of the house and . . . peep in the windows, for Christ's sake. A goddamn Peeping Tom. The desire was so strong, his feet moved until he was again standing in the shadows of a chestnut tree. He had a clear view of Jory's kitchen. She was handing out cookies. He could hear her voice but couldn't distinguish the words. What he could see was the smile on her face. The dogs were at attention like four little soldiers waiting patiently for their treat.

Ross wanted to run up the back steps and tell Jory she should be more careful about locking doors. Any crazy person could walk into her house. The puppies were no protection. Hell, they didn't even know he was out here spying like some low-life crud.

He wished he could share the bottle of soda pop she was drinking, light a cigarette to match the one she was puffing on. Smoking must be new. Jory hadn't smoked when they were married. Or had she?

She looked so pretty. So contented and so *normal.* In comparison, he felt ready for the white jackets and nets. She was moving again, the dogs on their feet. He watched as she set her pop bottle on the floor next to the refrigerator, held the cigarette under the water and then deposited it in the trash can under the sink. She was talking, the dogs' tails swishing furiously as they yipped and danced about the kitchen. He heard the door shut and thought he heard the bolt shoot home. He did clap his hands softly then and let his breath out in a long sigh. Gradually the lights on the first floor went out, one by one.

Bedtime.

It was one-thirty in the morning when Ross climbed the stairs to his own bedroom. He wished there was a four-legged creature following him. His steps slowed when he passed Woo's door. He looked down, hoping to see a ribbon of light, but there wasn't one. His hands balled into tight fists. Woo always came out on top. Always.

For four nights, until Saturday, Ross spent his evenings in Chestnut Hill hiding in the shadows, watching his wife. Then, on Saturday evening at nine-thirty, Ross got in his car and drove to Chestnut Hill, completely forgetting he had a date with Lena. The only thing different about this excursion was the light in the carriage house—Woo had moved in—and his hiding place.

He did the same thing Sunday evening, and again on Monday evening. On Tuesday he told himself he was behaving like a lovesick adolescent and stayed home. On Wednesday, Lena showed up at his door. She'd literally dragged him upstairs to his bedroom, where she fucked his brains out until four in the morning, when he had his own personal nightmare once again.

Ross managed to choke back his anger when he saw Lena trip down the steps at seven o'clock, as beautiful as any model. She joined him at the table, nibbled at buttered toast and drank three cups of coffee. She smoked four cigarettes before she kissed him lightly on the cheek. "I had a wonderful time last night, Ross. We should do *that* more often. I have no objection to getting engaged, if that's what you want. We can pick out the ring on Saturday if you like. I have to tell you I don't believe in long engagements, and I'm not even sure it's right for us to get engaged when you're still married to Jory."

What the hell was she talking about? Two bottles of wine must have been the reason he couldn't remember. Jesus, he had to say something. "I'll talk to my lawyer before we . . . I'm not sure either. You're going to be late, Lena." He wondered if he sounded as desperate as he felt.

"You're right, Ross. Your mother gets . . . hostile when . . . never mind. I guess I'll see you at the office."

"Hmm," Ross murmured. He waved halfheartedly.

At nine o'clock Ross was sitting in the waiting room of Fenster, Williams and Ryce, waiting for Arnold Ryce, his attorney. When Ryce finally arrived at nine-twenty, he said to Ross, "You look like something the cat dragged in and then dragged back out. Come into my office and let's see what we can do."

Arnold Ryce was a nice man and a good family attorney. Like Woo, he didn't believe in huge billable hours, preferring to try and talk sense into his clients before litigation was instituted. He was round like a basketball, a cherub of a man with rosy cheeks and snow-white hair. From time to time his eyes twinkled. Ross thought him amazing.

"So, what brings you here so early, Ross?"

"I'm not sure. I'm beginning to think you were right and I should have taken the time to . . . what I mean is, Jory is so . . . I don't want to rush into anything. Maybe I should . . ."

"Back off and take a breather." Ryce smiled. "It can't hurt, Ross. If you think this is a mistake, we can drop the proceedings. However, your wife seems so amenable to it, I think you have to prepare yourself for the fact that this is what she wants too. As you know, I personally do not favor divorce. Young people today rush into marriage, and then when they have their first fight they head for a lawyer. Marriage isn't easy, it's something that has to be worked at. Daily. Sometimes hourly. If you like, you can set up an appointment with your wife and yourself and we can talk. But again, I feel duty bound to tell you this rarely works. I'm due in court at ten to plead a motion," Ryce said, looking at his watch.

"Sorry," Ross muttered. "I shouldn't have barged in here without an appointment. I'll call you."

In the lobby, Ross called his office and spoke to Woo. "I'm going to be late this morning. There's nothing very pressing."

It was ten-twenty when Ross drove the Skylark up Jory's driveway. The din from inside when he rang the doorbell set his nerves twanging. The dogs yapped and yipped, and from somewhere he could hear a radio and the tap-tap of typewriter keys. He rang the bell again and then a third and fourth time, with no results. When the dogs stopped long enough to catch their breath, Ross shouted Jory's name. She came on the run, her face full of shock.

"Ross, what are you doing here?" She didn't look happy to see him. He wanted to tell her he'd been spying on her, but he didn't. He motioned to the stoop. Jory eased herself out the door, the pups slamming their fat little bodies against the screen in protest.

"I think we need to talk. Would you mind taking a walk around the yard? How can you think with those dogs making all that noise?"

"I'm used to it. The doorbell is a strange noise to them," Jory said coolly. "What is it you want, Ross?"

"I guess for starters I want to apologize to you for . . . that command performance and throwing the divorce thing at you like I did. I'm sorry, and I came to apologize."

"When will it be final?"

"By the end of the year. How are you managing here by yourself? Do you have a job?"

"I'm fine, Ross. I'm trying out for a job on the *Democrat*. Free-lance. I thought we settled everything the day I came to . . . your house. Is anything wrong?"

"No. No, nothing is wrong."

"Then I don't understand why you made this trip. You could have called me. I told you I'd sign whatever needs to be signed, and I don't want anything. I'm more than willing to take the entire blame for our disastrous marriage. You need to know something, Ross. I would have honored our agreement and stayed in Florida. I think it's good that we're finally going to dissolve our marriage and get on with our respective lives," Jory said breathlessly. "Is there anything else?"

Was there? Damn right there was. "Why did you rent the carriage house to Woo?" he blurted.

"Why shouldn't I? It was for rent, he saw my ad and wanted to rent it, and we struck a deal. It's a business arrangement, not that it's any of your business."

"You're changing your name. Why?" Ross demanded.

"Because it was the name I was born with. We were never *really* married. I'm not *going* to do it, I did it. Legally."

"Would you like to have dinner with me? Papagalo's is still in business." He waited, hardly daring to breathe, for her answer.

"No. Perhaps when the divorce is final we can celebrate. We need to break clean, Ross."

Ross shuffled his feet. There wasn't anything else he could do or say to prolong the meeting with his wife. He looked around. "You've done a good job out here. I came by once about a year after your father died and everything was overgrown. I wondered why you didn't sell it."

"Now you don't have to wonder any longer," Jory said tersely.

"Look, Jory, I was a jerk. I'm sorry about everything. I know I can't make up for those years. Look at you," he said proudly, "look what you accomplished, and you did it on your own. If we'd stayed together, do you think you would have gone back to school, gotten your degree, be the person you are now?"

She had to get back in the house before her eyes puddled up. Couldn't he see what this meeting was doing to her? Was he so blind? Too much, too little, too late. "You're about five years too late with your praise, Ross. You were a jerk, but so was I. No, you can't make up for what you did. I can't make up for robbing you of your life for a little while either. What we're doing now is the right thing. You'll meet someone who will fit into your life and your world will be right-side up. I really have to go now," she said, her voice breaking.

"Will you meet someone too, Jory? Or have you already met someone? Will you find someone who'll fit into your life?"

"Probably not. I don't think I'll ever marry again. Good-bye, Ross."

Her hand was on the knob of the red door when he called out, "Why did you get those dogs?"

"Because, like me, no one wanted them. They comfort me. They keep me company and they love unconditionally."

The red door closed. The yapping and yipping stopped immediately.

Inside, Jory's legs turned to rubber as she slid to the floor. Tears rolled down her cheeks, her arms outstretched to gather the puppies close. She allowed her emotions to take over, hiccuping and sobbing into the dogs' soft, furry bodies. Shaken with these strange happenings, the pups mewled softly as they tried to lick at her tears, demanding comfort for their own sake.

"I shouldn't still love him. I don't want to love him and I'm carrying on like this because I still have feelings," she cried heartbrokenly. "No, no, that's not it, it's because I'm . . . Why did he come here?" Ross had looked . . . like he really was sorry, and she'd been too cold, too reserved. "Oh shit," she said, wrapping her arms around the wiggling dogs. "Okay, okay, I'm going to pull up my socks and not think about this. This was something that was inevitable, something I have to work through. I can do it, I did it before. No more bawling and whining," she muttered as she wiped her eyes and nose on the sleeve of her shirt.

On her feet, Jory blew her nose lustily as the dogs circled her ankles, their tails swatting each other in the face.

In the kitchen, where she handed out puppy biscuits, she said loudly and clearly, "Only a fool would love Ross Landers, and I'm no fool, not anymore. So there!" She chomped on a Fig Newton as she made her way back to the study, where she was working on an article for *Redbook* on Florida honeymoon vacations. And when she was done with the article, she was going to tackle her checking account, and after that she was going to peruse the want ads in case the job at the *Democrat* fizzled on her.

"I don't *need* you, Ross Landers," she said, attacking the typewriter with a vengeance. "I don't *want* you either. So there!"

Even the dogs knew it was a lie.

Chapter 6

It was hard to believe these were the same offices he'd walked into months ago, Ross thought. The dust was gone, so was the heavy, outdated furniture. Loose-weave textured drapes hung at the windows now, drapes that matched the beige carpeting and California-style, low-slung furniture. Glossy magazines and green plants decorated the reception area. The desk was glass-topped, and so were the coffee table and end tables. Brass lamps and African violets added a homey touch, as did the colorful Moulin Rouge prints on the wall. The receptionist sitting behind the glass-topped table was so perfectly coiffed and made-up, she resembled, in Ross's opinion, a mannequin. Her lips barely moved when she said, "Good morning, Mr. Landers."

"Good morning, Astrid," Ross replied. He knew Astrid's real name was Josephine Takowsky because he'd seen her employment application. Josephine preferred to be called Astrid Hershey, and that's what the bronze name plate on the glass-topped desk read. "Everyone wants to be someone else, including me," Ross muttered as he made his way down the hall to his office.

Here too, renovations had taken place. The desks were polished light oak, the swivel chairs comfortable, with burlap-type fabric. A cluster of green plants filled one corner near the window. Woo wa-

tered them every Friday night. More than once Ross had seen the
big man pick off dry leaves and spritz the leaves with something
that looked like a perfume atomizer.

Ross looked down at his desk, which was so tidy, he knew the
cleaning lady had been in earlier. He assumed the manila envelope
catty-corner on the green blotter was from his father. He could just
picture Jasper standing in the open doorway tossing the envelope
onto the desk. He would have dusted his hands and walked out of
the building without a backward glance. Ross wished he didn't have
to look at it, wished he didn't have to take it down to his mother's
office, wished it would all go away. He sat down and opened the
envelope. His eyes expertly scanned the papers in front of him.
Then he laughed so hard and long, Woo came on the run.

"What's going on?" the big man demanded anxiously. Ross
handed the sheaf of papers to his friend, who quickly scanned
them. "I'm glad I'm not you," Woo said quietly.

"Hell, Woo, this is one of those rare times when I'm glad I am
me. I can't wait to see my mother's face when I show her this.
Wanna come with me?"

"I respectfully decline the invitation on the grounds that I might
embarrass us both. Good luck, Ross."

By God, maybe it was going to be a good day after all.

Ross jerked at his tie, removed his jacket, hung it over the back
of the swivel chair and then rolled up his sleeves to the middle of
his arm. He stacked the papers neatly before sliding them back into
the manila envelope. He was still smiling when he reached his
mother's office. He wiped the smile from his face the same moment
he rapped sharply on the door and then opened it. His mother, for
some strange reason, didn't insist on formality.

"Ross, just the person I wanted to see," Justine said cheerfully.

Ross blinked at his mother's severe hairdo, at the pinstripe business suit and crisp white shirt complete with string tie. She was
heavily made-up. He almost asked her if she was vying with Astrid
for the dead mannequin look. Be charitable, he told himself, this is
probably what the well-dressed businesswoman wore to the office.

"What do you want to see me about?" Ross asked, shifting the
envelope from his right hand to his left hand.

"If you'd been here at eight o'clock for our weekly meeting, I wouldn't have to go over it a second time. I wish you would *join* this team, Ross. You can't continue to be so aloof. This is a joint effort, we're all working toward the same goal, to outsell and outpublish *Confidential*. Actually, it's about Lena. This girl is so motivated she takes my breath away. The production meeting was more than beneficial. I gave her the go-ahead on the Duke and Duchess of Windsor story. You won't believe the dirt she's managed to dig up. And it's our exclusive. Of course, we have to pay for it, and she also wants a bonus. I agreed, subject to your approval, of course."

"Is this above and beyond the bonus system you outlined previously?" Ross asked coolly, sitting down in a chair facing the desk.

"Yes it is," Justine replied.

"Then my answer is no."

"On what grounds?" Justine snapped.

"On the grounds she's no one special. She does her job like everyone else. Do you want a mutiny on your hands? No good business person changes course in midstream."

"She can sell the story someplace else and get top dollar."

"No, she can't, Mother. She signed a contract with us. That's why you hired me, to protect you and the magazine. A year from now, when her contract comes up for renewal, she can threaten to take her material somewhere else, but not if she got it while she was working for us. I tied her and every other reporter up pretty tight. Woo dotted all the *i*s and crossed all the *t*s. If you agreed, you'll have to tell her it's no deal."

Justine seethed. "I find this all very strange. The girl inferred that you and she were . . . what she said was . . ."

"Yes, Mother?" Ross said coldly.

"Perhaps it was my imagination, but I thought she said you were considering an engagement. She didn't say it in so many words, but I can read between the lines. Are you saying it isn't true? I was trying to be kind and nice to her for your sake."

"Mother, I am still married. Do you really think I would do such a thing until the divorce is final? I wouldn't. We've dated, but that's about all we've done. Don't poke into my personal life."

"Very well, Ross. When will that divorce become final?"

"When I want it to become final. Don't concern yourself, Mother. You never approved of Jory or our marriage, so please don't pretend interest now." He tossed the envelope onto her desk.

"What's this?"

"Father dropped it off last evening." Ross sat down and crossed his legs to wait for the explosion he knew was coming. He fired up a cigarette and stared at his mother through a cloud of smoke.

"You approve of this?" Justine said tightly.

"It's not up to me to approve or disapprove, Mother. It's in order, it's legal, and there my responsibility ends. It's what you asked for. With a few strings. Now, if you want to negotiate, you can. As your attorney I wouldn't advise it, but you can do as you please."

"This is . . . blackmail. This is indecent, it's highway robbery. It can't be legal. Why didn't you protect my interests? I see, you're on your father's side."

"No, Mother, I'm not. You wanted to cut a deal with Father, and he agreed."

"This building *is* TIF. How can he charge me rent? Five thousand a month! Tell him to go to hell!"

"This is the Landers Building. *TIF* has always leased the premises from the corporation. Now that the building has been transferred to a new owner, you will be paying a new landlord. It's really very simple and very, very legal."

"I wanted this building!" Justine hissed.

"Then you should have asked for the building, Mother. You asked for *TIF*. Father has given it to you, lock, stock, and barrel. It's yours. No one can take it from you. You are the sole owner and publisher of *TIF*, but you do not own the building."

"Who the hell owns it?" Justine stormed. "What? Are you telling me Marjory Landers Ryan owns this building? Don't dare to tell me that, Ross! That is unacceptable. Totally unacceptable. You go back and tell Jasper it's no deal. Why would he do such a thing?" she wailed miserably.

"I believe it's all written down. Try the third page from the back. He goes into detail. If you agree, I'll go over to the courthouse after lunch and file the deed. If you disagree, you'll have to take it up with Father. If it's any consolation to you, Mother, I didn't know about this until a few minutes ago. I don't believe I'm being premature when I tell you I think this is a take it or leave it deal."

"So that's why she came back here. I should have known something was going on when I heard she'd taken over Jake's house and set up shop. Damn, I always liked that girl. She had guts," Justine blustered.

"Jory doesn't know, Mother. That's on the third page too."

Justine quickly scanned the page, then said icily, "This says that this building is being deeded to Marjory Ryan for all the mental anguish she suffered for the loss of her child and for sticking to her end of her bargain. And for agreeing to an uncontested divorce and no settlement. This is a goddamn settlement. Ross, say something."

"It's fair and it's legal. What else can I say? I was as surprised as you are. I think it's fair. I treated Jory terribly, Mother. She's been very kind and generous about all of this. She's going to be very shocked when she hears about Father's generosity."

"I damn well doubt that. Five thousand a month will help rid her of any shock. That's sixty thousand a year!"

Ross grinned. "A princely sum."

"I fail to see the humor in this, Ross. As Jory's husband, that means you are entitled to your half. You are on your father's side, you ungrateful snot!" Justine continued to bluster.

"My name is not Ryan, Mother. Jory took back her maiden name. The divorce is going through, it just takes time. I do not benefit from this in any way. Father is trying to straighten things out. He said when your separation becomes legal, he'll—"

"What separation!" Justine screamed. She was out of her chair, and around her desk in a second, to stand towering over her son. "What separation?"

"I assumed you knew, Mother. I'm sorry. Father told me last night when I stopped by the house. You weren't home. It's his way of absolving himself from this . . . business venture. Perhaps you should call him and arrange to sit down and discuss matters. There's no hurry in filing the deed. It's your call, Mother. If there's nothing else, I have work to attend to."

"You sold me out, Ross—my own son. You'll never convince me

otherwise," Justine said, returning to her chair, then glancing at him across her desk.

"You're wrong, Mother, but when did you ever listen to a thing I said?" Ross said sadly.

Back in his office, Ross noted that Woo had left for lunch. At odds now with what was going on, he kicked at the chair, bringing it toward him. He flopped down. He could see his reflection in the window across the room. He definitely did not look like a successful attorney. More like a wayward bum. At some point he must have raked at his hair, for it was standing on end. He smoothed it down.

What the hell was his father up to? Was he simply trying to make things right with Jory, as he said, or did the old rascal have an ulterior motive? If so, what was it? Who was going to notify Jory of his father's generous bequest? What would happen if she didn't accept Jasper's indulgent present, and it was indeed a present. He tried to put himself in Jory's place, tried to think as she would. He failed miserably. He didn't know his wife well enough to guess what she would do. Would she come down on the first of the month with the four dogs on their colored strings to collect the rent? The thought was so funny he burst into loud laughter. He was still laughing when his mother buzzed him and said, "File the fucking deed. I'll deal with your father in my own way."

Ross's fist pounded the desk. He hated to hear a woman use profanity, especially his mother. When he was younger, he'd tried to tell her it sounded terrible, especially in front of his friends. She seemed to take pleasure in doing it all the more. He'd gone to his father, who never so much as said a "damn," and asked him to intercede. He was told in his father's weary voice that his mother was not a lady like his friends' mothers. After that he didn't bring his friends home anymore. He'd carried it one step further and cultivated friends whose mothers were more like his own. Those friendships hadn't really worked out either because all they had done was bitch and moan about their parents and getting into trouble.

"A penny for your thoughts," Lena said quietly from the doorway.

"Right now they aren't worth that much," Ross said ruefully. He waited, fully expecting Lena to chastise him for his decision concerning her bonus. Or was it too soon for her to know? No, his mother would have told her immediately. He eyed her handbag. "Going somewhere?"

She grinned. "Hot lead. I just wanted to check on what time you're picking me up this evening."

"Seven okay?" He stifled a laugh. She'd zap home then or she'd get him in bed and work her wiles on him. "Womanly wiles" was a term his father used often.

"See you then. There's a great movie at the Roxy. Think about it, okay?"

"Sure. Lena?"

"Yes."

"Business is business and pleasure is pleasure. They're two different things. I don't want either one of us to confuse them now or at some point in the future."

Lena's eyes narrowed imperceptibly. "Please don't be silly, Ross. You can't blame me for trying, can you?"

"Guess not," he said airily. "Don't do it again. My mother feeds on stuff like that. I don't."

"Understood. See you tonight." She blew him a kiss that Ross did not return.

"So how'd it go with your mother?" Woo asked after Lena was gone. "I've been standing in the hall waiting for her to leave."

"All things considered, not too bad. Justine's going to deal with Jasper on her own. *That* could mean just about anything. Actually, Woo, I think this whole thing is funny as hell, and I'll be damned if I know why it's funny. Before you came in I was sitting here imagining Jory showing up on the first of the month with those four dogs on their colored strings to collect the rent."

"How'd you know about that? Have you seen Jory?" Woo asked casually.

"I saw her this morning before I came to work. Some divorce stuff. Our conversation lasted all of five minutes. Those dogs do create a ruckus, but I guess you know that already."

"I haven't seen Jory since I moved in," Woo said. "I did call her to thank her for having the electricity turned on and the phone installed, but that's it. Have things changed with you two?"

"No. Status quo."

"Do you want things to change, Ross? I'm asking friend to friend. I'm not being nosy."

"It's too late for all that. Guess you're going to have to hold down the fort. I have to go over to the courthouse and file the deed. I need to get in touch with my father and find out who's going to notify Jory of her . . . what's the word here, inheritance?"

Woo's homely face split into a wide grin. "Don't look at me. You rich people do things differently than us ordinary folk. I'm sure there's some kind of protocol involved. I trust you to find out what it is."

"Do you think she'll take it, Woo?"

"She'd be a fool not to," Woo said carefully.

"You didn't answer my question. Do you think she'll take it?"

"No. Yes. Hell, I don't know. If she gave you back the money you've been sending her, why would she keep the building?"

"That's a good question. It's hers for her lifetime. She can't sell it. It's a cushion for her if things don't go well. Single women have a hard time of it, according to my father. Lately, he . . . he's different."

Before he could stop himself, Woo blurted, "Maybe you never took the time to get to know him either." Then: "Jesus, Ross, I'm sorry. I didn't mean to say that. This is none of my business. Forget I said anything, okay?"

Their friendship was already starting to deteriorate; Ross could sense it. "Don't apologize for being right, Woo."

"I apologized for saying it aloud, not for thinking it, Ross. By your own admission, you didn't know your wife. And on many occasions you told me you didn't know the first thing about your father. You said he was weak and ineffectual. What he's been doing lately contradicts all those statements you made. At least in my eyes. I spoke out of turn and it won't happen again. I have no intention of getting involved in your family's business."

"You are involved. You work here, you live on my wife's property."

"Key words here—wife's property, not yours. Your mother signs my paychecks. Is this going to be a problem, Ross?"

"I'm a little tense right now, Woo. Let's just forget this whole conversation ever took place."

"Fine with me."

It was happening, things were changing. Ross felt like crying.

Chapter 7

On September 14, 1953, two days after Senator Jack Kennedy married Jacqueline Lee Bouvier, Jory Ryan opened a letter from the *Philadelphia Democrat* congratulating her on her new title of Auntie Ann. The job was hers, the letter said, if she wanted it. She was to respond by Friday the eighteenth of September, four days from now. The letter went on to say the editorial staff overwhelmingly voted to run the column three times a week instead of the initial run in the Neighborhood Life section on the weekend. An office, and then in parenthesis "cubbyhole," would be provided if she wanted to work at the paper instead of out of her house. The decision would be left up to her.

"I got it! I got it!" Jory chortled to the bemused dogs, who were silent for once, their dark eyes plastered on their exuberant mistress, who was dancing around the kitchen.

"I don't care if it's nine-thirty in the morning, cookies for everyone. Ice cream for me. I'm a reporter! I have a column! I get to work at home and take care of you guys. We aren't going to starve! Well, we won't starve, but things are going to be lean. Ten dollars a column won't get us very far. I'll mix noodles with your food and I'll eat hamburgers. God, I can't believe this! I wish there was someone I could tell, someone to share this with." Her exuberant mood dampened slightly, then lifted. A secret was more wonderful.

While the dogs gobbled their treats and she gobbled her dish of butterscotch ice cream, Jory's mind raced. She wasn't going to wait till Friday. She was going to change her clothes and go into town right now and accept the position, and then she was going to treat herself to lunch. Lord, it was all so wonderful! Thank God, this move back to Chestnut Hill wasn't a mistake. "I'm going to be the best Auntie Ann the *Democrat* ever had," she said to the dogs. "If they haven't had one, I'll set a precedent." She raised her eyes. "Thank you God, thank you God," she said over and over as she made her way up the stairs, the puppies struggling with the steps.

Low to the ground, their fat bellies tickling the carpet, the dogs watched Jory's fancy footwork as she raced about the room in search of just the right dress, just the right shoes, just the right earrings, just the right perfume. She finally settled for a persimmon-colored dress with white collar and cuffs and an elegant braided, leather belt she'd gotten on sale three years ago in Fort Lauderdale. Her pumps and handbag matched the belt perfectly. She added a splash of Arpège and a slash of lipstick. Her fading tan required no makeup. Thank God she'd tweezed her eyebrows two days ago. She debated for three whole minutes over three different pairs of earrings, finally settling for a delicate pair of gold filigrees. She worked at her hair, pulling it back into a French twist but leaving a feathering of shorter curls to frame her face. By God, she looked fashionable.

Downstairs, Jory barricaded the kitchen, laid down fresh papers and saw to the water bowls. A large bowl of puppy chow was set in the middle of the floor. "Share," she said, wagging a finger at the dogs. "I'll just be a few hours. We'll go for a long walk when I get back." To make her point, she pointed to the colored strings hanging from a peg by the back door. The pups understood the word walk and immediately scampered to the back door, their warm, wet eyes gazing longingly at the colored leashes. "When I get back." While their backs were turned, Jory stepped over the gate and left the house by the front door.

Jory was out of the *Democrat* office by noon, her arms loaded, her head buzzing like an active beehive. They were giving her two weeks to write six columns, set up a filing system, and recruit a team of "experts" to draw from when she needed expert advice outside the area of common sense. She was to pick up Auntie Ann's mail once a week. All letters would remain the property of the *Democrat*. She even had an expense account, though it was not to exceed twenty dollars a month. The last thing the editor-in-chief, a frizzy-haired, cigar chomping, overweight, overworked man, said was: "I want three months' worth of columns ahead, in case anything goes wrong." That meant she was going to have to literally work around the clock to get thirty-six columns ahead.

On her way to the car to unload her bags of supplies and reference books, Jory ran her end of the conversation over in her mind. She hadn't actually said much other than, "Fine, I can do it, thank you, I'll do my best, and yes I understand." She'd said fine about six times until the editor said sourly, "It will be fine when I see a ton of mail coming in here for Auntie Ann, and you're up thirty-six columns." Then she'd said, "Yes, sir, I understand, sir, thank you for giving me this opportunity." He'd just glared at her and pointed to the door.

My God, she really was Auntie Ann.

She thought about the celebratory lunch she'd promised herself as she locked the car, her bags and books neatly piled on the backseat. Should she go ahead with it or go back to the dogs and start to work? She opted for the lunch. She deserved it, but where to go? She was so excited she wondered if she'd be able to eat. Anywhere would do. Even the pub across the street or the deli on the corner. A pastrami on rye with lots of mustard and two pickles would be good. She headed for the In and Out Deli, which promised quick service.

Jory was down one pickle and starting on the second half of her sandwich when she heard a voice say, "Mind if I join you?"

"Woo! Of course not. Please, sit down."

"What brings you to this end of town, Miss . . . Ryan?" Woo asked, seating himself on the spindly chair opposite her.

"The *Democrat.* I had to pick up some things, and decided to treat myself to lunch. Oh, Woo, I just had the most wonderful news, but I can't tell you what it is. Walking over from the parking lot, I realized I have no one to share good news with. The dogs don't count," she said impishly.

Woo didn't mean for his voice to sound so sour when he said, "What good is a secret if you can't tell someone?" She must be referring to Jasper Landers's gift of the Landers Building, he thought. And he was so sure she'd turn it down. He felt cheated and angry that this girl, whom he really liked, could disappoint him like this. Ross would never let him live it down.

"That's how I feel." Jory grinned. "But this is a professional secret. It has to do with my job. Confidentiality and all that kind of stuff. Being a lawyer, surely you understand what I mean."

"You bet. Yes, of course. Well, that kind of secret you have to keep. Could I coax it out of you?" he asked jovially. Thank God, he thought.

"Not on your life. How are you, Pete? Do you like your job over at *TIF*? Is everything okay at the carriage house?"

"I'm just fine. The job at *TIF* is a job. It pays good and it's a light workload. I like the carriage house. I think I'd make someone a good wife. I can cook, I clean, my bathroom sparkles, and I hang up my clothes. I dusted last night," he said sheepishly. "I made a meat loaf, just like my mother makes. I'm not too good at gravy, though."

Jory giggled. "Gravy's tough."

"What do you do?" Woo asked earnestly, leaning across the table. She had remarkable eyes. Other than lipstick that was almost gone, she wore no other makeup. He remembered the pounds of pancake makeup she used to wear. He was remembering a lot of things suddenly.

"I strain out the lumps and add GravyMaster to give it the right color. I don't like dry meat or dry potatoes."

"Me either. I like to dip my bread in the gravy."

"Me too!" Jory gurgled. "I like stuff cooked in one pot."

"No kidding! I do too. That's how my mother cooks. There were so many of us, she had to stretch, and that's how she did it. I make real good chili. Real good. Would I be out of line if I asked you to join me the next time I make it?"

"If I'm not busy, I'd be happy to join you."

"When?"

"The next time you make it."

"I could do that tomorrow."

"You're making it sound like a date."

"Jeez no, I just hate eating alone. You can bring the dogs."

"Not tomorrow, how about next week?"

"What day?"

Flustered, Jory grappled with her tentative schedule. "How about Wednesday?"

"It's a date! I mean it's a . . . well, what the hell is it?"

"It's . . . for heaven's sake, I don't know. Lets just say we're going to eat together." Jory laughed.

Ross Landers had heard, "It's a date!" when he entered the deli. Now he approached their table and said, "Jory, how are you? Woo, I didn't know you liked the In and Out Deli."

"I come here almost every day," Woo said quietly.

"Well, if you gentlemen will excuse me, I have to be on my way." Jory winked at Woo before she snatched the pickle off his plate. Two pairs of eyes watched her leave. Woo attacked the remains of his corned beef sandwich. His eyes dared Ross to make a comment.

"It's been a hell of a day," Ross said, removing his food from the tray to arrange it in a geometric pattern. He shuffled the plates, but he didn't eat.

"Aren't you hungry?" Woo asked, digging into a slab of pie topped with two scoops of ice cream.

"Guess not. I tend to lose my appetite when I see my best friend having lunch with my wife and making a date."

Woo swallowed what was in his mouth before he laid down the fork. "As usual, Ross, you have it all wrong, and you know what, I'm not going to explain it to you either."

"I know what I saw," Ross said coldly.

"This is going to be a problem, isn't it?"

"Looks that way," Ross snapped.

"That's what I thought," Woo said.

Back in the office, Woo typed up his resignation. He put one copy in his briefcase and slid the other into one of *TIF*'s business envelopes. He placed it dead center on Ross's desk. There was no one he cared to say good-bye to, so he left the office, saddened that his friendship with Ross would end like this.

Jory was romping with the dogs in the backyard when he arrived home. The dogs ran to greet him. Jory remained where she was, a sick feeling settling in the pit of her stomach. "Is something wrong, Woo?"

"Depends on your point of view," he said tightly. "I just quit."

"Why?" She knew why, but still she asked.

"I think Ross thinks you and I are plotting behind his back or something like that. I guess he assumed our lunch was prearranged. Knowing Ross as I do, he would take that to mean I was trying to cut into his territory. He still considers you his wife."

"Well, I don't!" Jory said hotly. "This is ridiculous. You just . . . quit and walked out?"

"I left my resignation on Ross's desk. But yeah, that's pretty much what I did. God, all I felt was relief. I hated the job, but because of Ross I took it. The money was great. They were paying me three times what I'm worth. That's how I was able to buy this rattletrap of a car and move here. Looks like I'm going to have to go back to Lancaster with my tail between my legs."

"Oh, Pete, I'm sorry. Look, I can talk to Ross, set him straight. I'll tell him . . . whatever you want me to tell him. You've been such good friends for so long."

"That's just it, Jory. This never should have happened. Ross should have more faith in me. I would never have reacted the way he did. I think he cares about you."

Jory hooted with laughter. "Come inside, Pete, and I'll make us some coffee."

"Would you mind if I changed my clothes first?" he asked. "I think I'll work in the yard afterward and work off some of this hostility."

Woo was back in time to hear the last plop of the percolator.

"This is a nice kitchen, Jory. It's cozy, reminds me of home. You're happy, aren't you?"

"Pretty much so," she replied, pouring him a cup. "I was never happy growing up here, though. Coming back as I did, when I did, it was like . . . okay, now it's time, now I earned the right to come back. I know it sounds stupid, but that's how I feel."

"It sounds good. Hmmm, this is good coffee. You are a surprise, Jory Ryan."

"What are you going to do, Pete?"

The big man shrugged. "I don't interview well. I don't know why, but I tend to intimidate people. Christ, I hate billable hours and all that crap. You'd think I was an accountant instead of a lawyer."

"You just haven't found your niche yet. You could try my father's old offices. I still know a few people there, some of my father's best friends. Can you see yourself as an assistant district attorney?"

"I don't know. I hate the thought of going back home and answering all those questions. I should have my life in order by now. It's damn hard to be poor *and* ethical."

Jory burst out laughing. "Yeah, I found that out the hard way. I wonder what it's like to be rich."

"You mean like Justine Landers? She doesn't look like a happy woman to me. She's so busy hating everyone and everything, she doesn't even know what's going on with the world. All she's interested in is making money. That's just my opinion, of course. Poor isn't too bad as long as you don't have to go hungry."

"My sentiments exactly. Stop that, Murphy!" Jory said sternly. "No, no, Clancy, that's not nice. Down, I said down!"

"How do you know their names? Don't you get them mixed up? God, they look like four peas in a pod to me."

"I can't tell them apart. They all respond to whatever name I use. I mixed up the strings one day and it was all over."

"That makes life simple," Woo said, getting up. "Thanks for the coffee. Look, if you have something to do, I can watch the dogs for you. Fresh air is good for them."

"Okay, but if they get to be too much, just shoo them into the

house. They more or less stay together and don't go far. Thanks
Pete."

"My pleasure."

"Pete?"

"Yes."

"Don't worry about the rent. You can stay as long as you like. I
have a job, so you can take your time looking for something that
suits you. It's not charity, you can owe me. I feel terrible about Ross
and you."

"Well don't. Things usually happen for the best. I just might take
you up on your offer. I like it here. It's the first time I've ever had
my own place. Doesn't say much for me at my age, does it?"

"It says a lot, Pete. Guess I'll see you later."

"Yeah, later."

As she set the coffee cups in the sink, Jory muttered to herself,
"You're getting involved, this wasn't supposed to happen."

It was late in the afternoon when Woo stopped his yard work long
enough to have a beer. He was sweating heavily from his efforts.
The drink was refreshing. The pan of water he'd set out for the
dogs was almost empty. A grin stretched across his face when he
saw them sleeping in a ball, a jumble of legs and fur. They were
simply worn-out with all the running and chasing they'd done. He
liked the little rascals and realized they were becoming a part of his
life, just the way the carriage house was becoming his home.

It was a stupid thing he'd done, resigning and walking out on
Ross the way he had, with no notice. He was in no position to take
such a cavalier attitude, yet he'd done it. He'd never, ever, in the
whole of his life done anything so impulsive. He never reacted to
events on the spot, preferring to sit quietly and think things
through, to come up with a satisfactory conclusion, or at the very
least, a working method of dealing with a problem. He'd cut his
losses, burned his bridges, and here he was, doing yard work and
babysitting four dogs who were asleep at the switch. He threw back
his head and roared with laughter, his huge body shaking. The dogs
slept through the thunder of his emotions.

One eye on the sleeping dogs, the other on the row of forsythia bushes he was about to trim, Woo was aware of a weaving shadow to his left. He turned and nodded to Ross.

"I came to give this back to you," Ross said, holding out Woo's resignation letter. "I want to believe you reacted to the moment and don't mean this. I also want to apologize. I was out of line. I don't know what the hell got into me, Woo."

Woo shrugged his big shoulders. "I accept your apology. You're right, I probably did overreact, but I'm not coming back."

"Why don't you take a week off, with pay, and think about this before you make it definite? Jesus, Woo, what more do you want from me?" Ross said desperately.

"Nothing, Ross. I don't have to think about it. I knew it was a mistake the first week. Damn it, you did too. I was too gutless to quit, and too goddamn greedy. I appreciate the offer, but no thanks. You have this thing about me living here, and I like it here. I like working in the yard, I like these dogs, and I like your wife. I always liked Jory. No matter what you say, I'm not moving. I'm going to look for a job. Jory said I can stay and if I fall behind in the rent I can owe her. She's a nice person, Ross, a really nice person. You already have it in your head that something is going on between us, and you're wrong. Now that that's out of the way, how about a beer or some soda pop?"

"No thanks. Did you tell Jory about the building?" Ross asked tightly.

"Jesus, Ross, what do you take me for? Of course I didn't tell her, and I resent you asking me if I did. That's your family's business, not mine," Woo said coldly. "What the hell is happening to us?"

"I don't know. You're my best friend, you're like a brother to me. And now we're snapping and snarling at one another. I thought I was doing you a goddamn favor by getting you the job. I took it on for you. Shit, Woo, working for my mother was the last thing I wanted to do. I figured we'd give it a shot and go out on our own to hang up our respective shingles a year or so down the road. Things were fine until you stuck your nose in my business and moved here."

"That's what it's all about, isn't it, Ross? That friendship you speak of so highly obviously doesn't include trust. Stick it, Ross, I don't need that kind of friendship. If you have a problem with Jory, don't lay it on my doorstep. Deal with it."

"I am dealing with it. I filed for divorce. I'm going to knock on her door and hand her the deed and walk away. You're right, I can't accept you living here. There are hundreds of apartments in the city and on the outskirts, and you have to pick this particular one. Knowing the situation, I'd think you'd have more sense than to move here."

Ross had worked himself into a fury. "And as for this," he continued, holding up Woo's resignation, "this is what I think of your decision." He tore the paper into small pieces and dropped them, fluttering, at the big man's feet. "I'll see you at the office tomorrow morning at nine. You have a contract. I expect you to honor it."

"Sue me," Woo grated.

"Don't think I won't. Nine o'clock, Woo."

"Son of a fucking *bitch*!" Woo seethed when Ross had walked away. The forsythia bush fell under his wrath. He was a maniac as he raced down the line of overgrown greenery. When he was done he had nothing but stubble and a mountain of debris. Overhead a squadron of crows heckled him as they lighted like soldiers on the telephone wire stretching from the house. He continued to swear as he carried the severed limbs and branches to the back of the property. He'd bundle them and carry them to the curb over the weekend.

The dogs were still sleeping when Woo walked into the carriage house for a second bottle of Iron City beer. He fired up a cigarette, his eyes murderous. "Why is it everything you touch turns to shit, Ross?" He mumbled as he slugged at the beer bottle. He hadn't expected that business with the contract. "Which just goes to show, fellas, you never really get to know someone until you cross them." It would be just like Ross to sue him to make his point. So much for goddamn friendships sworn to in blood.

Ross looked around the comfortable living room, picturing Jory here at night with the dogs curled at her feet. It was a pleasant, contented picture, and he felt jealous. He wondered what the kitchen was like.

Jory was looking at him strangely, wondering why he was here. The vision of a fire with the dogs curled on the fire mat, Woo on the sofa, Jory next to him with a cup of hot cocoa, made Ross feel light-headed. She wasn't just looking at him strangely, she was looking at him suspiciously.

"I'm here for two reasons," he said, "three actually, if you count Woo. He resigned today and I came out to try and talk him out of it. He signed a contract, and if he breaks it I'll have to file a suit."

"You'd do that to your best friend?" Jory said in disbelief.

"Business is business. Friendship doesn't enter into it. Either you're professional or you're not. The second reason I'm here is to give you this. It was on my desk this morning. Everything's been taken care of. The third reason is, I'd like to invite you to have dinner with me on Saturday evening."

"What is *this*?" Jory said, backing up a step and refusing to accept the manila envelope in Ross's hands.

Ross laid the envelope on the coffee table. "You can read it at your leisure. What about dinner?"

"I don't think so, Ross. I thought we agreed to have dinner when the divorce is final. We discussed that this morning. What's in the envelope?"

"Open it. I want you to know I had nothing to do with it. My father . . . my father pretty much does what he wants. He's always been fond of you, Jory." Then he asked, "What's wrong with a simple dinner?"

"I'm sorry, Ross, I'm much too busy. Why are you insisting on this? We're getting a divorce. We haven't seen each other in five years to actually talk to one another. I don't need any problems in my life right now, so let's just keep things the way they are. What's in the damn envelope?"

"My father deeded the Landers Building on Andover Street to you. *TIF* will pay you rent to the tune of five grand a month. The building is yours for your lifetime. You can't sell it, you can't give it back. All you can do is collect the rent and maintain the building. I filed the deed this morning. Your first month's rent check is included. My mother fought like a tiger over this, but my father . . . well, he wanted to do something nice for you, and this is what he came up with. I guess he wanted to ensure your well-being. My father, as you know, is a very kind man."

"Is this some kind of joke? If it is, I don't appreciate it, Ross. Why would your father . . . yes, he is a nice man. You'll just have to tell him I can't accept it. Thank him, but I'll manage nicely without the old family building."

"You can't give it back, didn't you hear me? You have to pay the taxes, make arrangements to have the snow shoveled in the winter, maintain the shrubs and lawn, keep up the parking lot, things like that."

"I'll get a lawyer. I don't want it. You cannot tie me to your family. I won't tolerate it, Ross. I meant it when I said I don't want anything except to get on with my life. Please don't make this any harder on me than it already is. Undo it, you're a lawyer."

"Jory, I had nothing to do with this. My father's attorneys handled it. I have nothing to do with this. Call my father."

"I think you should leave, Ross, and take that with you," Jory said, pointing a trembling hand at the envelope on the coffee table.

Ross shook his head. "It belongs to you. I'm sorry you won't have dinner with me. I think if we set our differences aside, we could have a pleasant evening. Who knows, we might even come to like one another."

"You're five years too late, Ross." Was that admiration or approval she was seeing in his eyes? She felt like crying. There had been a time once when she would have kissed his feet to see such a look. She would have prostituted herself for a smile or a friendly pat on the head. Too much, too little, too late. "I'll walk you to your car, I have to bring the dogs in. Pete was kind enough to watch them all afternoon. Please don't come here anymore, Ross," Jory said, leading him through the kitchen and out the back door.

Jory's eyes burned as she bent down to gather the dogs close to her. Part of her wanted to call Ross back and part of her wanted to go to him and beat at him with her clenched fists. She turned her back on him and walked over to where Woo was standing.

"Is it true, can he really make you go back and work there?"

"He's right, I do have a contract, but contracts are made to be broken. I should know, I drew it up," he said ruefully. "But don't concern yourself with my problems, Jory. I'm sorry I said anything."

"I hate to see such a wonderful relationship go sour. I always envied your friendship. I never really had a close friend. I guess I was too wild and willful back then. I regret it now when I could really use a friend. I miss that," Jory said in a rare burst of confidence.

"Two people have to work at a friendship. I keep an open mind for the most part. Ross is going through some turmoil right now, and I understand that. I'll give him some slack and things will work out. If they're meant to work out. In the meantime I'll be your friend. Feel free to confide or weep on my shoulder at any time."

Jory laughed. "Thanks. Do you know about the Landers Building, Pete?"

"I heard about it this morning. Ross thought it was the funniest thing he ever heard. By that I mean he was happy for you. Something about his father outsmarting his mother."

"By using me," Jory said bitterly.

"Possibly, but I don't think Mr. Landers would deliberately do anything unkind to you, Jory. I think he wanted to provide for you in his own way. You turned him down, didn't you?"

"I tried to. Ross said I can't sell it and I can't give it back. That doesn't sound right to me. I have to pay the taxes and maintain the building. Mrs. Landers will be paying rent of five thousand dollars a month. Can you believe that? You're a lawyer, Pete, what can I do?"

He was right about her. He felt like singing. "If I give you sound, free advice, will you follow it?" Woo asked seriously.

"It depends," Jory hedged.

"Accept it. Bank the money. There's no law that says you have to *spend* the money. You can give it to charity if you want. You'll have to pay the taxes, add it on to your income, and maintain the building and keep up the insurance. All of which can be taken out of the rent. You'll have the security of a nest egg to tap if need be. Be gracious in your acceptance and forget about it. For a reasonable fee

I can act as janitor for you, and it won't embarrass me one bit to do blue-collar labor."

"Do you really think I should, Pete?" Jory asked, a frown building on her face.

"I really do. You don't have to decide right now. Give it some thought. These guys won't have to worry about their dishes being empty if you accept. Jasper Landers means well, Jory, I truly believe that."

"Looks like you got carried away," Jory said, pointing to the forsythia bushes. "By the time spring arrives, they'll be a foot and half high."

"I allowed the anger I was feeling at Ross to get the best of me. It was a dumb thing to do. I think I'm going to call it a day. The dogs are all yours. By the way, they did what they're supposed to do, all four of them. I gave them appropriate praise and we're buddies now. I can hand out cookies too." He guffawed.

Jory giggled before she called the dogs and took off on the run. "See you tomorrow," she called over her shoulder. "Oh, by the way, I called and spoke to one of my father's friends at the prosecutor's office. He said you should stop by for a chat. Tomorrow at two o'clock."

"What?"

"You heard me. I think it's in the bag. You can thank me by blacktopping the driveway. Whenever you get around to it."

Peeking out of the kitchen window Jory watched Woo leave. He looks like a huge grizzly bear, she thought. But grizzly bears didn't have endearing smiles that warmed one's heart. Grizzly bears didn't dispense good advice or pitch in with the chores.

"I'm glad Pete's living here," she said to the dogs. "Now, what should we have for dinner, leftover spaghetti or leftover pot roast?" The dogs waited for the refrigerator door to open, their tails swishing furiously, their noses quivering with delight. "Pot roast," she chortled, "with a tad of gravy for you guys."

She was happy, she realized. She was really happy! She had a new job, one she thought she was going to like; she'd set Ross straight; she now owned a building—if she decided to keep it—which meant money in the bank; and best of all, she had a friend. "I don't know what I did to deserve all this," she said aloud, "and I don't know how I'm going to repay you, but I'll think of something. Thank you, God, and thank you for these little guys." Jory dropped to the floor to tussle with the dogs. She laughed and giggled, and the dogs yapped and yipped as they rolled over and on top of one another.

Outside, his gardening tools under his arm, Woo watched his landlady and the four dogs through the screen door. He'd give anything to be inside on the floor with the romping dogs and happy young woman, he thought.

Anything.

Chapter 8

Lena Davis put the finishing touches to her makeup. She looked fetching, she thought. Today after work she'd rushed to Wanamaker's for a new dress. She felt prim, schoolgirlish in the blue-and-white-striped dress with the full skirt that swished seductively around her knees. She grimaced at the white piqué collar and narrow piqué trim on the elbow-length sleeves. It was too late in the season for such a summery dress, but it was on sale, and Ross seemed to like what she considered virginal-looking dresses. She added a narrow white rope belt that cinched in her twenty-four-inch waist. The platform-soled sling backs would add at least an inch to her height, to bring her to Ross's chin. Perfect for kissing position.

The coronet of braids was absolutely perfect, as were the small white earrings. "I look delectable." She made a kissing motion with her lips at her reflection in the mirror.

Men were such suckers.

Lena's smile was sweet and warm when she opened the door to Ross a few minutes later. "You're always on time, Ross. I like that. I don't like to keep people waiting either. You're very considerate. Did you decide on which movie you want to see? It really doesn't matter to me."

"Heads for *From Here to Eternity* and tails for *Roman Holiday.*"

Lena laughed, a tinkling, musical sound. Ross felt a chill go up and down his arms. "Tails," she said seriously. Ross flipped the nickel in his hand.

"Looks like we're going to see *Roman Holiday*. I thought we'd have dinner at Armand's and take in the second show. Is it all right with you if we walk?"

"It sounds wonderful, Ross. I'm relaxed already, just being with you. I really don't mind if you don't. All I need is a sweater."

"You're sure you don't mind?"

"I'm positive. I love to walk. Especially if I have someone to walk with. Do you like walking in the rain?" she asked, linking her arms with his.

"I can't say that I do or don't. When I was a kid, I'd get caught in it from time to time, but I don't suppose it's the same thing."

"All the big fat worms come out on the sidewalks. We used to catch them and put them in a can and go fishing. Have you ever gone fishing, Ross?"

"At a bazaar or fair."

"Let's go fishing on Saturday! I know how to bait hooks and everything. I'll fix a picnic lunch and we'll make a day of it. Oh, Ross, let's do it! Fishing is such fun."

"Why not? Okay, I'll pick you up at noon and we'll go fishing. I don't suppose you have poles."

"Heck no. We'll make our own. I'll pick up some string and a few hooks. Of course, I'm not promising we're going to actually catch our supper." She giggled. "How is it, Ross, that you've never gone fishing?" Without waiting for a reply she said, "Did you ever steal apples or pumpkins in the rain? Did you ever go to a fireman's carnival?"

"No to all your questions."

Lena pretended shock. "Truly, Ross?"

"Truly." There was such bitterness in his voice, Lena stopped and swung Ross around to face her.

"Let's forget the movie and go to the park and sit on a bench and talk about when we were kids. I have some wonderful stories, and if yours aren't wonderful, you can share mine. I'm not hungry.

Later, if you like, we can pick up a hot pretzel from one of the street vendors."

He'd been dreading the evening all day, more so after his visit to Chestnut Hill. Now things seemed better, lighter somehow. Lena was acting so nice, and she wanted to share. "That sounds good," he replied. "I more or less lost my appetite a little while ago, and to tell you the truth, *Roman Holiday* sounds like something that would give me an itch. The park sounds like a good idea."

"Good. Ross," Lena said suddenly, "have you ever gone square dancing?"

"No. Are you trying to tell me I missed out on the finer things in life?"

"You sure did. Next month they're having the annual harvest dance at West Chester. I'm taking you. You have to wear overalls and a plaid shirt. They are *soooo* much fun. I know you'll have a good time."

Later, in the park, Lena said, "I love it here. Sometimes I come and eat my lunch. Let's go on the seesaw, but promise not to keep me up in the air."

"Won't your dress get dirty?" He must have gone on one when he was a kid, he thought, but he couldn't recall it. He eyed the swings, remembering the fat bald tire hanging from a maple tree in Woo's yard in Lancaster. "Old tires make the best swings," he said, his voice ringing with authority.

"Yeah, I know," Lena said, straddling the seesaw. "Don't worry about this old dress. Besides, after tonight I won't be able to wear it again till next summer."

"It's pretty. I meant to tell you how nice you looked, but we got to talking. Okay, hold on now." Lena squealed as her end of the seesaw shot upward.

They played like children for over an hour, running from the slide to the swings to the merry-go-round and back to the seesaw. Exhausted, Ross spread his jacket under a tree. He leaned back against it, Lena in the crook of his arm.

"That was so much fun. I wish sometimes I was a little girl again. Life was so wonderful then. The only thing I ever worried about was what my mother would make for dessert. I have this sweet tooth, you see." Ross chuckled.

They talked for hours. At first Ross was reticent, but gradually, with gentle prodding from Lena, he opened up and revealed more about his life than he'd ever told anyone. He felt such an immense sense of relief, he hugged the girl sitting next to him. In turn, he learned about catching tadpoles; spitting on lucky stones; playing Red-light, Green-light and Simon says; exactly how to snitch pumpkins under the cover of rain; climbing trees, skinned shins, patching bicycle tires with bubble gum, and lordy, lordy, skinny-dipping in Miller's pond.

"What do you mean you never went skinny-dipping? *Everyone* has gone skinny-dipping. Did you go in your underwear? Not even in your underwear!" Lena said in mock outrage. "Well, we're going to take care of that before it gets too cold. We'll go on Saturday afternoon after we go fishing, providing it's warm enough. Buckassed naked, Ross. Just you and me. I'll bring a blanket and picnic basket. Deviled eggs, potato salad, fried chicken—the kind you eat with your fingers—wine, and a loaf of French bread. Some apples and cheese. Did I miss anything?"

"Not a thing. Who's going to get the worms?"

"We'll both dig them up. You have so much to learn, Ross. Do you know, it's a quarter to twelve. Fifteen more minutes and I'll turn into a pumpkin. We should be going."

Ross kissed her lightly, and she responded in the same manner. This was not going to be a night that ended in the wild, abandoned sex. This was a kiss-good-night-at-the-door evening.

As they walked along, hand in hand, Lena said, "You seem in a better mood now. You see, Ross, sometimes you have to play a little, be a child again so you can get a little more perspective on adulthood."

"Was I so transparent?"

Lena nodded. "Want to talk about it?"

"Woo resigned today. I got a little angry over it and went out to where he's living now and said a few things I regret. Sometimes I act on impulse."

"Sometimes I do too. As long as you're aware of it and make a conscious effort not to do it too often, it's okay. Why did he resign, or is that something you don't want to talk about?"

"It was a stupid thing. In his own inimitable way I think he was trying to tell me I'm an emotional cripple. I reacted, and then he reacted. End of story."

"Does this have anything to do with Jory?" Lena asked coolly.

"I think Woo had a date with her. Actually, I ran into them having lunch today. Woo tried to cover it up, and I don't know why. He said it was a chance meeting."

"Why would your best friend lie to you? Be more generous, Ross. Make amends. You said yourself Woo is the best thing that ever happened to you. Some people can go through their whole lives and not make one lasting, real friend. You're very lucky to have Woo. I hate seeing you unhappy."

"How'd you get to be so smart?" He was wrong about this girl, he thought. He was about to tell her the evil thoughts he had concerning her when she interrupted his thoughts.

"Ross, would it be so terrible if Woo dated Marjory? Now, be honest. You said your marriage is over and you're getting a divorce. Why shouldn't they date? You can't have it both ways. I think Woo was telling you the truth. Friends don't lie to one another. My sweet, on that thought I'm going to leave you. We are home, in case you hadn't noticed. I had a wonderful time, Ross." Lena stretched to plaster warm, wet kisses all over his face. "Sweet dreams," she said, laughing, tripping up the front steps.

" 'Night," he called softly.

Ross executed a two-step dance all the way down the street to where his car was parked. He thought about the evening, about Lena's words on the short drive home. He was still thinking about them when he put on his pajamas. It was possible he was simply a lousy judge of character. One minute he believed the worst about his friends, the next he compared them to saints.

Ross contemplated his bare toes. Tonight he'd talked more about his past, his childhood, than he ever had with Woo. Lena was such a willing, interested listener, ready to share her own experiences.

What was it she'd said? "We're going to go back in time and do all those things you missed doing. I'll be the really fortunate one because I'll get to do it twice, and it will be more fun now that we're all grown-up." She'd told him he was a taker and not a giver. You took from Woo, but what did you give back? she'd asked. She'd been appalled when he said he'd given friendship. In life you share *everything* with those you care about. "And," she said breezily, "I'm not talking about material things. Maybe," she had gone on to say, "that's what went wrong with your marriage."

As for Woo and Jory, well, he was going to have to live with that situation. The big man wasn't going to report for work in the morning. He'd known that when he issued his terse, tight-lipped ultimatum. He'd reacted in anger, wanting to have his own way. Lena was right, he gave with one hand and took away with the other. No doubt about it, he was a shit of the first order.

To the best of his knowledge, Woo had never lied to him. It was his own insecurities, his own guilt, that made him do what he did. Now he was going to have to go back there and apologize to both Jory and Woo. Shit, Jory told him not to come back. He could call, write letters. It wouldn't be the same. He could go to Chestnut Hill, stand in the middle of the road and bellow his apology.

What it came down to was, the old selfish, rich kid philosophy, what's mine is mine. Jory is still mine. The law said so. Woo's theory when he was stymied was, if you don't know what to do, don't do anything. "And that, Landers, is exactly what I'm going to do. Nothing."

Son of a bitch, he was going fishing. With a girl. And to a real honest-to-God picnic complete with ants, grass, and a blanket.

Ross slept like a baby, his sleep completely dreamless.

It was December before Lena Davis pronounced Ross's education complete. She presented him with a silly, little plaque with an engraved brass plate that said he was an expert angler, expert tadpole catcher, expert lucky stone spitter, expert game player, expert pumpkin snatcher, expert square dancer, and expert skinny-dipper. Ross laughed till his eyes overflowed. He hugged Lena and promised himself he was going to present her with an engagement ring the day his divorce from Jory was final.

It was amazing, he thought, how he'd turned his emotions around and come to terms with all the elements in his life that had been making him unhappy. And he owed it all to Lena. They were inseparable these days, and he wouldn't have it any other way. With Lena's help, he had his friendship with Woo back on track. He hadn't seen Jory or even spoken to her, and that was all right; Jory was handling her life just the way he was. He was even looking forward to the dinner he'd promised to celebrate the divorce. If Jory was amenable, maybe he'd invite Lena and Woo. It wouldn't exactly be a double date. His shoulders twitched. Jory probably wouldn't go for it at all. Woo would have something to say too, of that he was certain.

Ross smiled when he thought of Woo these days. The big man was making a name for himself in the prosecutor's office. His picture had been in the *Democrat* twice in one week. It looked like Woo had finally found his niche, and he was so happy, it was sinful.

Ross chuckled. Lena was right, time took care of everything if one had the patience to wait things out. Patience was the key to everything. Today he was full of patience, even though he hated the Tuesday morning meeting to discuss Philadelphia's secret skeleton. So far Justine had come up with three juicy stories about various bigwigs, as she referred to the county officials, that were so libelous Ross had to call in a battery of downtown lawyers to convince his mother she'd be out of business in a week if she ever *thought* about publishing the exposé articles she had on file. Malcom Collire, the head of the firm that had represented the Landers family from the beginning, took the brunt of his mother's hostility and left in a huff, but not before he told her she was a disgrace to the publishing industry and to the city of Philadelphia. Justine had backed down for now, but if there was one thing he knew about his mother, it was that she never let sleeping dogs lie. What she would do was find a way to print the same articles a different way and still say the same thing.

Once he told her how much court suits cost and what was involved in a lawsuit, Justine followed his advice. His mother was no fool, and she could read a ledger sheet in the dark. He'd explained to her that it was better to keep her profits, which were considerable, in her own accounts, than pay them out in court costs, court experts, outside legal firms, and settlement costs. He'd presented a hypothetical case to her, in which she lost a sizable amount of money. She'd been shocked speechless. Her favorite words after that were, "We must have three documented sources for every article we print."

Quietly and with little fanfare, Justine rented a warehouse on the outskirts of Philadelphia, where she was putting the finishing touches to *Keyhole*, a magazine so sleazy it was impossible to think of it as an actual magazine. Secretly, Ross referred to it as a rag. His mother simply called it money in the bank. The first issue full of supercharged sex and splashy pictures was scheduled to hit newsstands two days before Christmas.

He'd seen two of the feature articles earlier this morning, one written by Lena and the other by a reporter named Dick Thorne. Both used breezy, breathless prose that literally made his skin crawl. For one thousand dollars an article they promised, but didn't deliver, "the real goods." It was nothing more than cunning smears on starlets and leading men, saying nothing with finality. No claims were made in either one of the articles and both reporters left everything to the reader's imagination.

When it came to business and the almighty dollar, Justine had no equal, Ross thought uneasily. The money was pouring in so fast, they were having difficulty keeping track of it. *Keyhole* was going to bring in more money, even though the first issue was going out minus advertising, something his mother insisted on, saying, "we want to give them reading orgasms with this first issue, and we can't do that if we go with advertising. We'll recoup by the time the second issue is ready to go to press with the same customers who advertise in *TIF*." Ross didn't doubt the blasé statement.

Ross gathered up his reports and stuffed them in his briefcase. His mother would probably dance a jig when he informed her that production costs for *Keyhole* would be the same as *TIF*—eight cents a copy.

The new conference room was light and bright, even though the day outside was gloomy and overcast, with a prediction of heavy snow by nightfall.

Justine rapped her gavel, a gift to herself, on the fine oak desk. "This meeting will come to order," she said imperiously.

As usual, Ross sat in the back of the room, better to observe the small assembly. He also liked to watch the back of Lena's head. He prided himself on his astute observations. He could tell when something pleased or displeased her, when she turned anxious or excited, by the way she positioned pencils in her new, shorn hairdo.

Just last week Lena had shown him the severed pigtail she kept in a tin box to show her children someday. Her new "do" feathered and curled about her face like a nimbus of tarnished gold. She looked sixteen instead of twenty-three. There were days she looked wide-eyed and innocent, and others when she looked wide-eyed and calculating.

Ross's mind wandered. It was the twelfth of December, and as yet Woo hadn't invited him to Lancaster. With Christmas falling on Friday, it would be a long weekend. He'd done his shopping early for all the Woojalesky family. The washing machine for Woo's mother would be delivered Christmas Eve morning, complete with big red bow. A gift certificate for four new tires was already gift-wrapped in a huge box, with a bow as big as the one that would be on the washing machine, for Woo's father. For Woo there was a custom-made armchair and reading lamp Wanamaker's promised to deliver to the carriage house December 22 after five P.M. In his sun room at home, mountains of gift-wrapped boxes for the family lined the walls, all in silver and gold paper with monstrous red and green bows. How he was going to get everything to Lancaster was something he had to work on. Providing the invitation was forthcoming. Woo was late extending the invitation this year. Usually they had the holiday schedule firmed up by the fifth of December.

Lena had asked him if he'd like to go to Miami with her to meet her parents over the holidays. She'd pouted for days when he declined. He'd done his best to explain about Woo and his family. In the end she said she understood, but he knew she didn't. Nor did she understand about the dinner he promised Jory when the divorce was finalized two days from now. She'd called it indecent. The only thing she was really interested in these days was the Christmas party and the bonuses his mother would hand out.

Ross tuned in briefly to his mother's droning voice, then tuned her out. He had to call Jory sometime today and tell her about the court date. He should call Woo to tell him too. Maybe if the big guy wasn't too busy, they could have lunch at Mulligan's. And it would give Woo a chance to bring up Christmas, in case it was an oversight.

Ross wondered if he would feel any different when the judge granted the divorce. Would he feel relief, or the same shame and guilt every time he thought about it?

Ross tuned in to his mother again. She was addressing him. He felt like laughing when she said, "Your retired club members on the first floor left the lights burning all night. Electricity costs money. It might be a good idea to replace the seventy-five-watt bulbs with forty watts if they're going to keep on doing this." Ross deduced that meant he'd have to stay late and see to the lights himself. "And," Justine said coldly, "the roof is leaking on the south side of the building. If we get the snow that's predicted, we're going to have a major problem."

"Consult the landlord," Ross said coolly. "Repairs are written into the rental lease." Justine eyed him silently and let the matter drop.

"Is there any other business?" she asked offhandedly.

A reporter two rows ahead of Ross raised his hand. "Did anyone read the column in the *Democrat* about *TIF* and some of our competitors?"

Justine's eyebrows shot upward. "No, what did it say?"

"It's that new advice column that runs several times a week. There was a small article on the bottom of the front page of Friday's edition that said the column, because of heavy reader mail, was going to be a daily column."

"Yes, yes, what did it say?" Justine said sourly.

"Some woman's husband wrote to this Auntie Ann and said his wife was addicted to exposé magazines and all she did was read them, neglecting him, their kids, and the house. He wanted to know what he should do. He also didn't like the twelve dollars a month she was spending when they could be making payments on a television set. The husband said *TIF* was his wife's favorite. I suppose that's a kind of publicity," the reporter said lamely.

"And what did this . . . Auntie Ann reply?"

"She said magazines like *TIF* and other exposés owe their success to people who like vicarious thrills and who, physically, may be adults but never reached a grown-up level. She said the man should get his wife a library card."

Justine's eyes spewed sparks. "Ross, is that a libelous statement? Can we sue? Who is this Auntie Ann?"

"No, it's not libelous. It's Auntie Ann's opinion. No, you cannot sue, and I have no idea who Auntie Ann is," Ross replied coolly.

Justine eyed the reporter. "Does anyone know who she is?"

"I don't think so, Mrs. Landers. For all I know, it could be a man. What I do know is, the column has taken off like a rocket."

"Check it out and report back to me personally. Maybe we can give Auntie Ann a dose of her own medicine." To the others she said, "If there's no other business, we'll dispense with Friday's meeting and get an early start on the Christmas party."

Ross waited for the staff to file out when his mother gave him the high sign she wanted to speak with him. He winked at Lena, who winked back.

"Ross, I don't want those old coots at the Christmas party. See to it they don't show up. I don't care how you do it, just do it."

"Mother, they already have their Christmas tree up and decorated in the club room. If you didn't want them to attend, then why in the hell did you post a notice in the lobby? They can read."

"They're too damn senile to read. All they do is sleep and drink whiskey and then sleep some more. I don't like having them here, Ross, and it's all your fault. I want them out!"

"Mother, we have been over this so many times I've lost count. You cannot put them out. They're here to stay. They don't bother you, they don't traipse around, they don't make any noise. Let sleeping dogs lie."

"They're breathing, Ross. Or should I say snoring? You can hear them on the second floor if they leave the door open. Out!"

"No, Mother," Ross said patiently.

"All right, Ross," Justine said wearily. "I meant it about the lights, and I want their door kept closed. I've invited half the town to the Christmas party. God, I can see it now, all those gravy stains on their ties, their soiled shirt cuffs, and they always reek of alcohol. What kind of impression will they make?"

"Mother, compared to the crap you've been printing, those old gentlemen will hardly be noticed. All your guests will be interested in is who's going to be in the magazine next. I think we're both aware that in the past few months you've become, should we say, slightly feared?"

Justine preened. "Thanks in part to Lena and a few others. My reporters have noses for scandal I didn't think possible. You would not believe the articles we have on the back burner. It's enough to make you want to run screaming. Our pictures need to be a little more splashy. I'd like to see more lurid covers. Color sells. Red sizzles. Red and yellow together scorches. Do you know, Ross, this week we had to turn away advertisers? I'd like you to tell *that* to your father."

"Tell him yourself, Mother. I told you I would not be a go-between."

"Yes, you did say that," Justine said sweetly. "I guess I'll just have to write him a letter and give him an update. Jasper always loved to play with numbers. This set will drive him to the bottle, where his snoot is most of the time anyway."

"You really hate him, don't you?"

"Yes," Justine said bluntly.

"Shouldn't you be just a little grateful? You wouldn't be doing what you're doing if it weren't for Father. And you love this. You're eating, sleeping, and drinking this magazine. I bet you even dream about it," Ross said sourly.

Justine laughed. The sound was so bitter, Ross winced. "Not even a little, darling. Shoo, now, I have things to do, and I hope you do too. By the way, Ross, you are doing a tremendous job. Believe it or not, I appreciate it. Knowing how you feel about the magazine and me . . . it surprises me. I rather expected you to snafu things for me."

"That's not my style, Mother. You're paying me to do a job, and I'm doing it to the best of my ability. You're right, though, I don't like it, and . . ." He'd been about to say, I don't like you, but he held the words back. His mother looked disappointed.

"You're sure about that advice column, Ross?"

"I'm very sure."

"I think we should find out who writes it."

"For God's sake, Mother, why? The *Democrat* is a local paper. Leave well enough alone. That's my advice; I think you should follow it."

"Very well, Ross. Now, tell me, when is your divorce final?"

"Two days from now. I really don't want to discuss it, Mother."

"What about Lena? Are you serious about her? Christmastime is a good time to give engagement rings and to make plans for the future."

Ross's eyes turned cold and frosty. "What do you know about Christmas, Mother? We never spent one together. I was always at boarding school or military school, and not allowed to come home for the holidays. I'll bet you never knew I used to pretend I was Jewish rather than let anyone know I wasn't wanted at home."

"Where will you be this Christmas?" she asked.

"When I decide, I'll let you know."

"Sometimes, Ross, you are an impossible snot," Justine called to her son when he was halfway down the corridor.

Justine sat down with a thump. In two weeks it would be Christmas. She hated the holidays, hated the gift-giving, the decorating, the fucking happiness. She thought about Christmas when she was a child in the three-room shanty. There were no gifts, no oranges and nuts, no decorations or trees, and for sure there was no happiness. They were lucky they had Spam and beans on Christmas. She wondered, not for the first time, where all her sisters and brothers were. Probably if she found one of them, she'd be able to locate the others. If she wanted to. And her parents, were they alive or dead?

She'd gone back once after her marriage to Jasper. She'd dressed in her finest, filled the car with costly gifts and rich food, but the shanty was gone, an appliance store in its place. Her family was gone too, and she hadn't asked any questions. Jasper had looked at her with such pity in his eyes and said, "The Lady Bountiful image doesn't become you, Justine. You didn't go with generosity in your heart, you went there to gloat, to show off, and God simply would not allow you to do that." She knew he was right, and that hurt all the more. She couldn't do anything right in those days. Was that why she'd deprived Ross of love and Christmas? Was it because she didn't want him to be hurt and grow up tough?

Her own mother, the gentle, weary woman she remembered, wasn't that old, sixty-five at the most. She'd been married at fifteen, her father sixteen. She wondered if they were well, warm, and had food. Her eyes burned with her thoughts. It must be all the smoke in the room, she thought.

Justine returned to her office. To her secretary she said, "Don't take any calls for the rest of the day. I don't want to be disturbed. For any reason. Do you understand, Astrid?"

"Yes, Mrs. Landers, you are not to be disturbed for any reason."

Justine closed and locked the door. She walked to her ornate desk on shaking legs. She felt herself ooze into the chair. How did a person go about finding a family they hadn't seen in thirty-five years?

Ross looked at the pile of work on his desk. It was going to take him days to wade through it. He wished, as he did every day, that Woo was still working alongside him. Wishing was for fools, he told himself. He should know, since he was an authority on the subject. Jesus, he had to go over to the warehouse at some point, and he had a lunch date with his father. Maybe he could change lunch to dinner and bring Lena along. And he had to call Jory. Maybe this kind of news would be better presented face-to-face. If so, that meant a trip to Chestnut Hill. Should he tell her about Lena? Would it be better for her to hear it from him or someone else, namely Woo? He had to admit he didn't know. If the moment is right, I'll tell her, if it isn't, then maybe at the courthouse. Here he was, assuming she would be interested, which probably wasn't the truth at all.

Ross called his father, who didn't seem disappointed at all. Dinner, he said, would be fine. But Jasper's voice changed when Ross suggested bringing Lena along. "She probably won't be able to make it," Ross added hastily. "I just thought it would be nice."

Woo was in court and wouldn't be back in the office till after four. Ross left his name and number. His second call was to Lena, who said not to worry about her, she would wash her hair and give herself a much-needed manicure. "Stop by, if it isn't too late."

Ross reached for his coat, searched his briefcase for the folder he wanted, and was out of the office before he could think twice about what he was doing or where he was going.

It was snowing, the wind gusting, when Ross slipped the Skylark into gear to back out of his parking space. He loved snow. He craned his neck to look upward. If it continued, the world would be covered with a blanket of white in a few hours.

He drove carefully, aware of the drivers who came unglued at the first sign of bad weather. He'd gotten stuck in a snowstorm once during his third year at Villanova. He and Woo had been living in a rental house two miles off campus with four other students. His car had been in the shop for transmission trouble, forcing him to walk the two miles back and forth to school. Dressed in sweats and tennis shoes, he'd slogged his way home from the gym. Two days later he had a cold that turned into bronchitis and then pneumonia. Woo and the guys had taken care of him with the help of the school nurse and antibiotics. He hadn't even bothered to notify his parents. The guys had given him better care then a team of round-the-clock nurses. He remembered drinking greasy chicken soup by the gallon and rum toddies by the quart. It was one of his more memorable college experiences.

By the time he reached Germantown Avenue, the snow was battling Ross's windshield wipers with a vengeance. Visibility was terrible. "Shit," he said succinctly. This was not one of his better ideas. For Christ's sake, he didn't even know if Jory was home. "You aren't thinking today, Landers," he mumbled as he steered the Buick onto Graver Lane. He skidded when he made the turn, the car fishtailing across the length of the road to settle in someone's lawn. He slid again when he tried to back the car out to the road. Damn, he should have gotten the new snow tires he needed weeks ago. Procrastination these days was his middle name.

His breath exploded from his mouth like a gunshot when he finally managed to steer his car into Jory's driveway. He stepped into an inch of new crystal-white snow. A second later he was on all fours on the front walkway, the red door straight ahead of him, his slick leather soles giving out under him. "Son of a bitch!" he seethed as he picked himself up. A moment later he heard tinkling laughter from the side of the house. He turned, slipped, and went down again. Sixteen legs pummeled him. He felt one of his ears being nibbled, not exactly an unpleasant feeling. A tail swished in front of his eyes and then another. He cursed ripely before he burst into laughter as one of the dogs tried to nuzzle down into his jacket.

Jory laughed delightedly. "They don't know about friends and foes yet," she said. "You were in the neighborhood and thought you'd stop by, is that it, Ross?"

By now he was on his feet again. "Not exactly. Foe? Did you ever hear about rock salt? You could get your ass sued off if someone slips and gets hurt on your property. Do you know that?"

"I've heard of rock salt, I just don't happen to have any. Sue me."

"I'm probably bruised from head to toe," he grumbled. "I'm serious about the rock salt."

"And I'm serious about not having any."

"For God's sake, use table salt, then, before I manage to kill myself."

"You aren't exactly dressed for this winter weather," Jory said, pointing to his wing-tip shoes. "You can wait on the porch or in your car until I walk the dogs. Or I can get you a pair of my father's boots and his shearling jacket."

"Sure," Ross said as he shuffled toward the house, hanging onto her for dear life, the dogs snapping and nipping at his pants. "I can't believe you have four dogs," he said when they were finally on the porch.

"I can't believe you're out here in the middle of a snowstorm," Jory said pointedly. "Wait here and keep your eyes on the dogs. They like to scamper out to the road."

"And you think I can catch them with these shoes?" Ross asked disgustedly.

"I'd expect you to try. I'll just be a moment." She was as good

as her word and was back in five minutes with a stout pair of rubber boots and a heavy jacket complete with hood. "I think these are
fishing boots or something, the soles are grooved. You should be
able to stay upright." The laughter was back in her voice. When
Ross pulled the hood over his wet head, she gurgled again. "Na-
nook of the North. Well, come on, if you're coming with us. Don't
just stand there. These guys have been real patient."

"Do they have names? How do you tell them apart?" Ross asked,
falling into step beside her.

"I had color strings on them for a while, but it didn't do any
good. Now I just call one name and they all respond. Hey, it works,
and it makes life simple."

"How come you're home today? I was halfway here before I
thought about that. Good thing, though, you'd never get home
from the city at five o'clock. My tires are bald. I meant to buy snow
tires, but didn't get around to it. Story of my life these days."

"I have some chains in the garage you can borrow. You can give
them to Woo to bring home."

"Sounds good," Ross said carefully. "Wonder if Woo will make
it home in that little car he drives. Does he have chains?"

"I have no idea. He may have to stay in town tonight. I'm not
his keeper, Ross. The only time I see him is on the weekends when
he works outside."

"You didn't tell me what you're doing at home. I thought you
were working. Don't you have a job?" he asked.

"It really isn't any of your business, but yes, I have a job. I work
from home. Which brings me to my question, why are you here?"

"I came out to tell you our court date was moved up to the day
after tomorrow. I didn't want to tell you something like that over
the phone."

Jory sucked in a deep breath. She hunched deeper into her heavy
jacket. "Why?" was all she said.

Ross shrugged. "I don't know. Would you rather I told you over
the phone?"

"I don't suppose it makes any difference." Of course it made a
difference. She would have cried when she hung up the phone. She

wanted to cry now, but she couldn't let Ross see how much the divorce was hurting her.

"I didn't stop to think. It wasn't snowing so hard in town. Telling you on the phone seemed . . . I don't know, callous, I guess."

"I guess," Jory muttered.

"In less than forty-eight hours we'll both be free. It took a long time. Guess you're relieved."

"Are you?"

Ross chose his words carefully. "It's probably best for both of us. We need to get on with our lives. Don't you agree?"

"With which part?"

"About the divorce, you know, getting on with our lives and making futures for ourselves."

"That's one way of looking at it," Jory said quietly. "It's getting colder, don't you think?"

"Feels that way. Are you sure those dogs won't get sick out here in the snow? They don't look like they have a whole lot of hair on them to keep them warm, and they are pretty low to the ground. I got pneumonia once after walking home in a snowstorm. I was soaked to the skin. Maybe you should take them inside and dry them off."

The horror on Jory's face was so total, Ross reached out to her.

"Don't just stand there, Ross, help me. I never thought of that. I just . . . the first snow and all, I thought they'd romp and have some fun, a new experience for them. My God, what if they get sick? Hurry. For God's sake, Ross, they aren't going to bite you, and if they do, they've had their shots."

"They aren't going to let us catch them, they're having too much fun. Let's run, and maybe they'll follow us. I'll whistle. Do they respond to whistles?" he asked.

"How the hell do I know? I don't even know how to whistle." She ran, calling the dogs' names over and over. The hysteria in her voice brought the dogs up short as one by one they raced after Ross's lumbering body. The moment they were inside, Jory slammed the red door. "I'll get the towels. Take off your things and you can help me."

"Do what?"

"Take care of the dogs, for God's sake." Jory was kicking off her boots as she ran toward the hall and the linen closet. Her jacket lay in a heap with her mittens in the middle of the dining room floor.

"Rub them down and then warm the towel and wrap them tight. I think that will work, don't you?"

"Hey, I'm a lawyer. I never had a dog. I don't know anything about dogs."

"Well, guess what, Ross, I'm a journalist and I never had a dog either, so let's give it a try. You made good sense outside, so let's act on it."

He was enjoying this. Working as a team, they dried the shivering dogs and then warmed the towels in front of the fire screen. Jory sat back on her haunches to survey their handiwork. "How come the two you wrapped are neater than mine?"

Ross laughed. "I guess my hands are bigger. They're almost asleep. Which one is which?"

"I think that's Bernie and Sam by you, and mine are Clancy and Murphy." Ross guffawed. Jory giggled. "Now what?" she asked, looking at him intently.

"Chicken soup and a toddy worked for me when I got caught in a snowstorm," he replied. "Woo and the guys at school took care of me. My parents didn't even know I was sick. Of course, you'll have to give it in bowls versus spoons. I don't think it will hurt them."

"Okay, I'll make it. Watch them, okay?"

"This fire is nice," Ross said, indicating the oak logs.

"Oak is good, it burns steadily and lasts a long time. I curl up out here and work. The dogs like to snooze by the fire. Would you . . . would you like something to eat?"

"If it isn't too much trouble. After we take care of the dogs."

"Of course, after the dogs. The dogs come first."

Chapter 9

A bowl of soup in one hand, a bowl of tea with brandy in the other, Jory watched Ross from the dining room doorway. He was on his stomach on the floor, his face pressed against first one dog and then another. Pink tongues at his face. He looked happy. The dogs looked happy. She knew she looked miserable. She came in and set the bowls down. "You do the soup and I'll do the tea and brandy."

Fifteen minutes later Ross said, "Either they're drunk or they're out for the count. I'm no authority, but I'd say they're going to sleep for a good three hours. Look, there's steam coming up from the towels. I wish I could sleep like that."

"Me too," Jory said, gathering up the bowls. "Make yourself comfortable and I'll get us some lunch. Coffee or cocoa?"

"You make cocoa?" Ross asked in amazement.

"Yes, I make cocoa. Is that what you want?"

"Well, sure. Anything is all right. Would you mind if I called the office? It doesn't look like I'm going to make my three o'clock meeting."

"Be my guest."

It wasn't until Jory was adding lettuce to the chicken sandwiches that she remembered her pile of work on the end table. If Ross looked at it, he'd know she was Auntie Ann. Would he look at it? Damn, why had she carried her work to the living room? When the snow started to fall earlier, she'd thought a fire would be cozy and comfortable, and all she was really doing was reading the letters and choosing which ones to answer in the column. What might give away her secret, if Ross chose to look behind the sofa, was the sack of mail that said *Philadelphia Democrat* stamped in bold black letters on the burlap.

She wouldn't think about why he was here. She had to concentrate on slicing the chicken so the lettuce wouldn't make the bread cockeyed. She personally liked thick but flat sandwiches. She'd made the bread on Sunday afternoon. Every time she'd punched down the dough, she'd been punching Ross. The bread turned out perfect.

Jory parted the curtains to look outside. She could barely make out the carriage house at the back of the lot in the swirling snow. Would Ross be able to make it back to town? Her heart thumped in her chest as she placed the plates and bowls of soup on a metal tray that said SCHLITZ BEER. The thick mugs of cocoa were the last thing to be added to the tray.

He looks like he belongs, Jory thought sadly when she set the tray down on the round table in front of the sofa. She noticed his bare feet, and his wet socks hanging from the mantel. "A little early for Christmas, isn't it?" she asked tightly.

"I thought they'd dry quicker up there. I see you have your Christmas tree already. Where'd you get it?" he said, pointing to the corner where a giant Frazier fir leaned against the wall in a bucket of water.

"I went out to the country over the weekend and Pete chopped it down for me. They have these farms where you go and pick one out and cut it yourself. I was going to take a shot at it, but Pete said I'd be sawing and chopping for hours, so he did it for me. He got one for the carriage house too. I was going to decorate mine this evening. I assume the Christmas decorations are still in the attic. I even got enough evergreens to string a garland down the banister and over the mantel. Enough to make my own front-door wreath. Would you believe they want two dollars for a wreath and fifteen cents for a bundle of greens? What are you doing for Christmas, Ross?" God, why was she babbling like this?

"I haven't thought too much about it. It's more or less like any other day. Are you staying here?" he asked quietly.

"Yes. This will be my first *real* Christmas. I know that sounds rather silly, but it never seemed like Christmas in Florida. And growing up here . . . it was rip open the packages and get it over with. This year it's going to be different. This year I have the dogs. I'm going to make a turkey and plum pudding. I plan to make Christmas cookies and fruitcake. I even bought myself some presents I'm going to wrap so I have something to open on Christmas Eve. I like opening presents on Christmas Eve better than Christmas morning." God, she was babbling again. Why?

"It sounds kind of sad. What I mean is, your going to all that trouble when you'll be alone."

"But I'm not alone. I have the dogs. I think Pete is staying in town. He said something about going home for Christmas Eve and coming back after Midnight Mass. He may have changed his mind, though. He's got a pretty serious case he's preparing for court. He loves it at the prosecutor's office, but then I guess he already told you that."

"I haven't seen much of Woo lately. I did call and leave a message for him earlier this morning. Jory, this soup is the best I've ever eaten. Where did you get this bread?"

Jory laughed. "I made both of them, the soup and the bread, when I got back from the farm on Sunday. I figured I owed Pete a dinner for cutting down my tree and carrying it in here. Believe it or not, I'm a pretty good cook."

"The cocoa's good too. I guess you and Woo are hitting it off okay then," Ross said coolly.

"Yes. He's a very nice person, Ross, but then I guess you know that since you've been friends for years."

"They don't come any better than Woo." Then Ross blurted out, "What will you do after the divorce?"

"The same thing I'm doing now. It's not going to change my lifestyle at all. I suppose I'll feel sad for a while, but that's to be expected. What will you do? I heard you're seeing someone."

"Did Woo tell you that?"

"No, Pete did not tell me that. I was in town a few days after Thanksgiving and saw you walking down the street holding a very pretty girl's hand. I made my own assumptions. Will you remarry?" She busied herself with the dishes so she wouldn't have to see his face when he responded.

"Not right now. Someday. Then again, maybe not." He realized the words were true. And that meant he wouldn't be giving Lena a ring for Christmas. He felt like shouting in relief. "Our case is scheduled for eleven o'clock on Thursday."

"I'll be there, Ross."

"What's that wonderful smell coming from the kitchen?"

"Stew. I put it on early this morning so it could cook all day. I really have a schedule, even though I work at home."

"What exactly do you do?" Ross asked curiously.

"I write. I'm learning as I do it." He must not have looked at her materials or seen the sack of mail. "Listen, I wonder if you'd do me a favor, Ross," she said, trying to change the subject.

"Sure, what?"

"If I go to the attic for the tree stand, will you help me set up the tree? Pete trimmed the base before he put it in the bucket. God, doesn't it smell wonderful?"

While Jory was in the attic, Ross walked out to the kitchen to open the back door. Swirling snow smacked him in the face. There was no way he was going to make it back to town, chains or no chains. What he should do was call Woo and ask him if he would mind a roommate for the night. He wondered how Jory would feel about him staying on the premises. As long as he was under a different roof, he didn't think it would be an issue. He leaned halfway out the door, trying to see the accumulation of snow on the banister railing. Close to three inches, he surmised. With the wind blowing and gusting, the snow was already drifting. All about the backyard there were drifts that looked like desert dunes. He slammed the door shut to step back onto the small area rug by the door. His feet were freezing.

Ross looked around the kitchen. It was comfortable and cozy. Old-fashioned, like the Woojaleskys'. The green plant in the bright red bowl in the center of the table was pretty. So was the red-checkered place mat it sat on. A woman's touch. The red-and-white-checkered curtains at the double windows over the sink lent an air of coziness, as did the braided rug by the sink. Small pill bottles and tiny tubs of ointment filled the windowsill. He grinned when he saw scrawled names. Clancy, Murphy, Sam, and Bernie. The copper canisters gleamed beneath the fluorescent light attached to the bottom of the kitchen cabinets. A second plant in a bright red crock was curling upward and filled the corner perfectly. Next to it was a gleaming stainless steel percolator. He knew if he lifted the lid, he'd see coffee in the basket. He lifted the lid and smiled. The temptation to lift the lid on the stew pot was so great, he did it. He peered down at the gently simmering meal. The wooden spoon on the counter was a second temptation. He stirred and tasted, rolling his eyes at the delicious flavor. Every bit as good as Woo's mother's stew.

Jory Ryan was a homemaker. The thought stunned him. He wondered how many meals Woo had in this wonderful kitchen. *That* wasn't any of his business.

"Ross, is something wrong?" Jory called from the doorway.

"No. I wanted to see if the snow was drifting. It is, and it doesn't look good. Even with your offer of chains, I don't think I can make it back to town. I'll give Woo a call and ask him if I can camp out with him. The temperature seems to be dropping too. Listen, you wouldn't happen to have a pair of socks, would you?"

Jory held up a pair of her father's thick hunting socks. In her other hand she had a pair of heavy corduroy trousers. "I thought you might want to change. They should fit, my father was about your height. I brought down a sweater in case you want it. I left it on the couch. This house is pretty drafty. The handyman I hired back in September told me I needed new windows, but that will have to wait. There's a bathroom off the laundry room for you to change in."

"That's kind of foolish on your part, isn't it, Jory? If you need new windows, you should have gotten them. If your heat escapes, it ends up costing you money."

"I live on a strict budget, Ross. It does not allow for large expenditures like windows. Paying ten dollars more a month in heat is what I can afford right now," Jory said tightly.

"Jory, I'm sorry, I didn't mean to criticize. Thanks for the pants and socks. I'll accept the sweater too."

"I brought down the decorations and the tree stand. The dogs are still sleeping. How would you like to help me decorate the tree?"

He'd never decorated a tree before. The Woojaleskys' tree was always dressed in its finery when he arrived for the holidays. "I'd like that," he said honestly.

"You can stay for dinner if you like. There's more than enough."

"Thanks, Jory. I can clean up. I'm a whiz at doing dishes. I always do that part when I'm at Woo's house. I even wash off the stove," he said proudly.

"Good. I hate cleaning up. I hate doing dishes."

When Ross returned to the living room, Jory blinked in surprise. "I don't remember ever seeing my father in those pants or sweater. How did you like working for him? Did he ever say anything about me?" Jory asked curiously.

He wanted to lie and say yes, but he knew in his gut this woman standing in front of him would recognize the lie immediately. "Once, and I was the one who mentioned your name. He didn't really know who I was, just one of the many ADAs working under him. After I told him I was married to you, he came down on me like a bolt of thunder. He made my life miserable. I was going to resign, had my resignation all typed and ready to present to him the day he ... the day he died. I stayed on for another eighteen months and got out."

"Did you like him?"

"Jory, I didn't know him. I don't think many people really knew Jake Ryan. He was a legend in his own time, that much I can tell you. How about you, Jory? Did *you* like him?"

"I didn't know him either," Jory said sadly. "I think about him a lot, though. In his own way, he provided for me by leaving me this house and the car and a small bank account. If I'm frugal, I can live here quite nicely and not have too many worries. If new windows and a new roof are all I have to worry about, then I'm lucky. Don't look at me like that, Ross," Jory said, turning around to reach for the tree stand.

"How was I looking at you?" Ross said quietly.

"Like you pity me, like you feel sorry for me."

"Oh, no, Jory, I admire you. I'm sorry if that's what you thought." He wished she'd say she admired him too, but he knew there wasn't a whole hell of a lot to admire, and to top that off, she really didn't know him the way he was coming to know her. He wondered if it was possible to change that.

"What the hell are those things on your feet?" Ross said, bursting into laughter.

"My fuzzies. The dogs like to sleep in them. I got them at John's Bargain Store about a month ago. The dogs took to them right away. Would you like me to get you a pair?" She was giggling, unable to help herself.

"They look like they're still alive. I don't think I ever saw slippers like that."

"John's Bargain Store has tons of them. The floors are drafty. I'm ready if you are. I guess I should hold the tree and you fit it into the stand. Did you ever do this before?"

"As a matter of fact, no, but I don't think you need to be a rocket scientist to figure out the three screws go into the trunk. This is some hell of a big tree."

"The biggest one I could find," Jory said proudly. "Pete said I was nuts. He got this little, bitty thing you can sit on a table. One strand of tinsel, two balls, and one light will make that tree look overloaded, but it was what he wanted. I ribbed him all the way home."

"The Woojaleskys always have a big tree like this one. The kids make all the decorations. They string cranberries and popcorn, and when they take the tree down, they put it out for the birds. They have these real old decorations and things the kids made in school. They still have the one Woo made in kindergarten. Can you believe that?" Ross said, his face full of awe.

"Some parents are like that," Jory said wistfully. "I remember making something in the first grade with macaroni, and then we glued it to a wreath we cut from construction paper. We tied yarn on it. It was supposed to be a tree decoration. Did you ever make anything like that, or don't you remember?"

"Never. I'd damn well remember. Where is it?"

"Where's what?" Jory asked, puzzled.

Ross backed out from the beneath the tree. "You can let go now. The macaroni wreath, where is it?"

"I . . . I don't know. Christmas wasn't much of a deal around here. I guess it . . . I don't know, Ross," Jory said, flustered by his tone of voice.

"Your old man wouldn't throw something like that away, would he?"

"Listen, Ross, if you're trying to make me feel bad, you're succeeding. If you'd made a damn macaroni wreath, would your family have saved it?"

"Hell no they wouldn't have saved it. They'd have thrown it away while I was still looking, but then my parents are one of a kind. Your old man should have saved it. I bet it's in the box of decorations. Let's look."

"It's not important," she said quickly. "It was a stupid thing I made in the first grade. If you think it's in the box, you're crazy."

"If it's not in the box, then we're going to make new ones. You're going to make one and I'm going to make one. I'm putting my name on mine, and you're putting your name on yours. That's how you're supposed to do it. That's how the Woojaleskys do it," Ross said, wondering why he was making an issue of this.

Her eyes glistening with tears, Jory dropped to her knees to open the box of Christmas decorations. One by one she lifted the fragile ornaments from their cotton nests and handed them to Ross, who placed each one carefully and reverently in the same cotton batting on the floor. "I told you it wasn't here," Jory cried. "You made me do this knowing damn well it wasn't here. You haven't changed at all, you damn . . . you damn sadist." Tears funneled down her cheeks. She wiped at them with the sleeve of her sweatshirt. "You have no damn right to make me cry like this, Ross. You're a guest in my house, and don't ever forget it. Damn you!"

Tears continued to stream down Jory's cheeks as she followed Ross into the kitchen, and watched him open one cabinet after the other until he found a box of Muller's macaroni. He moved the table plant to the counter. The macaroni was placed in the center of the table.

"Where's your Elmer's glue and the scissors?" Jory pointed to a drawer under the counter. "Scissors, but no glue."

"I don't use glue," Jory sniffed. In a little-girl voice she hardly recognized as her own, she said, "You can make glue with flour and water. That's what we used when we made it in school."

"Yeah!" Ross said in stunned surprise.

"Yeah." Jory smiled tearfully.

"So, don't just sit here, whip us up a batch. I don't suppose you have any construction paper?"

"Not since first grade."

"Then we'll have to improvise. We need something of equal weight, and green in color. What do you have? This is important, Jory, what do you have?" Ross said seriously.

It was important suddenly, but to whom? "Why does it have to be green? Can't we color it green?"

"Do you have colors?"

"There's a box of colored pencils in my father's office. We can use the pencils and the backs of tablets," Jory said, getting into the spirit of things.

Overhead, the kitchen light flickered.

"This might be a good time to bring out the candles. Do you have candles, Jory? I think the power is going to go out. Do you have a flashlight?"

"There's a flashlight in the kitchen drawer, but the batteries are old," Jory said. "The Christmas candles are in the box with the tree lights and tinsel. I left the box at the bottom of the steps. Wait, there's a box of candles in the laundry room. They're big fat ones. I'll get them." She was back a moment later with a shoe box full of candles wrapped in cellophane.

"Listen, Ross, what exactly are we trying to do here? Are we going back to our childhood and trying to right old wrongs? Are we trying to make up for what we didn't have? What's the point? I'm not saying I don't want to do it, but . . . why, Ross?"

"Go get the pencils and the cardboard. We can talk as we work."

"Work? I seem to remember having fun when we made the wreath in school."

"We're going to have fun once we get organized," Ross said.

Later, as they worked at the kitchen table, Ross said, "In case you haven't figured any of this out, Jory, we're both fucked up." There was such sadness in his voice, Jory's eyes brimmed with tears all over again.

"I knew that the day I moved out of your house five years ago," she said. "How come it took you so long to figure it out?"

"Stupidity."

"Are you having fun?" Jory asked.

"Hell no. But that's going to change any minute now."

Jory giggled. "Says who?"

"Says me. Just as soon as the power goes off." Jory doubled over laughing. "See, I told you. You just have to lighten up. I do too," he said breezily.

"We need a cup and a glass," she said.

"Why?"

"To make the pattern. Unless you can draw a perfect circle. The cup makes the outer circle and glass makes the inner circle. It was a long time ago, but I remember."

"I guess that wreath was important to you after all," Ross said quietly.

"Yes, yes it was. I wish I knew what happened to it."

"It doesn't matter now. As long as you pull it out, look at it, talk about it, and put it all in perspective, it will be okay. We're doing that now," Ross said, his voice ringing with authority.

"I guess we are," Jory said, tracing a circle with the cup. When she was finished with it, she slid the cup across the table to him.

The lights went out at four-thirty. Ross lit the candles. Jory meticulously cut the macaroni into little pieces. "You have to do this so they look like holly berries. Three to a cluster. We have to color them red." Ross followed her instructions to the letter. Jory laughed. "Yours looks sloppy."

"You have a slight edge on me. You did this before. I didn't. Jory, do you want to talk about the divorce?"

"No."

"We should."

"It's too . . . it's best for both of us. We have to do what's best."

"Will we be friends?"

"That probably isn't a very good idea. If we meet on the street or somewhere, we should say hello, but that's it," Jory said carefully.

"I was jealous of Woo. I think I still am."

She felt pleased at his comment, but said, "That's silly."

"Are you jealous of Lena?"

"No," she lied.

"This thing we're doing here . . . making these wreaths—Lena helped me a few months ago. We had this talk once, and she was appalled that I had never done all the things most kids do growing up. We did them together, and I had a hell of a good time. I missed out on a lot. I suspect you did too. We grew up too fast, you on your own and me with too much money. I'd probably be in jail now if it wasn't for my mother and Woo. Early on, my mother bailed me out of jams. I have a pretty good grasp on things now, but not on my personal life. Lena wants to get engaged. I thought I did too. My mother seems to like the idea. That itself is reason enough to back off. I can't seem to get my personal life together," Ross said huskily.

"I think that's because we have unfinished business. Once the divorce is final, things will improve for you," Jory said solemnly.

"I wish I could believe that. If that's true, then why are you so much better off than I am? Emotionally speaking that is."

Jory put her pencil down and leaned across the table. "Ross, there is nothing more devastating to a woman than rejection. It's such a personal, degrading thing. It makes you look in the mirror to try and identify that thing, that . . . whatever it is that caused the rejection. It's not something you can see, you just feel it. Until you identify it, you can't do anything but wallow in self-pity. It seemed to me at the time I wasn't fit for anything. You didn't want me, I lost the baby, my father was too busy for me, my friends didn't want to have anything to do with me because I was pregnant. The only way running away helps is if you work at your problems and know that someday you'll return to the place you ran away from. In my opinion, that's when the healing process is complete. That's not to say there aren't still a few kinks to be worked out. Do you understand what I just said, Ross?"

"Every word. You did what I haven't been able to do. I'm sorry, Jory, I mean that."

"I am too, but we can't look back. We're doing what's right for both of us."

"Can I ask you a hypothetical question? If I call you for a date, say two weeks from now, will you go out with me? Is it possible for us to start over, clean?"

Jory thought her heart would leap out of her chest. "Didn't we just have this discussion? I don't know, Ross. Call me, and if I'm not busy, I'll consider it. I don't think we should be talking about this. Lord, listen to that wind. Do you think Pete will try to make it home tonight?"

"If he does, he's a fool. No, he'll stay in town. He'll probably go to my house. I think I'll give him a call."

Ross picked up the phone to hear silence. "The phone's dead."

Alarm spread across Jory's face. "You mean we're cut off from . . . from the world?"

"We're having a storm. For all I know, it could be a blizzard. You have food and wood and a roof over your head. You do have wood, don't you?"

"I have six logs on the back porch. Maybe we should bring them in. If they get wet, they won't burn. I did have a tarp on the wood-pile, but it wasn't anchored."

"Everything is going to be fine, Jory."

She believed him. "I'm glad you're here, Ross," she said shakily. "I hate the dark. When I was little I slept with the light on, and as I got older I kept the hall light on and left my door half open. I still do that." *My God, why was she telling him this?*

"This might surprise you, but I wasn't too keen on the dark myself. I had this blanket I kind of hung onto, you know, for comfort. It was something to . . . to sort of more or less hug," Ross said.

Jory's eyes widened. "I had a blanket too, but it finally wore out, so I ripped off the binding and put knots on it. I was a thumb sucker, and I would hold that string and feel the knots and that's how I was able to go to sleep. I found it when I came back. If someone had offered me a pot of gold for that string, I wouldn't have taken it. It's under my pillow." She didn't just say that, did she?

Disconcerted himself, Ross grappled for words that would take him out of the mine field of emotion he was feeling. "My wreath's finished," he said huskily.

"No it isn't," Jory said. "You have to put yarn on it so we can hang it on the tree, and you have to write on the back. You know, your name and all that. Wait here, I have some yarn in my knitting bag." She was off the chair like a whirlwind, to return a moment later with a ball of bright red yarn. She was flustered, her face flushed, her hands shaky when she snipped at the yarn. "You're supposed to use white ink. I found some in my father's drawer. We used toothpicks to write. I remember how hard it was. Guess my fingers were kind of fat or something." She sounded like a babbling idiot.

Ross accepted his toothpick. He pondered his wreath before he dipped the sliver of wood into the bottle of white ink. He wrote, *Christmas, 1953.* And then he wrote his name. "Jesus, I got it all on here." He looked so pleased, Jory smiled.

"I did too. You know, the dogs are still sleeping. It's cold out here, I think we should go back to the living room and build up the fire. We'll probably need two logs. That's your job, Mr. Landers," Jory said lightly.

"And one I'm capable of." Ross grinned. God, he was having such a good time. He prayed for the snow to continue. "What are you going to do about the dogs if they have to go out when they wake up?" he called from the back porch. "They'll get lost in the snow, it's deep."

"I'll do what I always do when I have to go into town. You aren't going to appreciate this, Ross," Jory said, taking a stack of papers from the pantry to lay on the floor. "I buy them for just this purpose." Ross howled when he looked down to see the blazing red letters rimmed in gold that spelled *TIF*. "In my opinion, this is the only thing it's good for," Jory called over her shoulder.

"It pays your rent, doesn't it?" He was still laughing when he added a log to the dying fire. "And I think you should know the roof is leaking. You're going to have to call someone in to fix it. My mother mentioned it early this morning."

"I'll put it on my list of things to do. Don't get me started on that Landers Building, Ross. I still haven't come to terms with Jasper's generosity."

The log caught fire as sparks shimmied upward. The snap-crackle of the pinecones Ross added woke the dogs. Ross watched their noses twitch as they sniffed the air. He himself felt drunk with the heady scent of the fir tree standing in the corner.

Jory lowered her voice and said in a stage whisper, "Watch this."

Ross sat back on his heels to watch the four dogs jockey for a straight line and then trot out to the kitchen, where they sniffed every inch of the floor before they squatted on the latest edition of *TIF*.

Jory giggled. "I think they go by the color."

"I'll be damned. My mother should see this. She'd probably say the paper is good for two things, to be read and then reused, or some damn thing like that."

"The magazine is a piece of crap, and you know it, Ross. I don't understand how you can associate yourself with it, even if it is your family's."

"Don't include my father in it. He signed it all over to my mother. He doesn't want any part of it. In fact, I don't like the magazine either. I'm not there on a forever basis. Temporary, at best, and then I'm going to try and get Woo to go into private practice with me. I'm simply trying to protect my mother. She doesn't always use good judgment. I have no trouble with your feelings in regard to *TIF*, none at all."

"That's good," Jory said stiffly. "I think it's a crime the way those exposé magazines attack people. Half the garbage they print is untrue." Abruptly, she changed the subject: "Are you ready to decorate the tree?"

Ross smacked his hands together. "This is the first tree I've decorated, so if you have any pointers, now's the time to mention them."

"Don't cluster the balls. Place them strategically. And the lights have to go on first. We should test them, but the electricity is out, so I guess we'll just string them and hope for the best. You start at the top and work your way down to the bottom. There's an extension cord here we'll plug into, and then it will go into the plug by the fireplace. See these little gizmos? You attach them to a branch. Do you think you can handle that?"

Ross snorted. "I'll have to stand on the hassock. I'm tall, but not that tall. Do you have an angel for the top?"

"The prettiest angel you ever saw. My father told me once that my mother made it when they first got married."

She talked nonstop as she watched Ross string the lights. How handsome he was, how perfect this scene was. How sad that it would end by morning, when Ross would leave, never to return. She couldn't allow him to return, she told herself. The divorce would make it all final, and to do anything else would be stepping backward. She'd come too far, worked too hard, to go backward at this point in her life. Today, this evening, was what it was, and nothing more. Tomorrow at this time it would be a memory. A Christmas memory.

"What's wrong, Jory?" Ross asked from his position behind the tree.

"Nothing, why do you ask?"

"You look so intense. Am I doing this wrong?"

Jory smiled. "No, of course not. I was just thinking about you, about us. Tomorrow this will be a memory. A Christmas memory. Memories are always sad, don't you think so?"

"Most of my memories are sad. My most pleasant memories are of college, law school, and visiting Woo's family. You're right, they're sad now because they're in the past. We can't ever regain them, but I guess we make new memories every day, some good, some bad. I believe they call it life."

Jory moved closer to the tree. "Do you know what first attracted me to you, Ross?"

Ross stopped what he was doing. "No, what?" he said hoarsely.

"You looked so vulnerable. You always appeared to be covering up something. You looked the way I felt. There you were, this tall, good-looking rich kid with the world at your feet, and there I was, this kid who only wanted to belong to someone. I thought you were the cat's whiskers. God, I would have crawled through fire for you. When you smiled at me, I was the happiest girl in the world. Why did you let it happen, Ross?"

Ross clipped the last light onto a branch and then plugged the end into the extension cord. "I thought you were easy, and I wasn't prepared for anything more than that. You were another notch in my belt. The sex wasn't anything special. A release and something to brag about. I'm sorry, Jory, but I can't lie to you. I'm sorry as hell that I was so shallow, that I used you the way I did. The plain damn truth is you were too good for me. I like to think today that somehow, some way, I knew it, and that's why I wouldn't let it matter. What about you?"

Something to brag about. Used. But then she'd known that. The only difference was, now Ross was putting it into words. Words she would rather not hear. "It meant something to me because I loved you as much as a seventeen-year-old could. I'd had . . . sex once, before the first time you and I did it, but I only did it so I would know what to expect. I wanted you to think I was experienced and not this dumb kid who didn't know her ass from her elbow. I'm the first to admit that was wrong, but I didn't know any better. I didn't have a mother who cared or anyone to give me advice." Her face was pink with embarrassment and shame. "I always wondered," she mumbled.

Ross walked over to Jory and put his arm around her shoulder. "I think, and this is just my legal mind here, that we both screwed up. I didn't know you and you didn't know me. It was my loss, Jory. I am just so very proud of you," he said huskily.

My loss. Later she would have to think about what *that* meant. "I'm kind of proud of me too. Now, let's get this tree decorated so we can eat. Remember, small balls on the top, bigger ones on the bottom, and the teardrops go in the front. You got that, Mr. Landers?"

"Got it, Miss Ryan."

It was seven-thirty when the last piece of tinsel was hung on the tree. Jory beamed her approval. Ross seemed to glow, she thought, or else it was the fire lighting his face like a thousand candles.

"We do good work, Miss Ryan," Ross said lightly.

"That we do, Mr. Landers. It is beautiful, isn't it? I don't think I've ever seen such a pretty tree. Wait till Pete sees it in all its finery. That little branch he bought is going to look pitiful compared to this. I hope he isn't upset. I more or less invited him to my tree trimming tonight."

"You like Woo, don't you?" Ross said quietly.

"It's impossible not to like Pete. Do you know anyone who doesn't like him?"

His answer was too quick. "My mother."

Jory snorted. "If I remember correctly, Ross, your mother doesn't like too many people. Besides your mother?"

Ross shook his head. "Woo is special, one of a kind."

"Yes he is. So, are you ready for dinner? I'm almost afraid to go into the kitchen. With the heat off, it must be freezing out there. I guess somebody has to go out there to get the dishes and the pot."

"If I knew where everything was, I'd do it, but I don't. I'll go with you though. I want to see what the temperature is on the thermometer on your back porch. Is it accurate?"

A moment later she called, "Well, what's the temperature?"

"Sixteen degrees."

"Lord, would you look at the snow!" Jory cried as she parted the kitchen curtains. "There must be eight or nine inches."

"It's drifting pretty bad. I hope you have a shovel."

"Several. They're in the basement. I don't want to think about that till tomorrow."

"Jory, when was the last time you *played* in the snow?"

"Years and years ago, and never during a storm. Why are you asking?"

"Want to go outside and have a snowball fight? We could jump in the drifts. Look at those drifts."

"Going outside in the snow . . . is that supposed to be therapeutic, like making the wreath?" Jory asked curiously. The blank look on Ross's face jolted her.

"I guess so. I take it you don't think it's a good idea."

"Heck no, I think it's a great idea. Let's do it!"

It wasn't until she was pulling on her boots that Jory realized she was doing the same thing she'd done five years ago. Anything for a smile, a pat on the head, a kind word. She took off her boots. "On second thought, Ross, it's not such a good idea. If you want to go out in the snow, I'll watch you from the window, but I'm not going out. Tomorrow I'll be shoveling all day. Besides, I'm hungry and I'm cold."

"But you said—"

Jory squared her shoulders. "I lied, Ross. Going out in the snow is the same as going backward. I don't expect you to understand, but I understand, and that's all that's necessary. So," she said, throwing her hands in the air, "do we eat or should I wait for you to play in the snow?"

Ross grimaced. This young woman with the defiant eyes standing in front of him definitely was not the Jory of old. He said so.

"Why thank you, Ross. You couldn't have paid me a nicer compliment if you tried. I take it we're going to eat."

"We're going to eat," Ross said quietly. "I'll light some more candles, and it might be a good idea if you bring down some blankets. We'll move the sofa closer to the fire."

"Let's do both. Does that mean you're staying here for the night and not at Pete's?"

"If you don't mind."

"No, I appreciate the company," Jory said honestly. "My life would be perfect if the dogs could talk. Some days I don't talk to anyone. Listening to yourself talk to four dogs can get a bit tiresome."

"But that's by your choice."

Jory met Ross's disconcerting gaze. "Yes, by my choice."

When they were finished eating, Ross burped enthusiastically and then apologized. "What about the dogs?"

"The dogs are eating the same thing. Mash it up fine and

scrunch up some little pieces of bread and soak it with gravy. By morning they'll all have the splats, but it can't be helped."

"What's that?"

"That's poop. By morning it will be all over. It happens every time I give them something strange to eat. I guess they have finicky stomachs."

"Oh shit," Ross muttered.

"Not to worry. I have a stack of magazines for just such an occasion," Jory said breezily. "Gee, I wish the tree lights were on. Tomorrow I'll wrap my presents and put them under the tree. It'll look even nicer with presents. I bought some stuff for the dogs. Squeak toys and rawhide bones. I'm going to wrap those too. They love to play with wads of paper. I wonder why that is?" she muttered.

They were sitting side by side on the sofa, wrapped in blankets, when Ross said, "Would you mind if I kissed you?"

"Yes. Yes I would mind." *Liar.* You don't ask a girl, if the moment is right, you kiss her.

"We could make love here in front of the fire. Sort of for old times' sake. You are so pretty, Jory, you take my breath away."

"That's a tired old line, Ross, and we don't have any old times either of us wants to remember."

"Are you telling me you don't feel anything right this moment?"

"As a matter of fact I do. One of the dogs is chewing the toe of my sock. It's not going to work, Ross, so forget it."

"You have to feel something. I feel something. The mood is right. This is the perfect setting. I'm very attracted to you, Jory."

"Really. Well, just unattach yourself. You're five years too late. We're going to be divorced in two days. . . . You're going to make this difficult, aren't you? I will not allow you to mess up my life again."

"But you feel the same attraction, admit it. Admit it and I won't say or do another thing. No lies, Jory."

"You're a handsome man, Ross. You're rich, you have an admirable profession. What that means is you're a wonderful catch for someone, but that someone isn't me. My life is going forward, not backward. So cut it out!"

"You didn't answer my question," Ross said lazily.

"What was the question?" Jory said sourly.

"The question was, are you attracted to me?"

"No. Now are you satisfied?"

"You're lying. You should never lie to yourself. I think I'm falling in love with you."

Jory closed her eyes to ward off her tears. She wanted to scratch his eyes out, to scream and yell and stamp her feet. Her voice, when she managed to speak, sounded hoarse. "You have no right to say things like that to me. If you leave now, you can probably make it back to town in time for the divorce hearing on Thursday. If you freeze to death along the way, I'll cry at your funeral. I'll make a beautiful young widow." Her voice was stronger now, angry and bitter-sounding.

"Jesus, you're heartless," Ross rasped.

"How does it feel, Ross?" she snapped.

"Is that what this is all about? You want to get back at me? Listen, damn it, I was telling you the truth. I do want to kiss you, I do want to make love to you. It wasn't a lie. I do feel like I'm falling in love with you. So what do you have to say to that?" Ross demanded.

"Plenty. There was a time when I would have bayed at the moon to hear what you just said. I was willing to cut this clean, it was you who sought me out. I did what you wanted. You never should have come here. I cannot give you what you think you want now." She was going to cry, could feel her throat tightening, feel the prick of tears on her eyelids. Damn him.

"I think I made a mistake. No, that's wrong. I know I made a mistake. I'd like us to try again. Let's forget the divorce, or at least put it on the back burner for now."

The blanket covering Jory sailed through the air, the pillow flew backward as she leaped to her feet to stand towering over Ross. The dogs growled their disapproval at such strange goings on. "You want to *try me out*, and if I don't measure up you'll bring the divorce to the front burner. Get the hell out of my house!" Jory raged. "Now, damn you! I don't care if you die in the snow. I don't care if you get pneumonia. I don't care if your body isn't found until *after* the divorce. Move!" she shrieked.

"Aren't you overreacting?" Ross said calmly. She wouldn't throw him out, would she?

"Out!" Jory cried dramatically. "And don't think you're staying in the carriage house. That's my property and I want you *off* my property. Get dressed before I take this poker to you," Jory said, grabbing the fire tongs and swinging them through the air. Out of the corner of her eye she could see the dogs scamper to the tree, where they squatted and peed in unison. "And you better be in that courtroom on Thursday, even if you're dying," Jory shrilled. She watched as one of the dogs pooped on a piece of cellophane. A second one missed the cellophane. The third one sat on a piece of tissue paper, while the fourth rolled a pinecone across the floor with his nose.

He was going. He was pulling on her father's boots and putting his arms through her father's shearling jacket. She watched as he buttoned it and pulled the hood over his head. Brandishing the fire tongs, she stalked to the door and pulled it open.

"I didn't mean that the way—"

"I don't give a damn what you meant. Don't tell me you didn't mean it, you lying worm. You haven't changed, Ross. Try me out! Like hell you'll try me out. I wasn't good enough for you the first time, and I'm not good enough for you now. Now leave!"

Ross felt dumbfounded. He would probably die in the damn snow. But he had the last word before the door slammed behind him. "Yes, Auntie Ann."

"You bastard! You living, breathing bastard," Jory shouted as she shot the dead bolt home.

"Don't worry, your secret's safe with me," Ross called from his side of the door.

Damn him, he was laughing at her. Laughing.

Jory waited fifteen minutes before she opened the door. Ross was sitting on the steps, huddled and shaking. "I've never been this cold in my life," he said, his teeth chattering.

"All right," she said, relenting. "Come in and sit by the fire. I'll get you some brandy. You owe me your life, Ross Landers," she grumbled. "But I don't want to hear another peep out of you for the rest of the night."

"Fine," he said as he settled in front of the fire. "But first let me say you need more logs. Your dogs pooped and the smell is making me sick. Aren't you going to clean it up?"

"You got them excited, you clean it up. You want more logs, you go out and get them. I'll get the brandy because I said I would. That's it, take it or leave it."

Jory watched him as he shuffled to the kitchen. He returned with two huge logs. He was shaking, his face pasty white. He was heading for the bathroom for the toilet tissue when she checked the thermometer on the back porch. Nine degrees. He'd been outside for fifteen minutes in nine-degree weather. Dressed warmly, she told herself. With aspirin from the pantry, she made her way into the living room. "Take these," she said, handing over the aspirin and brandy. "Lie in front of the fire. I'll put the screen up. You can move back after you get warm. You don't look well, Ross," she said coldly.

"I've been fighting off a cold for the past few days." His hand was shaking so badly when he brought the brandy snifter to his lips, Jory had to reach out and steady it. "I hope you feel like shit, Jory. What are you going to do if I die?"

"Bury you and collect your insurance. Go to sleep. You'll be fine by morning. I'll watch over you."

After a while he said, softly, "I really do think I'm falling in love with you, Jory."

"It won't work, Ross," she replied, just as softly. "We're two different people."

"Right, you're a girl and I'm a boy. That's the way it's supposed to be." An instant later he was sound asleep.

Jory sat on the sofa and cried. Too much, too little, too late.

The night was long and bitterly cold outside the perimeter of the sofa and fireplace. Wide-awake, Jory watched over the fire and her sleeping husband. She knew he had a high fever by the way he stirred restlessly in his sleep, his arms flailing the wood-scented air.

She got up three different times to draw the heavy blankets up to his chin. His forehead felt hot and dry. She worried.

Propped up in the corner of the sofa in her cocoon, Jory stared down at her husband. How boyish he looked, how vulnerable. She loved the way his unruly, dark hair curled around his head. It wasn't fair, she thought sadly, that a man should have such beautiful curly hair and sinfully long eyelashes. Curly hair and feathery lashes were meant for girls. Ross never seemed to realize how handsome he was, that much she did remember. When she first met him, she'd gushed and practically swooned at his good looks. She'd been dumb enough to say so, and he'd been embarrassed.

Jory's gaze moved to the fire. She groaned. She had to go out to the porch for another log, maybe two. The fire was low and would be nothing but smoldering embers in another thirty minutes. It was only three o'clock. She thought about throwing the dining room chairs into the fireplace, but negated the idea. If she burned the chairs, she wouldn't be able to have her Christmas dinner in the dining room.

The logs were heavy, necessitating two trips. She was blue with cold when she returned to the living room. She couldn't ever remember the temperature being minus two degrees. Would the pipes freeze and rupture? How did one unfreeze frozen pipes? She had no idea. A log caught fire, sending a shower of sparks up the chimney.

Jory eyed the aspirin bottle on the mantel. Should she wake Ross and give him some, or was sleep the best thing? She didn't know that either. She went back to her cocoon and snuggled deeper into the corner of the sofa, where she dozed fitfully.

At six o'clock Jory bolted from the warmth of the blankets when a sharp knock sounded on the front door. Pete must have made it home. She raced to the door to see a young man clad in a heavy lumberman's jacket, fur cap, and thick woolen gloves. "Yes?"

"Ma'am, would you like your driveway plowed? It's ten dollars, fifteen if you want me to go all the way to the carriage house."

"Uh, yes, of course. There's a car in the driveway, though. I'll pay you extra if you shovel it out and put chains on it. They're in a box inside the garage."

"Twenty, and you have a deal," the young man countered.

"How bad are the roads?" Jory asked fearfully.

"I never seen a storm this bad. The city plows are out. The plow is over on Evergreen Avenue. It should be on Gravers Lane soon enough. Don't go out unless you have to, that's my advice."

At seven-thirty all Jory could see from the kitchen window were mountains of snow. The young man had done a good job with Ross's car. It looked ready to go, and Ross had slept through the whole thing. The indoor thermometer said it was twenty-three degrees in the kitchen.

Shivering and shaking, Jory poured the water from the teakettle into the sauce pan and added coffee grounds. Boiled cookie was better than nothing. Breakfast would be the leftover stew. She stuck a loaf of Strohman's bread under her arm. It felt cold and hard.

Ross stirred and woke when she set the blackened cookie sheet on the log, along with the stew pot and sauce pan. "How do you feel?" she asked. She stood up to reach for the aspirin bottle.

"Like hell. Did I sleep through the night?" he asked in a deep, hoarse voice.

"You were restless, but you slept." She handed him three aspirin. "Breakfast will be ready soon. Do you think you can eat?"

He nodded. "Did the power come on?" He answered his own question when he looked at the pot on the cookie sheet. "How much snow did we get?"

"Well over a foot, and it's still snowing, but tapering off."

"Jesus, how the hell am I going to get out of here?" Ross asked, falling back onto the heavy blankets.

"I shoveled you out," Jory lied with a straight face. "The chains are on your car. I think I hear the plow now. If you're up to it, you can leave, providing you drive carefully. I expect you to return my chains."

"You did *what?*"

"You heard me. Take a look."

Ross tottered to the window in his stocking feet. "You couldn't possibly do all that," he croaked.

"Do you think some fairy came and did it while we slept? I spent the night out there shoveling so you can be on your way." Jory bent down to check on the boiling coffee so Ross wouldn't see the smile on her face.

"You really must hate me," Ross muttered.

"No, I don't hate you. You don't belong here, Ross. It's that simple."

"I could if you'd let me. Did Woo make it home?"

"Let's not go through that again. Pete didn't get home. The phones are still out, and God only knows when the power will come back on. There's probably power in town. If you stay here, you could get sicker. The best place for you is home in your own bed, and you should stop at the doctor's on your way home. Aspirin doesn't seem to be bringing down your fever. You need to drink a lot of fluids too. Unfortunately, I have no juice, and we used all the milk yesterday for cocoa."

"What about you? Maybe you should come back with me."

Jory snorted. "Look at me, Ross, do I look like I need you to take care of me? I'll be fine. I have plenty of food, and there's a lot of dry wood in the garage. I'll bring it in later. I come from hearty Irish peasant stock. All that shoveling should prove something. Eat!" she commanded.

"I see that. Do me a favor, Jory."

"If I can."

"Don't get so self-sufficient you turn out like my mother. You don't do much for a guy's ego, I can tell you that." He pushed his plate away. The dogs pounced on it immediately.

"That will never happen. Do you think your car will start?"

"All right, Jory, I'm going. Jesus, you'd think I was going to attack you or something. I'm sick, in case you hadn't noticed."

"I noticed. I seem to remember a time when I thought I was dying and I couldn't see your dust. I lost a baby. I didn't see you for five days. Your little head cold is your problem. The way I see it, I did a lot more for you than you ever did for me. I hope your car heater is working."

"You're never going to forgive me, are you?"

"I already forgave you. I just can't forget it. There's a difference. At the risk of repeating myself, you came here, you sought me out. You asked and I granted. Beyond that, Ross, I owe you nothing.

Nada. I'll get you a lap robe and another sweater. And to show you what a good sport I am, I'm going to start up your car. I want to know in my heart that when you leave here, you're leaving as well as can be expected under the circumstances."

At that precise moment the power came on. The tree lights sparkled. Jory clapped her hands. The dogs barked and then growled. Ross said, "Jesus, it's magnificent."

"You did a wonderful job stringing the lights. It looks perfect." A moment later the lights overhead flickered once, then once again, before the power went off completely.

"I bet that's some kind of omen," Ross said, getting to his feet. Jory wondered if he was right. "I'm sorry about the stew, but it hurts to swallow."

Jory had her boots on and was buttoning her jacket when Ross reached for her. "I'm sorry about everything. I came here and invaded your privacy. That wasn't my intention. You've been very kind to me, kinder than I deserve. I'm not going to bother you anymore. I just want you to know that I enjoyed last evening. Up until the part where you kicked me out. You misunderstood, but that's okay. In your place I probably would have done the same thing. I know you watched over me during the night. I felt you when you touched my head and brushed back my hair. I knew when you covered me. That's how I know you didn't shovel the goddamn snow! If there was ever a time to kiss someone, this is it, but because I'm a nice person I won't do it. I don't want you to get sick." He brought her close to him, so close he could smell the scent of her hair. It felt soft, the way his silk pajamas felt when he crunched them up in a ball. He felt like bawling. He pushed her away to head for the bathroom.

Jory did cry then, wet weepy tears of unhappiness. In a voice the dogs had never heard before, she ordered them to sit before she stormed outside, Ross's keys in her hand.

The frigid air smacked her in the face. She brought her mittened hand to her mouth as the cold attacked her layers of clothing. Attacked and won. She shivered violently as she crunched her way to Ross's car. Surprisingly, the door opened, and what was more surprising, the engine turned over on the third try. She waited a full five minutes with her foot on the gas pedal to make sure the car wouldn't stall. She turned the heater high. It would take at least twenty minutes for the car to warm up.

On legs that were so stiff they felt brittle, Jory started back to the house. In her life she'd never been this cold, this numb. It was still snowing lightly. Her world was winter-white and blindingly beautiful. She tried to walk faster in the crunching snow. She slipped twice. Nature's artwork would be more appreciated from a window.

Jory hunkered down by the fire. "Have some coffee, Ross. It's going to take a while for the car to warm up. It started on the third try. I know there's probably a window scraper somewhere in the garage, but it's too cold to look. I think the heater will melt the ice on the windshield. You'll have to use the side mirror instead of the rearview one. The ice is thick on the back window. Maybe you shouldn't go, Ross. It's bitter out there."

"I think you're right about this cold. I should see a doctor because my chest feels congested." The worry and concern on her face pleased him. He sipped at the coffee.

"Your cheeks are rosy," he blurted out. "You're very beautiful, Jory." He sipped again at the coffee.

"Thank you," Jory mumbled over the rim of her coffee cup. Why couldn't he have said that five years ago? Maybe she wasn't beautiful five years ago. She wasn't sure she was beautiful now either. "How will I know if you made it home safely? I'm going to worry. Damn this storm."

"I'll be okay. I filled the gas tank yesterday. I'll be on a main road. Relax, Jory, and enjoy that lovely Christmas tree."

"It is beautiful, isn't it? We did a super job decorating it. Thanks for helping. I think your wreath is better than mine."

Ross's chest puffed out. "For a first-time effort it's okay. You won't throw it away, will you?" he asked anxiously.

"Of course not. I'm the sentimental type. Every year I'll pull it out and think about last night. Together we have at least one nice memory." Damn, she was going to cry if she didn't get hold of herself. "If you get too warm in the car with the heater, open your coat, but don't take it off. Crack the window just a smidge. Drive in low gear," Jory said quietly.

Ross tied a thick woolen muffler around his neck. "Yes, Auntie Ann."

"Ross, that has to be *our* secret. Please promise you won't tell anyone. I really need this job, and if anyone finds out who I am, they won't take me seriously. You spied on me. That isn't nice."

"Jory, your secret's safe with me. Don't give it another thought. I'm hurt you would think I'd give it away. It's no one's business but yours. Well, I'm ready."

"Drive carefully, Ross, and make sure you go to the doctor."

"Yes, ma'am." He was stunned when Jory wrapped her arms around him. " 'Bye, Ross, and Merry Christmas."

He didn't know how to respond, so he just nodded. He knew she was watching him from the window, the dogs at her feet. He ached to be back inside, to belong, to be a part of Jory's new life. He must really be getting sick, he thought, because his eyes were burning and tearing like hell.

Jory watched the Buick's progress until the car was out of sight. She wiped at her eyes with the sleeve of her sweater. Too much, too little, too late.

Chapter 10

Woo paced the length of Ross Landers's huge living room. His hair was on end, his tie jerked loose from his big neck, his shirtsleeves rolled to the elbow. Every five minutes he parted the brocade draperies to stare outside, hoping for some sign of Ross. Where in the hell was he?

He wasn't a worrier, never had been. He took each day as it came and hoped for the best. Often he wondered if he was a fatalist. What it came down to, he thought, was you did your best, and if that wasn't good enough, then it was the other guy's problem. For most of his life his philosophy had worked fine. Until now. Now he was worried right down to the core of his gut.

He'd been up all night watching the storm from the wraparound windows in the sun room and answering Ross's phone. Four calls from Justine Landers, the last just short of hysterical. "Tell Ross to call me the minute he gets home, regardless of the time." He'd written down the message verbatim. Jasper Landers had called three times, but only said Ross was to call him. Nothing earth-shattering there. Lena had called twice and said the last time she'd seen Ross was before lunch and that he'd canceled their date, saying he was having dinner with his father. Jasper in turn said Ross never showed up and hadn't called. Ross hadn't gone to the warehouse and never returned to the office, according to Justine, who could only say his briefcase was gone and his car was not in the parking lot.

Woo fired up a cigarette he didn't want. He was on his tenth cup of coffee. Even his teeth were standing at attention.

Ross had to be at Jory's. It wasn't like him not to leave a message or a note saying where he could be reached. So he must have gone to Chestnut Hill with the intention of returning, and got caught in the storm and stayed over. He thought about the bald tires on the Buick. He thought about Ross and Jory alone in the house with the dogs. A wicked smile stretched across his face when he thought about the four-legged creatures that were Jory's roommates. They were fun, they made him laugh. But the thought of Ross frolicking with them on the floor wiped the smile from his face. It bothered him that Ross might be there at all. Maybe he had slept in the carriage house. Woo immediately negated the idea. Ross wasn't exactly a whiz when it came to making fires, unless it was a gas fire. Lack of central heat would definitely be a problem for his friend, one Jory would rectify by allowing him to stay in the house if the roads were impassable.

He'd tried to call all night long, but was told by the operator the telephone lines were down and she didn't know when they'd be back in service.

Woo had looked forward to last night for days. He and Jory were going to trim the huge Frazier fir and have dinner together. When she issued the invitation, he thought he was the luckiest stiff alive. They were good friends these days, and he still wasn't sure how it all came about. Secretly he thought it was because the dogs liked him. He'd kept his word and hadn't infringed on her privacy, and when they did talk, he never spoke of Ross. Maybe it was the pumpkin he brought back from Lancaster, which they'd cut out together and put on the stoop by the red door. Maybe it was a lot of things. Maybe she just liked him because he was a good person, a nice person. Maybe.

Tomorrow was *the day*. The day Jory's marriage would be dissolved. He was going to ask her for a real date then, movies and dinner at Dominic's. Maybe she'd accept and maybe she wouldn't. His life seemed to be made up of maybes these days.

Jory and Ross together in her house with the dogs. A blazing fire, some wine, dinner in front of the fire. If he'd been able to get back to the Chestnut Hill house, Woo thought, *he* would have been the one in front of the fire. He might even have kissed her, but he doubted that. He wouldn't do anything, say anything, until her divorce was final.

Woo sat down with a thump. He should be using this time to go over the final details of the case he was working on. He was going to win this one; he could feel it. He'd prepared an airtight case, and even gone over it with Ross several times. It involved two chop shops where cars were dismantled and reassembled and then shipped out of the country. He'd make headlines with this case, but that wasn't important to him; nailing the guys and presenting a good case was important. It had been dumped on him at the eleventh hour, when the ADA originally assigned the case went on leave with a case of bleeding ulcers. With a caseload heavy enough to break his back, Woo had taken on the extra work, staying all night at the office at least two nights a week. He was never going to be able to thank Jory enough for putting in a good word with her father's colleagues in the D.A.'s office.

Woo was at the window again, straining to see through the lightly falling snow. It was a hell of a storm, one that shut down just about every business in the city. It was rare for the courthouse to shut down entirely, but it had happened today. By tomorrow, with the road crews working around the clock, the city would start to get back to normal. Woo heard the clank of tire chains at the same moment he saw Ross's car pull into the driveway. The sense of relief he felt was so total he almost collapsed. He was at the door, holding it open, when Ross climbed the steps, his gloved hand on the iron railing for support.

"I was hoping you had enough sense to come here," Ross croaked. "I need a stiff slug of something and half a bottle of aspirin. Would you mind getting it for me, Woo?"

"No, of course not. Jesus, you look sick. Do you want me to call a doctor?"

"This is just a cold. I'll shower and change and camp out by the fire. On second thought, bring the bottle and a gallon of orange juice. Tell the cook to make me some chicken soup. Do you mind, Woo?"

"I'll take care of it," Woo said, relief surging through him. Ross hadn't just gotten sick, he must have been sick yesterday too. Ergo, nothing happened in Jory's house. He hated himself for the relief he was feeling.

While Ross showered, the housekeeper made the sofa into a bed with down comforter and two down pillows. A pot of tea, a bottle of brandy, and a huge glass of orange juice were on the coffee table. Woo set the bottle of aspirin next to the orange juice. The television set was on, the sound low. The fire burned brightly and the room was warm, but not stifling hot.

Ross settled himself between the covers, his teeth chattering. "Thanks, Woo."

"The housekeeper did it. I just carried in the aspirin bottle. How many do you want? Your chicken soup is being prepared as we speak."

"Four," Ross rasped.

"You should have a doctor look at you, Ross. Remember the last time you got sick like this?"

"As if I could forget it. If I'm not better by tomorrow, I'll call the doctor. Don't forget I have to be in court for the divorce."

"You could postpone it. What's another week?"

"It has to come off, Jory has herself all prepared. She more or less threatened me if I screwed it up. She's something else, Woo. She kicked me out and made me sit on the steps for fifteen minutes. She didn't know, at least I don't think she knew, that I was sitting on the steps. She thought I left. She really kicked me out. She would have let me walk all the way back to town. Do you believe that?"

"I sure do. That young woman rarely does or says anything she doesn't mean. What the hell did you do to make her kick you out?"

"I didn't *do* anything. I asked her if she wanted to try out the marriage again. That's it. This is what I got for my efforts."

"Try out! Are those the words you used?" Woo said quietly. "If I was Jory, I'd have kicked your ass out too."

"Jesus Christ! What the hell was wrong with saying that? The judge is going to ask both of us if we discussed trying the marriage again. I had to ask. She said no, so that's the end of it." He sneezed three times in rapid succession and then blew his nose. He leaned back, exhausted. "She wants nothing to do with me."

Woo felt a second surge of relief course through him at his friend's words. "Why'd you go there, Ross?"

"To tell her about the new court date. I thought it would be better to tell her in person than over the phone. Besides, I wanted to see her. What's so terrible about that?"

"Nothing, I guess," Woo mumbled.

"The phone and power went out early in the afternoon. The damn house was freezing."

"And you left her there with no heat, power, or water, with four dogs?" Outrage filled Woo's voice.

"In case you haven't been listening to me, Woo, I didn't have a whole lot of choices. She kicked me out. That girl is a survivor. You don't have to worry about her or those dogs. She can melt the snow for water, even I know that. She's got plenty of firewood and enough food for weeks," Ross wheezed.

Woo's disposition turned positive at Ross's words. He turned so Ross wouldn't see the smile building on his face. "I'll make a mustard plaster for you. My mother always used to do that when we got chest colds. I'll have the cook help me. By tonight you'll either be better or dead," Woo said cheerfully.

"Jory said she didn't care if I died, said she'd make a beautiful young widow and she'd spend all my insurance money. She goddamn meant it too. I think that was before she kicked me out. She's heartless. Look at me, I could die. Did she care? Hell no!"

"Take the aspirin, Ross, and I'll make the plaster."

The smile on Woo's face stayed with him for the twenty minutes it took him to make the plaster. Ross bolted upright when Woo slapped it on his chest, then wrapped a towel around him before he shoved him down between the covers.

"You have to work quick," Woo replied.

"Jesus, Woo, what is this? It burns like hell. I can't breathe," Ross gasped, his forehead beaded with perspiration.

"A little of this, a little of that, a lot of mustard and a lot of gar-lic. It's working already—your eyes are tearing and your nose is dripping. Old Polish remedies always work." Most of the time, he said under his breath. "Listen, I have an idea. How about I read to you? The latest issue of *TIF*." Woo grinned. "Maybe it will put you to sleep."

"Get the hell out of here, Woo, and let me die in peace."

"By the way, I've been meaning to tell you I won't be spending the holidays in Lancaster. But I am going up Christmas Eve, and coming back after Midnight Mass. You want to come?"

"Of course I'm coming. The presents are all wrapped and every-thing. I thought you weren't going to ask me this year."

"I wasn't," Woo said honestly. "I changed my mind. There's nothing in the rule book of friendship that says we can't have sharp words now and then. I expect us to be friends for the rest of our lives. I kind of lost sight of that for a little while. I'm glad you had the good sense to make it right, Ross."

"Me too," Ross said hoarsely.

"By the way, your mother called, your father called, and so did Lena. Everyone was worried about you. I said I didn't know where you were. Your mother wants you to call her no matter what time of day it is. Your father sounded terribly worried, said you had a dinner engagement. Lena merely said to tell you she called. Do you want me to call them for you?"

"Yeah, call my father and explain what happened. If my mother or Lena call again, tell them I'm sleeping, and don't let my mother intimidate you."

"Done," Woo said, heading for the library. "Sleep, Ross, it's the best thing for you right now. I'll put the phone in the hallway if you don't want to use it."

"Rip it out of the wall for all I care," Ross mumbled. His eyes closed wearily.

The first call Woo made was to Clyde Barrister, Ross's doctor. He explained the situation and said, "I can make it to the drugstore if you call the prescription in." The doctor said he would, with the understanding Ross would be in the following day for a thorough going-over, as he put it. Woo said he'd personally see that Ross got there by mid-afternoon. The second call was to Jasper Landers. The sigh of relief in the older man's voice tugged at Woo's heart. "He'll be fine, Mr. Landers. I'm going out to get some medication for him. I'll call you later in the day to let you know how he is. Of course I'll stay the night. Please, Mr. Landers, don't worry about Ross." The third call was to Jory. The phones were still out of order. Jory would be just fine, he was sure of it.

Woo checked on Ross before he dressed to head out for the drugstore. What should have been a ten minute walk each way took an hour. When Woo let himself back in the house, his eyebrows shot up as the cook motioned for him to be quiet. "Mr. Ross's mother is in the living room." That much he could have figured out himself. No one in the world had a voice like Justine Landers. She was doing all the talking. Woo wondered if Ross was pretending to be asleep. He walked through the dining room and brazenly listened behind the door. He grimaced when he heard Justine say, "I told that Polish person to have you call me. Why didn't you, Ross?"

"Mother, I'm sick. I'm running a fever. Whatever it is can't be so important it can't wait a day or two."

"This cannot wait, Ross. I set up the visit for tomorrow. You don't look sick to me, but you smell terrible. Don't playact with me."

"Mother, you wouldn't know if I was sick if I dropped dead at your feet. Go home, I'm not in the mood for this. I'll be lucky if I make the divorce tomorrow, and after that if I'm feeling better, I'm going to the doctor. Reschedule whatever it is."

"You're not listening to me. I can't reschedule. I've gone to a great deal of trouble to set up this meeting. It cannot be postponed."

"Yes it can, Mother." He rolled over to bury his face in the pillow. Justine jerked him around.

"I had . . . people arrange this meeting so you could meet your grandparents and your aunts, uncles, and cousins. It's supposed to be a surprise. Your presence is required. This is not a request, Ross, it's an order," Justine said firmly.

"Grandma and Grandpa are dead," he replied, staring up at her wearily. "I have a trust fund to prove it. What *are* you talking about?"

"I'm talking about *my* side of the family," Justine said coldly.

"What side? You said you had no family. You told me you were an orphan. Are you telling me now you lied?" Ross struggled to sit up on the sofa. "Why in the name of God would you do such a thing?" he demanded, a sick look on his face.

Behind the dining room door Woo took a deep breath.

"You make it sound like I killed someone. I need you to go with me to meet them. I said you would come with me. The people who arranged the meeting are expecting us. Please, Ross," Justine said desperately.

"No, Mother, I won't. I don't have the nerve to face a set of grandparents I never knew I had. What do you want from them? What is it you think they can do for you? Were you ashamed of them? Ah, that's it, isn't it? Now, suddenly, you want to resurrect this family and . . . do what? No, no thank you, Mother."

"I will not allow you to shame me, Ross."

"Shame!" Ross tried to bellow. His voice sounded like a frog in its death throes. He tried to clear his throat but was unsuccessful. Perspiration beaded on his face. He wiped at it with the sleeve of his flannel robe. "Put your best face on it, Mother, and pull up your socks. That's what you used to tell me. Wait, wait, you used to say, 'Only sniveling cowards cry.' I believed you when you said that because you were my mother. I wish now I'd never listened to you. You never once gave me good advice. Maybe if I'd cried a little more I'd be a better person today." Exhausted, Ross fell back against the pillows.

Woo pushed the door open. Justine backed up a step. "Is anything wrong?" Woo rumbled, his voice nearly carrying through the house.

"My mother was just leaving, Woo. Escort her to the door."

"It will be my pleasure," Woo rumbled again. One huge hand reached out to grasp Justine's arm. If he'd wanted to, he could have lifted her off her feet. Instead, the pressure on her arm forced her forward.

Justine tried to jerk free of Woo's tight grasp. "Either you meet me at noon or you no longer work for me," she said to her son. "Do you hear me, Ross, you're fired! Fired!"

Ross swung his legs over the side of the sofa. "Woo, break out the champagne! I'm a free man!"

For a man of his size and bulk, Woo moved with the grace of a cat. Justine was in the hall, then the foyer, and then out the door in a blink of an eye. The moment the door closed, he shot the dead bolt home. "Good riddance to bad rubbish," he muttered, using his mother's favorite phrase. Jesus, how was he supposed to handle *this*? Very, very carefully, he answered himself.

"You weren't serious about that champagne, were you, Ross?" Woo asked quietly when he returned to the living room.

Ross shook his head. "Did you hear it all?" he rasped.

"Yes, I was behind the dining room door." He held out the prescription bottles. "I thought we could get a head start on your visit tomorrow. You can take them with tea."

"You went out in this weather to get . . . thanks, Woo," Ross said. He gulped at the tea and swallowed the pills at the same time. Then he asked, "Are there any openings in the D.A.'s office?" a sickly grin on his face.

"I can check it out first thing tomorrow morning," Woo said lightly. "I don't think she meant it."

"She meant it. Look, I tried. Would you have reacted any differently? I have grandparents I never met, aunts, uncles, and cousins. You know how I feel about family. How could she not tell me? Now she wants me to . . . Shit!" he said succinctly.

Woo motioned for Ross to lie back. He'd only seen such misery, such fright, once before in his life. He'd been ten then and had gone along with his friends to check their hunting traps. His friends had crowed with delight at the sight of the small brown rabbit they snared. All he'd seen was the fear and misery in the animal's eyes. Because he was a head taller, and twenty-five pounds heavier, he'd squared off with his friends and let the rabbit go. Then he smashed the trap. He lost a lot of friends the year he was ten. His father said he was proud of him. His mother hugged him.

To this day he wondered what the rabbit thought. Relief probably. He wondered what Ross was thinking. He gave voice to the thought.

"Betrayed is too kind a word," Ross croaked. "That . . . that came out of nowhere. In a million years that was the last thing I expected."

"Listen, Ross, my mother always says God never gives you more than you can handle. Right now, this probably seems like the heaviest hand life's dealt you, but think about this—if your mother hadn't finally opened up, you'd never know about that side of your family. You know now. When the time is right, you can search them out and make things right. What's bothering me is your father. Why didn't he say something? Or do you suppose he didn't know?"

Ross shook his head. "I'm sure he knew. My mother is not someone you go up against. My father took the easy way out of most things. At least that's how I perceived it. He doesn't like to deal with problems. He had enough money to pay people to take care of things. He simply went on with his life and my mother went on with hers. That doesn't make it right, but I was forced to accept it."

Woo shook his head. "You *say* you accepted it, but you didn't. Not really. Hell, you turned out okay, and that's saying a whole hell of a lot for a kid who basically raised himself. So you screwed up with Jory and you made a bad call where Lena is concerned. Life goes on. Now don't take it wrong when I tell you I think Jory and Lena were important in your life. They both helped you get to this place in time. Now you have a chance to start a new life. You yourself said your father is coming around, that the two of you are on better terms and you truly like him. Your mother has given you a family you didn't know you had. The fact she fired you is probably the best thing that ever happened to you. Tomorrow you'll be a free man, like you said. I'm assuming you'll have a talk with Lena before too long and do whatever it is you have to do. The way I look at it, old buddy, is you got yourself life's tiger by the tail. You can let that tiger go to sleep or you can wake him up. Your call, Ross."

"Hmmm," Ross said groggily.

"I've just given you better advice than a psychiatrist would, and you fall asleep on me," Woo grumbled.

"I heard every word," Ross murmured.

Woo grinned. Famous last words. He poured the rest of the tea into his cup, added a squirt of brandy. He propped his feet on the coffee table and hunkered down.

During the night, Woo woke Ross three times, twice for the medication and once to change the mustard plaster.

At four o'clock Woo went into the kitchen for a drink of water. He blinked in surprise when he saw light snow falling outside the window. Would they close the courthouse again or would the municipal building open up for business?

Because he had nothing else to do, Woo reached for the phone to dial his own number at the carriage house. The phone was still out. Would Jory attempt to drive into town? Knowing her, she'd probably walk.

Woo made a pot of coffee and some toast, eating and drinking at the kitchen table. At five-fifteen he cleaned up his mess and headed for the shower. He was downstairs fully dressed for the day at six o'clock. He called the main number for the courthouse and was told court would be in session. At seven o'clock he called three different car services to see if they'd make the trip to Chestnut Hill to pick up Jory, and was told by all three companies there were no cars available.

Ross woke at seven-thirty. "Court's in session, I called," Woo said briskly. "It's snowing. I called three car services to ask if they'd pick Jory up, but they're all booked. The phones are still out. I guess it's a crap shoot. How do you feel?"

"Better," Ross lied. Christ, he felt like an elephant had his foot on his chest. "A hot shower and some breakfast will do wonders for me. Are you walking?"

"At least I'll get there. I picked up a pair of boots, and don't think that was easy. Very few people stock size fourteen. I'll be fine. I'd head for the doctor if I were you, Ross. You probably need a double shot of penicillin or something. Is it okay if I come back here for another night?"

"Hell yes. This place is yours, you know that. You don't have to ask."

Woo grinned. "My mother taught me to be polite. It's time for your pills. Make sure you wear boots. Dress warm. A muffler and some kind of cap. If you get another chill, you're headed for some serious sick time. I'm glad you're lying to me and saying you feel better. That's the Ross I know. You look like shit, so act accordingly."

"Yes, Woo. Whatever you say, Woo. Don't I always do what you say, Woo? Get going or you'll be late," Ross wheezed from his position halfway up the stairs.

"Ross?"

"Yeah, Woo?"

"Good luck."

"Thanks. See you tonight. Guess we'll have chicken soup, since I didn't get to eat it last night. Be careful walking or you'll break your neck."

"Likewise."

Damn, his eyes were burning again. In three and a half hours, Ross thought, he was going to be a bachelor. Which was worse, thinking about bachelorhood or thinking about how shitty he felt? A fucking tie as far as he was concerned. In the bathroom, he turned on the faucets and waited for the room to steam up before he shed his clothes. It was still snowing, he noticed, when he parted the curtains. Surely Jory wouldn't chance driving into town. Or would she? "Yeah," he answered himself, "she would."

It took Ross the better part of an hour to shower, shave, and dress himself. He didn't think it was possible to feel worse, but he did. Downstairs, he drank three cups of hot tea, doubled his medication, and added three aspirin to the pile of pills in his hand. He tried Jory's number and was told the line was still out of order. There was no way he could drive out to Chestnut Hill, drive back, and make court at eleven. No way at all, Jory was on her own.

It was snowing lightly when Jory backed the Rambler station wagon out of the garage. The car was toasty warm, the new tires crunching on the hard-packed snow. She didn't like the new falling snow because it was fine, almost like rain. The weatherman had predicted light snow later in the day when she turned the radio on at six o'clock. Damn. Thinking ahead, she'd strategically placed bowls of water and moist dog food bowls throughout the house in case she was late getting back. She'd also laid down thick wads of paper by the doors and at the foot of the stairs. Two hours to get into the city, thirty minutes in court, and two hours to get back. If Ross gave her the chains, she might get back sooner. She'd invite Pete for dinner, a big pot roast with potatoes and carrots and lots of gravy. Pete would like that. She'd set up a little table by the fire and they could look at the Christmas tree while they ate. They'd have a pleasant evening talking about his big family, and the big case he was prosecuting after the New Year. She'd talk about Florida. They'd play with the dogs, and Pete would go home, and she'd go to bed.

She cautioned herself to stay alert, to keep her eyes on the road ahead of her. She'd only driven in the snow twice in her life, and both times the snow was mushy and wet, nothing like what she was driving in now. The wipers swished furiously back and forth across the windows as they battled the fine, sandlike granules of snow. She drove in first gear, her left foot poised over the clutch. At best she was going less than ten miles an hour. She thanked God for the light traffic as she crawled along behind a fuel truck in low gear. She knew she was being a fool for even attempting the ride into town, since she didn't even know if the courthouse was open. She swore under her breath when the heavy truck ahead of her skidded to the right. She pumped her brake but didn't come to a stop. She was barely creeping now, the snow less grainy, but heavier. She called herself a fool and every other name she could think of. The court hearing had been canceled three times already. If Ross hadn't come out to the house, she wouldn't have known about this date today. She wondered if she should have gotten her own attorney, if it was a mistake to walk into court unrepresented. But with representation, what would she have gained? Nothing, she told herself, and I would have racked up a sizable legal bill.

It wasn't her imagination, the snow was heavier, visibility terrible.

The fuel truck was still ahead of her, its taillights a beacon in the gray-white gloom.

Her grip on the steering wheel was as tight as her clenched teeth. She knew if she relaxed her grip, she'd panic and the chances of an accident happening would be greater. She was going to be a mental basket case when and if she ever arrived at the courthouse.

She was going by landmarks now, the street signs invisible in the falling snow. Her wristwatch said she'd been on the road over an hour and fifteen minutes. Twenty more minutes crawled by and then fifteen more before she spotted the Landers Building. If she'd been religious, she would have blessed herself. She did offer up a prayer as she continued to creep along, looking for the entrance to the courthouse parking lot. The lot, she noticed, was partially cleared, with mountains of snow piled in the middle and along the sides. The number of parked cars had to mean court was in session.

God it was cold, she thought when she accepted her parking slip from the man in the small booth at the entrance to the lot.

"Is there a back entrance to the courthouse?" she asked the attendant, her teeth chattering.

"Go in through the basement. Turn left and take the elevator upstairs. One of the judges told me they're going to close at noon," the man volunteered.

That meant her case would be heard. It would be over and done with in thirty minutes, Ross had said.

Inside the cold, drafty basement, Jory shed her wool scarf and knitted hat. She stuffed her gloves in the pockets of her heavy coat. She needed to find a rest room to repair the lipstick she'd chewed off on her ride into town. Her nose was probably shiny, and she knew her hair was a mess. It wouldn't do to have a husband see his wife, even if it was at their divorce, at anything but her best, she told herself whimsically. She asked the first person she saw, a policeman standing by the elevator, where Judge Ryerson's courtroom was, as well as the ladies' room.

On the way up in the elevator Jory removed her coat. Either it was stifling hot or she was so overwrought she was experiencing hot flashes. One minute she was freezing and the next she was sweltering. It was all emotional, she told herself. She felt anxious now, worried that she hadn't fussed with her appearance before leaving the house. Was the simple navy-blue dress appropriate? In the rest room, she tucked a brilliant, crimson scarf around the neckline of her dress. After all, she wasn't going to a funeral. There was no need to look somber. She was being liberated, sent back to the ranks of eligible bachelorettes. She fussed with the scarf and brushed at her hair, fluffing it until the curls suited her. She readjusted the shell combs over her ears. She leaned across the sink to peer at her reflection. She was too pale, her eyes lusterless. She reached for a tissue, blotted her lipstick, then spread it across her cheekbones. Ah, that was better. At least she *looked* like she was alive. Right now it didn't matter how she felt.

Twenty minutes of eleven. Should she stay in here until five minutes of eleven or go outside and sit in one of the leather chairs?

Would Ross be early? Would Pete be in the courtroom? The only way she was going to find out was to walk to the hallway and wait. She took a seat at the far end of the alcove and watched a middle-aged couple spit and snarl at one another. A youngster of sixteen seated four seats away looked at her and rolled his eyes. "Don't mind them, they do this all day long, that's why they're getting a divorce." He went back to reading what looked like a back issue of *TIF.* Jory continued to watch the boy's parents. Once, they must have loved one another, and now it looked like they hated each other. She wondered where the boy's loyalties were, with the mother or the father? How would he fare with the divorced parents?

"How do you feel about it?" she asked quietly.

The boy raised large dark eyes full of pain. "Anything is better than listening to this all day. The judge is going to ask me who I want to live with. I haven't decided yet. My mother says my father has a chippie on the string. My father says my mother drove him away because all she wants to do is listen to the radio and read trashy magazines like this one. I've been reading it since we got here to see what it is she finds so fascinating."

"Have you come to a conclusion?" Jory asked.

"No. My grandmother says you have to have a screw loose to

read this trash. I think she's right. I think I'm going to tell the judge I want to live with my grandmother." He lowered his eyes to the paper, his expression mystified at what he was reading.

When she saw Ross, he looked so ill, Jory rose from her seat. "Ross, over here. Are you all right?" He was carrying her father's shearling jacket over his arm.

"I'm here," Ross whispered. "I'm a little hoarse and I'm running a fever, otherwise I'm fine."

"Did you go to the doctor?"

"No, but I'm going this afternoon. Woo called him and picked up several prescriptions last night. I've felt better and I've felt worse. I appreciate your concern. Did you have any trouble driving into town? Woo called a car service for you, but they were all booked up. Did they turn on the phones and power?"

"The power's on, but the phones are still out. I wasn't sure if court would be in session, but I took a chance. My tires are new and they have good tread. I drove in low gear at ten miles an hour. As you can see, I made it. The man in the parking lot told me they're closing the courthouse at noon."

Ross nodded. "I'll put the chains on your tires before you leave. I parked in the lot."

"Oh no you won't. I'll be fine. You're in no condition to be here, much less outside working in the snow and freezing temperatures."

"Are you going to fuss about it?" Ross asked wearily.

"No. And that's my final word. If they're closing all the municipal buildings, Pete might want to drive with me. He can put the chains on. Have you spoken with him today?"

"Earlier, before he left. They're calling us, Jory."

The couple was still wrangling when Jory walked past them. She heard the man say, "There's so much crud on the frying pan, I'm afraid to eat anything you cook in it."

Jory sat through the proceedings in a trance, answering and speaking only when she was called upon. She could barely hear Ross's hoarse responses. She half expected the judge to say, "I now pronounce you divorced." Instead he said, "This divorce is granted." The entire proceeding took exactly twenty-five minutes.

"I guess that's par for the course," Ross croaked. "Our marriage took seven minutes, if I recall."

"I always thought it took nine minutes," Jory said, just to hear herself speak.

"No, it was seven. I remember thinking this is the longest seven minutes of my life. At the time that's how I felt," Ross apologized.

"Why does it take longer to end a marriage than it does to start one?" Jory asked quietly.

"Beats the hell out of me. Paperwork, would be my guess. You know, he said, she said, they said, and so on."

"Which courtroom is Pete in?"

"I think it's 407. Judge Cameron. Up one flight."

Woo was packing his briefcase when Ross opened the door to Judge Cameron's courtroom. He looked up, his eyes going from Jory to Ross. "I hope you're going straight to the doctor, Ross. Glad you got here in one piece, Jory."

"I'll get there," Ross said. "Listen, Woo, help me put the chains on Jory's tires, okay? Maybe you should drive back with her. Court's going to be closed tomorrow, and you won't want to hang with me over the weekend. The decision is yours, of course. If you want to stay, you know you're welcome. And yes, I'm going to the doctor at three. Sooner, if you guys get yourselves in gear. How'd the case go?"

"I got 'em by the . . . very well," he said, looking at Jory. "I'll put the chains on the car. I'll stick around until you get back from the doctor. In fact I'll drive you myself to make sure you get there. I'll pick up a set of chains and drive out later on. Does that meet with everyone's approval? Do you think you can make it, Jory?"

"I got here without chains, so with chains I should be fine. There won't be much traffic. We're divorced," she blurted out.

Both Ross and Woo looked at her.

"We are," she said. "It just . . . registered. I feel like crying."

Ross wanted to tell her he felt the same way. He looked helplessly at Woo before he handed Jory his handkerchief.

Damn him, he should have said something, Jory thought. Her back stiffened. "I said I felt like it, I didn't say I would." She thrust the handkerchief back at Ross. "I came in through the basement. My car's in the lot. Ross said he parked there too. How did you get here, Pete?"

"I used my brains and walked. I'm ready if you are."

"That's how we're getting home too," Ross muttered. "Who cares if they tow my car?"

In the basement, Woo pushed open the door. "Jesus," he said, stepping back into the corridor. "Give me your gloves, Ross, and that muffler. I'll tie it around my ears. I need the keys to your trunk, yours too, Jory." A moment later he was outside. Cold air swirled about their feet as the door closed behind him.

"You really are going to the doctor, aren't you, Ross?" Jory said.

"I'm going to try. It doesn't look good out there."

"Just because we're divorced doesn't mean I won't worry about you. I will."

"Just because we're divorced doesn't mean I won't worry about you getting home. Are the dogs okay?"

"They were when I left. I've never really left them for more than a few hours. I put down lots of paper and dog food. My worst fear is they'll miss the papers and leave me a mess."

Ross's voice was almost a growl when he said, "Do you leave the tree lit up all evening?"

"I did last night. It's breathtaking. Your wreath is right in the front. It adds a certain dash to the tree. The dogs sit and stare at it. I think they like it. Thanks for helping, Ross."

"Thank you for allowing me to help. Listen, I'm sorry if I got out of hand."

"And I'm sorry I made you leave. I guess I wasn't prepared for you. Your visit was so unexpected. I thought . . . what I mean is, I didn't expect you to tell me our case was moved up." She held out her hand. "Friends, Ross?"

"Sure. By the way, I don't know if this will mean anything to you or not, but my mother came by last night and fired me. If I hadn't been so sick, I'd have danced a jig. Instead I rolled over and went to sleep. I felt like a thousand-pound weight had been taken off my shoulders."

"Your mother fired you! I don't understand. For heaven's sake, why would she do such a thing?"

Ross tried to clear his throat. The best he could do was whisper: "She told me I have a set of grandparents, uncles, aunts, nieces and nephews. She wanted me to go with her to see them today. I refused. Until last night I thought my mother was an orphan. All of a sudden she has parents, sisters and brothers. I felt cheated. Don't misunderstand me, I'm happy as hell I suddenly have all these relatives, but to find out like I did . . . how could she do that, Jory?"

"Oh, Ross, I don't know. Your mother . . . your mother is different than most people. She must have had a reason. What about your father? Did he ever say . . . allude to the fact . . ."

"Not a damn word. I had this feeling she hasn't seen any of her family for a very long time and she wanted me with her because she didn't have the nerve to go alone. That's just my opinion, of course. She didn't care that I was sick, she didn't care about anything. She up and fired me. I had Woo show her to the door. I do not lead a charmed life, I can tell you that."

"My dogs liked you," Jory said shyly.

"They did, didn't they? Woo's dog and cat liked me too." Ross beamed.

"Animals are astute judges of character. The vet told me that." Jory smiled. "If you need support, moral or otherwise, when and if you decide to look up your mother's family, call me and I'll go with you. I don't think I could handle something like that alone. Maybe men are different."

"I'll take you up on that, Jory. Thanks."

"Don't mention it."

"It's done," Woo said, barreling into the basement. "It's bad out there, Jory. Are you sure you want to leave? There's room at Ross's house if you want to stay over." He looked at Ross, who nodded vigorously.

"I have to get back," she replied. "What if the power goes out again? The dogs will freeze. We almost froze night before last. I'll be careful and drive slow. Thanks for putting the chains on, Pete."

"The engine's running and the heater is on. If I don't make it home tonight," Woo said, "I'll be there sometime tomorrow."

"No, no. You have to tell me one way or the other so I don't worry. Which is it?"

"Tomorrow," Ross rasped.

"Okay. Tomorrow." Jory reached out both hands to Ross. He hugged her. Woo did the same. "Take care of him," she whispered to Woo.

"I will," he whispered in return.

"We'll go back upstairs and leave by the main door. It will save us a block of walking," Ross muttered.

A second later Jory was out the door.

"We shouldn't have let her go," Ross growled.

"I know, but which one of us do you think could have stopped her?"

"We should have damn well tried," Ross grunted as he punched the elevator button.

Ross and Woo walked arm in arm for support, their heads lowered against the driving snow, each busy with his own thoughts. There were few pedestrians on the sidewalk as the two men lumbered on. They stopped at the corner of Andover and Mitchel streets to wait for a traffic light that was no longer functioning. They were half-way across the street when Ross saw a Fieldcrest milk truck jump the curb and careen around in a half circle until it was headed in the opposite direction, sliding straight for Jory's Rambler, whose headlights blinded the driver. The Rambler swerved to the right on impact, the Ford behind it crashing into the back end before it swerved back to the right, going over the curb, the right front bumper pinning Woo to the electrical pole. Ross felt a shove to his side, stumbled and ended up facedown in the snow. He rolled over, saw Woo's agonized face and Jory slumped over the wheel of the Rambler at the same time. He was on his feet a moment later, try-ing to shout as he struggled with the Ford's bumper.

Was he talking or thinking? He didn't know, didn't care, as he put every ounce of strength he had into shoving the Ford backward. He thought he was going to die with the effort until a man dressed in heavy snow garb bent to help. Woo slid to the ground. "It's gonna be okay, Woo. It's gonna be okay," Ross whispered. He wanted to yell, to shout and scream for an ambulance, but he couldn't get the words out. There was no way he could get to Jory, so he didn't try. Woo needed him, and he could hear other people around the Rambler and the milk truck. He heard somebody say an ambulance was on the way. He heard someone else say the girl's alive.

Ross leaned closer to Woo's ear. "An ambulance is on the way. I think Jory is okay. I can't get to her. You saved my life, you son of a bitch, and look what happened to you. I should slug you right here. Damn you, Woo. Don't tell me you didn't see it coming, you did, and you pushed me out of the way. Why'd you do that, you dumb shit? Now what the hell am I gonna tell your parents?" He cradled the big man in his arms, saying anything that came into his head. When he exhausted his litany of curses he was about to start over when he heard the wail of the ambulance.

"Ross, don't tell my parents it's serious. Promise me," Woo whispered.

"I have to call them, Woo. They'll never forgive me."

"Please, Ross," Woo whispered. "Not yet. Maybe later. I want your promise."

Ross tried to speak again, to tell the ambulance attendants to be gentle, but again the words wouldn't come. He ran alongside of the stretcher, trying to speak to Woo, to tell him he'd hitch a ride in the second ambulance, the one carrying Jory and the driver of the milk truck.

"Sorry, bud, there's no room," one of the attendants said, slamming the door of the ambulance in Ross's face.

Dizzy with exertion, Ross tried to make sense out of what had just happened. The police cars, their red and blue lights flashing in the swirling snow, forced him to look away. He could still hear the sound of the shrieking ambulances. How had it happened? One minute he was walking along, and the next Woo was pinned to the light pole. Jory. He looked at the holocaust around him. He counted eight cars in the pileup. Tow trucks were arriving. Jory would never drive the Rambler again. She just had to be alive. Woo . . . Woo had to be all right too. He'd been so still, so *dead*-looking when they placed him on the stretcher. He hadn't been able to see Jory all that well when they pulled her out of the wreckage.

A policeman was shouting to be heard over the din, pulling at Ross's arm. "Did you see what happened, sir?" Ross nodded. He tried again to talk, but couldn't. He motioned to his throat, tried again to speak. He mouthed the words "ambulance, wife, friend." He reached into the breast pocket of his suit jacket for a business card. He mouthed the word "hospital."

"John, come over here," the officer called out. "Take this guy to the hospital. He can't talk. Maybe you can have him write out his statement. His wife and friend were in the accident." He turned to another policeman. "Clear this goddamn area. What the hell is this? Get rid of all those looky-looks. What the fuck are they doing out in weather like this anyway? Move it, Spenser, before the chief shows up."

Ross climbed into the patrol car, grateful for the warmth it afforded. He leaned back, closed his eyes, and prayed. Thirty minutes later, siren still wailing, the patrol car pulled to a stop underneath the canopy of the hospital's emergency entrance. He was out of the patrol car before it came to a complete stop. He waved his thanks as he rushed through the wide double doors.

An hour later he was still waiting for someone to tell him what was going on. At two o'clock he demanded answers on a written tablet. At three o'clock he asked one of the aides, again on paper, to call his father to ask him to come to the hospital.

It was four-thirty when Jasper Landers arrived, apologizing as he shook the snow from his overcoat and woolen cap. He put his arm around his son and led him to a chair against the wall. "What happened?"

Ross scribbled furiously.

"What can I do?" Jasper asked helplessly.

Stay with me, Ross wrote on the tablet.

Jasper squeezed his son's arm. "Of course I'll stay. This might be a good time for you to be seen by the staff doctor. You look awful, Ross," Jasper said, his voice full of concern.

I feel awful, Ross wrote. *I'll see the doctor. I have to go to Chestnut Hill and take care of the dogs. Jory will never forgive me if I don't. I need to know they're all right. I'm going to need your car, Dad.*

Jasper's eyes rolled back in his head. His son had never, in the whole of his life, called him Dad. At that moment he would have promised to gift-wrap the moon if he could find a way to get it for his son.

At five-fifteen, after being examined by the staff physician, Ross returned to the waiting room to take his seat next to his father. *I have a fever,* he wrote, *my chest is congested, and on top of that I have a head cold. Got a double shot and these pills. I took two of everything. I'll be okay.*

Jasper patted his back. A moment later he was on his feet when he saw Lyle Mortimer, the chief of staff, approaching in his operating room attire. They nodded to one another. Jasper's arms went around his son's shoulders again. "How are they?"

"Not good, Jasper. I'm not going to soft-pedal this. Mr. Woojalesky has internal injuries, a broken pelvis. His right leg is broken in three places, his left in two places. We have him on a twenty-four-hour watch. His spine suffered damage. We're not sure how extensive his injuries are at this time."

Ross groaned.

"Jory?" Jasper said quietly.

"Not as bad. She's got a concussion, four broken ribs, two fractured ribs, fractured hip, damage to her left kneecap, ruptured spleen. They're both in a lot of pain and have been sedated. I ordered round-the-clock nurses. There's nothing either one of you can do, so I want both of you to go home. We'll call if there's any change. They're not going to die, if that's your next question."

He looks like I feel, Ross thought.

"Can we see them?" Jasper asked, anticipating Ross's next scrawled message on the tablet.

The doctor shook his head. "Tomorrow. Go home now, and for God's sake be careful. The emergency room is full right now. We don't need any more patients. I'll be here throughout the night."

"Thanks, Lyle," Jasper said, extending his hand. Ross did the same.

"Don't thank me, Jasper. It's my job. I treat each one of my patients like it's my father, my mother, my son or daughter. Now, take your son home and leave the worrying to me."

Chapter 11

Jasper drove the high-powered Cadillac like it was a bus. "I cannot allow you to go to Chestnut Hill in your condition," he said flatly.

Ross wanted to tell him he was years too late in expressing concern for him. Then he remembered his father's comforting presence at the hospital.

"I know, I know, you aren't going to listen to me," Jasper said. "At least you're going to eat before you leave, and take another dose of your medicine. I'll be here waiting for any phone calls. What about Woo's parents?"

Ross grabbed his father's arm and shook his head vigorously.

"That must mean we aren't to call them. I don't think that's wise, Ross."

"I promised," Ross rasped.

"All right, I understand a promise. However, if things look . . . if things don't look good, you must call them. They'll never forgive you, and rightly so. I know how much you love that family. Sometimes promises have to be broken. That's all I'm going to say on the matter."

He should have been a commanding general, Ross thought as his father issued orders to the cook on their return to the Landers house.

"Rosa, get all the flashlights, all the candles and lanterns we have. Pack up all the food in the refrigerator for Ross. Get him my woolen socks, my sheepskin boots, my cap with the fur earmuffs, that lap robe for the car, and anything else you can think of. Water too, in case the pipes freeze."

"Yes, Mr. Landers," Rosa said, scurrying off to do his bidding.

"I'll make some hot cocoa and put it in a thermos for you. Coffee too, for when you get there. Who knows, you might be lucky and the power will be on, but I doubt it. For years Chestnut Hill has gone without power at the first sign of a storm. They've never been able to remedy that, at least that's what I've been told, I don't know it for a fact." Jasper realized he was babbling. He clamped his lips shut and headed for the kitchen.

Ross went upstairs to change into the heavier clothing Rosa had laid out on his father's bed. As he changed he wondered where his mother was. He didn't care enough to ask the housekeeper. All his father had said was that Justine lived in the front of the house and he lived in the back. Which was the way it had always been. As if he cared.

Back in the kitchen, his father stared at him, his eyes full of concern and worry. "I should go with you." Ross shook his head violently. Jasper screwed the caps on the thermos bottles as if he'd been doing it for years. Picnics with Helen Halvorsen, Ross thought. He smiled, enjoying the concern in his father's eyes. His father was worried about him. The thought stunned him. "I just don't understand all this. I do understand the animals have to be taken care of. Of course you have to go. . . ."

Ross reached for the tablets. He wrote: *No one wanted the dogs. Jory says no one wanted her. Go to the hospital early and tell her I went back to take care of them. She loves them. They love her and depend on her.*

"You could bring them here tomorrow," Jasper said, a frown of worry building across his brow. "If the power and phones are out on the hill, this would be the best place. How will I get in touch with you?" he fretted. "And you're ill, Ross. I've never interfered in your life before, but this time I feel like I must. For your own good, of course."

Ross bit down on his lower lip. "Maybe you should have. Interfered, that is." His voice was so raspy, so hoarse, it was almost indistinguishable. Nevertheless, Jasper heard the words. He looked away.

Ross refused to apologize. *I need lots of paper. For the dogs. I'll come back tomorrow morning. Guess that's it. You'll see me when you see me,* he scribbled.

Rosa's husband appeared in the dining room doorway. "Will there be anything else, Mr. Landers?"

"Do you have any old newspapers?" Jasper asked.

"Quite a pile, sir, in the basement."

"Load them into the car for Ross, as many as you can fit in."

"I think," Ross said in his raspy voice, "I should leave you with a smile on your face so you won't worry. Jory bought *TIF*, not to read, but to put down by the doors for the dogs to poop on. She said that's all it's good for."

"I always liked that girl. She has a real head on her shoulders. She's astute. If I had a dog, I'd do the same thing. She's going to be all right, Ross. You're right, a smile will be on my face all evening when I think of that. I might even leave a note on the dining room table for your mother to that effect, not mentioning names, of course."

"Okay, Dad, I'm leaving." How easy it was to use that word when things started to crunch up.

There it was, that wonderful sounding word, Dad. Jasper almost swooned a second time. This father-son stuff was heady indeed. He clapped Ross on the back. "Drive carefully, son. I'll take care of things here. I might go back to the hospital tonight if the weather lets up."

Ross nodded. Christ, his throat hurt. His ears were buzzing too. On the ride to Chestnut Hill, Ross cautioned himself over and over not to think about Woo or Jory. Concentrate on the road, on this monster car you're driving. Think about the dogs and on making a fire when you get there. Think about spending the night in your ex-wife's house. Think about anything but the two people lying in the hospital.

It was eleven o'clock when he arrived in Chestnut Hill. The sand trucks were out, following on the heels of the plows. The houses were dark except for pinpoints of light shining from a few windows. The power was out again.

The night was quiet, with an ominous feel about it, Ross thought as he got out of the car to step in snow up to the middle of his calves. He could feel it sliding down into his boots.

He carried box after box to the back porch. Relief coursed through him when he saw the pile of wood on the porch. Jory must have carried it in from the garage yesterday or maybe that morning. He pushed open the kitchen door and stared into darkness. No happy yelps of surprise greeting him. He tried to whistle. God, they didn't freeze to death, did they? He called the dogs by name, hoping, expecting, to see four furry streaks circle his legs. Nothing. He kicked the door shut.

Jesus, the house was cold. He lit two candles and set them into two cups from the drainboard, then carried them into the living room for illumination. The fire was out, the room ice-cold. So cold he could see the vapor from his mouth when he breathed.

They were huddled together by the hearth for warmth. He tried to coax them from their cocoon, but they wouldn't budge.

"Okay, okay, just give me a few minutes and I'll have things shipshape. Stay there. I'll have a fire going and supper on the table before you know it." Jesus, was he really talking to these dogs like they were people? Yeah, he was.

The fire took some doing, but he finally managed to get it to spark. He added an extra log and a wad of newspaper that flamed so bright he stepped backward, startled by the shower of sparks shooting up the chimney. "Good, good," he chortled. The dogs watched him. "I have the situation in hand. I think." He headed for the bathroom off the kitchen, one of the candles in his hand for light. He grabbed a pile of towels from the shelf next to the tub. In the living room he fanned them in front of the fire until they felt warm to his touch. One by one he wrapped the dogs in the fluffy towels. He wasn't sure if it was his imagination or not, but he thought they looked grateful. A tiny pink tongue licked at his hand. He felt dizzy with the display of affection. He fanned a fifth towel in front of the flames until it felt hot to his hands. He spread it near the hearth, but not on the cold fieldstone. Carefully, he carried the dogs over to the towel. A second tiny tongue licked him, then a third and a fourth. "See, I'm not such a bad guy," he crooned. "I'm gonna be moving around here until I collapse so you guys stay tight." He halfway expected a response.

Then Ross carried in the boxes and stacks of papers. He piled everything in the corner, away from the fire and the Christmas tree. He lit five more candles, setting them on the table and mantel. He made three trips back to the porch for more logs. By God, no one was going to freeze while he was in charge. The room was warming up from the blazing fire. He removed his heavy jacket, hat, and gloves, and kicked off his boots. He peeled off his socks and put on heavy dry ones. His feet were cold as ice. Cold feet, cold heart. "Not true," he muttered. While he was at it, he changed his trousers too, pulling on a thick flannel-lined pair from his college days. Where in the hell his father found them he had no idea.

He was almost warm.

"Time to eat! Let's see what we have here. Ah, chicken, roast beef, and what have we here, gentlemen? It looks like duck, tastes like duck, so it must be duck. My father eats well, you see. We have soup in this thermos, tea in this one, coffee in this one, and a whole bottle of plum brandy. We'll drink first to warm our innards and then we'll eat, but first I have to find saucers so you can . . . lap at it. Lick? Whatever it is you do."

The docile pups, drunk with warmth, licked daintily at the chicken soup and then at the tea laced with brandy. Ross picked at a fat chicken breast and hand-fed the dogs. By God, their eyes *were* grateful. In his life he'd never been more pleased with himself. The elation he'd felt the day he smacked a solid home run at Woo's family picnic paled in comparison to what he was feeling now. "One more slug of tea and that's it for you guys." He filled the saucer again. The dogs lapped obediently, their eyes closing as they finished. "I don't suppose any of you have to . . . *go*. So, it was a stupid question. I'm entitled," he muttered wearily.

Ross swallowed his medicine, drank some soup, poured brandy in his coffee and took it in two quick swallows. He felt his insides spring back to life. He took another swig of brandy straight from the bottle. He liked the feel of it going down his throat. He took a second and then a third swallow before he capped the bottle.

Outside, the wind shrieked and howled, the snow beating at the windows like giant claws. The fire burned brightly. He added two more logs before he spread the blankets and pillows from the couch onto the floor. He stretched out next to the dogs, reaching out one long arm to draw the four little bundles closer to him.

Lyle Mortimer said they weren't going to die.

He slept.

Ross woke at five-thirty, instantly aware of where he was and what had transpired the evening before. He was also aware of four snuggling fur balls under the blankets with him. He lay perfectly still, loving the feel of one tiny head burrowed into the warmth of his neck. One pup was on his chest, another snuggled under his arm. He closed his eyes, trying to feel the fourth one. He could feel the beginning of a panic attack when he located a soft wiggle in the bend of his knees. The relief he felt was so overwhelming he grew light-headed. He realized he felt somewhat better, though not good. Time for the pills. Time to do whatever it was you did when dogs woke up. Only they weren't waking up. They were probably on Jory's schedule and didn't get up till she did, around seven, maybe six. He wished he knew her better.

He had to think about it now, the accident, the hospital, and what was going to happen next. The Woojaleskys. They had to be told. Damn Woo. No, not damn Woo. A promise was a promise. What was this accident going to do to Woo's job in the D.A.'s office? Surely they wouldn't fire him. Nothing mattered except Woo's recovery. Hell, for that matter he could take Woo's place if push came to shove. Jory and her job was another matter.

The dogs stirred at the same time the doorbell rang. Ross struggled to his feet, his heart pounding, certain when he opened the door he would see his father standing there with a sorrowful look on his face. He yanked at the door, his lips pulled back into a snarl.

"Mr. Ryan?"

"No."

"Oh. Is Mrs. Ryan here? I wanted to ask her if she wants me to plow out the driveway again. There's a big car out there that's pretty much snowed in. Driveway, carriage house, and digging out the car is twenty bucks."

"Did you say *again?*"

"Yeah. I did it the day before yesterday. I do just about everybody around here. The road's been plowed, so if you need to get into town, you'll make it. They've been sanding the roads all night."

"Sure." Ross handed the young man twenty dollars, and as he closed the door said to himself "I knew she didn't do it, but she sounded so damn believable."

Inside, he reached for a thick stack of papers and carried them to the far corner of the room, where it was still warm, spreading them in a wide circle. The dogs scampered over to their haven, dancing around the edge of the papers.

"In the middle, in the middle," Ross said sternly. They ignored him, squatted, and ran back to the fire, where they curled up in the nest of blankets. They were asleep when he made his way to the bathroom to brush his teeth with Jory's toothbrush. When he was finished, he threw the brush in the wastebasket. He made a mental note to buy her a new one.

Back in the living room, he finished the lukewarm coffee that was left in the thermos. The caffeine gave him the surge he needed to pull on his boots and wool cap.

The dogs continued to sleep. He poured the rest of the chicken soup into the saucer, wondering which dog would put his feet in the dish. He told himself they would be fine if he added two more logs to the fire, secured the fire screen, and extinguished the smoking candles. His chores completed, he pulled on his father's jacket and closed the door quietly so the dogs wouldn't wake. He could make it to town, check in with his father, go to the hospital, and be back here by early afternoon.

Jasper opened the kitchen door for his son. The relief on his father's face stunned Ross. He clapped Jasper on the back. "Hot coffee and some eggs would taste good right now. Any news?"

"I called Lyle early, around seven. He was making rounds and called me back at seven-thirty. We can see Jory and Woo anytime you're ready. I sent Henry over to your house for clothes and toilet articles. Everything is in the bedroom next to mine. Your breakfast will be ready by the time you get down here. How'd everything go?"

"The house was so cold you could see your breath steam. The dogs were almost frozen. As the saying goes, I got there in the nick of time. I'm going back as soon as I see Jory and Woo. I'm going to need more food and a way to heat it in the fireplace if the power doesn't come back on. Figure out something, Dad."

"Rossssa!"

It was twelve o'clock when Ross was escorted to Jory's room by a nurse in a uniform so stiff it crackled. Her white, serviceable oxfords made hard squashing sounds on the floor. Outside the door she whispered, "Five minutes, not one second longer. Miss Ryan is very groggy and still in a lot of pain. Do not, I repeat, do not say anything that will upset her." Ross nodded as she looked pointedly at the watch on her wrist. He knew she would time him to the second. The white uniform crackled angrily as she squashed back down the hall to the duty station.

Ross didn't know what he expected, but the sight of Jory helpless in the sterile hospital bed wasn't it. He swallowed hard, his tongue thick in his mouth. "Jory, are you awake? It's Ross. Jesus, Jory, I'm so sorry. The nurse said I could only stay five minutes. She means it too."

"Ross, what happened to me? All I remember is the bright lights," Jory said softly. "What time is it? The doctor was in here, but he wouldn't tell me anything. The nurse is worse. What time is it, Ross? They won't give me anything to drink."

"Shhh, it's okay. You have a concussion, some broken ribs, some fractured ones. I think they fixed your hip and spleen in surgery. I'm not next of kin anymore so they wouldn't tell me anything," he lied. "The doctors said you would be okay, it will just take time."

"How much time, Ross? Please, don't lie to me," she whispered.

"Probably a very long time, a month, maybe two. That's just a guess on my part. Don't worry about anything, just get well."

Jory cried. "What about my dogs, Ross?" Jory said, alarmed. "They only know me and Woo, and Woo works all day. I didn't think there was this much pain in the world." Tears trickled down her cheeks. Ross wanted to wipe away the tears, to hug her, to tell her he'd make everything right.

"I went to your house last night and took care of the dogs. I'm going back after I stop and see . . . later. The power is off and the phone is still out. I don't want to leave the dogs too long. We got along real well. I know how to put down papers. They ate a lot. They like sleeping by the fire. I'll stay there, if you don't mind, and come in once a day to see you and give you a progress report. Now, what about your job?"

After they talked, Jory quickly fell asleep, her face ashen.

"*Mister* Landers, your time is up," the nurse hissed from the doorway. "Did I just hear you *cough?*" Ross shook his head, his eyes cloudy with unshed tears.

The nurse on Woo's floor was friendlier. "He's in pain," she told Ross, "but holding his own. He's groggy. Try not to let him talk."

Ross pushed the door open and immediately reached for the jamb to support himself. He could barely see Woo for all the wires, tubes, pulleys, and monitors attached to the big man. His eyes filled. He swiped at them with the back of his hand. Woo's eyes were closed. "Woo, it's Ross. Can you hear me?"

"Yes."

"Listen, you're going to be fine. It's going to take time, but the end result is what counts. I'm only allowed five minutes, so I have to talk fast. I'm going to have my father call the police commissioner and the mayor to make sure the D.A. lets me take over your caseload. This way you stay on the payroll. I'll try your murder case after New Year's. By the time I win that one for you, you'll be able to go on disability.

"Jory is okay, Woo, but it's going to take her a long time to recover. I don't know how long either one of you will be in here, so I've decided to . . . take over for you both. I'll do my best. I think

I can count on my father to help out. The dogs kind of like me. They probably like anyone who feeds them and cleans up their messes. They take a lot of work.

"I need to know something, Woo. Why'd you do it?"

Woo worked his tongue around the thickness in his mouth. "You're my friend," he whispered.

"You dumb son of a bitch. Look what you got for your efforts. I'm walking around and you're . . . you're here," Ross growled, tears gathering on his lashes.

"I wouldn't have it any other way," the big man whispered. "Ross, remember your promise, don't scare my parents."

"I've never broken a promise in my life. I think you're wrong, but then you always were bullheaded. I wish there was something I could do for you. I'd cut off my arm, you know that. When you're feeling better, I'll think of something."

Woo reached for Ross's hand. "Just say a prayer I don't end up in a wheelchair. I don't think I could . . . besides, they don't make them for big people like me."

"Yeah, yeah. Sure." Pray? He didn't know how. He couldn't ever remember praying. Praying meant you came out in the open where God could look at you and hear you. It meant calling attention to yourself. He'd had no religious upbringing. No one ever told him to say prayers at night, and he never went to church. You had to know a particular prayer to pray, didn't you? Once when he was at summer camp his bunkmate, a skinny little kid two years younger than himself, always kneeled down by his bed and said a prayer that started out, "Now I lay me down to sleep . . ." At the time, he remembered thinking the kid was saying the prayer to protect himself while he slept from the bigger kids who loved to torment the younger ones.

"Your five minutes are up, Ross," said a voice from the doorway.

"Yeah, I guess they are. I'll be back tomorrow." He wanted to lean over and kiss the big guy, to hug him, to tell him what his friendship meant to him, but there were too many things in the way. He had to say something meaningful, something he felt, something from his heart. He felt his lip start to quiver. Another minute and he'd be yowling like a baby. "Woo, that God you pray to, I . . . do you think he pays attention to us Protestants?"

"Probably, though Protestants are second-class religious citizens. . . . That's a joke, Ross. Of course he does."

Jasper was sitting in the waiting room when Ross was through talking with Woo. He was reading a tattered magazine, a paper cup of coffee in one hand. Jasper set both aside when he saw his son. "How is he?"

"He's . . . worried about ending up in a wheelchair. He still doesn't want me to tell his parents. Another thing, he wants me to pray for him. So he won't end up in a wheelchair. Stupid, right? Like God is going to listen to me. I don't even know any goddamn prayers. You never took me to church. Do you know any prayers?"

"A few," Jasper said quietly. "I've been thinking, Ross . . . I'm going back to Chestnut Hill with you. I don't know what good I'm going to be, but I'm certainly willing to do whatever is necessary to get you three young people over this crisis. Can I do that for you?"

Ross was touched, and didn't trust himself to speak. He merely nodded.

"Come along then, son," Jasper said, getting to his feet, "we have our work cut out for us. By the way, I called the power company and the phone company. Both utilities are on as of an hour ago."

Ross blew his nose, a gusty sound in the quiet waiting room. "I'm ready," he said, standing up and squaring his shoulders, his head inching higher. I'm going to give it my best and if that isn't good enough, I'll try harder, he thought as he walked outside with his father.

It was mid-afternoon when Ross opened the door to Jory's house again. He whistled. Four streaks of fur circled his feet. He watched, a smile on his face, when the four dogs sniffed his father's feet, growling fiercely. "Scratch them behind the ears," Ross said. "They love that. I'll carry in our stuff. Could you go around and collect all the poop papers and put down clean ones? Check their water bowls. They stick their feet in them. Look at that tree, Dad! I helped to decorate it," Ross said proudly.

"It's magnificent," Jasper said sincerely. "Christmas must be very special to Jory."

"Yes. She might be able to come home by Christmas, maybe New Year's. Woo's mother says you have to keep water in the stand. And we have to keep the fire burning all the time. This house is drafty as hell, and the dogs are low to the ground. There's a lot of wood in the garage. We have to carry it to the porch, okay?"

"Okay," Jasper said, nodding.

"I'll cook breakfast, because that's the only thing I know how to cook. Dinner is your responsibility. I'm not fussy. If you are, you're going to have to change your eating habits. You can always call Rosa for hints. Tomorrow I want to call around to get some estimates for replacing the windows in this house. I'll call someone to look at the roof too, and I'll get an estimate on the roof for the Landers Building. It's leaking on the south side. Jory was going to do it, but . . . it has to be done soon. Jory will have a fit over this because she can't afford it, so I'll need to strike a hard bargain. She can pay me back in installments."

"Ross, you're interfering in her life," Jasper said. "I'm not sure you have a right to do that. You aren't married now. Even when you were, I don't think you would have had a right. I'm not opposed to doing any of this. I just don't want Jory to be angry with you."

"I'm prepared for her to snarl and sputter, but if it's done, what can she do? She didn't like that business with you giving her the Landers Building, but she's living with it, Dad, if not profiting from it." Abruptly, Ross, observing the dogs, changed the subject: "Aren't they something?"

"They certainly are," Jasper replied as one of them peed on a piece of soggy paper. "Where do all these . . . papers with their . . . poop go?"

Ross laughed. "There's a barrel on the back porch. I don't know when the garbage is picked up. We'll have to call and find out. I have to tell you, it stinks."

Jasper chuckled. "Duly noted." Damn, he was enjoying himself. Ross was counting on him. This was his second chance, he couldn't afford to foul things up. God, he liked this young man. No, he *loved* this young man who was his son. "What now, Ross?"

"Now we settle in. There are four bedrooms. Jory's room is the first one on the right. Take any of the other three. There's only one bathroom upstairs, but there's a second one off the kitchen. I'll replenish the fire and bring in more wood. After that it's your job. If you don't let it go out, you won't have a problem. Put the food away, and I'll make us some coffee. We need to talk about something else that's a little more . . . involved, and I think we should be sitting down when we discuss it. I think it might be a good idea to start with the papers," Ross said, wrinkling his nose.

Jasper bent to his task, the dogs trotting alongside him as he crunched their papers into tight balls. He felt the cross drafts immediately. He wasn't sure, but he thought the dogs were shivering. The papers deposited according to Ross's instruction, Jasper headed for the bathroom and the linen closet. He returned to the living room and stuffed hand towels and washcloths around the base of the window and a large dark brown towel at the bottom of the door. He dropped to his knees and he smiled with satisfaction. He'd eliminated the draft. He did the same in the dining room and kitchen.

Ross was poking at the fire, the logs burning brightly.

"A wood fire is a bit different from a gas one," Jasper said.

"Quite a bit different. You have to work at it. The flames are kind of mesmerizing, don't you think?"

Jasper thought of all the lonely evenings he'd spent over the years in front of his gas fireplace watching the flames. "More than you know, Ross," he said sadly.

At six o'clock Ross pronounced their situation under control. Rosa's contribution of roast chicken, scalloped potatoes, and a bean and onion casserole was warming in the oven. The dogs were fed, papered, and snoozing. The fire burned bright and steady. A pile of logs rested on the hearth. Jasper had turned the couch so they could look at the tree and the fire. Both men were silent as they sipped their coffee.

"It's kind of nice, isn't it?" Ross said.

"Very nice," Jasper conceded.

"Why wasn't it ever like this at home?" Ross asked.

"I don't know, Ross. It would be easy for me to blame your mother for everything, but I didn't want to be bothered either. For a long time now I've regretted those early years. Tell me, what is it you wanted to talk about that's involved and required us to sit down? You're feeling better, aren't you?"

"Yes, I guess I am," Ross replied with surprise. "With everything that's gone on, I didn't have time to think about myself. I took the pills and kept moving, hoping for the best. More coffee?"

"To the top. This is good coffee, Ross."

Their cups refilled, Ross reached behind the couch to pull the sack of mail onto his lap. He looked at his father for several seconds before he undid the drawstring.

"In here, Dad, is Jory's job. She writes a column for the *Democrat*. She's Auntie Ann. You get the *Democrat*, you must have seen it. She can't afford to lose the job. I'm going to take over Woo's caseload at the D.A.'s office providing you can pull some strings to get me reinstated. Woo will still get his salary for now, something he needs as desperately as Jory needs her job. I can't try two criminal cases that Woo has prepared and write Jory's column too, so you're going to have to do it."

"Me?" Jasper gasped. "Ross, I can't type. I don't know the first thing about . . . good Lord, I could get her fired. Ross, you're asking the impossible!"

"I know, but there's no one else I'd *trust* to do it. Auntie Ann's identity is supposed to be a secret. Even Woo doesn't know. I found out by accident and gave Jory my word I wouldn't tell anyone. In this instance I think she'll forgive me. Will you at least try? I can type, the hunt-peck method. You can write the column in longhand, and if I have time I can type it up for you at night. I know it's a lot to ask of you."

"All right, Ross, I'll do my best."

"You have to read all these letters and pick out the ones you want to answer. Jory keeps a file in her father's office. You'll probably have to go through it and read the older columns to see how she does it. You know, get a feel for it. She has a style of her own, so you'll have to follow it. I think you should know, one of the reporters at *TIF* mentioned Auntie Ann to Mother and her nose started to twitch. I didn't know at the time Jory was the columnist. No one outside the paper knows."

"I'm forewarned. Ross, there are hundreds of letters here." Jasper groaned. "Do I have a schedule?"

"I'll have to find out. Dad, I know nothing about this. I told you, I found out by accident. Let's get our dinner ready, and after the dishes, you can start to work."

"Did you say dishes?"

Ross grinned. "Someone has to do them."

"Can't we get a temporary domestic?" Jasper pleaded.

"No. Look at it this way, this is where they separate the men from the boys. If I can do it, so can you. View all of this as the ultimate challenge." Ross clapped his father on the back to make his point.

In the kitchen, Ross covered his mouth so his laughter wouldn't carry into the living room. He had no doubts at all about his father being up to the tasks he'd outlined for him. No man likes to fail, no matter how simple the task.

At midnight Ross announced it was time to go to bed. The dogs stirred, their ears at attention. He pointed dramatically to the mound of paper by the front door. In single file the dogs trotted over to the paper. Jasper voiced amazement.

"Where do they sleep?" he asked.

"That's a good question. They kind of line up, if you know what I mean. It's like they're waiting for orders. They probably sleep with Jory, so maybe we should let them use her room. They must miss her."

"They seem to adapt to strangers rather well," Jasper remarked.

Ross turned the tree lights off, banked the fire, and closed Woo's briefcase. "I'm leaving the heat on," he muttered as he headed for the stairs. "It's drafty as hell up here. If you want to stuff the windows, feel free. Jesus, I'm tired."

"Me too," Jasper said, rubbing his eyes. "What would you say to a woman who doesn't want her mother-in-law to come and live with her and her husband?"

"I suppose I'd tell her to ask herself why she doesn't want her there, and whatever that answer turns out to be is what she has to work on. Woo's mother told me two women in one kitchen doesn't work. The mother-in-law will want to cook for her son, the daughter-in-law will be jealous. Maybe you should pick another letter."

"They're all like that," Jasper grumbled.

His jaw dropped when the four dogs followed him to the room he'd chosen. He could hear his son laughing as he closed the door. "I don't need a diagram to tell me what comes next," Jasper said to himself. He undressed, the silk pajamas so cold he thought he would faint from the shock. He scooped up the dogs, dumped them at the foot of the bed, and pulled down the covers. One by one the dogs inched upward, until all four were nestled on the pillow next to him. He did laugh then, heartily, loving the sound. He pulled the covers higher before he rolled over. He was still laughing when he said, "Justine, you should see me now. You'd piss those fine lace panties you wear."

Chapter 12

The days passed, routines were established and adhered to. New windows were installed and life moved forward. Christmas and New Year's came and went. During the second week in January a carpenter repaired the back porch, fixed the roof, installed ramps at the back of the house and at the carriage house, and put a furnace in the carriage house. During the third week a motorized, custom-built wheelchair was delivered and placed in the garage. At the same time, Ross summed up Woo's case and closed the file.

A month had transpired since the accident when Jasper Landers drove Jory home from the hospital. She walked with the aid of a pronged cane, her face full of pain with each step she took. Jasper wanted to carry her, but she wouldn't hear of it. "I have to learn to take care of myself," she said, tears rolling down her cheeks.

"You can't stay here alone, my dear," Jasper said quietly. "Please come back to town with Ross and me. You have to go three times a week for therapy, and you have no car. You need more time, Jory."

"I know," she said weakly, leaning her head back against the cushion of the sofa, the dogs cuddled in her lap. "I'm lucky to be alive, I have to keep remembering that. I'll manage. I can have the physical therapist come here. I need to be home, among my own things."

"We can stay on and help. We've got a routine that works," Jasper said proudly. "It took some doing, but we pulled together. Woo is coming along. He should be discharged soon."

"His injuries were more extensive than mine," Jory said. "I didn't know he'd been injured until the day after Christmas. Ross should have told me."

"What could you have done, my dear?"

"That's not the point." Jory frowned, annoyed with herself for seeming less than gracious. "I want to thank you for doing the column," she said.

"I'm only too happy to relinquish it to you," Jasper replied. "Will you be able to keep it up?"

"I think so. If not, can I call on you?"

"Absolutely. It's amazing no one discovered our secret. I did just what you said, I mailed ahead and used those little slips. Ross or I typed everything and scrawled your initials at the bottom of each column. Your checks and other mail are on your desk in the basket. Woo's rent check is there too. I can make a deposit at the bank for you if you like."

"I would appreciate it, Jasper."

"You haven't said anything about the new windows. Does that mean you're going to accept them or does it mean you didn't notice them?"

"I noticed them. I'm just too weary to argue. I'll pay Ross back. I know he meant well."

"He said he did it for the dogs. The drafts on the floor were terrible, and those dogs are low to the ground. Please, accept the windows in the spirit they were meant. Well, now that my job is done, I guess I'll be heading back to town. If you need anything or if I can be of any help, don't be shy about calling."

"My deposit tickets are in the top drawer of the desk, Jasper. Is Ross coming back tonight?"

"I believe so. His jury went out and said it would be a few days before they arrived at a verdict. He's certain he's going to win. For Woo's sake, I hope he does."

"Will Pete walk again, Jasper?"

"I don't know, Jory. His parents still don't know about the accident. He persuaded Ross to tell them he's out of town on a big case. I don't think it's right, and neither does Ross, but who are we to take matters into our own hands? I prepared the dogs' dinner. It's on the counter. I've been feeding them at five o'clock. Are you sure you'll be all right? I can stay longer if you need me."

"No, no, Jasper, I have to get back to the business of living. I'll never be able to thank you enough for what you've done."

"Then don't try, my dear. I'm glad you're home."

Then Jasper Landers was gone and Jory was alone. Exhausted, she stretched out on the couch and was asleep within minutes, the dogs curled next to her. She woke a few minutes past five, when the dogs grew restless. "Dinnertime I guess," she muttered, struggling to a sitting position. She clenched her teeth as pain from her hip shot down her leg. Her eyes filled with tears when the first problem of the day presented itself. How was she to get the dogs' plates on the floor? She tried placing all her weight on her good leg, with one hand holding onto the counter, the other balancing the dish. It simply wasn't going to work.

Food in sight, their noses twitching with anticipation, the dogs clamored around her feet. She knew she was going to fall, knew the dish was going to slip from her hand, but there was nothing she could do about it. She went down on her backside, the food scattering in every direction, the plate shattering in a dozen pieces. She cried with pain and humiliation and then cursed, using every dirty word she'd ever heard.

Goddamnit, she was crippled. She rolled over onto the braided rug by the sink and cried, her fists pounding the floor.

Ross watched his ex-wife from the back porch. His first instinct was to rush in, to pick Jory up, cradle her in his arms, and croon soft words to her. How hard this must be for her. He opened the door. "Having a tantrum?" he drawled. He knew she hadn't hurt herself or she'd be writhing in agony instead of crying. He hoped his assessment of the situation was right.

The dogs quieted, sitting back on their haunches, their ears straight up, their eyes bright and curious. Jory rolled onto her back to stare up at Ross. His leg was only inches from her right hand. If she wanted to, she could reach out and yank him to the floor. She bit down on her lower lip. "I slipped. I can't get up."

"Sure you can. You haven't tried. What would you do if I weren't here? Would you lie there and waste away or would you try and get up? Is this for my benefit, to make me feel sorry for you? I know in my gut my father offered to stay, but knowing you, you probably told him to leave, saying you could manage by yourself. So, Miss Independence, get off your ass and on your feet," Ross said, walking away, the dogs on his heels.

"You miserable, rotten son of a bitch!" Jory screamed. "Damn you, Ross, come back here and help me!" Silence. Fresh tears rolled down her cheeks. "You better be packing your things, because when I get in there I'm going to boot your ass out the door like I did last time. Do you hear me, Ross?"

"Clear as a bell!" Ross shouted from the living room.

Hands spread on the floor, Jory managed to get up on her knee. She crab-walked with her hands and knee until she was next to the kitchen table. She grabbed for the table leg to bring herself to her feet.

From his position on the other side of the doorway, Ross watched her, mouthing silent encouragement. Come on, you can do it. You're almost up. Move your right hand, ah, that's it, now reach for the edge of the table. He watched as she lost her grip and then regained it. He nodded his approval. She was wobbly, her grip on the edge of the table tight. He backed up a few steps and shouted, "What's taking you so long?"

"You better be out that front door when I get in there, Ross Landers, because I'm going to kill you and burn your body in the fireplace," Jory shouted. Ross smiled to himself. He moved closer to the door.

Jory looked around. She needed the pronged cane, but it was next to the sink. She swayed dizzily as she eyed it.

"I'm waiting," Ross singsonged.

"You're a low, stinking bastard, is what you are, Ross Landers. You wait, you just wait!"

"I am waiting. How the hell hard is it to walk from the kitchen to the living room?"

Jory reached for the back of the chair nearest her, her weight on her good leg. Her left hand inched out. Ross heard her sigh of relief. Okay, now move the chair, he silently urged her. Easy, go slow, push it with your good knee, that's it, you're doing fine. I knew you could do it. Pick it up, swivel on your good leg. Move the chair, easy now. Ah, you did it. He moved quickly then, to sprawl on the couch, his head turned toward the kitchen door. He waved one hand lazily. "Yoo hoo, over here." He cringed at the murderous look on her face.

Jory looked at the expanse of dining room floor she had to cross, and then the same distance in the living room until she could collapse onto the wing chair closest to the couch. She could feel her eyes fill, her lip start to tremble. I can't make it, she thought. If I try, I'm going to fall. She brought her left hand up to wipe at the tears rolling down her cheeks. "I can't make it, Ross," she cried pitifully. "I *need* your help. I'm sorry I didn't listen to you and the therapist in the hospital. I didn't want to admit . . . I should have tried harder, stayed with it instead of caving in and saying the hell with it. It was stupid of me to insist on coming home. I'm sorry. Please, Ross."

Suddenly she was swept into his arms. She closed her eyes to ward off the dizziness engulfing her. The cushions being propped around her felt like feathers, cotton batting, the most soothing balm in the whole world. Exhausted, she closed her eyes. She didn't see or hear Ross run up the steps to return with the knotted string from under her pillow. He placed it in her hand.

"Oh, Ross, what am I going to do?" she cried, grateful for his concern. "I'm crippled. I didn't plan . . . count on something like this. I had my life mapped and charted. Why me, why did this happen to me?" She was blubbering, crying hysterically, her fingers feverish on the knots of the string.

"You were at the wrong place at the wrong time," he replied. "But you're lucky compared to Woo, you're at least walking. Woo may never walk again. So you're going to have a slight limp, so what? You aren't crippled, Jory. That's the word that's bothering you. And you're right, you'd be farther along if you'd cooperated with the therapist, but instead you allowed yourself to wallow in self-pity. I'm not saying I wouldn't have done the same thing. You're right about coming home too soon too. But you're here now, so you'll have to make the best of it. There's nothing wrong in asking for help. It's the decision to ask that's hard. I'm here, I'll stay on and help you if you want me to. I know I was hard on you a little while ago, but I was on the other side of the door. There was no way I would have let you fall again. When you were in the doorway, I didn't let you fall. Now, do you see what you're up against?"

"I'm sorry I yelled at you like that."

Ross laughed. "No you're not. You had to take out your frustration on someone. I was that someone. Do you want me to stay?"

"Yes, of course. The dogs need you." She looked up at him through tear-filled eyes. "I need you too, much as I hate to admit it."

"Okay, this is the plan, then. I have to be in court until the jury comes back with their verdict. Two more days at the most. I can have my father come back or I can arrange things for you so you don't have any more bad episodes. Who knows, the jury might come in tomorrow. If they do, we can set things up so you have a schedule. I can call the therapist first thing in the morning—I'm sure your insurance will cover it, and if not, I'll tack it on to the window money you owe me. I figure three bucks a month for thirty years will just about do it. You can afford three dollars a month, right?"

"Yeah, I guess so. I'm not in a position to be proud right now. Three dollars a month is fine with me. What about those ramps I saw when I came home?"

"Premature on my part. I thought, still think, Woo will want to come back here. He'll be in a wheelchair for a while. I didn't know if you would be or not. They can be dismantled with little trouble."

"You really did take over, didn't you?" Jory said wanly. "Your father wrote my column, both of you took care of the dogs, the new windows, the ramps . . ."

There was an edge in Ross's voice when he said, "You thought we were just rich people who breathed air other people needed to live. I suppose you're right in a way. Believe it or not, my father distinguished himself—in my eyes at least. He had this system, and by God it worked. We were like a well-oiled machine. Watch this!"

"Murphy!" The four dogs pranced over to the couch and lined up. Ross snapped his fingers. To Jory he said, "Don't laugh or you'll spoil it." A moment later the dogs returned, each dragging a colored sweater. Ross bent down and slipped them over the dogs' heads. He snapped his fingers twice. The dogs trotted over to the corner and returned with colored leashes that matched their sweaters. They waited patiently until Ross put on his coat. "We'll be back in exactly ten minutes. Hey, you ain't seen nothing yet. Wait."

Giggling, Jory waited for their return.

In exactly ten minutes they were back. "Everyone did what they were supposed to do in their designated spot," Ross said. "If you'll notice, Miss Ryan, there are no papers scattered about." He removed the sweater and leashes. The dogs dragged them back to the box by the hat rack and returned again to line up at the couch.

"You can fetch it now." The dogs trotted off obediently, to return dragging a paper sack with a string around the top. "Treats!" He handed out four chew bones. "For some reason they won't take the sack back."

Jory smiled, the color back in her cheeks. "I don't believe this."

"I didn't either until my father demonstrated. He really worked with them. Jory, he hunkered down, cooked, did dishes, tidied up, even washed clothes. In his life he'd never done anything like that. I believe he had the time of his life. He did your column while the dogs worked on their chew bones. It takes them exactly an hour to devour them. He had it down to a science. At night after dinner, I took over and he typed up the column himself, using two fingers. Sometimes he worked until three in the morning. We got along swell, really got to know one another. There's more to my father than what you see. You look tired, Jory."

"I'd like a drink, Ross. A glass of wine. A big glass."

"Now, before we eat?"

"Yes. I think we should make a toast to your capabilities."

Ross's chest puffed out. "Let's not spoil this with a bunch of accolades, okay?"

"Okay." Jory raised her glass. "To a job well done. Thanks, Ross."

Ross took a sip and raised his glass a second time. "To your complete recovery. One that won't happen overnight."

They both sipped, then Jory asked quietly, "What's going to happen to Woo?"

"I don't know," Ross replied. "He's stubborn, like you. I think we'll know more in a few weeks. I filed a lawsuit on his behalf. Yours too."

"You did?"

"Of course. Your auto insurance gave you blue book value for your car. It was completely totaled. It wasn't all that much. I showed them the four new tires, so they added a little to the payout. I took the liberty of ordering you a new station wagon. It makes your monthly payment, spread out over thirty years as discussed earlier, five dollars a month. Maybe it's six. I have it all written down somewhere. Anyway, they'll deliver the car anytime you feel you're ready for it."

"How many cars were involved in the accident?"

"Eight altogether. I've had two offers to settle Woo's case, but I turned both of them down. I won't let Woo settle until I know if he's going to be permanently disabled. Their last offer was seventy thousand. I'm jamming his profession down their throats. How does a lawyer do trial work in a wheelchair? I'm prepared to go to court, and the company knows it. What's more, I was involved. Me, another lawyer, a respected Landers. Woo will do all right financially, I guarantee it."

"Pete is lucky to have a friend like you, Ross."

"I'm the lucky one. You ready for dinner?"

"Depends. What is it?"

"Roast pork, potatoes, carrots, and salad. Dad made it earlier and it's warming in the oven. He always cooked early. I'm telling you, he had this routine that wasn't to be believed. I *like* my dad."

"I guess this . . . accident wasn't for nothing, then. God does work in mysterious ways. You and your father have made peace and actually like one another. I'm sorry for Pete, for myself too, but I'm happy it worked out for you, Ross. I mean that."

"I know you do, Jory. Dinner's in the kitchen. You'll have to walk out there. Can you manage?"

"You bet. By the time you set the table and put the food out, I'll be there. I'm really hungry. Is Jasper a good cook?"

Ross laughed. "No. I think it's because he cooked so early in the day and then warmed it for hours. Usually everything is dry. I told him it was good, though. He preened like a peacock."

As she was finishing her meal, Jory said, "If you drink enough wine it doesn't seem dry at all." In fact, she didn't care what it tasted like as long as she didn't have to stand over the stove and cook it. Soup and sandwiches would have to suffice from now until she was back to normal. *If* she was ever back to normal.

Jory sat back, content for the moment as Ross prepared to leave the table. "This might be a good time, Ross, for you to tell me what else you did for me around here."

"Well," he said, as he cleared, "you *really* needed the roof fixed. Even my father said so, and he knows diddly about things like that. I know less. We shored up the back porch, it was sagging on one end. There's a new floor on it too. My father was afraid the dogs might slip through. Something like that. It doesn't matter." He grinned. "We'll add it all to your monthly bill."

He was half kidding, but Jory wasn't when she said, "When do my payments start?"

"Start?" Ross said stupidly.

"Yes, when do I start to pay you back? Do I owe for January and December, or do I start in February? And how much interest are you charging?"

"Ah, February is good. I haven't had much time to . . . you know, make it legal and all. How does twenty dollars a year sound for interest?"

"That's robbery! Are you trying to take advantage of me? Ten!"

"Deal!" Ross said as he finished clearing the table. "Coffee by the fire okay? I'll bring it in."

Minutes later they were both settled in the living room. "This is nice," Jory said. "I love sitting in front of the fire. I thought a lot about it when I was in the hospital. It was nice of you to stop every day and let me know how everything was going. I guess your father had his hands full. Have you made peace with your mother?"

"Nope. My father pointed out something to me so I could point it out to you. My mother has not paid December's or January's rent. You can't let her get away with that, Jory."

"What do you propose I do, Ross? Go down and beat it out of her? I can't do that to your mother. Maybe she forgot."

"My mother never forgets anything, except maybe her family. When I get Woo settled, I'm going to look into *that*. I haven't had time for anything but this case of Woo's. He worked so hard on it, I couldn't let him down. Sic a lawyer on her or a collection agency. She's digging in. Better yet, evict her!"

"Ross, she's your mother. I'll think about it. I won't let her get away with it. Who took down the tree?"

"My father. Your presents are upstairs in the bedroom. We bought a few things and my father wrapped them. They looked nice under the tree. We took some pictures. They're in your room. Are you going to sleep upstairs or down here on the sofa?"

"I can't manage steps yet. The couch will be fine."

"I can carry you up. You might want to sleep in your own bed. You know, to prove you're really home. There's plenty of hot water. If you want to take a shower, I'll take you up. You can't weigh more than a hundred pounds." He inched closer to feel her arm.

"A hundred five. I lost ten pounds." She leaned against his arm, liking the feel of his heavy sweater. He smelled good. She said so.

Ross smiled. "You smell like antiseptic and bandages. Don't get me wrong," he said hastily, "I like that . . . fluffy smell you had on when I was here last."

Jory snorted. "That was soap. More likely it was Prell shampoo. I don't waste my money on perfume," she said coolly.

"You should. Men like perfume. I like perfume."

"Then why didn't you buy me some and add it to my thirty-year bill?" Jory snapped.

"Actually, I did buy you some. It's gifted-wrapped in your room. It smelled good."

"What's it called?"

Ross laughed. "My Sin."

"What are you going to do, Ross?"

"You mean about a job?" he said, putting his arm over the back of the couch. "I'm going to open my own office. Hopefully, Woo will be a partner. I mentioned it three different times, but he didn't express any enthusiasm."

"That's understandable. I wouldn't pressure him if I were you." Was that Ross's arm on her shoulder? Of course it was, she could feel the nubby material of his sweater on the back of her neck. She was too tired to get herself riled up. Too tired to protest. An arm around her shoulder didn't have to mean anything. No, she thought—Ross Landers's arm meant something. Her shoulders stiffened.

Ross's fingers toyed with a tendril of hair next to her ear. She shivered, but she didn't move or tell him to stop. "I won't pressure him," Ross said. "Woo has to make up his own mind. Do you know what I want to do right now?"

"Are you going to spoil this, Ross? I'm not in any . . . I don't . . . you can't take advantage . . ."

"Whoa, back up here. You don't even know what I was going to say. This may surprise you, but I was going to ask you if you wanted me to make some popcorn."

Jory burst out laughing. He kissed her then, a sweet, wonderful kiss of promise. Flustered with the intimacy she'd been avoiding, Jory murmured, "Popcorn sounds good."

When he left, she pretended to sleep, snuggling into the pillows, her face flushed, her nerves twitching. She wondered if Ross would be disappointed when he returned with the popcorn. What would he do? Would he stay in the living room or would he go upstairs? She burrowed deeper into the pillows, the dogs alongside her. How good they felt, how warm and comforting.

She heard him moving about, setting the bowl down on the table, carrying the coffee cups to the kitchen, steps coming back, the poker being taken from the rack, another log added, the fire screen being fitted into place, the snick of the light switches being turned off. And then nothing. She lay still, afraid to open her eyes. Where was he? Was he watching her? She felt a blanket placed over her huddled form. The added warmth felt good. The light touch of his lips on her cheek made her want to cry out, to reach for him.

"Good night, Jory, sleep well," Ross whispered.

She heard the bedroom door close at the top of the stairs. Her eyes snapped open. The fire was the only light in the room, the flames dancing and stretching upward. It all looked so normal, so peaceful. Why was she feeling this inward tension, this unbearable heat rush coursing through her body? You were *that* close to doing something you promised would never happen, she told herself.

Ross was so different, so . . . helpful and caring. What would she have done without him and Jasper? Everyone needed someone, and she was no exception. Sometimes, according to the doctors and nurses at the hospital, you had to have what they called a backup, someone to help smooth the way in tight spots. Ross had certainly done that. She had new windows, a new roof, ramps, a new porch, all thanks to her ex-husband. Maybe she was wrong about Ross. Maybe if she wanted to participate, things could change course. *If.* The kiss had been expected yet unexpected. What she hadn't expected was to like it, but she had.

Now she was obligated to both Ross and Jasper. She owed money to Ross that would take a lifetime to pay back. She owed Jasper her job. She swore again under her breath. Some job. If Jasper Landers could do it cold, anyone could do it. She'd thought it special, something only she could do well, but Jasper did it equally well, so well that no one seemed to know the difference. If anything, the mail was heavier since he'd taken over.

Is this what I want? she asked herself. A dead-end job giving advice to people who, if they used common sense, could figure out their own problems? Did she *want* to do this for the rest of her life? God, no. For now, however, it was what it was: a job.

But would anyone else hire a cripple? Not likely. Personnel directors, employers, didn't like deformities. She'd just read that recently in a slick magazine someone had left in the hospital. If she remained in her present condition, this job was ideal; she could continue to work at home and no one would ever see her. No one at the food market would care if she limped. The dogs didn't care. She'd make herself get used to the stares of other people. She'd become reclusive and never marry. Who in their right mind would marry a cripple? She'd end up being an old maid living with four dogs in a house empty of love. She'd be writing Auntie Ann until she was ninety. She'd *become* Auntie Ann, a little old lady with a gray topknot, spectacles perched on the bridge of her nose.

Ross was being kind to her when he kissed her. Trying her out, checking to see if she . . . what? Worked, was all in one piece? Emotionally and physically.

Pity. There it was, the hateful word she'd thought about for weeks but was afraid to say aloud.

It wasn't fair. Pete was such an exuberant, viable person, so full of life, so full of feeling and compassion. What would happen to him? Would Ross be able to work his magic for Pete, to make him come out of the depression she knew he was feeling? It wasn't fair that just as she was getting her life in order, just as she was divorced, that this should happen to her. Why was it fair for Ross, who had everything handed to him, to walk away unscathed? Where was the justice? Where was the fairness? Why? Maybe she was being punished. For what, past sins? Why did God do this to her and Pete? Maybe she should go to church, pray more, try to be a better person. Maybe she wasn't measuring up in God's eyes. When things went awry, people always turned to prayer, to God. After the fact. She'd never been one of those people who bargained with God: do this for me and I swear I'll never do this or that. I'll be good, toe the line, never make waves. I'll pray and donate to the church, just do this one little thing for me and I'll never ask for anything else. Until the next time. No, she hadn't been one of those people. She'd taken all life's lumps, tried to be a good person, thanked him when things worked out. She said her "God blesses" at night. Well, most nights.

What is it you want, Marjory Ryan? she asked herself.

To be contented and happy, and not necessarily in that order. To look forward to waking up with a smile on my face because the new day will be whatever I make it. I want a bunch of kids like the Reynoldses have, with pets and the house in disarray from time to time. I want friends who stop by for a cup of coffee, and a husband who loves me unconditionally. I want to fight with him, express my opinions, fight

some more, and then make up with both sides satisfied with whatever
resolution we come up with. I don't care about having a lot of money
or a fancy car. Please, God, give me someone to love, someone who will
love me back, and I'll do the rest. If you can't see your way clear right
now, will you take it under advisement?

Before she fell asleep, Jory made a pact with herself. She would
give the therapy sessions every ounce of energy and courage she
could muster. If she failed and remained a cripple, then it was
meant to be. Only a fool believed fate and destiny could be tam-
pered with. And five years ago she stopped being a fool.

January came to a close with above-normal temperatures. The
mountains of snow melted to make way for February when Pennsylvania's famous groundhog, Punxsutawney Phil, didn't see his
shadow. Valentine's Day passed as just another day for Jory, as did
Washington's birthday. The following morning Ross carried his two
suitcases down the stairs and placed them by the front door. They
were the first thing Jory saw when she brought the dogs in from
their morning walk.

"Time to say good-bye, Jory. I am so very proud of you. I knew
you could do it. Another month and you'll be good as new." It was
all true. He was proud of her, and she had distinguished herself
with the intensive therapy and the endless, grueling hours she put
in on her own. Once or twice he'd thought demons were on her
back, forcing her to push herself to the limit. He pretended not to
see the tears in her eyes when he hugged her. "If you need me, just
give me a call. I'll be in my new office waiting for my new partner
to join me, whenever that might be. At which point," Ross said
lightly, "we will both wait for new clients to knock on our door. I
hope everything works out the way you want it to, Jory."

He was going. Really going. She'd gotten used to him, had even
paraded around with her hair in curlers and in her old fuzzy robe.
The last few weeks they'd laughed, talked, shared confidences, and
held hands. And now he was walking out of her life. She had to say
something. He looked like he was trying to think of something to

say too. They both spoke at the same time. She said, "I'm going to miss you."

He said, "I'm going to miss these guys."

Damn, what had she expected? Hearts and flowers of course, "I think they're going to miss you too. They went absolutely wild when Jasper came out last week. If you come back, they'll give you the same kind of greeting. They say dogs never forget a kindness done to them, and you have been more than kind. I think they know you're going. Good luck with your new office, Ross. Are you sure you don't want to wait until Pete gets here?"

"I'm sure. Speaking for myself, it's killing me that I can't be here to help him, but I know Woo and how proud he is. He won't want me to see him struggling. You see, he has all this pride. If he slips and falls, he'll make it personal. You'll be able to help more than I ever could because you've gone through it. About all I'm good for is picking up the pieces and trying to glue them together. My lot in life," he said sadly.

"Ross," Jory said, her eyes welling, "I couldn't have done it without you. I will be eternally grateful." Damn, she wasn't going to cry, was she?

"Eternal means something lasts forever," he replied. "Wrong choice of words, eh?" He bent down to pick up his bags. "I do love you. I played by your rules and now the game is over. Take care of Woo for me. He's all I have left to care about these days."

"Ross, I . . ." But she was talking to the door. The dogs circled her feet, growling softly. Growling *at her.* She threw her hands in the air, her eyes fire-bright. "Don't you *start!*" she yelled at the dogs. "So he left, so what! It's not the end of the world." Yes it is. For you it is. He walked out of your life. Just the way he did a long time ago. Over with. Finished. You don't get a third chance. If she wasn't crying, she would have laughed when the four dogs scurried to the corner to bury their heads in their paws.

Jory sat down on the couch with a thump, realizing for the first time how she looked in the morning. Like a bedraggled vagabond. Her mind raced, her thoughts tumbling over one another. Ross had redeemed himself. He'd stepped in, taken charge so effortlessly it seemed natural for him to continue taking care of things. Her comfort, her health, her financial problems, her dogs. All while he was trying to set up his own office, taking care of hers and Pete's lawsuit, dealing with his new affection and respect for his father, and dealing with the hatred he had for his mother. He'd done it all and hadn't complained once. He'd come into her life and made it a much better one. He'd taught her to deal with adversity on a gut level, taught her about compromise, taught her how to laugh again, taught her about herself. He'd shown her his vulnerability, trusting her, asking for nothing. And now he was gone.

I really am going to miss him, Jory thought. I got to know Ross, really like him as a person, and now he's out of my life. That's what I said I wanted, and now that he's given me my freedom, I'm not sure it's what I want. Her silent, running conversation ground to a halt. She snapped her fingers twice. The dogs scurried to the corner for their respective leashes.

Ross was out of her life and getting on with his own life.

"It's just us now," she said to the dogs, "but I couldn't have done it without him. I really am going to miss him," she said softly.

Chapter 13

Ross stood on the sidewalk and stared at his new storefront office. The brass lettering on the door said, LANDERS AND WOOJALESKY, and underneath, in smaller letters, *Family Law.* They were going to be lucky if they made the rent every month. It was Woo who said family law paid off in service or chickens and produce, and once in a while, money, but it was the big man's dream. Helping families who couldn't pay their bills or had to pay in monthly installments meant they'd both be making a commitment to become part of the community, to do their best for those who needed their services.

Woo had agreed, under pressure, to form the partnership, saying his half of the start-up costs would have to come out of his accident settlement. He'd insisted on only one thing: no bills to clients, saying people knew when they owed money and they didn't need a bill to prove it. Ross thought it a naive way of doing business, even stupid, but he'd agreed to test it for one year. If they were in the red at the end of the first year, they'd resort to semiannual billing, and if that didn't work, then quarterly billing. They hadn't gotten to the monthly part and probably never would. Basically, Ross thought, they would be doing pro bono work.

Ross fit the key into the lock. Time to begin this new part of his life. Everything smelled new and unused. The furnishings were not just inexpensive, they were cheap. Woo said the kind of clients they'd be dealing with would be intimidated by costly furnishings, so the carpet was flat as opposed to nubby, the chairs a mixture of vinyl and leather, with a lot of wood trim. The desks were bought at an auction, sanded down, and restained. The bookshelves were made from pine, the shelves reinforced to hold heavy law books. There were only six comfortable chairs in the five-room suite: two client chairs in Woo's office, two in his, plus his chair and Woo's. Woo's was custom-made, but the big man didn't know that. Ross had told Woo he'd been lucky to find an oversize chair belonging to a retired judge at an estate auction. He wondered if Woo would notice the doorways were extra wide to accommodate a wheelchair. Things were looking good, though, and if Woo persevered and prevailed the way Jory had, he might not need the chair.

Ross walked around the office trying to imagine a thriving law practice. The file cabinets were ready, the phones installed, but as yet there was no secretary or receptionist. The supplies in the small storage room hadn't even been unpacked.

Ross whirled when he heard a sound behind him. Clients? "Dad, what are you doing here?"

"I came to see if the drapery people hung the drapes yesterday. Ah, I see they did," he said, wrinkling his nose. "They smell new. I had to pay ten cents more a yard for the material. Because you get the morning sun, I wanted to be sure they didn't rot. I stayed within your budget," Jasper said proudly. "What do you think, Ross?"

"I think you did what I could never have done, just the way you took charge at Jory's. Thanks. Woo hasn't seen this yet. I did tell him about it, though. I described it to him the way you described it to me. He listened, but he wasn't interested. Until he can walk through those doors, he isn't going to be a participating partner. I'm beginning to doubt . . . what I mean is, maybe I shouldn't have pushed for this, but I owe him my life. This doesn't seem adequate compensation. Sometimes it seems I'm just interfering in my best friend's life, making decisions for him, trying to . . . Jesus, what if I'm wrong?"

"Would-haves, could-haves, should-haves—there's no place for words like that, Ross. You believe in what you're doing. If for some unfathomable reason it doesn't work out, then you'll start over. Woo isn't thinking rationally right now, the way Jory wasn't thinking rationally. Your method worked with Jory," Jasper added quietly.

"That was different. I love Jory. I do, you know."

He said it so wistfully that Jasper felt he had to respond: "Sometimes, Ross, you have to become friends before you can progress to that next stage."

Ross stared at his father as though seeing him for the first time. "Dad, did I ever say thank you for all you've done? I really needed someone, you came through for me. I have to be honest, I didn't want to ask, but you just pitched in. I do thank you." Then Ross blurted out, "Did you ever go fishing, Dad?"

"No, have you?" Jasper asked curiously.

"Once, with Lena. I was sort of thinking, if things get slow around here, after we get going, of course, it might be nice to hang a sign in the window that says, 'Gone Fishing.' I could teach you to bait a hook. You gotta throw the fish back after you catch them," Ross said authoritatively.

Jasper's head bobbed up and down. "I thought the object was to catch and eat them."

"I don't know how to scale, gut, and fillet them." Ross grinned. "That's lesson number two. I don't think either one of us can handle that yet, so we'll concentrate on catching them and throwing them back."

"I'm not adverse to that," Jasper said happily. "Did you just stop by to check on things or are you here to work? If you're going to stay, I can make us some coffee. I stocked the kitchen. I was going to unpack the supplies for you. A few green plants should be delivered this morning. The florist told me women like plants. I didn't know that, did you, Ross? Flowers yes, everyone knows women like flowers."

Ross smiled. Life was suddenly becoming a learning experience for his father as well as himself. "No, I didn't know that."

"This place is kind of austere, manly, superior, if you know what I mean. The woman at the florist suggested a garden dish for the table in the reception area. You're supposed to keep magazines and ashtrays and maybe a dish of mints on it. It sounded right to me," Jasper said. "What do you think, Ross?"

"I say we do it."

The relief on Jasper's face was almost comical. "I hoped you'd say that. I have everything in the trunk of my car."

"You're doing good, Dad," Ross said. He realized he meant it sincerely.

His father realized it too, his chest puffing out proudly. "Ross, I was wondering if I . . . I've been thinking about something. You're going to need some type of office management, someone to keep your books. I'd like to apply for the job." He held up his hands at the shocked look on his son's face. "Hear me out, Ross. After leaving Jory's, I realized what a miserable, unrewarding, uneventful life I've been leading. I didn't know what to do with myself. I missed the dogs, the cooking, the column. I missed *belonging*, being a part of something. I have a business as well as an accounting degree. Not that I ever applied my knowledge to anything in my life. I also realized my business acumen is probably quite rusty if not archaic in today's business world. Based on that assumption, I hired myself a . . . tutor to bring me up to date. I've been studying since I left Jory's. I feel confident enough to offer my services if you and your partner feel you can use me." His shoulders squared imperceptibly when he concluded, "I of course want to be paid."

Ross gaped at his father. He *was* serious. "I don't have any problem with hiring you, and I don't think Woo will either. It's the compensation that might be a problem. If you're prepared to take your salary in produce and other services, like we will, then it's a deal."

Jasper beamed. His hand shot out. Ross grasped it. The old man's bone-crushing shake made Ross's eyes water. "By services, you mean if a client comes in who's a mechanic and he's short of cash, he'll service your car as payment, something like that?"

"Exactly. Woo says we cannot intimidate our clients in any way. What that means is we dress down, and your car has to go too. Are you prepared to give up cashmere and a luxury auto?"

"Of course. Those are just trappings. I'm prepared to move here if necessary. I can see myself living in a small house like Jory's. But that's in the future. Woo has to agree. So, I'll make that coffee now. If you want, you can carry in the things from the trunk of my car."

Ross, his face full of shock and awe, watched his father strut down the hall to the kitchen. He broke into a wide grin when he heard Jasper whistling. "I'll be damned," he muttered.

The morning passed swiftly, and it was mid-afternoon when Jasper said, "I think I heard the door open and close, Ross."

"I'll check it out."

The woman sitting in the reception area with two children next to her looked tired. All of them were sucking on the hard candies Jasper had put on the table. An honest-to-God client. His and Woo's *first* client. He felt giddy. He smiled and stretched out his hand. "I'm Ross Landers, can I help you?"

"Are you open for business?" the woman asked hesitantly.

"Next week is our official opening, but I have time now, if you're prepared to step over boxes and cartons."

The woman rose to follow him. She turned to caution the children to be quiet and not to take any more candy.

Ross reached for a yellow legal pad. His first client in his own office. Jesus. He hoped his expression was reassuring.

"I picked the children up from school and thought I would stop and make an appointment. I appreciate you seeing me like this. I want to sue someone," she blurted.

"All right, Mrs. . . . ?"

"Newton. Eleanor Newton. My husband and I contracted to have a garage built, and this man, Duncan Pfeister, agreed to do it. We signed a contract. My husband signed it," she said, pulling it from the depths of an oversize handbag. "Mr. Pfeister built the garage, but it's crooked. It looks like Jack Sprat's house. The windows are crooked and the roof leaks. He didn't measure anything right. There's . . . this belly in the concrete. You know, a hump of some kind. We asked him to correct the situation, and he says there's nothing wrong. He needs glasses," Mrs. Newton said vehemently. "He's an . . . older man, and doesn't take . . . suggestions or criticism well. I know he might carry insurance. We want our garage fixed. We can't even get our car inside. My husband has talked to him, I've screamed at him, but it doesn't do any good. He won't talk to us on the phone anymore. Foolishly, my husband paid him. I told him not to, but he wouldn't listen. We've always paid our bills, and Oliver, that's my husband, said we aren't going to start stiffing people. That means not paying them. How much will it cost to sue this man, and what are our chances of us getting our garage redone?"

Ross was scribbling furiously. He looked up. "Of course, you are within your rights to sue, but I always like to try other means before I resort to filing suit. Why don't I write him a letter using very strong language? We'll give him ten days to respond, and if he doesn't, then we'll resort to other measures. I can type up the letter myself this afternoon and mail it on my way home. We don't have a secretary yet, as you can see. I can also search Mr. Pfeister out and speak with him personally. Will that be satisfactory?"

"I think so. Mr. Landers, my husband and I aren't the type of people who go around making trouble. We don't want to sue Mr. Pfeister, but I don't see that we have any choice. I'll tell Oliver what you said. A letter will be fine. How much will that be?"

"Five dollars, but you don't have to pay me now," Ross said.

"No, we always pay our bills. Five dollars sounds fair. Oliver doesn't like anything on credit." She laid a wrinkled five dollar bill on the desk. "He'll want to see a receipt."

Ross wrote out a receipt, took her address and phone number. "I'll send you a copy of the letter I write to Mr. Pfeister."

The giddiness was still with him when he ushered Mrs. Newton to the waiting room. He was stunned to see the children sitting quietly with their hands folded. He also expected the glossy magazines to be scattered about and the candy dish empty. He was almost disappointed, and didn't know why.

Jasper wore a wide grin when Ross made his way back to the kitchen where he was cleaning the coffeepot. "My first client," Ross said proudly. "I'm going to write the letter now, but before I drop it in the mail, I'm going to drive by the Newtons and take a look at the garage on my way home."

"Do lawyers do things like that?" Jasper asked.

"This lawyer does. This is Woo's kind of law. He jumps in with both feet, both arms flailing, which means I go check out the garage. It's ten minutes out of my way, and when it comes right down to it, what else do I have to do?"

"Ross, how would you like to take in a movie? We can catch a bite of dinner first downtown. Of course, if you have other plans or if you think hanging out with your father is not fashionable, I'll certainly understand."

"It sounds good to me, but I want to stop by the house. I called earlier, and my housekeeper said I had three calls from Lena. I'll call her from home. Do you want to pick me up or shall I pick you up?"

"I'll pick you up. Is eight o'clock okay with you? Ross, I thought, and this is none of my business, but you did say it was over between you and Lena, didn't you?"

"It is. Her heart wasn't broken, and neither was mine. Mother dangled the California carrot under her nose, and Lena sniffed it just the way Mother thought she would, then she yanked it away. Lena was devastated. I talked to her a few weeks ago and she was about ready to resign. She's transferring to the University of Wisconsin for the fall term. I think she's fed up, but that's just my opinion. I think the call is to say good-bye."

"The girl used you, Ross," Jasper said coolly.

"But I used her too. We talked about that and had a good laugh. It was all part of my learning process. I figured *that* out on my own." Ross chuckled. "Now, I have to get this letter drafted. It won't do to keep my first client waiting one minute longer than necessary."

Jasper retreated as Ross made a notation in his brand-new appointment book to follow up on the Pfeister letter in ten days.

Ross was so intent on the letter he was writing, he didn't see his father leave. He didn't notice the darkness creeping into the offices or that he was typing with only the light from the street shining through the windows. When he finished, he turned on the brass lamp to look for the roll of stamps he'd seen earlier. His job done, the letter on top of his briefcase, Ross leaned back in his new chair to prop his feet on the desk.

His thoughts weren't on his father, Woo, or his first client, they were on Jory and the look on her face when he'd left the house earlier in the day. He closed his eyes to try and imagine the scene back at the house. The dogs were probably lined up waiting for dinner. Jory was cutting up the chicken gizzards and mixing them with noodles. While the dogs ate, she'd drink her pre-dinner cup of coffee and smoke a cigarette.

Was Jory thinking about him? God, she was pretty. She was everything he wanted in a woman. A wife, if she'd have him again. He missed her already, dreaded going back to his lonely house. Dinner and a late movie with his father would only take care of one day's loneliness. What was he to do the other 364 days of the year? Work, work, work, he thought morosely.

He thought about Jory's warm, golden eyes when he dialed Lena's number at five-thirty. He thought about light brown tendrils of hair that curled around his fingers, thought of pain he'd seen in those golden-brown eyes, of the perspiration soaking the curly hair as Jory struggled to do the therapist's bidding. He admired her dedication, her thoroughness in wanting to get well. What surprised him most was the way she could swear at herself when she was too tired to go on with her therapy. She didn't give up, though. He hoped Woo would do as well.

"Lena, this is Ross. I just got your message today. Is anything wrong?"

"I guess that depends on your point of view. Yes and no. I called to say good-bye. I'm leaving tomorrow for Wisconsin. How's everything?"

"Jory is coming along nicely. Woo was due home today. He has to undergo extensive therapy. There's no real guarantee he'll walk again. Everyone is hoping for the best. I opened the new offices today and had my first client. I made five bucks!"

"Ross, that's wonderful. I expect to hear great things about you in the future."

"All the way in Wisconsin?"

"You could drop me a line from time to time. If you don't, that's okay too. I'll write you a card just to stay in touch. Ross, I don't know if you want to hear this or not, but I thought . . . I feel someone should know your mother is . . . well, what she's doing is, she's printing some pretty powerful exposés. There's a story that came in two days ago, from a tipster, about . . . a well-known judge who, according to the informant, solicits call girls from his car. Justine wanted me to pose as a . . . as a prostitute and trap him. There's a lot of things I'll do for a story, Ross, but that isn't one of them. I quit on the spot."

"Good for you, Lena. Have a good trip, and take care of yourself."

Lena laughed, a warm, trilling sound. "It's perfect weather for ice-skating. Draper's Pond is frozen. Do you know how to skate?"

"No. Do you?"

"I used to, but I have weak ankles. It's fun. Maybe you should think about taking Jory," she said lightly.

"Playing matchmaker, Lena? I don't think Jory is in any condition to ice-skate."

Lena laughed again, the sound just as warm as before. "Me, play matchmaker? Ross, you are so hooked on Jory it's almost pathetic. As for her condition, get her a pair of skates with double runners. I'd recommend the double runners for yourself too. When people get cold they tend to huddle together, if you get my meaning. See you around, Ross."

Ross grinned to himself when he replaced the phone. He thought he could hear Lena's laughter long after he'd hung up.

He placed two phone calls then, the first to his father, canceling their evening. The second call was to Lieberman's Sporting Goods store, where he ordered two pairs of double-runner ice skates, saying he'd pick them up within the hour.

At seven-thirty he was knocking on Jory's front door. "Get your clothes on, we're going ice-skating!"

"Ross, are you out of your mind? I can't skate. What if I fall?" She was giggling, her golden-brown eyes sparkling.

Ross held up the double-runner skates. "You can't fall with these. Little kids three years old skate on them. What do you say?"

She wasn't an impetuous person. She never did anything on impulse. Well, maybe it was time she did. "I'll get my jacket."

"What's good about these," Ross said later, "is they buckle on over your shoes. We'll stay on the edge and hold hands. I never did this before. Have you?" he asked anxiously.

"When I was real little, and I seem to recall being on my rear end most of the time. Don't you dare let go of me, Ross!"

Ross snorted, his face a mask of anxiety. Maybe this wasn't such a good idea. "Don't you let go of me either."

"Race you, mister," a youngster on single blades said.

"Some other time," Ross said, sliding forward, Jory giggling at his side.

"I don't think we're really skating," Jory said later as two five-year-olds whizzed by. When the five-year-olds passed them for the second time, Ross steered Jory toward a bench at the side of the pond.

"I think you're right. We're—"

"Shuffling our feet," Jory said, finishing his sentence for him. "I feel incredibly old at this moment. I think we should go around the pond one more time and call it a night."

"God, I thought you'd never say that," Ross said, getting up and pulling her to her feet. "Hans Brinker I'm not."

"The next time you get a brilliant idea like this, don't include me. Swear to me, Ross," Jory grumbled good-naturedly.

"Don't worry, this will cure me for the next hundred years. It is good for you though, admit it. How'd Woo do today?" Ross asked, to change the subject.

"It's hard to watch my feet, breathe, and talk too, Ross," Jory muttered. "I wanted him to stay in the house so I could help him and watch him, but he wouldn't. I made up the fires and carried in the logs. I took dinner over. He didn't seem to want me to linger, so I didn't. He has the house phone number and can call me if he needs me. I think he was pretending to read a law book. It was nice of you to get him a television. The therapist comes tomorrow. I can call you and let you know how it goes," Jory said breathlessly.

"Okay, we're finished," Ross said, his voice full of relief. "Sit down and I'll take off your skates. Should we throw them away now or later?"

"God, do it now. I want to see you do it, Ross, because I don't ever want to have to do this again."

Ross tossed the skates into a barrel at the entrance to the pond. "I'm sorry, I thought it might be fun, you know, an experience. I wanted to spend time with you. Would you like to go someplace to get some hot chocolate or coffee?" Ross asked hopefully.

"I'd love some. The dogs miss you. After you left, they kind of scrunched up by the front door. I think they thought you were coming back. They've been in the carriage house with Pete since dinnertime. I thought they'd be company for him."

"What about you, did you miss me too?"

Jory chose her words carefully. "Of course. The house seemed very quiet after you left. I allowed myself to depend on you. I shouldn't have done that. It's not that I don't appreciate what you've done. I do. If it wasn't for you forcing me to help myself, I'd probably still be sitting there sucking my thumb. I'm very grateful to you. I wish there was something I could do for you. I'm not a taker, Ross. I don't like to be beholden or obligated."

A long time later, after they'd driven to the house in Chestnut Hill, Jory said, "It was a nice evening, Ross, despite our inability to whiz around the pond. I felt so darn old out there."

Ross chuckled softly. They were in front of her door, the soft yellow light of the carriage lamp casting them in golden shadows. He wanted to kiss her, to have her melt in his arms, to whisper words that meant he was to come inside and upstairs. Instead he said, "I wasn't going to come back here unless I was invited. To see Woo, yes, but I wasn't going to invade your privacy. Tonight seemed . . . the truth is, Jory, I missed you and the dogs. I allowed myself to feel like I belonged here. I didn't want to leave this morning. Part of me wanted you to ask me to stay, and the other part of me wanted to trench in and tell you I was staying. I know you feel something for me, just the way I feel something for you. I told you I loved you, and I meant it."

"Have you ever been in love before, Ross? You know, that heartstopping feeling that your world won't be right unless the person you love is right next to you?"

Ross stared down at her eyes. "Not till now. That's what I've been trying to tell you. I'm new to this. Heart-stopping is a good way to describe what I'm feeling. My world is almost right-side up. It would be perfect if you were in it. I'm not that same person I was years ago. Thank God for that. Why can't we act on our feel-

ings? Why can't we set it all aside and start new? You said you forgave me, but you couldn't forget. What will it take to make you
forget that awful time in our lives?"

"I don't know, Ross. I wish I did. I want to trust you, I really do,
but . . . I guess it's my own insecurities. You have to understand,
Ross, it was a terrible time for me. I used to walk down the beach
in Florida to think and stare at the water for hours at a time. One
particularly bad day I told myself I had nothing to live for, so I
swam out as far as I could go. I was going to let the tide carry me
. . . wherever. I didn't want to live anymore. But the tide washed
me to shore. That's when I had to take a good, long, hard look at
myself. I wish I had a rotten memory, but I don't," Jory said
miserably.

"Jesus, Jory, I'm sorry. I—"

"Look, it was as much my fault as it was yours. I try to put it
behind me, I really do. I wish there was another way to say this,
but there isn't. I'm affraid to trust you."

Ross cringed. "What you mean is you won't let yourself trust me.
What will it take to make you trust me? I'll do it, Jory. I'll turn
cartwheels, stand on my head, strip naked in the courthouse at high
noon." How desperate his voice sounded, Ross thought.

"None of those things, Ross. It's me. It's not a physical thing. I
don't know what it is. I can't hold out a promise to you that maybe
tomorrow I'll feel differently. Maybe next week I'll look at you and
something will happen to me and I'll rush to you saying I love you,
I want you, I need you." Her voice was full of anguish when she
said, "I've tried so many times to figure out why I feel the way I
do, and the only thing I can come up with is the miscarriage."

"And all I felt was relief that you miscarried," Ross said quietly.

"I know. Tonight when I saw all those little kids skating on the
pond, I thought . . . our child would be five and a half years old.
I know I would have made a good mother. Maybe not in the beginning, but later on, when I got the hang of things."

"We weren't ready to be parents then, Jory. God . . . Woo says
everything happens for a reason. He says God acts in mysterious
ways. If we'd stayed together for the sake of a child, we probably
would have ended up with a marriage like my parents. Our child

would have had a childhood like mine. I wouldn't wish that on anyone. You and I would have hated each other. When you left, I felt like I was given back my life. But Jory, that was then, this is now."

Jory was lost in her memories. Then she said, "It's a beautiful night, isn't it, Ross? It's so quiet you can hear yourself think. Isn't it strange, growing up here, I never felt anything. Too young, I guess. Listen, I can hear the dogs yipping. They must know I'm home. The snow's almost gone. The air is crisp and cold. A perfect evening."

"Are you going to go in and sit by the fire with the dogs and have cocoa?" Ross asked wistfully.

"Not tonight. I have some work to finish, and one cup of cocoa a night is enough for me. I liked it with marshmallows, didn't you?"

"Hell yes." At that moment he would have agreed to anything she said just to see the smile on her face.

" 'Night, Ross," Jory said, reaching up to kiss him on his cheek.

"Good night, Jory. Thanks for going skating with me. Tell Woo I'll call him tomorrow to brief him on our first client."

How sad he looks, Jory thought as he walked away. How alone. She couldn't let him go like this, she thought, not after all he'd done for her. She ran after him, calling his name. "Ross, wait." She reached for him, took both his hands in hers. "I like you, Ross. I mean that sincerely. For a long time I loved you and hated you at the same time. I'm trying to be honest with you. Hug me, Ross," she whispered.

He did.

Chapter 14

Jory kept her eye on the carriage house as she prepared lunch for herself. How had Pete made out with the physical therapist? The therapist had left thirty minutes ago; she'd heard his car in the driveway. She'd wanted to rush out, to check on Pete, until she remembered how limp and exhausted she'd been after her first session. She looked down at the sandwich fixings and made two extra. She would take over all three, and if he wanted company, they could eat together. She added a thermos to the grocery bag along with napkins and two Sno Balls for dessert.

Should she take the dogs or not? No, she decided, Pete wouldn't be in the mood for the dogs' hijinks. They yapped their disapproval as Jory closed the kitchen door behind her.

Jory knocked loudly on the door to the carriage house. "Pete, it's me, Jory, I brought you some lunch."

"Door's open," he called.

"How'd it go?" Jory asked. She didn't look at him, not wanting to see his haggard face, the defeat in his eyes. She busied herself removing lunch from the bag and setting it on the paper plates she'd brought with her. "I have coffee here, but if you prefer soda pop, I can go back and get it. Ross said he was stocking your cupboards, but I didn't check to see what he got. Knowing him, I don't think he missed anything. He's so . . . thorough. I've seen beavers when I was a kid at Draper's Pond who weren't half as busy as he's been. He's so worried about you, Pete. He feels responsible for your accident. Okay, here we go," she said, setting the plate on a little table next to Woo's chair.

"My appetite's off these days," Woo said. "Maybe it was the hospital food."

"I brought my lunch too, but if you'd rather be alone . . ."

"No, of course not. Stay, I like your company. How's the column going? You aren't sorry you confided in me, are you? I didn't mention it to anyone. I laughed myself silly in the hospital when I read Jasper Landers's responses. He did a good job."

"He certainly did, which just goes to prove anyone can do what I'm doing. I thought I was unique, you know, one of a kind, dispensing advice no one else was capable of giving. I'm grateful I have a job and grateful to Jasper. It's not what I want to do with the rest of my life, though."

"Ross and his father are getting along," Woo said. "He seems in awe of the whole relationship. Mr. Landers came by to see me, and he seemed to be . . . different. He made me laugh so hard a couple of times with stories about the dogs I almost fell out of bed. He used the word 'routine' a dozen times. So I guess you could say that something good and positive came out of the accident. You and Ross are friends. Ross and his father are getting to know one another. Ross opened a business and included me in the partnership."

"And what about you, Pete?" Jory asked, biting into her chicken sandwich.

"What about me? Well, my parents came to see me two weeks ago. I finally realized I had to tell them what happened. My father is very emotional. After all the crying, after all the recriminations, do you know what they said to me?" Jory shook her head. "They said," Woo said tightly, "Ross will make things right. I don't think I wanted to hear that. They made it sound like this accident was Ross's fault and it's his duty to make things right. It's not that way at all."

"I know that, Pete. I think Ross would die if he couldn't help. He had workmen here at dawn making sure everything that could be done to make you comfortable was done. It was all his idea, the new shower to accommodate your wheelchairs—he had them custom-made for you, one for the shower and one for regular use. He said there wasn't anywhere you couldn't go in that chair. He said it goes seven miles an hour. I like the whirlpool bath. Maybe sometime when I get stiff and achy I'll ask to use it. When it's damp or it rains, I start to ache. When you start going outside you'll appreciate the ramps."

"It's going to take me the rest of my life to pay him back," Woo said.

"Didn't he give you a thirty-year deal like he gave me? I'm to pay ten dollars a month for thirty years. Listen, Pete, Ross had to . . . it was his way. He's carrying a very heavy load. Neither of us are ever going to be able to convince him he wasn't responsible for what happened to you. Like all of us, he needs to be needed. You won't believe what he did to my house. My roof's been redone, I have a new back porch, a new floor, ramps, and all new windows. Oh, he told me to tell you he's going to call you today."

"He did call," Woo said, "early this morning, to tell me we had our first client and we made five dollars. His father is going to be doing the bookkeeping and handling the business end of it. Ross said he wanted my approval, so I gave it. Jasper Landers is an okay guy in my opinion."

"Yes he is. When do you think you'll be going in to the office?"

"Whoa. That's a long way off. I don't even want to discuss it now."

As they were talking, Woo had absently reached for and eaten one sandwich, then another. Now he dabbed at his mouth with his napkin. "This was an unexpected pleasure, Jory. It was nice of you to do this. How are things with you and Ross?"

"I don't know how to answer that, Pete. Last night he showed up at the house and took me ice-skating. Double runners. Turns out he's never skated, and I only did it once or twice when I was little. We more or less shuffled around on the ice, and when we were finished, Ross threw the skates away. I'm very grateful to Ross," she said carefully.

"Ross is a terrific guy. For a long time he's had lots of demons chasing him, the biggest being a young woman named Jory. He seems to be coming into his own of late."

"Thanks to you, Pete," Jory said.

"You too, Jory. Everyone's life seems to be on an even path but mine," Woo said quietly.

"Is that self-pity I hear in your voice, Pete?"

"Probably," Woo said curtly. "Have you taken a look at me? A good look?"

Jory squirmed in her chair. "As a matter of fact I have. I see a man who's lost forty pounds that needed to be lost. I see someone who is kind, generous, warmhearted, and a true friend. I see a man who is . . . temporarily laid low. A man who, with the help of his friends and the therapists and doctors, will be as good as new one of these days. I still limp, Pete, and I've accepted that when I get tired the limp will be more pronounced. There are a lot of things I can't do as well as I did before. However—and this is the most important part—I no longer think of myself as a cripple. I did for a while. What are these poles with the hooks on them?"

"Canes. There's a name for them but I forgot what it is. Those circles or bands hook around my arms, and someday I may be able to walk using them. Actually, the word 'walk' is the therapist's word. You sort of shuffle yourself along with the weight on your arms. The therapist is a very positive person. We do it to music. It makes it a little easier to bear."

Jory threw her arms around Woo. "I know you'll get better. I just know it. God could never punish you like this for doing something so good for Ross. You have to believe that, Pete."

How it happened, she didn't know. His lips closed over hers gently, softly, sweetly, as though he were drinking from a cool spring. Her arms closed around his neck, answering his embrace, her mouth tasting the soft, cool sweetness.

When Jory lifted her head, she looked into Woo's pain-filled eyes. There was a curious glistening there. She cradled his head against her breast, then pulled back and gently wiped the tears from his lashes. "Now you have to get better," she said. In turn, he drew his finger gently underneath her eyes and smiled. "Do you think you can hug me without crushing me to death?" Jory whispered.

"I can try," Woo whispered in return.

"This is probably going to sound strange," she murmured, "even unbelievable, considering my past circumstances, but I've wanted to kiss you for a long time. I wanted you to hug me. Everyone needs a hug sometimes. I haven't had too many in my life. Hmmm," she sighed as he hugged her gently. A long time later she said, "Thanks, Pete."

Woo stared at her a moment, then grinned. "Anytime," he said. He watched from the window as Jory walked back to her house. "I'll be damned," he muttered.

He fantasized then, his imagination running wild. He was walking in the rain, in the moonlight, in the snow, through sweet-smelling autumn leaves, a pretty young woman at his side, four dogs trailing behind. He was coming home from work to a house full of fragrant cooking odors, to the same pretty woman greeting him at the door with a smile on her face. A pretty woman who smelled like Ivory soap, lemon, and vanilla, the most heady perfume in the world. He envisioned a picnic with fried chicken, hard-boiled eggs, cheese and wine, ants and a soft blue blanket. The Woojalesky family reunion sprang to life, all the aunts, uncles, cousins, and friends telling him in unison, "You're homely as a mud fence, how did you get such a pretty girl?" And his laughing response, "She loves me." A garden wedding under the chestnut trees, he in a dove-gray tux, Jory in a long white trailing gown with something old from his mother, something blue from his sister, something borrowed from one of his aunts, and the something new would be from him. But what? A locket? His mother had a locket, so did his sisters. A picture of him on one side? The dogs? Ross? A picture of Jory and himself smiling into the camera, he thought triumphantly. Yes, yes, a locket, a tiny gold one on a fine gold chain.

A best man. Five brothers would solve that problem. But would it really? Ross should be his best man. Ross was his best friend. It was the kind of friendship they would both carry to the grave. If the truth were known, he loved Ross more than he loved his brothers. Ross was family.

The reality of his situation slapped Woo in the face, his

fantasizing over. There was no way for him and Jory to be anything but friends. He was crippled; that wasn't going to change.

Another operation, even two, might give him back his old life. All the therapy in the world wasn't going to change his spine, his legs. He looked at the canes, his eyes burning unbearably. His mind raced. "Handicapped" sounded better than "crippled." He brushed at his burning eyes. Think positively, Woojalesky, you still have your mind and your hands and arms. And you can feel. Everything.

All this from a kiss and a hug.

"The hell with this," he muttered. "I can love anybody I want."

He wheeled his chair to the sofa, where he grasped the thick padding on the arm and dragged himself onto it. He laid back, his physical body exhausted with the morning's activities. He cradled his big, shaggy head into the mound of pillows. There was no one to see the glistening tears on his lashes, no one to wipe them away, no one to say, "Shhh, everything's going to be all right."

He slept fitfully, his dreams full of tiny gold lockets that were threatening to choke the life from his body as he twirled his wheelchair into tight, crazy circles to elude the monster chain of lockets.

He cried out in his sleep, but there was no one to hear, no one to soothe him, no one to whisper, "Shhh, it's just a bad dream."

There was no one.

It was the end of May before Woo's therapist told him he was ready to try the canes.

Woo grunted. "My big day, huh?"

"Physically you're ready. We're going to do it for five minutes, not one minute longer. It will be painful at first, but I believe you're up to it. Every third day we'll increase the time by one minute. If Miss Ryan is amenable and you feel you want to try it later in the day, you can attempt it. If it proves to be too tiring, then you'll stop."

Was he ready? Maybe physically, but was he ready psychologically? "Let's get on with it, Arthur," Woo said through clenched teeth.

Arthur Nelson held out the canes. This was the part he hated the most, fixing the canes on his patient's arms. The patients expected so much, and as much as he prepared them, they were never ready for that first fall, that realization they weren't going to literally ·dance across the room. It was always at this moment that he wished he were in another profession.

The canes were locked in place. All he had to do now was get up. And walk. Try and walk, Woo corrected the thought.

If determination was the only barometer of success, then Peter Woojalesky would succeed, Arthur thought.

"I'm not going to be able to do this," Woo said, his forehead beading with perspiration.

"You won't know unless you try, and keep on trying. We discussed this at great length, Peter. It's not an overnight miracle, as you well know. Remember what I told you. Get a mind-fix on an event you want to participate in later on when you're well." Arthur's tone changed to almost a monotone: "You're in the courtroom summing up a case you've worked on for over a year. Your thumbs are hooked in your vest pockets. Your back is to the prosecution, you're facing the jury. You've got it locked tight, you know you're going to win. The other side doesn't have a chance. You prepared, you ate, slept, and drank this case for a year. You were brilliant in your cross-examination, even the judge showed his approval. Now *strut!* You earned this moment."

What the hell was Arthur talking about? Woo thought. He'd be lucky if he saw a trial in ten years of family law. Sweat rolled into his eyes and down his cheeks. He shook his grizzled head, seeing his perspiration flick off into nothing. He had his mind-set. He was in a dove-gray tux and he was *standing* at the front of the church waiting for his bride. Did brides limp? This one did. He leaped over the communion rail and was running, *running,* and he was goddamn falling, on his face, in front of his bride-to-be.

"Three steps, Peter. That's good for the first time. I'm very pleased. Get up and we'll try again. The clock doesn't tick until you're on your feet. Let's pick up where you're hooking your thumbs in your vest."

The hell with his vest. He saw her stumble and right herself, and then the heel of her pump 'caught in the long white dress. He was moving toward the communion rail, shouting words of encouragement as Jasper Landers helped to untangle the hem of the dress from her shoe. Past the communion rail, arms outstretched, his face wreathed in a smile, he said, "I knew you'd make it."

Arthur clapped his hands. "I knew you could do it, Peter. Well done. Steady now, don't lose your balance. Let the canes take the weight. How do you feel?"

"Like someone whipped me."

"Did you win your case?" Arthur asked.

"Hell no! But I got married!" Woo hooted. "The bride stumbled twice, but I was right there to catch her. She didn't need my help, though." He hooted again as Arthur bent down to remove his shoes and socks.

"I like my scenario. You are a lawyer. I work very hard on these scenarios," Arthur grumbled.

"I'm a man first, a lawyer second," Woo replied. "We both knew I would have won, so what was the point? Neither one of us knew if I could get married."

"The point," Arthur said testily, "was you were supposed to *strut*. I wanted you to strut and win your case."

"And I wanted to get married. I wore a dove-gray tux. What do you think of that, Arthur?"

"Who was your best man?" Arthur asked sourly.

"You were," Woo lied.

"Really." Arthur preened. "Congratulations. Now, let's get you into the whirlpool where you can relax. Don't fall asleep, Peter."

"At my wedding! You must be joking. Go make your phone calls, Arthur. Report my progress, call your next patient, and have a cup of coffee. I made it right before you arrived so it's fresh. I'd like to be alone for a while."

"Do you want a book or magazine?"

"Nope."

"Something to drink?"

"Nope."

"All right, I'm going. Hold onto the edge."

"I know the drill, Arthur," Woo said, leaning back against the headrest.

He dozed, his grip tight on the edge of the whirlpool.

He was half asleep, the swirling water washing away the pain, leaving room for dreams of wedding cakes, dancing brides, showering rice, and airborne floral bouquets caught by . . .

"Peter, you aren't supposed to sleep in the bath. You said you understood. What that means to me is I can't leave you alone anymore."

Arthur Nelson was a feisty man of sixty-two who was so thin he was stringy. He was exceptionally strong and was always assigned the most difficult cases. He preferred to work with men because he could bully and cajole them into things they didn't want to do or thought they couldn't do. He wasn't married because his job didn't allow for much free time. When he did have an extra hour or so to call his own, he spent it checking on old patients, charting their progress and wishing them well. He was likable in an odd sort of way, even though he never smiled. He never allowed any of his patients to quit on him. He'd say, "If you give up, if I can't work with you, I'll be fired. Where am I going to get a job at the age of sixty-two? This is all I know, all I'm trained for. Do you want me to starve? Just remember, I'll be on your conscience. They don't pay me enough to have savings. Do it for me." And usually they did. Arthur realized that Peter Woojalesky would see through his strategy immediately, which was why he was going to have to come up with something even better than the stories he'd been using for forty years. Woo grimaced. Using his hands, Woo hoisted himself onto the ledge of the bath. Fifteen minutes later he was back in his chair.

"Was I really your best man, Peter, or did you just say that?" Authur asked fretfully.

"Do you think I'd lie about something so important?" He struggled for his best injured look for Arthur's benefit.

"What's wrong with my story? I spent over a week on it. I write them up and file them away. You're supposed to go along with the stories, it's part of the therapy." He was still fretting.

"You can't always be right, Arthur. We learned that in law school. I can try your story when I've progressed more. How's that?"

"You're probably just saying that to make me feel better. I've got your number, Peter, and from now on I'm going to watch you. I'm also going to tell Miss Ryan to keep her eye on you. Is there anything I can get you before I leave, something to drink, a book, or would you like me to turn on the television?"

"I can do these things myself, Arthur, but thanks for offering. I'll see you tomorrow."

The days and weeks passed slowly, the seasons changing gradually. It was November before Woo was using his cane more than he was using his wheelchair. He still had a long way to go, and two more operations before he would be able to walk with *one* cane.

A week before Thanksgiving, when he was feeling particularly low and depressed, he dressed and walked across the yard to Jory's house. She smiled when she opened the door. The dogs barked happily as they circled both canes, sniffing and licking the prongs. "I think I need some cheering up," he said. "A cup of your flavored coffee might do it."

"How wonderful of you to walk over here. As a matter of fact I can use some cheering up myself. I was going to come over later on to invite you for Thanksgiving dinner. Do you think Ross and Jasper will come if I ask them?"

"Absolutely. What are you feeling depressed over?"

"My life, my job. I don't know what I want, Pete, but this job isn't it. That much I do know. I haven't made any friends since coming back. All I do is work and take care of the dogs. I don't have time for anything else. I've thought about taking a vacation, but I don't know where to go. I don't even know if that's what I really want to do. I was so happy when I came back here, got the job, the dogs, and fixed up the house. I thought it was enough, but it isn't. But that's not important. How are you doing? I can't believe you walked across the yard, up the ramp, across the porch, and you're sitting here. You've made so much progress, Pete. You must be almost ready to go into the office."

"By the first of the year. For a little while each day. The insurance company is going to give me a customized vehicle to drive. It's part of the settlement. Ross pushed them against the wall, and they're giving me two hundred thousand and the van. It's enough. We'll settle next week. It was my idea to settle. Ross wanted to hold out and go to court. I think this is fair. I can still work. Family law won't require me being in court, and by court I mean trials. I think I can make a decent living even if I'm in a wheelchair. It was an accident, and even if the insurance company is paying, I can't gouge them. The settlement is fair. How's yours going?"

"With what they gave me for my car and the rest, I came out of it with fifty-three thousand. That's not shabby. I expected ten thousand at the most. I feel sinfully rich. I'm going into the office to sign the papers tomorrow. I thought I'd ask Ross and his father to Thanksgiving dinner then. It will be nice, don't you think? All of us around the same table, giving thanks."

"If you don't mind me asking, what are you going to do with your money? You should think about investing it and making it work for you, giving you income. I *know* this is none of my business, but how are you handling the income from the Landers Building?"

Jory snorted. "What income? Mrs. Landers hasn't paid a dime in rental. I sent her two reminder letters, but she ignored both of them. Ross told me to evict her, but I can't do that."

"Does Jasper know?"

"No. I knew this building . . . the gift of it, was going to be a problem. I didn't want it. I still don't want it. I don't think Jasper wants anything to do with it. I really don't know what to do. It's a year now, and she should have paid sixty thousand dollars in rent. My original intention was to simply let the rent accumulate. Ross must be paying the utilities, and that's not fair to Ross. I certainly don't have that kind of money to shell out every month." Jory rubbed at her temples. "Every time I think about it, I get a headache. I just want it to go away."

"I can write a letter for you, if you think it will help. Or you can hire an outside attorney to do it for you. You should do something, Jory. Sixty thousand dollars is an awful lot of money."

Jory stretched her neck muscles. "I know," she said wearily. "What bothers me the most is I'm obligated to Ross now, and I hate the feeling."

"What about the taxes?" Woo asked.

"Pete, I don't know. I assume Ross has paid them. I never wanted that damn building," Jory said vehemently.

"Where do the bills go?"

"I have no idea. For a while there I didn't exactly have all my ducks in a row. Ross took over. Maybe they go to Justine, maybe he had them diverted to . . . wherever."

"I can call a friend of mine and dictate the letter for you. I think a letter from me on Landers and Woojalesky stationery will carry about as much weight as the ones you've written. You're within your rights to give her ten days to pay up the back rent or eviction will be the next step. It's your decision."

"If you were me, what would you do, Pete?"

"Business is business, Jory. She wouldn't get away with it if she was paying rent to a corporation or another landlord. You either pay or you move. That's the law. Extenuating circumstance normally would be taken into consideration, but not in this case. She's raking in fistfuls of money, so she can afford the rent. This is a spite case. Do you want me to call my friend Brian Kelly?"

"Yes," Jory said miserably.

Ten minutes later Woo said, "It's done. Brian will type up the letter today. It will go out in the mail tomorrow, certified. Mrs. Landers will have ten days to respond with her check. That will bring it to December first. Brian will give her two extra days to allow for the mail. If she ignores the letter and doesn't pay up, he'll get in touch with the sheriff's office, and within twenty-four hours she'll be on the street. It's called taking charge of your affairs. I think she'll pay up."

"I don't," Jory said sourly. "Jasper is going to be upset. I imagine Ross will be too. What if it gets into the papers? Jasper lives in fear of scandal. This may surprise you, but I like Justine. She ignored me, but she was never ever unkind to me."

Woo laughed. "That was the old Jasper. The new Jasper seems to be going out of his way to right old wrongs, taking life by the tail and swinging that—whatever it is he managed to get hold of— overhead. He'll cheer you on. You said yourself Ross told you to evict her. They're on your side, honey. Ross did tell me once his mother liked you."

Honey. "More coffee, Pete?" she said, her head lowered over the pot. *Honey.*

"To the brim. The house is toasty these days. It used to be pretty drafty here in the kitchen." He wondered why she was suddenly so busy, opening and closing drawers, moving things on the counter, shuffling the papers on the table. He remembered the feel of her lips, the comforting hug. He wondered if she was remembering it too. "Am I making you feel uncomfortable? I can leave," Woo said, setting his coffee cup down on the table.

"No. Yes . . . kind of. I was thinking . . . don't leave. I have a leg of lamb in the oven. You're welcome to stay for dinner if you like."

"Mint jelly and those little potatoes?" Woo asked wistfully.

"The potatoes aren't exactly little. They were sort of big and I cut them into pieces. Carrots too. I made bread early this morning. I'll take the butter out of the refrigerator so it's soft." She was talking too much, aware of Woo's intense gaze. What was he thinking? All she had to do was ask. She gave voice to her thought.

"Do you want me to lie, or will the truth do?" Woo asked quietly.

At the sudden sexual tension, something in Jory's stomach jumped upward. She felt her heart take on an extra beat as a warm flush crept up to her neck.

"What were you thinking?" he asked, noticing her discomfort.

Her ears felt as warm as Woo's looked. She found her voice, the words startling her. "Probably the same thing you're thinking."

Woo ran his hands through his hair. It felt like it was on fire. "I sure as hell wasn't thinking about the oven temperatures and your chopped-up potatoes. Or carrots."

"I wasn't either. I did give a passing thought to the fact the lamb might burn if we—"

Woo leaned over and turned the oven off.

"It's been a very long time. I, ah . . . I'm not . . . agile," Jory said, looking everywhere but at Woo, her hands massaging her hip.

"If it's agility you're looking for, I guess I better turn the oven back on," he said, reaching out one long arm.

Jory's arm shot out to grasp his. She shook her head. "I'm not looking for agility. I'm not even looking for a lot of . . . of energy. The fire's nice. My comforter is on the couch because I slept down-stairs last night. It's difficult going up and down the steps."

"I can't manage steps at all," Woo said.

"I know."

Woo stared at Jory. He thought he'd never seen a prettier young woman or a nicer one. He wanted to ask, Why me? She smiled then and there was no reason to ask.

"Do you think you can get down on the floor?" Jory asked breathlessly.

"Hell yes," Woo said just as breathlessly. "I think if we keep this up, we're going to talk ourselves out of whatever it is we're *thinking* of doing."

"Then I think we should march into the living room and . . . *do it.*"

"That's what I was going to say, but you beat me to it. However, I'm not the marching type. You march and I'll shuffle."

Jory marched.

Woo shuffled.

They did it.

"I think," Jory whispered in Woo's ear, "this will definitely go into my memory book. If you like," she teased, "I can sew up a sampler for you with the time and date."

Woo groaned as he nestled her more comfortably into the crook of his arm. In his life he had never felt what he was feeling now. He forgot about his handicap, forgot about everything except the girl lying next to him. He should be saying something to her, some-thing that would let her know how he felt, but the words wouldn't come. A sigh escaped him when Jory burrowed deeper into the nest his arm created. "It's all right not to talk, to just feel, isn't it?" Woo whispered against her sweet-smelling hair.

"Oh, yes."

A lifetime passed, and she gave an involuntary shiver.

"Are you cold?" Woo whispered. He shifted his upper body weight until she was stretched out next to him. He liked the feel of her nakedness against his own, loved the feel of her warm skin against his hands. He wanted her again.

His mouth was gentle, his touch delicate, as he explored and caressed. He could feel passion quicken within her, and he calmed her with his touch and soothed her with words known only to lovers.

He was gentle with her, so gentle, evoking in her a golden warmth that spread through her loins and tingled her toes. His movements were familiar, reassuring, his touch on her naked breasts light and lingering.

He gentled her with a sure touch and a soft voice, quieting her whimper with his mouth and yet evoking moans of passion with his caress. When passion flamed again, it burned as pure as the fire that warmed them.

Woo cradled Jory in his arms, his expression full of awe. This young woman matched his ardor, and without reservation gave herself totally to him. How beautiful she was in the dim glow of the room, how gentle she could be, and then she could become a raging riptide, swirling and crushing his volcanic outpourings until the molten lava and thundering waters were a marriage of one.

Imperceptibly, his embrace tightened. Jory smiled into his dark eyes, which mirrored his soul. Woo's thumb traced the delicate skin over her golden lashes. He thought of her as a sleepy angel. She belonged to him. For now.

His tone when he spoke was a husky caress. "You're the most beautiful woman I've ever seen. Lovemaking gives you the aura of an angel and the soul of a lioness."

"I feel wanton," Jory whispered softly. She sighed deeply. She never wanted to leave this place, leave Woo's embrace. His hard, manly body that molded itself to hers was so comforting, so right.

Was it possible that she loved this man? Even as she thought it, she knew it was possible, if she allowed it.

She stirred, affording herself a better look at his face. He appeared sleepily relaxed. A sudden surge of desire and longing stirred within her. She wanted him, needed him again, and again. She shifted her position slightly and leaned toward him. Strong arms pulled her body on top of his. Hungry mouths searched, found, and conquered in the dimness of the firelight.

Tenderly, his fingers lifted her chin, raising her lips to his own. His arms tightened about her, pressing her close to his chest, crushing her breasts against him. His body was hard and muscular. Jory's arms encircled his back. Without reason or logic, she felt safe and secure in his embrace, and she faced her tumultuous emotions with direction and truth. She wanted this man just the way she'd wanted him before. Wanted him to make her the woman she knew she could be . . . the woman Ross had never known existed.

Looking into his eyes without a trace of shyness, she was aware that she could drown in that incredible dark gaze and emerge again as the woman she wanted and needed to become.

When he released her, his eyes searched hers for an instant, and time became eternal for Jory. From somewhere deep within her, she felt a desire to stay forever in his arms, loving the touch of his mouth upon hers as passions began to build to a crescendo, threatening to erupt like fireworks. Thick, dark lashes closed over sparkling golden eyes, and she heard her own breath come in ragged little gasps as she boldly brought her mouth once more to his, offering herself, kissing deeply, searchingly, searing this moment upon her memory.

She kissed him as she had never kissed another man . . . a kiss that made her knees weak and her head dizzy. She knew, in that endless moment, that this man, this giant of a man, belonged to her in a way no other man could ever belong to her, for however brief this time together would be. She had found him, a man who could make her senses real, her passions explode, who could promise the fulfillment she had only dreamed could be hers.

Woo's gentle fingers caressed her cheek softly and seemed to know what she was feeling. "There are needs of the soul that go beyond the hunger of the body." His voice was deep, husky, little more than a whisper.

Gently, in the firelit room, he nuzzled her neck, inhaling the heady fragrance that was hers alone. Blazing a hot trail from her throat, his lips covered her unguarded breasts, and she shivered with exquisite anticipation. She became unaware of her surroundings, oblivious to time and place; she only knew her body was reacting to this man, pleasure radiating outward from some hidden depths within herself. She allowed herself to be transported by it, incapable of stopping the forward thrust of her desires, spinning out of time and space into the soft, consuming vapors of her sensuality.

Her emotions careened and clashed, grew confused and wild, her perceptions thrumming and beating wherever he touched her. And when he moved away from her, leaving her, she felt alone and grieving. When he returned, she was whole again, wanting, needing, wanting to be needed. The feverish heat of his skin seemed to singe her fingers as she traced inquisitive patterns over his arms and back and down over his muscular haunches.

She had never touched a man this way, not even before or during her short marriage to Ross. But somehow she knew she could touch a thousand men this way and none would feel the same to her as this man. None would have unexpectedly smooth skin that tantalized her fingers and tempted her to seek the hard, rolling muscles that lay beneath. No other man could possess this soft furring on his broad chest that tickled her nose and brushed her lips, nor the long, hard length of thigh that her wandering hands had found and explored.

Suddenly the room was almost dark, the fire at last dying, jealously keeping the sight of him from her eyes. She wanted to see him, to know him, behold the places her fingers yearned to find and her lips hungered to kiss.

The fire flared then, lighting the room again. "I want to see all of you," she whispered throatily.

He was filled with an exhilarating power that came from the knowledge that she wanted him, unabashedly and unashamed . . . the power that only a woman can give to a man when she reveals her desire for him, welcoming him into her embrace, giving as well as taking, trusting him to take her to the realms of the highest plains, where passion is food for the gods and satisfaction is its own reward.

His hands found and undid the ribbon in her hair, eager to see the golden-brown wealth tumble around her shoulders and curl around her breasts. Silky, dark gold hair, scented and clean, rippled through his fingers, tumbling and cascading, following his hands down the smooth length of her back and onto the soft coverlet. She lifted her head, looking up at him, her golden eyes heavy with passion. Her lashes created shadows on her high cheekbones, upward-winging brows delineating her features. The slim, lithe body tempted his hands, invited his lips.

Her teasing touches fleetingly grazed his buttocks and the backs of his thighs, slipping between them and rising higher and higher. She watched him as she touched him, aware of the masculine hardness of him, feeling it pulsate with anticipation of her touch. And when her hand closed over him, a deep rumbling sounded in his chest, coming from his lips in a barely audible groan.

He reached for her, covering her breasts with his hands, seeking them with his lips. But her appetite for him had not been satisfied, and she lifted herself onto her elbow, leaning over him, her hair falling askew over her shoulder, creating a curtain between them.

Hesitantly she touched him again, running the tips of her fingers down his chest, hearing his small gasp of pleasure. The flat of her palm grazed his belly, and her lips blazed a trail following her hand's downward sweep.

The swell of her hips and the rounded fullness of her bottom filled him with a throbbing urgency. Nothing short of having her, of losing himself in her, would satisfy. He was afraid the touch of her lips would drive him over the edge, past the point of no return. Impatiently, he drew her upward. He wanted to plunder her, to drive himself into her, to quench his thirst, knowing that his needs could be met only by her.

Her mouth was swollen, passion-bruised and tasting of himself. Her arms wound around him as she moved to straddle him, holding him close as she pressed her nakedness against him. His hands made an intimate search of her shoulders, skimming the long, silky length of her back, following the curve of her spine.

A golden warmth spread through her veins, heating her erratic pulses. Her hair became entangled around her neck, and he lightly brushed it aside before resuming the moist exploration with his lips. His mouth lingered in the place where her arm joined her body before tracing a patternless path over her full, heaving breasts. She clung to the hard, sinewy muscles of his arms, holding onto him for support, afraid she would fall into a yawning abyss where flames were fed by passion.

His hands spanned her waist, tightened their grip and lifted her above him. His mouth tortured her with teasing flicks of his tongue, making her shudder with unleashed passions. She curled her fingers into his hair, pushing him backward, away, pleading that he end the torment, only to follow his greedy mouth with her body, pushing her flesh against it, relieved when it encircled the whole peak.

A throbbing ache spread through her, demanding to be satisfied, uncontrollably settling in her haunches, making her seek relief by the involuntary roll of her hips against the length of his thigh. He held her there, pulling her toward him, driving her pelvis against him.

A single, pale tear glistened on her cheek. She was triumphant, powerful, a woman. In this man's arms, she knew she had been born for this moment, that all her life had been leading up to what she was experiencing with this wonderful man she called friend. He had taken her out of herself, revealed a world of wonder to her, where arms and lips and bodies were meant for loving. He had shown her secrets of the universe, and she had learned them. He had taught her what it meant to be a woman, carrying her with him to the heights beyond the stars.

It was totally dark when Jory woke in her cocoon of warmth. She felt warm, cozy, and slightly disoriented until she remembered where she was and what had transpired. A heat rush engulfed her as she stirred to look at the man sleeping next to her. He looked peaceful yet vulnerable, exactly the way she herself was feeling. A wave of tenderness unlike anything she'd yet experienced engulfed her. She reached out a hand to smooth the hair back from Woo's forehead. She smiled when his eyelid twitched.

It was time to get up, to let the dogs out of the office where she'd barricaded them earlier. Time to feed them, time to turn on the oven and the lights. Time to replenish the fire or turn up the thermostat.

Carefully, so as not to disturb Woo, Jory crawled from beneath the covers to gather up her clothes. She ran naked to the bathroom off the kitchen to dress. She yanked on her clothes, brushed her hair, and then splashed cold water on her face. She avoided looking in the mirror, afraid of what she would see reflected in her face. A wave of giddy euphoria washed over her. What was she supposed to do now? How was she supposed to react when Woo woke and looked at her? Five hours of intense lovemaking made one stand back and view things in a totally different light. What did it mean to her? More important, what did it mean to Woo? Where was she prepared to go from here? Woo was a gentleman, she thought. He would take his cue from her.

She raised her eyes to stare at her reflection in the mirror. She was stunned at the flush on her cheeks, at the sparkle in her eyes and the silly smile on her face. Surely this wasn't her. She wiped at her cheeks and eyes, remembering gentle kisses that had fallen on them. The smile refused to go away. She had no idea sex could be so wonderful, so powerful. What she'd experienced with Ross when she was in her teens was nothing compared to what she'd just experienced. Back then she'd thought of herself as experienced in a cockamamy kind of way. She'd felt loved this afternoon, but what did she know about love? Maybe what she felt and experienced was just plain sex, and that's the way men and women who were experienced in the art of lovemaking behaved. Maybe in Woo's eye this was just a romp in the covers. How was she to know?

When no answers came back to her from the mirror, Jory walked out to the kitchen. She turned on the overhead light and then the oven. On her way to rescue the dogs from their exile, she turned up the thermostat in the hallway. She tried to be quiet when she gathered up the dogs' leashes and her jacket. A long walk in the crisp November air might help clear her head. If not, she would wait to see how Woo reacted and then act accordingly.

The moment the door closed, Woo shot upright, his eyes searching the covers next to him and then the empty room. He rolled over, Jory's scent still in his nostrils. It wasn't a dream, it had been real, so real that he could still feel her presence. He reached for his watch on the raised hearth. Seven o'clock! Jesus. Five hours of love-making with a short nap in between. Arthur would never believe his stamina. Hell, he didn't believe it either. Jesus!

Using his hands, he dragged himself to the couch, where he struggled into his clothes. Now what? His head fell back against the arm of the sofa. Now what, indeed? He didn't have the foggiest idea what he should do next. Should he go back to the carriage house? Should he wait for Jory to come back? Of course he should wait. But what did he do, how was he supposed to act when their eyes met? Did he say, Jesus, it was great? Let's do it again soon. Should he read the word love into what happened? Was it just one of those spontaneous things that happened sometimes between two people? Was this the right time to tell her he loved her, had loved her from the day he moved into the carriage house? It was one thing to have sex with someone who was crippled, as he was. Marrying or committing to such a person was something totally different. Maybe she felt sorry for him, made love with him just to prove to him he was a total man. Jory would do something like that. He didn't know how he knew that. Maybe he felt it and didn't really know.

Woo let his mind soar as he explored the possibilities of a serious relationship with Jory. He thought of Ross, his best friend, who was still in love with Jory. "Shit," he said succinctly. Why was he always the last one out of the gate? "Because you're stupid, that's why," he muttered.

They were on him all at once, licking his hands and bare feet as they crawled up his chest to snuggle against him. They yipped and yapped, their fur cold to his touch. He laughed as he always did, the sound booming out in the room. She was standing at the back of the couch, which meant he had to crane his neck to see her. He had to say something. Something that would take away the uneasiness.

"Is it cold out?"

"Very cold," Jory said, removing her jacket. "I wouldn't be at all surprised to see snow flurries by morning."

"Really," Woo said brilliantly.

Jory bobbed her head up and down. "Uh-huh," she said, just as brilliantly.

"I can't believe it's seven-thirty," Woo said.

"I was surprised myself to see the time," Jory said carefully. "I turned the oven up. I'll bring in some wood. You are staying for dinner, aren't you?"

"Can I take a rain check? I didn't know it was so late. I have some reading I have to do." He turned to see her better, but she was out of his range of vision. He couldn't see the way her shoulders slumped or the tears forming in her eyes. What was that crap about a rain check?

"Okay," she called back. She damn well wasn't going to cry. They could punch her eyeballs in and she wouldn't cry. The cold air on the back porch smashed her in the face. She gathered up an armful of wood. She had her cue.

He hadn't moved, Jory noticed when she dropped the load of logs into the basket. She built up the logs in the grate and added wads of paper in between the pyramid of wood. The paper sparked, as did the slivers of wood jutting out from the logs. She had to turn now, had to say something. Something to take the edge off what she was feeling. "I've got to get back to work myself, but first I have to feed the dogs. Are you leaving by the front door or the back?"

Woo blinked. Front or back? It sounded to him like the most important question in the world. "Is it important which door I use?" Of course it was. Ross used the front door. He was relegated to the back door. He felt like smashing something.

"If you aren't using the front door, I'm going to lock it and turn out the front light. If you're using the back door, I'll see you out. I won't be in the front end of the house for the rest of the evening."

It made sense. He liked his version better. Was he supposed to say, I had a wonderful afternoon? Sorry I can't stay for dinner. It wasn't just wonderful, it was the most memorable afternoon he'd ever spent in his life. He was about to tell her so when she opened the back door and then stepped aside. She couldn't wait to be rid of him. Then he'd damn well accommodate her and leave. He did turn just as she was about to close the door. "I don't know what the rules are. We should have set them up in advance, and maybe both of us wouldn't be behaving this way." The door opened a little.

"Behaving in what way?" Jory mumbled.

"Behaving like we did something wrong, like it didn't mean anything. It meant something to me. I wouldn't have . . . you acted like . . . it was some . . ."

"What you're trying to say but having trouble saying is, if I hadn't made the first move, you wouldn't have persued me. Well, Pete Woojalesky, I already figured that out. Now you think I hop in the sack any old time I feel like it. The word you're probably looking for is one your friend Ross used. Easy. Well, now you can go back and tell him I haven't changed. Are you leaving or not? I want to close the door."

Woo slammed at the door with his cane, driving it backward, fully exposing the trembling young woman whose face was a mask of cold fury. How could something so wonderful change so drastically with just spoken words? "Just a damn minute here. I never said any such thing. No, I wouldn't have had the nerve because . . . because I'm like I am. I have feelings. Just because I'm big and ugly doesn't mean I don't feel and hurt the way other people do. You mean something to me, and because of that I didn't want to screw things up. I didn't know what to say to you when you came in, I didn't know what I was supposed to do. You acted like it didn't mean anything. Well, it meant something to me. I don't need your past problems, I have enough of my own. Don't ever, ever, confuse me with Ross Landers. Your problems are yours, not mine. *Now* you can close the damn door!" Woo stormed as he made his way across the porch and down the ramp.

"Pete." It was an iron command. He turned, his face miserable. He waited. "I need to ask you something. One question. I want your answer in three seconds."

"Shoot."

"Will you tell Ross about us first thing in the morning? Are you prepared to snatch me away from him? Three seconds, Pete."

"Not right—"

The door slammed in his face.

"That's what I thought," Jory cried, stumbling through the house and up the stairs to her room, where she threw herself on the bed, crying heartbrokenly.

Chapter 15

Jory rubbed at her aching shoulders. She'd been sitting here at her father's desk working on her column since dawn. It was now twelve-thirty. The calendar her eyes kept straying to said it was December sixth. A little over two weeks since the legal letter written by Brian Kelly went out to Justine Landers. Four of those days had been added to Justine's deadline because of the long Thanksgiving weekend. A little over two weeks since she'd spent the afternoon with Woo.

Her Thanksgiving dinner had never materialized. Instead she'd made a pot of spaghetti, large enough to last a whole week. At the last minute she'd made a pumpkin pie to ease her conscience. Coward that she was, she'd written a note saying she was too busy to prepare a big dinner and stuffed it in Woo's mailbox.

Jory looked around the dark-paneled office. She was spending entirely too much time in this room. What kind of life was this? All she did was work, eat, sleep, and go to the market three times a week. The only fresh air she got was when she walked the dogs or went food shopping. She was bored and angry at the same time. She hated what she was doing, hated the way she was forced to wait for Brian Kelly to call her, hated Woo's silence, hated the circumstances she'd created for herself.

In a few more weeks it would be Christmas, and then New Year's. A year since the accident.

What was it she wanted from life? Better yet, what was it she expected? Happiness and contentment? But then everyone had a right to expect happiness and contentment. One either worked at it or fell into the trap she now found herself in.

Jory yanked at the paper in the typewriter. She scanned the jumble of words and then crunched it into a ball. "Enough!" she shouted. "I quit!"

She was a whirling dervish then as she gathered up her files and the letters she'd been working on. The sack of mail next to the desk made her clench her teeth. It took her an hour to sort and carry her boxes of files to the front door. She dragged two mail sacks and set them alongside the boxes. Another hour was used up changing her clothes, applying makeup, and fixing her hair. At three-thirty she was in the *Democrat*'s office surrendering her files and the two mailbags. "This is consuming my life and I can't do it anymore. You don't pay me enough money. I appreciate your kindness to me in the past, but I need to do other things. My columns are three months ahead, which will give you ample time to find a replacement. Mail me my check!"

Outside, it was snowing lightly. It looked wonderful and it felt wonderful. Her shoulders felt pounds lighter. She felt like singing.

The streets were busy with Christmas shoppers carrying colorful bags and beribboned boxes. Maybe she should do some shopping, she thought, and immediately changed her mind. She'd come to town to do other things, and she wasn't going home until those things were taken care of. She stopped long enough to get her bearings as she tried to decide if she should walk or go back for the car and drive to Brian Kelly's office. She opted to walk when she realized she was only a block and a half away.

"You timed your visit perfectly," the young attorney told her. "I just got back from court. Please, sit down. Can I get you coffee or a soft drink?"

"No thanks. Have you heard from Mrs. Landers or her attorney?" Jory asked.

"Not a word. I called the sheriff two days ago, but he was out sick with bronchitis. His aide said he would be back in the office today and would take care of things. I would imagine by now the building has new locks on all the doors and Mrs. Landers is . . . someplace other than the building. Let me give the sheriff a call."

He seemed nice, the kind of young man Woo would call a friend. He was tall and thin, with round horn-rimmed glasses he kept pushing up on his nose. He looked so ordinary she couldn't help but wonder how he did in court. Maybe he was a scrapper, or maybe he was just a fine attorney. His offices were neither plush nor shabby. Comfortable and easy on the eyes. She particularly liked the tropical fish tank against one wall. She'd read somewhere once that watching fish was supposed to be relaxing. They were certainly colorful. She jerked her eyes back to the attorney when he hung up the phone.

"I'm sorry, but it wasn't done today. The sheriff did try, but Mrs. Landers wasn't in the office and her staff said they didn't know where she was. He's going back at nine o'clock tomorrow morning. If you wish to go along, he says you're welcome. He'll meet you in the front lobby. If your next question is, is she avoiding him, the sheriff said he didn't announce himself and her car wasn't in the parking lot. We have a court order."

"I'll be there," Jory said firmly. "How much do I owe you?"

Brian waved away her words. "Nothing. I did it for Woo. He'd do the same for me. I'm sorry it's running into overtime, but that's the way it works out sometimes. How is Woo?"

"He's making progress. The therapist comes out every day and works with him. It will take a while, but I think he's making good progress."

"Ross did all right by him. I heard about his handsome settlement. He really held out and brought the company to its knees, and deservedly so. I'm particularly glad about the van with the hand controls. That should buoy old Woo. Tell him I asked about him."

"I'll do that, and thanks again."

"It was my pleasure. I hesitate to ask this, but does Ross know about the . . . eviction?"

"I didn't tell him. I don't know if Woo did or not. As a matter of fact I'm driving over to Ross's office when I leave here. I planned on telling him, because I thought . . . I expected the eviction to . . . what's the right word here?"

"To have taken place?"

"Yes. Well, if I want to make it before Ross leaves, I better go now. Would it be too much of an imposition for me to ask you to call him and tell him I'm on my way and to wait for me?"

"Not at all. If anything goes awry tomorrow, Miss Ryan, call me. I'll be in the office all day. Give my regards to Woo."

"I'll do that."

The snow flurries had ended while she was in Kelly's office, with no accumulation. If the snow had started to stick, Jory knew she would have headed for home immediately.

On the ride to Ross's office, all she thought about was Woo and the last two weeks. She'd been so certain during the first few days that he would call her or come over to the house, but he hadn't. More than once her hand had been on the phone to call him, but she didn't know what to say to the big man. Now, two weeks later, she still didn't know what to say.

When exactly had her feeling for Woo changed from friendship to something more? Before the accident? After the accident? Before Christmas, before Ross's visit that night when they put up the tree?

Did she love Pete Woojalesky? Woo. In her thoughts he was Woo, always Woo, but when she spoke his name or called him, it was Pete. She thought it strange, but she'd never dwelled on the matter. Pete was Pete. Maybe it had something to do with Ross, since it was Ross who'd nicknamed him Woo in college and the name had stuck. When he'd introduced himself to her that first time, eons ago, he'd said his name was Pete Woojalesky.

Did Pete have feelings for her? It seemed like he did that night; that afternoon, she corrected herself. She remembered the way he stood in the doorway, the miserable look on his face. She hadn't helped matters at all. He didn't want to be a part of her problem. That was all fine and well, but she'd been willing to overlook his handicap, *had* overlooked it, simply because it wasn't important to her. Didn't that come under the heading of problems? Evidently it didn't, at least in Woo's eyes.

Damn, she hated it when she got to this part of the memory. She was doing the same thing she'd done with Ross, taking all the blame. God, didn't she learn anything during those long years? What *were* the rules? Why did they need rules anyway? They'd done something that was natural and spontaneous. Who thought about rules at a time like that? It had been so wonderful, those hours she spent in his arms, and then it soured so quickly, she was at a loss to explain it.

"The hell with it," she muttered.

She drove slowly, her eyes searching for Ross's office number and a parking space at the same time. She spotted the storefront office and then a parking space two blocks away. She walked back, her hands jammed into her pockets, her collar pulled up around her neck. She hated the cold, more so since her accident. Every bone in her body seemed to ache when it got cold or it rained.

The warm air of the office seemed to slam against her. Her breath exploded in a loud *whoosh*.

The receptionist, a middle-aged woman with gray curly hair and round circles of rouge on her cheeks, looked up. Purple barrettes held back the curls, and her earrings, the size of pennies, were purple too. Her smile was warm and friendly. Two purple plastic bracelets clicked against each other when she motioned for Jory to take a seat. "Are you Miss Ryan?" Jory nodded. "Mr. Landers will be with you momentarily." The moment the words were out of her mouth, the phone at her elbow buzzed.

"She's here now, sir." To Jory she said, "You can go in now, the first door on the right."

Each time she saw him, he seemed to grow more handsome. His tie was jerked loose, his shirtsleeves rolled to his elbow. Ross reached for his jacket, a tired smile on his face.

"Jory, it's wonderful to see you. I can't imagine what you're doing here, so I have to assume you came just to see me. Can we have dinner? How's Woo?"

"No dinner, Woo is coming along, and yes, I came here on a . . . personal . . . business matter. Is Jasper here?"

"He was a few minutes ago. I'm not sure if he left or not. I can find out in a minute." Jory heard him ask the receptionist to tell his father he needed to see him.

Jasper, his sleeves rolled up, his tie askew too, walked into the office a few minutes later.

Jory waved aside the amenities. She took a deep breath. "Please, both of you sit down. I've come here to tell you something. I don't know if you'll be upset or not, but you, Jasper, placed me in this position, and now I've been forced to act on your generosity. And you, Ross, gave me the go-ahead. For the past year I've been writing notes to Justine asking her to pay rent. She didn't see fit to answer any of my notes, nor has she paid me. Brian Kelly, an attorney in town, sent her a certified letter on my behalf telling her if she didn't pay rent she would be evicted. The sheriff was supposed to act on it days ago, but he was sick with bronchitis. He went there today to do it, but Justine wasn't available. He'll go back tomorrow morning. Now you know," Jory said tightly.

Both men gaped at her, their eyes wide, their mouths open.

"What I want to know, Jasper, is this: Did you give me that building as a way to get back at Justine for something she did to you?"

"My dear, Justine had nothing to do with my gift to you, other than the fact she was a paying tenant. I wanted you to have some measure of security. She still hasn't paid you anything?"

"No, Jasper. If I go ahead with the eviction, will it harm you in any way?"

"Absolutely not. We're legally separated," Jasper said. "I hope this doesn't offend you, Jory, but I didn't think you had the guts to do something like this."

"I didn't think I did either, but I did it. Ross, what do you have to say?"

He grinned. "Well done, Jory. I might just go into town to watch the proceedings myself. What time?"

"Nine o'clock. Am I doing the right thing? Justine is your mother, Ross, and she's still your wife, Jasper, even though you're separated. I feel terrible," Jory mumbled.

"You're taking charge of your property. Think of Justine as you would any other tenant. Would you let anyone else get away with nonpayment of rent if they were raking in over a million dollars a year?" Jasper said quietly.

"Well, no, but . . . I feel like . . . it doesn't seem right."

"Justine believes she's a law unto herself. It doesn't work that way. She chose to ignore your requests for payment, and she's ignored the letter from the attorney you hired. Now she's going to have to deal with the result of those decisions. My advice is to follow through."

"And that's good advice," Ross said, seconding his father. "Why can't you have dinner with me?"

"I have to get home, Ross. I've been in town since three o'clock. I don't like leaving the dogs too long. I quit my job this afternoon," she said.

"We should talk about that. We never did have that dinner you agreed to, the one where we were going to celebrate our divorce. Woo is ambulatory now, can't he let the dogs out?"

"Not really," Jory said, a catch in her voice. "If they run off, he can't go after them. Four leashes are something even I have trouble with."

"The most they'll do is make a mess by the back door, said Ross. Their dinner's been late before. I'm sure you left a bowl of dry food for them. I think you've just run out of excuses. Now that I'm looking at you a little closer, I'd say you look like you need a drink and a nice dinner. There's a very good restaurant not far from here. As a matter of fact it's so close we can walk. You haven't taken your coat off, so you're ready to go. I'm ready," Ross said, reaching for his topcoat. "So, let's go."

"Go along, children, I'll close up. I'm almost finished, but today is the day I water the plants, so I stay later. Don't worry about tomorrow, Jory. You do what you have to do and go on from there. Neither Ross nor I will blame you for anything."

"All right. You talked me into it, but we can't dawdle. One drink, dinner, and then I have to be on my way."

Out on the street, Ross linked her arm with his. "This is great, just great," he said. "You know, we have things to celebrate. It's almost a year since the accident. Look at you, you're here and in good health. Reason enough to celebrate."

Jory gasped as a cold gust of wind buffeted her backward. "It was snowing earlier and I panicked. I mean I really panicked. By the time I left the *Democrat*, it stopped. I think my heart did too. I am mortally afraid of the snow these days," she confided.

"Don't dwell on the past, Jory, it doesn't do any good. I'm the living proof. It took me a while to learn that, but if I hadn't, I wouldn't have the relationship I now have with my father. We went fishing this fall. Can you believe that? We all learn from our mistakes," Ross said.

"I suppose you're right, I try not to look back. How much farther, Ross?" Jory asked.

"A few more steps." Half a block later he said, "We're here," relinquishing her arm to open the door.

It was a charming little restaurant with checkered tablecloths and wine bottles on the tables. Jory sniffed, her nostrils flaring at the rich scent of garlic and cheese.

Ross grinned. "Garlic will ooze out of your pores for three days, but the food is worth it. Everything on the menu is great, but the ziti is superb. They wrap the leftovers if you want them. Meatballs on the side. The wine has the kick of a mule. Be warned. You look great, Jory."

Flustered, Jory thanked him for the compliment. "So do you. I guess family law agrees with you."

"You wouldn't believe the satisfaction I get out of it. I can't wait for the first of the year when Woo comes into work. We have quite a client list. We aren't exactly making the rent, but we're close. By this time next year I think we'll be in the black, and if we aren't, who cares?"

"It's fortunate you have outside income. Do you take a salary?"

"Nah. I'm just banking the checks. Half the time we don't get paid in money. We've accumulated quite a roster of clients, though. I get free car maintenance for the next five years, and anytime I need carpentry work done, it's mine for the asking."

Jory laughed. "I can picture Woo doing that, but not you. You were always so . . . Landerish. And I simply cannot get over Jasper, now that I think about it. He looks and acts like a normal person. I'm sorry if this offends you, but it's the way I see it."

"A couple of rich stuffed shirts, eh? It's all true. I never wanted to be that person. I'm happy now with who I am, who my father has become, and glad that I'm in a position to do what I really want to do. I probably never would have done any of this if it wasn't for Woo. That guy has been such a positive influence in my life. I owe everything to him. I mean that sincerely. Now, what should we drink to?" Ross said, pouring the Burgundy into thick wineglasses.

"Freedom of choice, options, good friends, or all the above," Jory said, holding her glass aloft.

"To all of the above," Ross said, clicking his glass against hers.

After they drank, Ross asked curiously, "What are you going to do now that you've quit your job?"

"I've been thinking about going into business for myself. The one thing I did like about doing the column was working on my own, for myself, with no one breathing down my neck, issuing orders. I'm the first one to admit working at home is not ideal in many ways. I've made no friends, I haven't participated in community affairs at all. When I first came back I wanted to do some volunteer work at the children's hospital, but I couldn't find time. I can't continue to lead such a narrow existence. Before you know it, I'll wither and die on the vine." Jory smiled. "I don't know what kind of business I want to go into, if that's your next question. I plan to think about it from now till the first of the year. That's my personal deadline."

"I approve. In case it hasn't occurred to you, you will have a perfect base of operations if you go through with your plan to evict my mother. The whole damn building will be available to you. There's over twenty-five-thousand square feet of space, did you know that? There's space in the parking lot for seventy-five cars. It's a handsome piece of property, Jory. You aren't going to boot out the old gentlemen, are you?"

"Of course not. I like what you said. I'll think about it. Rent-free. I like that too." Jory smiled.

"I thought you would. Tell me, how is Woo doing? I haven't talked to him much lately. He's . . . different these days. He'll chat for a moment or two and then say he has to hang up. What the hell is he doing besides therapy? I have this feeling he's . . . avoiding me. Is anything wrong?"

Jory shrugged. "I haven't talked to him much myself. He seems to prefer being alone. He's getting around very well. Maybe you should drive out and see him. Surely there's a lot you have to discuss, with the New Year just weeks away. It's not good to be alone so much." Jory grimaced.

"Maybe he's starting to worry about getting back into the work harness. Let's not talk about Woo. Let's talk about *us*," Ross said, filling her wineglass a second time.

"Ross, there is no us."

"There should be. There could be. Why are you being so stubborn? Why won't you give me a second chance? I know in my gut you'd give one to Woo, to anyone else. Why am I so damn different? Now that I've been rehabilitated, what's not to like about me? Jesus, I don't beat up on little old ladies or children. I pay my taxes, I do pro bono work. I even go to church once in a while. I believe I'm a worthwhile person."

Jory leaned across the table. "Oh, you are, Ross. I'm so very proud of you and so grateful for the way you stepped in to help me. I'll never forget it," Jory said sincerely.

"Then what is it? What's wrong with me? I know you feel something for me, I can see it in your eyes, in your face. I'm not exactly ugly, and I don't smell. Jesus, I just don't understand," Ross complained.

Jory gulped at her wine. She held up her empty glass. Tears momentarily blurred her vision. "It's not you, Ross. It's me. Well, it's both of us. I don't know what I mean," she mumbled.

"If you'd tell me, maybe I can sort it out. I'm supposed to have this sharp, legal mind. Give me a chance to use it," he pleaded.

Jory gulped at the wine again. "I can't have children." There it was out, the words finally said aloud. She watched the piece of meatball on Ross's fork drop to his plate, saw the red sauce splatter against his white shirt, saw the look of horror on his face and knew it reflected her own expression. She jabbed at the ziti on her plate with such force the pasta skidded off, landing in the sugar bowl in the center of the table. She stabbed again, this time making contact with the ziti.

"You're blaming me," Ross said quietly.

"No. I did for a while. Blame isn't something we should be talking about. There were two of us. I haven't been able to reconcile it in my mind because I feel so terribly cheated. I always wanted a houseful of children. Men usually want children, sons especially, to carry on their name. Mothers want little girls to dress up in bonnets and little boys who look like their father. It's more like, why did God do that to me? I cannot explain it any better than that, Ross. I never would have told you if you hadn't . . . maybe it was the wine," Jory said miserably.

"All these years and you never said a word. You should have told me, Jory," Ross said tightly.

"Back then you didn't care. Later it was too difficult to talk about, and then when I came back here, it was worse. Talking about it doesn't help. Now you're going to blame yourself. It's not something either one of us should dwell on. We can't do anything about it."

"Are you sure? There are wonderful doctors out there making new advances every day," Ross said desperately.

Jory locked her gaze with Ross. "You don't understand, Ross. If you don't have the necessary body parts, it doesn't make any difference what kind of advances they make," Jory said sadly.

"Oh."

"I'm not really very hungry." Jory said. "Do you mind if we leave?"

"Yes. I mind. I think you owe it to me to let me try and make up for what you've gone through. You should have told me. I can't believe I wouldn't have tried to do something to ease your pain," Ross said.

"I didn't see it that way at the time, Ross. To show you how dumb and inexperienced I was, I thought, even after speaking with the doctor, things could be *fixed*. I was seventeen, what did I know? I try not to think about it, and for the most part I succeed, but then when I see you, it all comes back. I don't want it to be this way. I hate feeling like this, but that's the way it is."

Ross reached across the table to take her hands in his. "I'm so very sorry. I wish there was something I could say for both of us. Whatever it takes, I'll do."

"Too much, too little, too late, Ross," Jory said quietly.

"It doesn't matter to me that you can't have children. What I mean is, if we ever got married, it wouldn't matter. What I'm trying to say here is, I'd marry you in a heartbeat if you'd have me. I'm proposing. Will you marry me so we can live happily ever after?"

Jory forced a smile she didn't feel. "I'm flattered, Ross, but no. I admire what you're doing with your life, and I truly believe you respect me. Let's not tamper with what we have."

"Look me in the eye and tell me you don't feel something for me. Right in the eye, Jory, and tell me there can never be anything between us because once, a long time ago, we were two dumb people who didn't know what they were doing. I think that's stupid thinking on your part. I know I'm not a woman and don't think like a woman, but I think and feel and hurt just the way you do."

She sighed. "I have to leave, Ross."

"I can't let you drive back alone. You've had too much wine. Either come back to the house with me or I'll get you a hotel room. Barring that, you can sleep in the office and leave when you're sober. In case you haven't noticed, we've had two bottles of wine."

"The dogs—"

"You left food and the heat's on, so there's no problem. You'll clean the mess tomorrow and that will be the end of it. What's it to be?" Jesus, he felt like his eyes were crossing.

"Do you have a sofa in the office?" Jory asked, slurring her words.

"No. Just chairs."

"Then where would I sleep?"

Ross shrugged. "Sitting up in the chair. I have a picnic blanket in the trunk of my car. The floor? I'm not sure I'm in any condition to drive myself. I suppose we could sit up all night and drink coffee. There's a small kitchen at the office and we have plenty of coffee."

"Let's go back to the office. Maybe the cold air will sober us up. I'm not drunk, mind you, just . . . not moving on all cylinders."

Ross peeled some bills from his money clip and put them on the table. "Maybe you're not drunk, but I think I am. Come on, let's see if the cold air snaps us to attention."

Jory reared back. "I don't think I should go with you if you're drunk. I'll sit in the car until I feel well enough to make the trip home." She struggled into her coat. She wondered if she'd fall once she started to walk. A vision of herself facedown on linoleum on the restaurant floor flashed before her. She bolted from the tiny restaurant.

Ross took that moment to pluck the carnation from the bud vase on the table.

Outside in the cold air he looked at Jory solemnly for a second before he presented the lone flower to her. "You're as pretty as this flower," he said, enunciating each word carefully.

"Really, Ross! No one ever gave me flowers before. When we got married I bought my own bouquet of violets. Do you remember that?"

"No. Did you save them?"

"For a week or so, then I threw them away. I wish I'd saved them." They were walking now, holding onto each other, both of them shivering in the frigid air.

"You should have saved them," Ross mumbled.

Jory stopped and shook off his arm. Her fist shot upward. "Well, maybe I would have if you'd bought them for me, but since you didn't, I threw them away." Ross swaggered sideways, coming to rest against the lamp post.

"You hit me!"

"Damn right I hit you. You keep bringing up all this stuff. Stuff I don't want to remember, stuff that's too damn hard to deal with. You deserved it," she said, kicking him in the shins.

Ross yowled with pain. " 'Stuff' . . . you call it 'stuff'!" Ross yelled in outrage. He reached for her.

"Don't you dare touch me, you—you—"

"What? What am I? Ha! You can't even think of a word to describe what I am. That's because," he said, leering at her in the lamplight, "there's nothing bad to say about me. You're the one who isn't a nice person. You've been trampling on my emotions for years now, and you're going to keep on doing it. I can see it in your eyes. Go ahead, tell me it's not true," Ross bellowed.

"Shut up, Ross," Jory bellowed in return. "Jerk. Jerk is what you are. So there. You're a crud, a lousy crumb, is what you are. Were. Probably still are under that . . . that persona you're presenting to the world. You ruined my life and now you want to . . . what the hell is it you want, Ross?"

"You, goddamnit!"

"Ha! I'm not for sale. Once I was, and you got me cheap. For nothing. Then you threw me away!" Jory cried.

"Do you have to tell the whole damn world?" Ross hissed. "People are on the street, watching us. Don't you have any shame?"

"Don't you talk to me about shame, Ross Landers!" Jory shouted.

"You won't talk about anything else. What should we talk about? Get it through that stupid, dumb head of yours. I'm not like that anymore. Nothing is forever, Jory," Ross blustered.

"Oh no!" Jory's fist shot up a second time, landing square against Ross's left eye. "Well, I am damn well forever. I can't have children, so that's forever. Go ahead, you . . . jerk, stand there and tell me that isn't forever. Forever, Ross!" Jory yelled so shrilly, a cop on the corner meandered over, his nightstick tapping his leg as he walked.

"Now you've gone and done it. There's a cop heading our way," Ross grated.

Jory kicked him in the shins so hard her shoe fell off. The cop retrieved it and handed it to her.

"Is there a problem here? Mr. Landers, is that you?"

"Yes, it's me, officer. I seem to be having a difference of opinion here with my ex-wife."

"Ma'am?" the officer said, looking to Jory for clarification.

"The only part of what he said that's right is I am his ex-wife. The rest is a lie. We're having a . . . fight. We're settling an old problem. Don't interfere."

"Are you inebriated, Mrs. Landers?"

"Yes she is, and it's disgusting," Ross said virtuously. "I've been trying to quiet her down. I'm taking her back to the office."

"Take your disagreement indoors and keep it off the street or I'll have to run you in," the officer said sternly.

"I'm not Mrs. Landers. My name is Ryan. My father was Jake Ryan, the district attorney. Don't call me Mrs. Landers. I hate that name. I always hated that name. You don't have any right to call me Mrs. Landers. Tell him he doesn't have any right, Ross."

Ross rolled his eyes for the cop's benefit, as much as to say, See what I have to put up with. "Don't worry, officer, I'll take care of her." A moment later Jory was slung over his shoulder like a sack of flour.

"Put me down, Ross! Put me down this damn minute! Do you hear me? You're jiggling my stomach, I'm going to throw up if you don't. Ross, put me down!"

"Are you going to shut up?"

"Yes. Yes, just put me down."

"I can't stand a drunk woman," the officer said, taking one of Jory's arms. Ross took the other and between the two men they dragged Jory to the office doorway.

His shins burning with pain, his left eye swelling to twice its size, Ross said, "Why do you think we got divorced?" The cop nodded sagely as Ross unlocked the door. "Thanks for your help, officer. I'll see that she sleeps it off. Just because we're divorced doesn't mean I don't care what happens to her," he said virtuously.

"You stinking bastard," Jory screeched the moment the door closed.

"Just shut up. That cop could have dragged both of us down to the police station. I could have talked my way out of it, but they would have locked you up to sleep it off and you'd be in the morning papers. Now sit down in that fucking chair and don't move until I tell you to move. I have to put some ice on my eye and leg. I should paddle your rump good for this. I have to be in court tomorrow. This is all your fault, Jory."

"Ask me if I care. I don't care. A black eye is too good for you. I should have socked you in the other one so they matched," Jory snarled.

"I told you to shut up. Go make coffee. Everything's in the kitchen. I don't want to hear another word," Ross said menacingly.

"You told me not to move," Jory said sweetly. "Make up your stupid mind."

"Make the coffee! I'm keeping my eye on you so you don't get frisky with me. Take your coat off, it's warm in here. First thing you know, you'll catch a cold and blame that on me too. I like my coffee strong with just a little cream." Ross reached past her to remove the ice cube tray from the refrigerator. He yanked at the metal handle. Ice cubes showered upward to land on the floor. Jory laughed. She kept on laughing at the expression on Ross's face.

"Serves you right, smart aleck. Ohhh, I'm going to be sick."

"Jesus Christ!" Ross groaned as she rushed down the hallway to the bathroom. "You get it on the floor, you're cleaning it up!" he roared.

Ross leaned against the wall, his grin stretching from ear to ear as he listened to her retch. "That's an enriching vocabulary you have, Miss Ryan."

Silence. Then, "I'm going to kill you, Ross. First I'm going to blacken your other eye, then I'm going to cut off your . . . oh shit!"

"Tsk tsk tsk," Ross said, clucking his tongue. He headed back to the kitchen, where he measured coffee into the pot and gathered up the scattered ice cubes. He packed them into a dishcloth, slapping it against his eye. He was contemplating the pain in his leg when Jory tottered out to the kitchen. Ross stared at her with his good eye. "You look," he said searching for just the right words, "a mess."

"Shut up, Ross," Jory muttered, her eyes on the coffeepot.

"Let's call a truce here. I'm the one who's maimed and injured. I'm the one who has to appear before a judge tomorrow morning at eight-thirty. I'd think you could have a little compassion here. I also saved you from a night in jail. Let's start over. Let's talk about Woo or the weather. Better yet, let's talk about Christmas, it's just a few weeks away. Where are you going to get your tree this year? If you like, I can go with you to cut it down," Ross said generously.

Jory poured two cups of coffee. "I have no desire to discuss your friend or the weather," she said coldly. "I'll think about the tree part, but not tonight. You should keep toothbrushes in the bathroom."

"Why?"

Jory threw her hands in the air. "Because my mouth feels . . . awful. Toothpaste washes away the taste of the wine. If you had toothpaste, I could have swished it around in my mouth. Mouthwash would be good too."

"Shut up," Ross said wearily.

"I feel terrible," Jory said.

"Well, guess what, I don't feel like I could run the mile. Take a good look at me. Let's just sit here and drink our coffee."

"This coffee is too strong. I feel like my hair is standing on end." Ross laughed. "It is." He laughed again, to Jory's irritation.

"Well, your eye looks like a peanut butter and jelly sandwich. More grape than peanut butter. I hope you limp for a week."

"C'mere and kiss me," Ross whispered.

Jory's heart started to pound. "Why would you want to kiss someone whose hair is on end and looks like a racoon?" she asked.

"Because I love you. I don't care how you look. I don't care if you can't have children. I don't care about anything but you. And don't tell me it's too late. It's never too late if you're willing to set aside past differences and move forward. I told you before, I'll do whatever it takes to convince you. I'll work at it for the rest of my life. I mean it, Jory."

He sounded so sincere. Her heart was pounding so hard in her chest she was sure Ross could hear it. What would it be like to be in his arms, to make love with him here on the floor in the office? Would it be as wonderful as she always imagined it would be? Would she be able to let go of all her inhibitions, all the hurt she had stored inside of her? And when it was all over, then what? She took a tentative step and then another. Ross reached for her hand, fearful she would change her mind. She sat down next to him on the kitchen bench, her hand still in his. The ice cubes scattered a second time.

"Do you believe me when I tell you I love you and want to marry you?" Ross whispered against her cheek. She nodded. "Tell me how you feel about me."

"I don't know, Ross. I'm afraid of you, of what you can do to me. I can't help it if I keep remembering . . . I don't want to be hurt again. I don't ever want to go through that again. Maybe what you think you feel for me is . . . lust. That's not good enough for a lifetime together."

"Oh, I feel lust all right, but that's not why I love you. Well, part of it. I just want to be with you. I want to see you in the morning when I wake up. I want to eat breakfast across from you. I want us to walk the dogs together and play with them after dinner. I want to be the one to cut down the Christmas tree and help trim it, to put the angel on top. I want to hand out the presents under the tree. I want to be the one to make you smile. I swear, I'll never make you cry, Jory. I'll take care of you if you get sick. I'll stay home from work and make a mustard plaster for you. I want to be part of your life. Please, think about it with an open mind. I have all the time in the world. I'll wait forever if it takes that long. But do me a favor."

"What?" Jory whispered.

"Invite me for Christmas."

"Okay. I'll think about everything you said."

Ross put his arms around her shoulder to draw her close to him. She didn't resist.

They talked all night long, often seriously, though at other times silliness overcame both of them and they laughed together. The intimacy she'd always hungered for was there. She could feel it.

"It's getting light out, Ross, I have to leave," Jory said a long time later.

"Me too. I have to go back to the house and get fresh clothes. I keep saying I'm going to bring a stack of clean shirts, but I always forget. How does my eye look?"

"Awful. Do you really know how to make mustard plaster?"

"Yes. Woo told me how to do it. He made one for me. I swear that's how I got better last year before . . . before you had the accident. Woo's in love with you, but then I guess you already know that. I'm jealous. I imagine all kinds of things. It's none of my business, I know. I had to say it out loud."

"Do you feel better now that you said it?" Jory asked quietly.

"No," Ross replied, getting up. "I think you're right, I'm going to limp for a week. Aren't you going to wash your face?"

Jory laughed. "With what? There's no soap in the bathroom. I'll see you later, Ross. Saturday is good for me, if you want to go with me to get the Christmas tree."

"What time?"

Jory shrugged. "Come for breakfast and we'll go from there."

"All right," Ross said, helping her on with her coat. He kissed her lightly on the tip of her nose. "I meant every single thing I said last night. By Saturday I'll think of a lot more. Should we ask Woo to go with us?"

"No. Just you and me. 'Bye, Ross. I'm not sorry about the black eye and your shins."

"I know, but I forgive you anyway. Drive carefully."

"I will." She didn't look back.

Chapter 16

Gravel spurted upward as the tires of the station wagon crunched to a halt. The moment Jory opened the car door, she could hear the dogs barking by the back door. Guilt rushed through her. She'd take them for a long walk the minute she brushed her teeth and washed her face. She didn't look to the left or the right or toward the carriage house as she hurried up the back steps to the porch. A moment later she was inside, scrooched down with the dogs, hugging and crooning softly.

Across the yard in the carriage house Woo watched Jory climb the steps to the back porch. All night he'd watched for her return, wishing for a key to let the dogs out. It wasn't like Jory to stay away all night. Not that it was any of his business. He wanted to stomp his way over to the house, to demand to know where she was, *who* she'd spent the night with. Demand to know *details*.

He needed to know where she had been. And when he needed to know something, he asked. He was out in the driveway, walking slowly, when Jory emerged from the house, the dogs on their leashes. He was feeling belligerent, and his heart felt sore when she stopped long enough to say "Good morning" in a voice so neutral that he winced.

"You're up early," he said carefully. "Were the dogs upset last night? They kept barking. I suppose there was a cat or maybe a squirrel in the yard."

He didn't think it possible for her voice to sound even more neutral and bland, but it did. "I hope they didn't keep you awake."

"I couldn't sleep, so it didn't matter."

"Then why did you mention it?"

"To make conversation. I don't understand what happened. One minute things were . . . wonderful, and the next minute you acted like . . . it didn't mean anything. I guess I just wanted to understand. If it was just to pass the time, just to make me feel good about myself, then tell me that. If I did something, if I said something, tell me."

"It meant a great deal," Jory said, bending down to untangle the dogs' leashes from around her ankles. "I waited for you to come over, to call, to make some kind of move."

"When you came in that evening from walking the dogs, you acted like I was there to pay the rent. Sometimes I'm not too astute. I figured you were already regretting making love with me, so I went home. Then when you didn't come over or call, I figured my theory was right. I know you didn't come home last night. The house was dark, so that's not exactly a brilliant deduction on my part. The dogs did bark, though. I thought something happened to you, and then I decided you were with Ross. You were, weren't you?"

Jory bent to untangle the leashes again. "Where I was last night is not your concern. I'll share something with you, Pete. I quit my job yesterday, and in just a bit I have to head for town because the sheriff is going to evict Mrs. Landers. I have to walk these dogs." She raced off, the dogs yipping and yapping happily.

Woo returned to the carriage house, his shoulders slumped, his face full of misery. He made two phone calls, the first to Arthur to cancel his therapy, the second to his parents. "I'm leaving as soon as I get my things together," he told them. "I'll stay till New Year's. No, Ross won't be with me this year."

The second thing he did was write a note to Jory that he would put in her mailbox on the way out. As he wrote, scratched out, erased, he wondered if it was possible for someone his size to have a broken heart. He decided it was possible when he signed his name to the note.

Dear Jory,

I've gone to Lancaster to spend the holidays with my family. I turned the thermostat to 65 degrees. If you get a severe cold spell, the pipes won't freeze. Feel free to use any of the food in my refrigerator if you want.

If you see Ross, wish him a Merry Christmas for me. I tried calling the office, but his secretary said he was in court.

Have a wonderful holiday, and I'll see you after the first of the year.

Pete

Now he wasn't sure what he should do with the gift he'd bought on his excursion to town with Arthur in his new van. It wasn't much, more a remembrance than anything else. Jory was probably going to think the four little pewter dogs clustered around a Christmas tree was silly and tacky. He'd thought it endearing when he picked it up. "What the hell, so she'll laugh and I'll never know about it," he muttered.

His suit for Midnight Mass in a garment bag and one carryall of underwear and assorted day clothes was all he was taking with him. On his last trip to the van he carried the small gift-wrapped package and the note. He slid them into the mailbox and raised the red flag.

"Merry Christmas," he whispered.

Justine Landers looked around her room, which had never been called anything but a boudoir. It looked, Jasper had said at one time, like something in an expensive cat house. Looking at it now, Justine thought it was one of his more astute judgments. "Tacky" was probably a better word. Maybe sleazy or cheap. Whatever the hell it was, it was giving her nightmares, had been giving her nightmares for months now. When she was able to sleep, that is, which wasn't much of late. Mostly she spent her nights drinking coffee or pacing, or drinking brandy and pacing.

She was pacing now, a coffee cup in her hand. Twice the coffee slopped down between her breasts. She looked down at the chantilly lace on her peignoir and shuddered. Damn, she even spilled some of the coffee over the feathery tendrils on her mules. She kicked them off as she ripped at her negligee. She sat naked on the small satin bedroom chair, contemplating her past and her future.

At some point she was going to be literally out in the cold. Evicted. Unwanted. Where was she to go? To the warehouse where *Keyhole* was printed? Her eviction would probably be in tomorrow's paper. Already, half the city of Philadelphia was out of business. In the past six months she'd personally ruined so many politicians and bigwigs, she'd lost count. God, how she'd loved it when they came sniveling to her offices begging her, promising her anything not to print *their* story. Some of them had even given her juicy stories about their colleagues just to get out from under. She'd accepted money. She hated the word "bribe," but that's what it was. She'd taken the bribes and the stories, banked the money, and then a month or so later, when the politician was breathing easier, printed the story she'd promised to withhold. Payback time.

By God, she sold magazines, though.

One of her few remaining reporters had tipped her yesterday that the sheriff was on his way. The same reporter had called her again last night. He'd signed off by saying he expected five hundred dollars more in his paycheck at the end of the week. She'd agreed. What would happen if she wasn't at the office at nine o'clock? Did she dare call Ross and ask him? The Landers Building was supposed to be hers. Ross had screwed things up and then tried to make her appear stupid by saying, "If you wanted the building, you should have asked for the building. You asked for *TIF* and you got it. Don't be greedy." But she was greedy. She had every right in the world to be greedy. She loved seeing all those zeros in her various bank accounts.

It occurred to her then, for the first time, that she could buy a building. But she would lose weeks, months, until the deal was finalized. She'd long ago negated the idea that anyone would rent to her, not with every politician in the city gunning for her. When one of her reporters said the fix was in, she didn't know what it meant until he explained it. No, renting was something she could not do.

All she had to do was pay the money to Marjory Ryan, as much as it galled her to do so. All she needed was one more month.

Naked, Justine padded over to the Victorian desk she'd gotten at an auction. She hated the desk, but it matched the ruffles and frills she adored. Maybe it was time to think about redecorating. Time to think about a lot of things, like all the pending lawsuits she was involved in. She struggled with the bottom drawer of her desk until it opened. Stacked haphazardly were complaints and summonses. District Court, Civil Court, Federal Court. Nine different lawsuits with nine different lawyers representing her. She wrote a check to one or the other of them every day. Her response to all complaints filed against her, and to the nine different lawyers, had been and still was to threaten, cajole, stress the First Amendment, and if that didn't bring results, tell all those other lawyers she'd attack with a vengeance and print another story worse than the first one. She knew she was in very hot water, because all nine lawyers said so. She rifled through the stacks of complaints, trying to calculate the vast amount of money she was being sued for. She'd done it once before in the middle of the night when she couldn't sleep, and the amount had been so staggering she'd gone downstairs and drank half a bottle of brandy. If even two of the suits went against her, she'd lose everything. The following morning she'd used an adding machine to be sure she hadn't made a mistake. Two days later she'd been on a plane to the Cayman Islands, where she kept a bank account.

Justine swore then. What were all these people going to get from her? Nothing but judgments. Jasper had never, in all the years of their marriage, put anything in her name. She personally owned nothing except her car. *TIF* had no accessible assets, she'd made sure of that. As fast as the money came in, it went back out. Operating funds and lawyers' fees were all she kept in the business account.

One of the more bitter, adamant plaintiffs was trying to seize *TIF.* And, according to the attorney, he might well succeed. So maybe she should vacate the premises at nine o'clock when the sheriff arrived. At best, she could get out three more issues before the ax fell. Three issues would net her, if she went with the stories she planned, at least $800,000. More like $1.1 million. With what she had deposited in foreign accounts, plus the three weeks' net, she could live in splendor for the rest of her life.

Could the authorities extradite her? She'd been afraid to ask. First they'd have to find her. She thought of Jasper then. Was there a way to gouge money out of him? Of course there was. He'd do anything to keep the Halvorsens' name out of print. She'd been saving the judge and his wife for just the right moment. How much would Jasper pay? A lot, she decided.

Justine's eyes fell on a thick manila envelope with the name Q. T. Investigations stamped in the corner. She'd paid handsomely for the contents of the envelope, because Quentin Thomas, the private detective, said he would have to put all his other cases on hold if she wanted the information in thirty-six hours. Not that she'd acted on the information. Coward that she was, she hadn't gone to see her parents or any of her brothers and sisters. But she had pictures now. Pictures she looked at almost every day. A good psychiatrist would probably say she was obsessed with the photos. Maybe she was. But then again, maybe she wasn't. She liked the word "curious" better than the word "obsessed."

Justine looked at the onyx clock on her dressing table. She had enough time to look at the photos again and still make the office at nine o'clock. She kept the pictures in order, her mother, her father, and then the oldest to the youngest of her siblings. Then all the nieces and nephews. All told, she had forty photographs. The first two pictures were of her parents and her oldest sister, Mary Ellen. She'd cried in the privacy of her room when she saw Mary Ellen's picture. The prettiest of all the girls, Mary Ellen was now crippled with arthritis and in a wheelchair. The nieces and nephews of all ages were dressed neatly, but poorly. Candid shots with a zoom lens didn't show clear features, but she could see the family resemblance in each black and white snapshot. The pictures of her parents were the ones that left her the most fearful. The camera captured them as they were leaving the church, her mother holding onto her father's arm. They looked so old, dressed in their best, her mother with a kerchief on her head, her father carrying his fedora.

Justine wiped away the tears to stare at the elaborate furnishings in her bedroom. The cost of the lace spread and fancy flounces on the imported draperies could have supported her parents for at least three years. She looked at her mother's feet, at the black-laced ox-fords with the one-inch heel. She knew they would pinch her feet, give her blisters and corns, but she'd wear them one day a week to church no matter what. At home her mother had always gone bare-foot, because she had flat feet and hated shoes. The only time she remembered seeing anything on her mother's feet was when one woman she ironed for gave her a pair of men's slippers. She'd worn them till they wore out, and even then she'd put cardboard over the inner soles and kept on wearing them. Justine looked across the room at the feathered mules. One hundred twenty-five dollars, and she was going to throw them in the trash because she'd spilled cof-fee on them.

She held the photos of her parents against her bare chest. "I'm sorry, Mama. Maybe it's better I didn't go to see you and the others. You would be so ashamed of me. You'd go to church and pray for me, saying prayers better said for someone else." The photos went back into the brown envelope. A moment later she opened the middle drawer of the desk and withdrew Ross's law school gradua-tion picture. She slipped it into the envelope. Her family. She slammed the drawer shut with the palm of her hand so hard, one of her nails broke against the brass pull.

A packet of photos, millions of dollars in foreign banks, and a heart full of misery. That was all she had.

Things could be worse, she thought on her way to the ornate marble bathroom. I could be poor. She turned on the gold faucet, remembering the tin tub her mother used to bathe her in. She and Mary Ellen in the same tub. In the same water, the same washcloth, the same towel. The soap had been hard and brown and smelled like disinfectant. Justine sprinkled fragrant bath crystals under the gushing water. The soap was perfumed, the same scent as the bath crystals. Imported. The thick, extra large towels were a far cry from the threadbare towels that hung on the back of the door in the shack she'd grown up in.

"You have no right to be ashamed of me," she said aloud. "None of you had any gumption, any wish to better yourselves. I did. You were all content to make excuses, to simply exist and to depend on public welfare to take care of you. You have no damn right being ashamed of me. None at all. Damn you. Damn the whole bunch of you."

Her bath was a quick one, little more than a dunking. She dressed quickly and carefully in a navy blue suit with a flared skirt that swished about her knees. Her blouse was high-necked and silk, perfect for the single strand of pearls she slipped over her head. She added pearl studs to her ears and powder to her nose, instead of the pancake makeup she usually wore. She peered at herself in the mirror, her breath catching in her throat. She swore she was looking at a younger version of her mother. The thought didn't exactly displease her, but it did bother her.

If ever anyone was prepared to be evicted, she was that person.

At exactly two minutes to nine Justine Landers walked through the front doors of the Landers Building. She didn't bother with the elevator, preferring the steps. She wasn't in the least surprised to see the sheriff and Jory sitting in the reception room, each of them reading the latest issue of *TIF.* She allowed a small smile to play around the corners of her month.

"Sheriff, and you must be Marjory," Justine said coolly as she held out her hand to receive the eviction notice. "My staff and I will be out of here by four o'clock. Will that be satisfactory?"

The sheriff looked at Jory. Jory nodded.

"Mrs. Landers, would you like to discuss this?" Jory asked. "Perhaps we can come to terms, make a new agreement. If the rent is too high, I can lower it. I didn't set the terms. You need to know I never asked for or wanted this building. Jasper . . . Jasper just did it. I believe it's part of some kind of trust or something. I don't want to evict you. Truly I don't. I'd like us to sit down and talk about it."

"You turned into a very pretty young woman, Marjory," Justine replied. "My instincts tell me Ross was a fool for divorcing you. He's incredibly handsome, don't you think?" she asked dryly.

"Yes he is, and thank you for the compliment. It was a compliment, wasn't it?" Jory said, puzzled.

"Yes, it was, dear. I don't think what Jasper did was right. And because of that I couldn't pay you the rent. It no longer matters what his reasons were or still are. I am a Landers by right of marriage, and by that right, even though Jasper has filed for a legal separation, I am not paying *any* rent. You may have this building. It's more than kind of you to want to discuss or negotiate new terms. If you think about it, I believe you'll understand my position. If you don't, let me repeat it. It is unfair and I refuse to pay one dime. My secretary probably has coffee on by now, would either you or the sheriff like a cup?"

The sheriff looked at Jory. "Do you want me to oversee Mrs. Landers . . . the removal of office property. . . ?"

"I won't be taking anything but the files, Sheriff," Justine said coolly. I understand Marjory's rights as well as my own. You are, of course, welcome to stay. I guess that means neither one of you want coffee."

"No thank you," Jory said.

"I'll check back at the end of the day, Miss Ryan," the sheriff said.

"Will there be anything else?" Justine asked coolly.

"Do you have a place to go, Mrs. Landers?" Jory asked.

"Yes. To a very cold, drafty warehouse. But that's not your concern. I hope you find a good tenant. By the way, how is your Auntie Ann column doing?" Justine asked slyly.

Jory's eyebrows shot upward. "You know about that?"

"Of course, since the day after that column appeared, when you said something sarcastic about *TIF.* You can get that kind of information if you're willing to pay for it. If memory serves me correctly, it cost us two hundred dollars. The recipient was the personnel director of the *Democrat.*"

"But Ross said if you found out, you'd . . . crucify me and the paper. Why didn't you?"

"Crucify you? You never did anything to me, Marjory. Whatever was between you and Ross had nothing to do with me. All of us make mistakes at one time or another during our lives. It helps if you're wise enough to correct them. If not, you learn to live with those mistakes. I've certainly made my share."

"Stay!" Jory blurted out. "I can't put you out on the street."

Justine snorted. "And here I've been thinking you're one smart cookie. That's not good business on your part. But thank you anyway. If I tell you something in confidence, can I depend on you not to repeat it to *anyone*?"

Jory thought about the question for a full minute before she nodded.

"Come with me, we'll have coffee while I start my packing."

Justine poured coffee into two fragile cups. She handed one to Jory. Instead of drinking hers, Justine opened the wall safe and pulled out duplicate copies of her complaints and summonses. "These represent lawsuits. Against me, against *TIF*. If they go to court, they could wipe me out. I have three more issues to publish, and then I'm going to . . . there's an expression: take it on the lam."

Jory burst out laughing. Justine joined her. "I really am. This sleazy magazine was my way of getting back at every single person who ever put me down, wronged me, insulted me, and talked about me behind my back. I was never good enough for Jasper's crowd of friends. I didn't have the finesse, the polish. I wasn't Main Line Philadelphia, whatever the hell that's supposed to be. It's just another way of saying I was from the wrong side of the tracks, I suppose. I tried to fit in, tried to teach myself, because Jasper couldn't be bothered to help me. I swore one day I would get even. You know that old saying, 'Don't get mad, get even.' I took *TIF*, ostensibly to do exposés on movie stars, starlets, and anyone else in filmland that would make good reading. I planned to gradually work into the last few months of . . . what you were reading in the reception area. I took all those people who hurt me, and I hurt them back by exposing their insidious little secrets, and they did have secrets. They groveled, Marjory. I had seeds, nuggets of information, and built on that. I felt so powerful when they came here pleading with me. Sometimes the men sent their wives, who would show me pictures of their children and beg me not to ruin them.

I turned a deaf ear to all of them. I got even. As I said, I have three more issues, and then I'll be out of everyone's life."

"Where will you go, Justine?" Jory pointed to the pile of legal papers on the desk. "Will they be able to make you come back?"

"I certainly hope not." She sipped at her coffee. "No one knows about this but you, Marjory. I don't know why I'm telling you. I think it's because you have guts."

"Mrs. Landers," Jory said, "maybe you should talk to Ross. He's a fine attorney. He might be able to help you. You'll be in . . . exile."

Justine turned her back to pour more coffee into the cup. "In a sense, I've been in exile a good deal of my life," she said wistfully. "I don't expect you to understand. The fact that I finally understand is all that's important. More coffee, Marjory? Ross can't help me," she went on, "but you're right, he's a fine attorney." She smiled again. "If my sources are right, Jasper has turned into a worthwhile human being."

"Justine, if you want to stay on here one more month until you publish your next three issues, it's all right with me," Jory said generously. God, did she just say that? "I take it the last three issues are the most important."

"How did you guess? What will you do now that you have no job?"

"I've been thinking about going into business for myself. I have these four dogs, you see. I need to be self-employed, where my hours are my own. Ross managed to get me a very handsome settlement from my accident last year. I'd like to use it to start up something."

"Why not start up your own magazine? Everything is right here. I can leave it for you. I did it on my own, so you can too." Justine smiled. "Maybe this is fate."

"You'd do that for me?" Jory asked, astonished.

"Why not? You never did anything to me. As I recall, you were always nice to me back in those early days. I more or less thought of you as a brainless twit with good manners."

"And I more or less thought of you as a woman with brass balls."

Both women convulsed in laughter.

"Do you want to stay on?" Jory asked.

"Why the hell not? If I have to take off suddenly, will you clean up the debris I leave behind?"

"Why the hell not?" Jory said, sticking out her hand.

Justine reached for it. "You'll look out for Ross?"

It was a question Jory wasn't prepared for. She shook her head. "No promises."

Justine smiled. "I accept that."

"Can I ask you a personal question, Justine?"

"You can ask it, but that doesn't mean I'm going to answer it."

"Did you love Ross? Do you love him now?"

Justine sat down, the china cup in her hand, refilled for the fourth time. "I was afraid to love him, afraid he'd hurt me the way . . . yes, in my own way I do. I wanted Ross to grow up independent and . . . tough. You need to be tough as steel to survive in this world. I didn't want him to turn out like Jasper. I didn't want him to turn out like me either. All those affairs and functions he said I never went to . . . I was there, he just didn't see me because I didn't want to be seen. When he had his appendix out, I was there too. Of course it was the middle of the night after Jasper and his amour left. I sat with him till it got light out and then left. Does that answer your question?"

"Yes, it does. Maybe you should think about telling Ross how you feel."

"And maybe you should think about minding your own business, Marjory. Ross will be fine. He has Jasper now. I don't plan to worry about him." Her voice was not unkind.

"I wish you luck, Justine. Brainless twit, huh?"

Justine grimaced. "Marjory . . ." she said hesitantly.

"Yes."

"Don't think—this is going to come out of left field—I mean, you came here to evict me, and here I am—we are—talking like we like each other. I'd like to tell you about a dream of mine. Do you have a few minutes?" she asked.

"I have all day, Justine," Jory said gently.

"Hear me out. I'm not an educated woman. I think that's why I went into the exposé end of publishing. I didn't trust myself.

Sleazy journalism I understood, and then there was that get-even thing I had to clear out of the way. I did some stupid things I'm going to have to pay for. I'm digressing here. . . . What I wanted to do was start up a magazine, a really first-class operation for the older woman, women like myself. I tried to talk to Jasper about it, but he told me I was crazy. He told me it would cost millions to do what I wanted. He took great pleasure in telling me no one wanted to read about over-the-hill women. I didn't believe that then and I don't believe it now. But at the time I didn't have the financing. I have it now, but circumstances . . . these," she said, tapping the piles of legal papers, "are raining on my parade.

"I've always been a reader, all the trashy magazines, even the good ones. Everything is geared to young women like yourself. As women grow older, they tend to be forgotten. I personally take that as a grievous insult. If you believe what you read, life is over the moment you reach thirty-nine. I wanted to take a shot at proving all those people wrong. I spent a lot of time working up numbers, and Jasper was right, it would be very expensive to start something like that. I have everything right here in this folder. If you . . . you're young, but if you want . . . God, you know how to write, you have a college education . . . it would be yours, I'd just put up the money. If you agree with me that there is a need for such a magazine. Maybe I'm ahead of my time, but I don't think so. Will you at least think about it?"

"Justine . . . I don't know what to say," Jory replied. "I know what you're saying, I even understand it, but are you just going on instinct here, gut feelings?" At Justine's nod, she continued, "You should do some test marketing, hire someone to do some market research. That's not something I feel I can do. I don't have that much money. What if it doesn't sell?"

"It probably won't at first. Any new business needs a year, maybe two, before it gets off the ground. I've allowed for all of that in my business plan," Justine said proudly.

"You have a business plan?" Jory said stupidly.

"More or less. I told you I had numbers. It's my own version of a business plan." She waved her hands, airily dismissing the money end of things. "What do you think of my dream? Do you think older women would be interested in buying a magazine that tells them they're worthwhile and not second-class citizens? I hesitate to mention this, but one day you're going to be thirty-nine. You could do articles on what happens to women when their husbands die. How to cope, who handles their finances . . . who takes charge of things. I'd like to see articles about *wrinkles*. Women taking charge of their lives."

In spite of herself, Jory wanted to know more. "Why me, Justine? I came here to evict you, and here you are . . . my God, we must both be insane."

"Probably. You didn't evict me, though, did you? You . . . are more like me than you know, Marjory. I'm just sorry we didn't take the time to get to know one another before this."

"I'm sorry too, Justine." Jory realized she meant it. She really liked this vulnerable-looking woman. "What I don't know about magazine publishing will fill a book . . . but if you're really serious, I'll do it. I don't have to think about it."

"I knew I was right about you," Justine said happily. "Brass balls, eh?"

Jory laughed, a genuine sound of amusement. "Only a twit like myself, with her own set, would do what I've just promised to do. I'll see you around, Justine."

"I'd like that, but don't wait too long. There is every possibility I could end up in jail. How would that look? 'Older woman behind bars.' I'm sure there's an article in that somewhere."

Jory laughed all the way out to the reception area, to the elevator, and down to the first floor. She was still laughing when she got behind the wheel of her car.

"Why do I feel like we just did this a few days ago?" Jory said, standing back to admire the angel on top of the tree.

"It does seem like that, doesn't it? It's been a hell of a year for all of us. I think, and this is just my opinion, that next year is going to be the best yet. Jory, I want you to marry me."

"This *is* just like last year. Let's not spoil anything, Ross." Her heart was pounding. What was wrong with her? Why did she always draw back, refuse to acknowledge Ross's feelings? Her own too. For so long she wanted nothing but Ross Landers, wanted to hear the words he was now repeating on almost a weekly basis. He was definitely a good catch, as they said. He was handsome as sin and he was *nice*. He was also a good friend, and if one started out with friendship, according to the slick magazines, marriage had a chance of succeeding. Her tongue felt thick in her mouth. She reached for her glass of wine and sipped at it, her eyes on Ross atop the ladder.

"Is that a yes or a no? I'll settle for a maybe. If there's someone else in your life, tell me."

How miserable he looks, Jory thought. How unhappy. If she were to nod her head even slightly, he would smile.

"If there is or isn't, it doesn't concern you, Ross. Are we going to dwell on this now?"

"I'm not giving up," Ross said, coming down from the ladder.

Jory smiled. She allowed him to kiss her, and it was as wonderful as all his other kisses. She said so, to Ross's amusement.

"And now for the *pièce de résistance*, or however you say it," Ross said, whipping out the macaroni wreath he'd made the year before. He pretended to study the tree, holding up the little wreath against first one branch and then the other. "Aha, right here in front. Perfect!" he chortled.

"It does add something," Jory laughingly admitted. "Quick, turn out the lights so we can see it in all its splendor," she ordered.

"Ahhh," Ross said.

"Ooohh," Jory said.

The dogs barked in unison.

A long time later Ross said, "What's that little package under the tree?"

"It's my first present. Woo left it in my mailbox before he went to Lancaster."

"I didn't think he was going to go home this year," Ross mused as he stared at the present beneath the tree. "I guess he just wanted to try out the van and be on his own. He's been dependent on too many people this past year. New Year's is a big milestone for him. It's going to be great working with him again. I've really missed him." Ross watched Jory carefully. "I wish he'd find some nice girl and fall in love and get married. Woo is perfect husband and father material. He's just so damn shy when it comes to women."

Jory snorted. "I find that almost impossible to believe with you in the wings. Casanova himself, meaning you. Didn't any of that rub off on Pete?" Jory said lightly.

"Not on Woo. He takes it all very seriously. Don't go getting the wrong idea here, I take it seriously myself. Woo is . . . deathly afraid of rejection. He thinks he's big and ugly, and now he's . . . lame. If somebody loved him, they'd love him for the person he is. Don't you agree?"

"Absolutely, and Ross, I know what you're trying to do here, so just stop it. It's time for you to leave, isn't it? You did tell me to remind you when it was eleven o'clock. It's five minutes past eleven. Time for me to walk the dogs."

"So it is. Am I being invited for Christmas? I'm only asking because my father asked me. If you have other plans . . . or if it's too much bother . . . or if you're going away, say to Lancaster . . ."

"Will you stop it, Ross? If you and your father want to come for dinner, consider yourselves invited. I think I should tell you I invited your mother. Do you and your father still want to come?"

Ross's jaw dropped. "*You* invited my mother *here*? For God's sake, why? I still don't understand why she's still in the building. You get yourself into a flap, hire a lawyer, involve the sheriff and take up the taxpayers' time, and then change your mind. If she's coming, then we'll decline your invitation," Ross said sourly.

"You more or less invited yourself, Ross. It's not necessary for you to know my business. I don't have to report my affairs to you. Furthermore, I can invite whomever I damn well please to my house."

"She's going to hate these dogs. She's never happy with the food that's served to her, she never takes wine or flowers to the hostess, and she hates Christmas," Ross snarled.

"Perhaps. I'll find a way to muddle through. If you change your mind, let me know. I find it rather curious how close you and Jasper have become. There was a time when you couldn't stand him.

Then, all of a sudden, you changed your mind. You call him Dad, you go to dinner and the club with him, and you went fishing together. He works for you. I think it's wonderful that you're both making new lives and you've come to some . . . agreement about the past. Why haven't you done that with your mother? You gave your father a second chance, why can't you give your mother one?"

"Because she doesn't deserve one," Ross said bitterly.

"You want to know something I've found out the past seven years, Ross? There are two sides to everything. As a lawyer I would think you'd be aware of that. In law don't they say there's three sides—both sides and then the truth. Something like that. Hatred is like a dreaded disease," Jory said quietly.

"Now that's funny coming from you, Jory. Isn't hatred right up there with forgiveness?"

"Don't be nasty, Ross, it doesn't become you. I said I forgave you. I also said I couldn't forget. There's a difference. 'Night, Ross. Thanks for helping me trim the tree."

The moment the door closed behind Ross, Jory's breath exploded in a sound so loud the dogs ran for cover. They peeked at her from behind the corner of the chair. "I don't know what possessed me to say that," she moaned. "I feel like there's a devil perched on my shoulder these days." The dogs ran to her, circling her feet until she snapped her fingers. "Leashes. On the double!"

The walk was short and uneventful, to Jory's relief. The moment they were back indoors by the fire, Jory reached for her address book next to the phone. Maybe she'd be less of a liar if she called now, even though it was almost midnight.

The phone rang seven times before Jory heard Justine's voice on the other end of the wire. "Justine, it's Marjory. I'm sorry to be calling so late. If this is a bad time, I can call you tomorrow."

"Not at all. I go to bed late. Is something wrong?"

"No. I'm calling you to . . . I know how you feel about . . . holidays. I'd like to invite you to my house for dinner on Christmas, if you aren't busy."

"I have no other plans, Marjory." Justine's voice turned hesitant when she said, "Are you sure you want me to come? I'm not exactly popular these days. Are you having other guests?"

"I didn't invite anyone else. Ross more or less invited himself and Jasper, but when I told him I was inviting you, he declined. I hope that doesn't hurt your feelings, Justine."

"I have the hide of a buffalo," Justine said quietly.

"I think you want to believe you have the hide of a buffalo," Jory replied gently. "You don't have to pretend with me, Justine."

"That's a relief," Justine said, her voice catching on the last word. "What time do you want me to come out?"

"I'm up with the birds. You can come anytime. I'll put the turkey in around eight o'clock and we'll eat around two, if that's all right with you. Ah, Justine, do you like turkey?"

"Very much. I probably like the stuffing more than the turkey. I eat most anything."

"One other thing, Justine, I have four dogs. They aren't big. They're like a mini herd when they move all at once. They're very lovable. If you don't like animals, I can put them upstairs."

"No, no. I don't actually like or disdain animals. I never had a pet of any kind. It's possible they won't like me. Please don't lock them up on my account. I'll adapt."

Jory laughed. "Is that a smile I hear in your voice, Justine?"

"I believe it is, Marjory. There hasn't been much to smile about of late. I appreciate the invitation. I think I'm being truthful when I say the last *real* invitation I had was some nineteen years ago, and it was a half-assed one, to say the least." Jory laughed again.

"Then I guess I'll see you whenever you get here. Come early so you can admire my tree."

"Will noon be too early?"

"That's perfect. Justine, you're welcome to stay the night if you like. It'll seem more like Christmas if you stay. It's up to you."

Justine giggled. "You mean a slumber party?"

"Sure."

"I might do that."

"Justine, how is everything going?"

"You don't want to know. At least not now. You didn't say anything to Ross did you?"

"No, of course not."

"Good night, Marjory."

" 'Night, Justine."

Chapter 17

Justine checked the diamond-studded watch on her wrist. The time was 10:45. Christmas Eve. She was going to Midnight Mass at Holy Trinity Church, the church her parents and her sister attended. She took off the watch, her earrings, and her rings. She was dressed simply in a caramel-colored dress and dark brown walking shoes. On her head she wore a navy-blue scarf that matched her dark blue coat. Her car keys went into one pocket, money and driver's license into the other. She had no rosary or prayer book, but she knew how to pray on her fingers so it didn't matter.

The church was in South Philadelphia, thirty minutes away. If she didn't run into traffic, she would be in time to get a seat in the back of the church so she could watch the parishioners as they entered. All she wanted was to see her parents and Mary Ellen. In the trunk of her car were ten gift-wrapped shoe boxes she planned to drop off at her parents' home when she left the church. Hopefully, ahead of her parents.

During the past week she'd driven the route she planned to take this evening dozens of times. By now she knew every traffic light, where to turn to avoid other lights, and her timing was so accurate that she was only off a minute or so each time she made her dry run. For the millionth time she wished she'd done what she was about to do sooner.

Justine drove carefully, her eyes on the road, not wanting to make any mistakes. One mistake and she would be late and her plan wouldn't work. And she had to get a good parking space in front of the church so she could leave immediately after mass to make it to her parents' home without being seen.

Justine turned up the volume on the radio. Christmas carols. "Oh Come, All Ye Faithful." She hummed along under her breath, tears blurring her vision when "Silent Night" was played. "Play 'Jingle Bells,'" she pleaded, her eyes starting to ache with strain. She thought about the shoe boxes in the trunk that she'd wrapped with shiny green paper and tied with huge yellow ribbons. Don't think about the last Christmas before you left the shack, she told herself. Don't think about the wieners and canned sweet potatoes mixed with rice so it would stretch far enough to feed us all. Don't think about the faces on the little ones when they woke and there was no tree or presents, and no breakfast either. Don't think about that. Don't think about little Billy's face or Mimi's tear-filled eyes. Don't think about the lies, the bare table, the ironing your mother had to do on Christmas morning. Don't think about your mother saying, "We must pray now for those who have less than we have." Well, she hadn't prayed. Her eyes had been defiant, challenging her mother, who refused to look at her. Don't think about any of that.

Her relief when the church came into view drove away all her memories. She was in time for the parking space she wanted. She parked the big car carefully and sat a moment or two longer than necessary, measuring with her eyes the distance she would need to maneuver the big car into a U-turn in the middle of the street so she could head back the way she'd come. She would have no extra time to go around the block and possibly get lost. Satisfied with her calculation, she got out of the car and locked it.

God, it was cold. Maybe that had something to do with why she'd always hated Christmas. It had always been cold in the shack at Christmas, forcing all of them to sleep pressed against one another.

Inside the church, Justine removed her driving glasses, which had steamed up the moment the door closed behind her. The glasses went into the pocket with her money. She hadn't been in church in over thirty years. She felt pleased with herself when she saw the holy water font. She quickly blessed herself, genuflected, and slid into the last pew. She sat at the end, forcing people to scowl at her and crawl over her legs. She didn't care. Each time the door opened, she turned to stare at the people entering the church. What if they didn't come? What if the detective was wrong? It had to be at least ten minutes of twelve. Mass started at midnight. Where were they? Later, on the drive home, she came to the conclusion God had answered her prayers at the same precise moment she wondered if her family was attending mass.

The door opened and was held open longer than usual as a young man pushed a wheelchair through. The woman in the wheelchair looked just like the picture in the brown envelope. The young man was handsome, the young girl next to him was pretty. Steven and Eleanor, Mary Ellen's children. They moved up the center aisle, but Justine's eyes didn't follow them. Then she saw them. Her parents. Oh God, how very old they looked. How worn and tired. Her hand moved and she would have reached out to her mother, but the boy sitting next to her took that moment to struggle past her. Her eyes followed them down the aisle, her mother holding onto her father's arm, leaning against him. She was on her feet, ready to run down the aisle after them, when the boy pushed his way back into his seat. She sat down, trying to see where they were sitting. All she could see was the wheelchair next to the third pew.

She meant to pray, wanted to pray, but the words wouldn't come. *Look back here, it's me, Ethel. I'm here. Can't you feel me here? Mama, I'm here. I know it seems like I forgot about you. I did for a while. I'm sorry. Mama, forgive me. I'm so sorry. Mary Ellen, I'm sorry you're in a wheelchair. I'm sorry you're a widow. I'm sorry about everything. Forgive me, Mary Ellen.*

She did bow her head then. "God, forgive me all my sins. I'm selfish in wanting them to see me, to recognize me, to say my name. I don't deserve a kind word. I don't deserve anything. If you can't see your way to forgive me, make life easier for them. I can help out a little in that respect, but you have to do the rest. I won't invade their lives. Thank you, God."

Justine crept from the church, her eyes full of tears. For the first time in her life she felt free of herself. She'd just inflicted her own punishment; never to see or speak to her family again. She waited a moment to see if God would change His mind. When nothing happened, she stuffed all the money in her pocket into the poor box.

On the walk to her car Justine swore her shoulders were lighter, her heart less heavy. If she were religious, which she wasn't, she would have said it was her cross to bear, because all of it was of her own making.

She had time now, there was no need for a mad rush to her parents' home. It took her no time at all to reach the small house where her parents lived. The porch light was on. She knew the door would be open. Her mother never liked locked doors. Justine parked in front of the house next door, away from the streetlight. The carton of presents in the trunk wasn't heavy, but it was awkward to handle. She ended up dragging it down the sidewalk and tugging it up the front steps to the front porch. She tried the door and smiled when it opened to her touch. A small lamp burned in the living room. How neat it was. How very warm and comfortable. The heady scent of the small balsam was overpowering. She took a deep breath. Cinnamon and bayberry scents wafted through the house. She wished she'd worn her watch. How much time did she have? She worked quickly then, taking the gift-wrapped shoe boxes out of the carton and placing them under the tree. She moved several of them until she was certain they looked pretty enough to her eyes. She had to remember to take the carton with her. For now, she wanted to walk around the little house, and for just a few minutes be part of it all.

The kitchen was tidy, a braided rug in front of the sink. Blue-and-white-checkered curtains were crisp and starched on the kitchen window and the back door. An apple pie was on the counter. She bent over to smell it. Cinnamon. She opened the refrigerator. Plenty of food. She lifted the lid on the coffeepot. It was full, ready to be perked after church. She wondered if there was ice cream in the freezer. There was, a quart of vanilla. Tears pricked her eyelids. She saw the leaf for the kitchen table leaning up against the back door. There would be company for Christmas dinner. She felt pleased.

There was no dining room, but there were two bedrooms on the first floor. Both were neat and tidy. Spare rooms. Guest rooms. She ran upstairs. The bathroom was blue and white. Her mother must like the color blue. There wasn't a drop of water anywhere, not a stray hair, not a speck of anything on the floor.

Her bedroom. Her parents' bedroom. Double bed, blue chenille spread, not a wrinkle anywhere. A crucifix on the wall over the bed. Two rag rugs on the polished floor, one on each side. A dresser with an embroidered scarf on it. A statue of the Blessed Virgin, a hairbrush and comb.

It was the picture on the wall that took her breath away and made her clutch at her heart. It was about two-by-three feet, and framed. Inside were her brothers' and sisters' school pictures, her own included. "We all looked alike," she whispered. "Thank you God, for letting me see this."

Justine looked at the small alarm clock at the side of the bed. Lord, she had to get out of here. She ran down the steps, stopping just long enough to grab the carton. Outside on the porch she looked through the front window at the tree with the presents underneath. Each package had a name on it with a note inside. She didn't want any of her family to think the packages weren't for them. She spelled out nieces and nephews, mentioning other dates they would reconcile with their gift. She hadn't signed any of them, instead she wrote "Merry Christmas" at the bottom.

She was in her car, the carton in the backseat, ready to turn on her headlights when she saw the car pull in front of the house. She had to wait now, wait for Mary Ellen to be taken into the house by Steven and Eleanor. Her parents followed. Would they see the presents right away? Was the rest of the family going to join them this evening or tomorrow? She wished she knew. She rolled down her window. She could hear them now. Everyone was cold. It was

Christmas Day, her mother was saying. Steven carried his mother up the steps onto the porch. Eleanor unfolded the wheelchair. She swayed dizzily when she heard her father say he thought it was going to snow. And then her mother said, "I'm glad we went to mass tonight."

Then there was confusion. They were all on the porch, but light spilled from the open door. "Someone's been here! Look at this!" It was Eleanor. What a sweet voice she had, much the way she remembered Mary Ellen's.

Before she knew what she was doing Justine was out of the car and on the front porch. She stood to the side and peered through the sheer curtains. She could see everyone gathered around the tree. She pressed her ear against the glass and could hear faintly.

"There's ten of them," Mary Ellen said. "How pretty they look."

"Look, here's one for Uncle Billy, one for Uncle Marty, one for Aunt Helen. Here's yours, Mother, and yours, Grandma and Grandpa."

"Who brought them?" her mother asked.

"What should we do?" Steven asked.

"I think you should call everyone and ask them to come over," Mary Ellen said.

"No. Tomorrow will be soon enough," her mother said.

"Aren't you curious, Mother?" Mary Ellen asked.

"Of course, but I can wait until everyone is here. They're all wrapped the same and they're all the same size, so they must all contain the same thing. If we open them now, it will spoil it for the others. I think we should have our pie now and later we'll open them."

"Your mother is right," her father said. "It's time for the pie."

Her mother turned to stare across the room. Justine's heart thumped in her chest. Could she see her through the sheer curtains? She backed up one step and then two, until she was at the top of the steps. She raced down them and was in the car when the front door opened. Her heart pounded in her chest. They were all on the porch again, she could hear them plainly.

"I thought I saw someone by the window," her mother said.

"You always see things at this time of year, Mother," her father said. "You always think you see Ethel in one of the department stores or in church or in the backyard peeping in the windows."

"It's just that she always took Christmas so hard," her mother said.

"Now, Mother, you know Ethel is dead. If she wasn't dead, she would have come back long before this," Mary Ellen said. "I always think more about her at Christmastime too. I think we all do. I have an idea," she said cheerfully. "Let's all guess what's in the packages. Each of us gets three wishes. We can do that while we're having our pie and coffee."

The car door slammed shut.

Justine bawled until her eyes burned and her throat was sore from sobbing. When her feet and hands grew numb with the cold, she turned on the ignition. It wasn't until she was halfway home that she realized her car window was wide open.

It was Christmas Day.

Justine drove around to the back of the house and entered from the kitchen, something she'd only done once or twice in all the time she'd lived in Jasper's family home. Still in her coat, she did something she'd never done before. She brewed a pot of coffee. She tapped her foot impatiently as she waited for the coffee to perk, her thoughts far away. Her family thought Ethel Pullet was dead. Ethel Pullet, aka Justine Connors Landers.

Light-years ago she'd thought the name Pullet sounded like some kind of chicken and she'd been ashamed of the sound of it, so she'd changed both her names. She's seen the name Justine in a *True Confessions* magazine and liked it. She'd christened herself Justine Connors a week after she left her family. Why shouldn't they think Ethel was dead? People with intelligence and a heart didn't do what she'd done. She deserved to stay dead. She was more certain than ever that her decision was best for everyone concerned.

It was Christmas Day and Ethel Pullet was dead.

Justine listened to the last plop of the percolator. She unplugged it, slopped cream into a large heavy mug, something she would normally never drink out of, and carried both the pot and the mug upstairs to her room.

She wondered if she would ever be warm again. She longed for a warm, ratty, flannel robe and thick fleece-lined slippers, but all she had was silk and ruffles. There wasn't one damn thing in the whole of the house that was comforting or familiar. Everything was for show, right down to the skimpy underwear that no one ever saw.

Justine made a nest for herself in an uncomfortable chair. Two full packs of Chesterfield cigarettes lay open on the table next to a handsome leather-bound book of poetry. She'd never opened the book, never perused the poet's writing. It was on the table because the color of the leather matched a picture she'd once seen in a magazine. The Tiffany lamp had been in the same picture. Which meant, she thought, it hadn't been her own taste; she'd copied theirs.

And nobody cared.

It was going to be a very long night.

Toward morning Justine dozed, her dreams invaded by demons from her past. She was on trial, sitting in a courtroom, defended by her son Ross. She was in the witness chair screaming at the jury of her peers, her brothers, sisters, and parents. Nine siblings and two parents made eleven.

"Where's the twelfth juror?" she screamed. "You can't judge me unless there are twelve people!"

"And where's the alternate juror, Your Honor?" Ross shouted.

Jasper settled his black robe more comfortably around his shoulders. He peered down at Justine in the witness chair. "It really doesn't matter if there are twelve people or not. An alternate isn't going to help you either. You're guilty, we all know it. But since your attorney insists, we'll fetch the twelfth juror and the alternate. No tricks, counselor. Just because Justine Landers is your mother and my wife doesn't mean this jury or myself will tolerate any shenanigans. Bailiff, fetch the alternate and the twelfth juror."

Justine watched in horror as Marjory Ryan was seated as the twelfth juror and Peter Woojalesky was seated as the alternate.

"That's more like it," Attorney Landers said, smacking his hands together.

"No more outbursts, counselor," Jasper said, rapping his gavel for order.

"Now, Mrs. Landers, tell us what happened."

"They said I'm dead? I'm alive. Look at me! I'm breathing. How can I be dead? They hate me. They're ashamed of me. You all hate me. They only think about me on Christmas."

"Who?" Ross said.

Justine pointed to the jury. "I changed my name. That's not a crime. I didn't want people to think of chickens when they heard my name. Justine Connors sounded pretty. I never had a pretty name. Ethel Pullet stinks," she said huffily. "I went back once. They were gone. You can't find me guilty, I went back."

"How do we know that's true?" Mary Ellen Pullet Akers shouted from the jury box. "Why should we believe you?"

"Order, order!" Jasper shouted. "Jurors are not permitted to make comments. I'll disqualify you if you make another outburst. Proceed, counselor."

"Do you regret what you've done?" Ross asked.

"I refuse to answer that on the grounds my answer might tend to incriminate me. You have no right to pry into my personal life even if you're my son."

"I have every right. You neglected me, you robbed me of a normal childhood. You sent me away. You were never a mother! You're guilty as hell. Ladies and gentlemen of the jury, I recommend you find the defendant guilty. Judge, what do you have to say?"

"I say she was never a wife to me. I say she married me for my money. I didn't know she changed her name. I did love her. Once. Ladies and gentlemen of the jury, I second Mr. Landers's recommendation that you find the defendant guilty as charged."

Justine screamed as Jasper read his instructions to the jury. She was still berating her son and husband as the jury filed out of the room. She deflated when Marjory winked at her.

In the hallway, waiting for the jury to return, Justine felt like a pariah as she smoked one cigarette after the other. Unable to stand the loneliness a moment longer, she marched over to where Ross and Jasper were standing. "What about me?" she asked quietly. "All you had to do was talk to me, Jasper. All I wanted was to be treated like a person, like I was worth something. You did pick me off the streets, and you never let me forget it. You were just as ashamed of me as I was of my family. And as for you, Ross, I didn't want you to grow up to be like your father. Or me. I wanted you to be your own person, and you succeeded. I know I did it all wrong, and if I had to do it over again, I might do things differently. I'm not sure, though, maybe I wouldn't. Everyone makes mistakes. I certainly made more than my share, as you did, as your father did. Marjory seems to be the only one who's come out of this intact. Marjory understands me because she's been through all this too. You can't break her, Ross. She'll never marry you again. I can see it in her eyes.

"I don't care anymore. I don't care what you think of me. I don't care what anyone thinks. You can have all this. It was a means to an end, and now it's ended. You used me, I used you. We all use one another, feed off each other's insecurities, and then we moan and groan when things don't work out right. Each of us has to take responsibility for our actions. I'm taking mine, you both do whatever you have to do."

"The jury's in, Judge," the bailiff called from the doorway.

"This isn't a real court," Justine said to Ross. "You aren't permitted to discuss this with the judge. I could have you disbarred for such actions."

"Then do it, Mother. Stand up to hear your sentence."

"We, the jury, find the defendant Ethel Pullet aka Justine Connors Landers . . ."

"I don't want to hear your damn verdict!" Justine whimpered as she tried to extricate herself from the blanket she was wrapped in.

Tears rolled down Justine's cheeks. It was a dream. A very bad dream.

Christmas Day.

She got up stiffly, her joints stiff and achy. She turned the thermostat up to eighty-five degrees and wondered why she hadn't adjusted it the night before instead of shivering all night long. "Because I'm stupid, that's why," she muttered on the way to the bathroom to draw a bath.

Shortly before noon Justine snapped the lock on her small overnight case and walked out to the hall, where she stood at the railing looking down into the massive entryway and into the richly decorated living room. She saw Jasper approaching out of the corner of her eye.

"There should be a Christmas tree down there somewhere," Justine said quietly. "One of us should put one up. Merry Christmas, Jasper," she said, starting down the staircase.

"Are you going away?" Jasper asked curiously.

"I've been invited out for Christmas dinner." She turned midway down the steps and turned to face her husband. "I think this is the first real invitation I've had in close to twenty years. Will you be staying home or going out? Are you going to file for a divorce, Jasper? The reason I'm asking is, if you don't do it, I intend to. Will you be seeing Ross today?"

"I'll be home today. Christmas to me is much like any other day. I hadn't thought too much about a divorce, but you're right, one of us should file. I invited Ross for dinner. He invited me to his house. We finally settled on his coming here. Where are you going?"

"To Marjory's house in Chestnut Hill. She asked me to spend the night. This is just a guess on my part, but I think the child is looking for a mother image. I'm the first to admit I'm a very poor choice, but sometimes one gets a second chance at things. Whatever her reasons, I plan to enjoy myself. I just hope I remember how to do that," Justine muttered. "I didn't buy you a present, Jasper. There didn't seem to be much point."

"I didn't buy you one either. As you said, there didn't seem to be much point. Tell Jory I wish her a Merry Christmas."

"Coming from me it's secondhand. It will mean more if you do it yourself."

"Perhaps you're right. I envy you, you know."

Justine stopped on the bottom step. Startled at his words, she turned around. "You envy me. For heaven's sake, why?"

"It's not important. Enjoy your day."

"Jasper, what happened to Helen?"

"Nothing happened to Helen. She's alive and well. I . . . how do I say this . . . ? I gave her up when you threatened me. I couldn't risk you harming her or her husband. I wish I could say I gave her up for love, but I didn't. We were in a comfortable relationship that wasn't ever going to go anywhere. You brought it to a head. I think it was a mean, underhanded thing for you to do."

"Jasper, you're going to find this impossible to believe, but Matthew Halvorsen is a sick man. By sick I mean he likes young children. Very young girls. There was a time when he wasn't fussy and included very young boys in his little inner circle. Didn't you ever question why Helen never had children? I can prove this, Jasper. Three sources of documentation and signed affidavits. Helen knows, has always known. He doesn't deserve to sit on the bench. In my own way I did you a favor. You certainly don't want to be part of that scandal. You are, after all, a Landers," Justine said bitterly.

"Are you going to print that story?" Jasper asked.

"No, I'm not," Justine replied. "I got wind of it from one of my reporters who got it from a source close to the big man at *Confidential.* They're going to print it. As I said, I did you a favor. Don't rush to thank me, Jasper, I couldn't handle it today."

"I don't believe you," Jasper sputtered.

Justine slipped into her coat. "Yes you do. If there's one thing I'm not, Jasper, it's a liar, and we both know it."

Jasper was still sputtering. "I remember a time or two when you told a few lies."

"Ah, well, Jasper, we all pay for our mistakes one way or another." She had her hat and gloves on and was searching for her car keys when she remembered putting them on the kitchen counter when she got home.

"I put them on the table," Jasper said, pointing to the table in the foyer. "Justine, I don't like to ask this of you, but will you do me a favor?"

"It depends on what it is, Jasper," Justine said coolly.

"I have all these presents I was going to take out to Jory's. Some are for the dogs, most of them for Jory, and there are a few for Woo. Will you take them out to the house? People should have their presents on Christmas."

"Yes, I'll take them. My car is in the back. Where are the presents?"

"In my car. It's parked in the back too. I'll transfer them."

Outside, Justine's eyes widened when she saw the gifts. "My goodness, Jasper, did you buy out the store?" she asked in amazement.

Jasper shuffled his feet. "It's supposed to be better to give than to receive," he muttered.

Justine smiled. "Yes, I've heard that." Her eyes turned misty.

"It's supposed to snow this evening. Not a lot, but the roads might be slick in the morning, so be careful. I didn't see any chains in your car. Do you want a set?"

"That might be a good idea. However, I don't have the faintest idea how to go about putting them on, so what good will they do? Thanks for the offer, though."

Jasper shrugged. "Justine, were you telling me the truth in the house about Matthew Halvorsen?"

"I swear to you, Jasper, on the life of our son. You might want to warn Helen that someone else might print the story. She deserves to know. I'm sorry, Jasper, I really am. Enjoy dinner with Ross."

Jasper stood in the driveway watching Justine's car until she was out of sight. They'd actually talked, and looked one another in the eye. Her eyes had misted, and been bare of the heavy makeup she usually wore. He wondered why she wasn't wearing any. She'd been wearing a cloth coat instead of her luxurious mink. She looked plain, almost dowdy. He wondered about that too.

Jasper was in the kitchen when he remembered Justine's declaration that she was going to file for divorce. If he didn't do it first. Obviously that was something he was going to have to discuss with Ross. After dinner. After they opened the presents they bought for one another. Damn, he should have gotten a tree. Frantically, he looked around.

"Rosa!" he called. When she came, he said, "Where's your husband? I want to cut that tree down in the backyard and put it up in the living room. Where are our tree decorations? Do we have any? Find them, Please! I want that tree up before Ross gets here!"

"It's picture perfect, just like in the family magazines," Justine said quietly, her eyes on the huge, fragrant tree. "You bought into the whole thing, didn't you?"

There was no point in pretending not to understand what Justine was saying, Jory thought. "Yes, it works for me. It didn't when I was growing up. I thought it would when I married Ross, but it wasn't right. For me, now, at this point in my life, it works nicely. I hope it never changes for me. I'm contented, and at times I'm happy. I don't believe there's such a thing as total happiness or being happy all the time. If you stop and really think about it, it simply isn't possible. Happiness as we know it are those little bits of time we're granted from time to time when things seem perfect."

"Today was very nice," Justine said. "I can hardly believe it's eight o'clock. I can't ever remember not being aware of the time. I'm always looking at my watch expecting something to happen. Dinner was wonderful. You're a very good cook. I could have done without the dish-washing part, but I did my share." Justine chuckled.

Jory smiled. "Yes you did. You seemed surprised that the dogs liked you. Were you afraid of them?"

Justine lit a cigarette and blew a perfect smoke ring. "I was afraid of their reaction to me. Not physically afraid of them. Supposedly, dogs are very good judges of character. We did a piece on a starlet who owned several dogs about eight months ago, and she said she never allows anyone into her home that the dogs don't like. I know that sounds kind of bizarre, but for some reason I believe it. Not too many people like me, my husband and son included, but then I guess you already know that."

Jory interrupted the older woman. "Is this the part where you confide in me and then I confide in you?"

"Good Lord, no. I merely stated a fact. One I've accepted. I used to be amused when Ross called me—to my face, mind you—the 'Dragon Lady.' " She was so busy fondling the dogs' ears, she didn't see Jory's smile.

"I do have a favor to ask of you," Justine said. "I won't be offended if you think it's something you don't want to do. I'll be leaving after the first of the year. From time to time I'd appreciate it if you'd let me know how Ross and Jasper are doing. The last issue of *TIF* is ready to go. All I have to do is clear up my files, store them, and be on my way. I do have a few legal matters to take care of, but I'll be doing that in New York. I have a feeling we'll be talking to one another on a daily basis once you start up operations."

"I would be comfortable doing that, Justine. Are you sure you're going to be happy being away from here? Are you ever coming back?"

"I thought you said there was no such thing as real happiness." She smiled wryly. "No, I don't think I'll come back. There's nothing left for me here. I did what I set out to do. I admit, it's my loss, and I'll have to live with it. Jasper finally turned himself into the man I thought he was when I married him. Ross is steady on his feet. He'll never forgive me. He's a lot like you, Jory. Of course you don't see that now. Revenge is not sweet, take my word for it."

"Justine, I did not say there was no such thing as real happiness. You understood what I meant. Aren't you going to . . . to tell Ross and Jasper you're leaving? You're just going to let them find out . . . however they find out?" Jory said, grappling for words.

"Exactly. I can't change my stripes now. I was thinking about you on the ride out here. I thought up a name for the magazine. It's not going to be as hard as you might think. It's all there for you, Marjory. Hire good writers. Don't be afraid to pay for the best. Go slick, the best paper money can buy, write about things that are happening *now*. Be bright and innovative with it, as you young people say. Go out there and print what the other magazines are afraid to tackle. But for God's sake do it in good taste. Don't do it low-down and dirty the way I did it. Develop your own style. Slick and sophisticated is the way to go. I have a whole file on advertisers you're free to use. You'll have to do some selling. Of yourself. You have the guts. I saw those guts the day you came to the office. You never should have backed down. You should have booted my ass out on the street. You'll have to get tough, but not as tough as me," Justine said sourly.

Jory laughed. "I have fifty-three thousand to add to the kitty. I wouldn't have that if it wasn't for Ross. And a few thousand more left to me by my father, but I've been dipping into it."

"I'm lending you the money at regular commercial business rates. Perfectly legal. The year's rent I owe you will be factored into the payback. I owe it; I'll pay it. At first I wasn't going to, but I never stiffed a creditor in my life. Using Jasper's money, of course. No one need know, Marjory. If you decide to do it, there's one last piece of advice I want to give you, and that is, change with the times, don't be afraid. Don't lock into any method no matter how successful it seems. Stretch, reach out and do it. For yourself. Not for me. You don't have to prove anything to anyone but yourself."

"Why Justine, why me?" Jory asked suspiciously.

"I like your suspicion. That's very good. Let's just say I'm doing it for . . . Ethel Pullet."

"Who's Ethel Pullet?"

"Ethel Pullet is . . . someone I used to know. She had dreams and aspirations. She probably would have been a nice person if other people had stopped to get to know her, helped her a little, been just a little kinder," Justine said sadly.

"Did she die?"

"Yes, Ethel Pullet is dead. It's definite, you're going to do it, right?"

"I'm thinking. What's the name you came up with? I have to admit, I've been thinking about it a lot since that day in your office."

" 'Serendipity.' It means, oh, it means a lot of things, like finding agreeable or valuable things not sought for. You can make it work for you. I love the name. Picture it on a magazine cover, bold dark script. Write it out on a piece of paper. It will look lovely. Women will adore it."

"I'll do my best. I made up my mind that day in your office."

"I know. I wanted to make bushels of money. And I did. I'm too old for that type of magazine publishing now. *TIF* in the old days was boring. The new *TIF* was so loud and sleazy it would never put you to sleep. It was all my doing, Marjory. I have no one to blame anything on, but myself." She laughed then, a light, trilling sound that tore at Jory's heart.

"Let's go for a walk," Jory said, getting up to add another log to the fire.

"I'm game if you are," Justine said, struggling up from the sofa. "Oh, look, it's snowing."

"A white Christmas. Well, sort of white, but it's sticking to the ground. The dogs like snow. Jasper got them sweaters last year."

Justine doubled over laughing. "Marjory, have you ever heard the expression, too much, too little, too late?"

Jory busted out laughing. "It's my personal favorite. I say it to your son every time I see him."

"He doesn't hear it, does he?"

"No, Justine, he doesn't."

"Jasper wouldn't understand it either. Well, I'm ready," she said briskly.

"Me too," Jory said, buttoning her jacket.

"Then let's . . . hit the road."

Justine walked through the Landers Building one last time, her eyes raking the far corners of every room. She was going to miss coming here every day. But most of all she was going to miss the anticipation of each new issue hitting the streets and the public's reaction to the stories she printed. Would she miss her name being mentioned on the evening news? In the beginning she'd kept track until the broadcasters started referring to her as the estranged wife of Jasper Landers. She stopped watching the news entirely when the broadcaster began asking other publishers for their opinions of her brand of journalism.

She no longer laughed on her way to the bank. Grim-faced and tight-lipped, she'd pumped money into one bank after the other, banks owned by Jasper's blue-blooded friends, only to wire it out the day the checks cleared. She couldn't remember which one of the blue bloods said, on the evening news, "She slits our throats and then drains our blood." She'd been overjoyed the night she'd heard that comment. Let them bleed to death.

Her desk was bare with the exception of one white envelope containing the rent check to Marjory Ryan. In the middle drawer of her desk was a list of instructions, two thick journals she'd kept from the time she walked into the offices of *TIF* when it was a staid, dull, boring, noninformative magazine until this last issue of the new *TIF.*

Marjory Ryan was the only one who knew she was jumping ship. Her skeleton crew had been told she was taking a brief hiatus in South America because she wanted to get a new perspective on turning the magazine into a serious publication. Handsome bonuses had been handed out, new contracts signed that promised nothing if the fine print was read. One last check would be issued to the staff by her attorneys in New York after she was gone, along with a letter saying Marjory Ryan would be starting up a monthly magazine and to seek her out for employment. She'd been pleased when Marjory told her she would give it a try. Maybe she would succeed and maybe she wouldn't, but if she didn't, it wouldn't be for lack of trying. The girl had guts, spunk, and *ethics.*

"Mrs. Landers, is there anything else you want me to do?" Clarence the maintenance man asked from the doorway.

"I don't think so," Justine said vaguely as she looked around her office. "Be sure to keep watering the plants. You did hang all those pictures didn't you?"

"Yes, ma'am, just the way you said. I cleaned them up and polished the frames. They're hanging all in a row in the conference room."

"Did you have a nice holiday, Clarence?"

"Yes, ma'am, I did. The extra bonuses you gave me throughout the year helped me pay my taxes. We had a large increase this year. The Christmas bonus was a godsend. I wanted to thank you personally before you left."

"Clarence, that's our little secret. You aren't to talk about it to anyone."

"No, ma'am. You aren't coming back, are you?"

Justine felt the temptation to lie, but this kindly man would see right through her. "No, Clarence, I'm not. You've been a good friend to me."

"And you've been a good friend to me, Mrs. Landers. I won't forget your kindnesses to me."

"It's alright for you not to forget, just don't mention them to anyone. I'd just as soon keep my rotten image," Justine said briskly. "By the way, how are the gentlemen on the first floor?"

"Nodding or asleep. I'll keep my eye on them."

"Keep your eye on Miss Ryan too. She's going to need a good, loyal friend when she starts up her magazine. I guess it's time to say good-bye, Clarence." Justine extended her hand.

"I'm going to miss you, Mrs. Landers."

Justine's eyes burned. She pretended to look away. "No one ever said that to me before, Clarence. No one." She cleared her throat. "Good-bye, Clarence."

"Good-bye, Mrs. Landers. Have a safe trip wherever you're going." He knew she didn't hear him, she was running too fast and crying too hard.

Clarence inched Justine's chair away from the desk to wipe a speck of dust from the sofa leather. He sat down to relieve the ache in his legs. His varicose veins were bothering him lately. He massaged them carefully. He was wearing special shoes and special hosiery made just for him, thanks to Mrs. Landers. She'd even sent him to her own doctor and paid for the visit.

They were the same age; she'd told him that once. In confidence. Everything she said to him, as far as he was concerned, was said in confidence. He'd cut out his tongue before he said one bad word about Justine Landers. In his opinion, he was the keeper of the secrets. Just because he was a janitor didn't mean he was stupid. He could read, and he and his wife both read each issue of *TIF* from cover to cover and then discussed it between themselves at great length. It was his wife, though, who figured out what it was Mrs. Landers was doing with her paper. "She's getting even, Clarence," she'd said. "Those high and mighty muckety-mucks did something to her at some time in her life and now she's paying them back." Tillie, his wife, read all the papers, especially the social pages, and there was never a mention of Mrs. Landers. That, Tillie said, was significant. Mrs. Landers wasn't one of *them*. When Tillie said that, he'd started to keep his eyes and ears open. He'd made it his business to be dusting the hall or sweeping it when the parade started with bankers, politicians, lawyers, and even doctors. He heard the raised voices, seen the fear, and heard Mrs. Landers's soft, bitter laughter.

Once he'd had respect for Jasper Landers and Ross, but that fell by the wayside when Tillie said no self-respecting man or son would allow their wife and mother to be treated the way Justine Landers was treated, and so what if she was sharp and bitter and nasty from time to time, who wouldn't be with what she must have gone through?

He knew about the lawsuits, the threats too. He'd worked late one night and he'd found Mrs. Landers crying in her office. She'd told him what was going on. He'd tried to console her, but he was out of his depth. He talked it all over with Tillie, and Tillie was the one who came up with the idea. What it came down to was, she should take the money and run. He'd expected her to do it months ago. Why she waited so long, he had no idea. Maybe Christmas had something to do with it. People didn't like change or trouble over the holidays. The first of the year seemed to be the time to do things, make new beginnings. Clarence felt pleased with his assessment of the situation.

Now, Clarence got up stiffly. He pushed the chair back against the desk. He looked at the picture of Justine Landers on the opposite wall. Mrs. Landers told him to take it down and put it somewhere. She hadn't meant hang it someplace else. What she meant was throw it out or store it in the basement, but he wasn't going to do it. He was going to let it hang where it was, and when Miss Ryan came to work, he was going to lie and say Mrs. Landers said the picture was to stay right where it was. Besides, he thought, rubbing at his eyes, he wanted to be able to see it from time to time so he wouldn't forget all she'd done for him and his family.

No sir, that picture was staying right where it was.

Clarence closed the door to Justine's office. He would dust it every day until the new occupant arrived to sit behind the polished desk.

Justine Landers loved New York. She would have done well here in this busy city, but Philadelphia was nice too. Here, people seemed simply too busy to be snobs. Maybe she was wrong about that, she thought fretfully.

"This is it, lady, 122 East Forty-second Street," the cab driver said. Justine paid the fare along with a generous tip and stepped from the cab. Ten minutes later she was seated in John Fried's office.

"Mrs. Landers, I'm John Fried. What can I do for you?"

He looked nice. A family man, Justine decided when she noticed the picture of a smiling woman and two little girls on the low cabinet across from his desk. She wondered how he liked his profession. She asked him.

"Somedays I do and somedays I don't. What do you do, Mrs. Landers?"

Justine smiled. "Not much of anything these days. I'm leaving town later this afternoon and . . . well, here's everything you'll need to take care of matters for me in my absence." The lizard-skin briefcase snapped open. She withdrew three thick envelopes. She spoke in a low, even monotone. Attached to the first envelope was a bank check made out to cash from the Morgan Guarantee Trust Company in the amount of $300,000. "This money is from the estate of Ethel Pullet," she said. "On the first of every month I want a check sent to each of the ten people whose names and addresses are inside the envelope. Send a letter the first time explaining the situation. I would expect the account to draw interest. Three thousand to each of them. I'll know when the money runs out and wire more to your offices. Is there any problem with what I've said so far?"

Fried shook his head when Justine handed him what she thought was a suitable retainer. He smiled.

"This second envelope has a list of instructions. It's pretty cut and dried, in my opinion. I'm lending money to Marjory Ryan at the lowest rate of interest possible. She can take the money all at one time or in payments. Whichever way she decides is fine with me. Two million dollars. If she needs more, she's to ask and you will give it to her. There's an additional two hundred thousand I want you to put into an interest-bearing account. She's to make her payments directly to the bank, and I want you to monitor the account." She handed over another retainer check. Fried smiled again. "Do you see any problem with what I just outlined?"

"No. It's a relatively simple matter. Has Miss Ryan been advised of all of this?"

"Not really. We discussed it, but not in detail. Write her a letter and explain it in detail. I assume the bank will charge a fee for handling the account." She handed over another check. Fried eyed the last bulging envelope. And then he looked at his new client. Her eyes were steely cold, her face stiff and unsmiling.

"Whatever we say," she said, "is client privileged, or however you say it. Which means you cannot divulge anything we discuss here today. Is that right?"

"Yes it is."

Justine handed over the third packet. "I'm choosing not to respond to any of these lawsuits. Other attorneys are handling them. What I'm doing is . . . flying the coop and taking my money with me. As far as I'm concerned, the first two matters have nothing to do with the contents of this envelope. There are diaries in this envelope, journals, if you don't like the word 'diary.' The lawsuits, all of them, are documented in the journals, and the sources of my information are the sworn affidavits in the back. I have no stomach for what's going to happen in the coming months. I printed the truth. That's all I'm concerned with. I'm choosing not to pay out thousands of dollars in legal fees, since I did nothing wrong. I have no desire to have a jury of my peers get up on the wrong side of the bed and find me guilty of destroying all those fine blue-blooded bastards. That's all you need to know, Mr. Fried. Will *this* be a problem for you?" She passed an additional check across the desk. "Nuisance money."

"How can I reach you if I need to get in touch with you?" he asked.

"You can't. I'll check with your office periodically. My personal advice, and I certainly don't want to tell you how to conduct your business, would be to lock away this third envelope. I think of it as 'for your eyes only,' that kind of thing."

Justine stood up. "Look after Miss Ryan for me."

Fried stood and offered his hand. "You wouldn't by any chance have a death certificate for Ethel Pullet with you, would you?"

"No, Mr. Fried, I don't," Justine said coolly. "Happy New Year."

"The same to you, Mrs. Landers," Fried said.

The attorney rang for his secretary. "Mrs. Peters, take these checks to the bank. Deposit them in our escrow account and ask Mr. Bellamy to call me so I can set up some new accounts."

John Fried sat back in his comfortable chair to read all the documents on his desk. When he locked everything away at seven o'clock, he felt sorry for the woman who'd stared at him so coolly across the wide desk. But who was he to judge her, legally or morally? he asked himself. As instructed, he locked everything in his office safe. He never looked at the contents of the third envelope again.

On the second day of the new year, as John Fried boarded the train for Scarsdale, Justine was presenting her passport to the ticket agent at La Guardia Airport. "Have a good trip, Miss Pullet," the agent said, handing back her passport and first-class ticket.

Justine smiled. "Thank you, I will."

Chapter 18

Woo could hardly believe it was January second. He'd counted days and then hours and finally minutes while he was in Lancaster. He'd slept a lot while he was at his parents, dreaming about returning to the carriage house, *leaping* from the van to run to Jory and the dogs. In every single dream, and there were many of them, she smothered him with kisses, hugged him, smiled with her eyes and shared every minute of her time since he'd left. The dogs climbed his legs, begging to be picked up and cuddled. They were wonderful dreams, and he always woke up with a smile on his face.

He'd meant to stop at Jory's, to knock on the door and say "I'm back," but the house was dark, the draperies drawn. He'd waited the way he had once before. He'd meant to check the garage to see if her car was safe inside, but once he was in the carriage house, he didn't have the stamina to trek all the way back to the garage. Instead he tortured himself with her whereabouts. The dark house convinced him she was somewhere else. It had been New Year's Day, after all. He'd spent the night on the couch, his ear tuned to the window and the sound of a car's engine, which never materialized.

He couldn't go on like this anymore. All he did was think about Jory and the future. One way or the other he had to know what she felt for him. Tonight, after his first day at work, he was going straight to her house the minute he got home. Damn, maybe he should make an appointment with her, leave a note in the mailbox telling her he'd stop by. That's exactly what he would do. He scribbled off a note that said, *I need to talk with you. Seven o'clock.* He signed the yellow slip of paper, *Pete.*

He was in love. The realization was so heady he wanted to dance, to shout the words aloud. More important, he needed to tell Ross, to clear the way, before he announced his feelings to Jory. All during the holidays he'd practiced speech after speech. None of them sounded right, none of them said how much he loved Jory. How in the goddamn hell did you tell a woman's ex-husband how you felt about his ex-wife, when that ex-husband loved her too? How did you say "I love her, I'm going to ask her to marry me. We had sex. It was wonderful, for both of us. I don't want to hurt you, Ross. Can we still work together?" Was it Ross's business? That was the key question. When Woo showered and dressed, he still didn't know if it was Ross's business or not, he just knew he was going to tell him because to do otherwise would be . . . disloyal. If he didn't tell, Ross would view it as a betrayal.

Woo struggled into his overcoat, turned out the lights and lowered the thermostat. He would get breakfast in the café three doors down from the office and still arrive in time to look at the caseload of work Ross said was on his desk.

Woo felt almost whole when Ross entered the office at ten minutes to eight, Jasper five minutes later. Both men clapped him on the back, pumped his left hand and grinned like kids catching their first trout. He pretended the same enthusiasm.

"We're celebrating tonight," Jasper said. "Dinner on me. Ross and I have been planning this since before the holidays. Don't even think about saying no."

"We've got a lot to talk about, buddy," Ross said. "I've got some news, my father has some news, and we damn well want to share. That's what this partnership is all about. So, what do you think of your new office? Is the chair comfortable? Your first appointment is for ten o'clock. We ordered lunch sent in around one o'clock. There's doughnuts and coffee in the kitchen. Jesus, Woo, you don't know how glad I am you're here and that you *walked* through the door. I said you'd do it, remember?" He almost knocked Woo off his feet with his exuberant bear hug. Self-consciously, he backed off. "When it comes to you, I always get carried away," he said, embarrassed.

So he would call Jory and explain the situation, Woo thought. He wouldn't stay at the celebatory dinner one minute longer than necessary. Nine o'clock wasn't too late to talk, at least for him. Midnight, two in the morning, wouldn't be too late.

"Sure," Woo said lightly. "I got here early, couldn't sleep. You know, my first day back and all that. The chair's great. I really like the plants. Any advice on the files you left on my desk? By the way, what happened with Mrs. Landers? Did she leave or pay the rent? Of course, if you think it's none of my business . . ."

Jasper wore a disgusted look on his face. Ross grimaced. "As far as I know, she's still there," Ross said. "Jory backed down. I don't know if Mother paid the rent or not; Jory won't discuss it. However, get this, Woo, Jory invited her for Christmas. They spent the day together."

Woo's eyebrows shot upward. "That sounds like Jory. For some reason, I thought you and Jasper would spend Christmas with Jory." Woo's heart fluttered in his chest.

"Jory is a very kind, giving, caring person," Jasper said quietly.

"I'll second that," Ross said, grinning. "It must have been a hell of a day."

Woo turned to walk to his office. As long as it wasn't with you, Ross, he thought jealously.

Woo tried the number in Chestnut Hill seven times during the course of the day. Late in the afternoon he looked up the number of *TIF*'s offices and called to ask for Jory. It was just a hunch.

"The office is closed, sir," a male voice said.

"You mean they're closed for the holidays? Has Miss Ryan been in?"

"No sir, the office is closed permanently. Mrs. Landers has stopped publishing her magazine. Miss Ryan, according to Mrs. Landers, will be taking possession of the building either today or tomorrow. I'm Clarence, Mr. Woojalesky. Perhaps you remember me."

"Yes, Clarence, of course I remember you. Was this a sudden decision on Mrs. Landers's part?"

"Mrs. Landers didn't confide in me, Mr. Woojalesky," Clarence said coolly.

"Clarence, if Miss Ryan should come in today, will you tell her I called and ask her to call me?"

"It's rather late in the day, Mr. Woojalesky, I leave in forty-five minutes. I can leave a note on the desk if you like."

"Please do that."

A frown started to build on Woo's face. Why would Justine Landers stop publishing her magazine just when her circulation was hitting an all-time high? And what did Justine Landers and Jory have in common that would make the young woman invite her to spend Christmas with her? An ex-mother-in-law. Ross said he had news to discuss with him. Jesus, he was dumb. It all made sense now. He was a dumb shit, just the way Ross said he was. "Son of a fucking bitch," he growled.

"You talking to yourself?" Ross said, sticking his head in the open door. "How'd it go today?"

"I didn't turn any clients away. I probably made us fifty bucks. If we collect, that's something else," Woo mumbled.

Ross stepped into the office. "You okay, Woo? You look kind of . . . whipped. Listen, if a full day is too much, cut back to half a day. I don't want you having a setback. You've come too far to have a relapse. I think this dinner we have planned is just the ticket for you. You can stay at home with me instead of making that trip back to Chestnut Hill. Come on, the hell with all this shit, let's close up now. I think we both need a drink. We don't have any other clients coming in. Don't worry about cleaning up. My father does that. For some reason," Ross said, lowering his voice, "he likes watering the plants, emptying the trash, and cleaning the ashtrays. But the biggie is, he loves sharpening pencils. You should see this place in the morning when I walk in. You'd swear a cleaning crew went through it. He works cheap too. Some weeks he doesn't get anything. Last week I paid him fifteen bucks. That's the most I've paid him, and he works from eight to five."

"Okay, Ross. I just have a call or two to make and then I'll meet you in the reception area. Are we walking or riding?"

"Either/or. It's a block and a half away. It's your call, Woo."

"Let's walk. The exercise is good for me."

"Okay. I just want to pack up my briefcase. I have a couple of things I need to read over this evening. I have oral arguments tomorrow at nine."

Woo nodded. That had to mean it was going to be an early evening. He dialed Jory's number again and listened to it ring eleven times before he hung up the phone. Where the hell was she? Or was she simply not answering her phone, and if so, why? He wished he was a little kid again so he could run to his room and cry until he fell asleep.

"It's a new year, Woo," Ross said happily on the way to the restaurant. "I think it's going to be great for both of us. You're walking, which is the best thing of all. Woo," Ross lowered his voice, "I prayed like hell for you. I went to the Catholic church and asked the priest how to do it, what prayers to say. He showed me how. I started going to a Catholic church on Sundays to see what it was all about. I never did get the hang of the beads, so I just read all those little cards the priest gave me. Church on Sunday was for you."

"You mean the mass?"

"Yeah, yeah, the mass. He said it for you. Everyone in church prayed for your recovery. Out loud. We did it out loud. When I was sitting there, I knew you'd make it. Really knew. Hell, I know you have two more operations to go through, but in the end you're going to be walking all by yourself. That priest tried to sign me up, but I said I wasn't ready. I'm no churchgoer. I guess you have to be psychologically ready for a commitment to something so serious. I'm serious about the praying, for you, but that other stuff, I don't know if I can handle that. Do you know what I mean, Woo?"

"Sure," Woo said quietly.

Ross stopped. "Listen, Woo, do you ever wish it was me instead of you? It's okay to think that. Sometimes I think you must hate my guts that I'm walking around and you need a cane. I'd cut off my arm for you, breathe for you if I could, if it would help you. You have to believe that, Woo. Whatever you want, whatever you need, it's yours. I mean that from the bottom of my heart, Woo. Jesus, you're the best thing that ever happened to me, the best friend a guy could want."

Give me Jory, let me have her all to myself. Don't stand in my way. "I feel the same way, Ross," Woo said, and he did.

"Here we are," Ross said, holding the door open for Woo to go through ahead of him. "My father will join us as soon as he finishes up. It will give us time to have a drink by ourselves and to talk and catch up. How was Christmas?"

"Very quiet. My parents went to Florida to see my oldest sister. She had a baby the week after Thanksgiving. They've never been out of Lancaster. Mom loves the palm trees, and Pop said he would never get used to swimming in a pool on Christmas Day. They don't seem to be in a hurry to come home. We all told them to stay until spring. They might," Woo said, sitting down with a thump.

"Did you guys miss me?" Ross asked wistfully. "I thought about all of you all day long. Why didn't you ask me, Woo?"

"I needed to be by myself. I wasn't even going to go, but then I . . . it was the spur of the moment. I thought you'd understand."

"Yeah, I figured it was something like that. Did you have a nice tree, were there lots of presents?"

"Sure. From you. You don't have to do that you know. We called Mom on Christmas Day and told her about her dishwasher. She was so excited. My brother read her the model number and she was going to the store down there to look at it. That was real nice of you. Last year she cried over that washing machine. You're a kind man, Ross Landers," Woo said sincerely. Ross flushed.

"So, what is it you want to tell me?" Woo asked carefully, knowing he wasn't going to like what he heard.

"You really want to hear?"

"Isn't that why we're here? Come on, spit it out!"

"I asked Jory to marry me. She didn't say yes, but she didn't say no either. She's weakening, I can feel it. We have so much in common these days. I want you to be my best man. That's what I wanted to tell you . . . ask you. Will you? Be my best man? Hell,

I can't get married without you as my best man. Look, I know you like Jory a lot and she likes you a lot, but you two aren't in love, are you? I thought about that and I know you, Woo, you'd never go behind my back and do something like that. I need to know if . . . Am I wrong, is there something between you two, and is that why Jory is taking so long to say yes? And no, we haven't had sex. Sex isn't what this is all about. Well it is, but it isn't. We just talk and hold hands and once in a while she lets me kiss her. She's nervous about me. I told her I don't care if she can't have kids. I'm perfectly willing to adopt or not adopt. I know something like that would matter to you, because you said you want a whole houseful of kids. Some men can't accept not having an heir, a son. I don't care about that, that's how much I love Jory. So, will you be my best man if she says yes? You don't think she'll turn me down, do you, Woo?"

Woo swallowed his wine in one gulp. "She'd be a fool to turn you down, Ross. I didn't know she couldn't have children. But then, why would she tell me?"

"I didn't know it either. She had an . . . oophorectomy when she miscarried. We had a fight right out on the street. She goddamn gave me a black eye and kicked my shins so hard I limped for two weeks. She had too much to drink that night, and we ended up staying here in the office. That's when she really let me have it. I didn't know what to do or what to say. She said she wanted lots of kids. I told her it didn't matter. I think she believes me. What do you think, Woo? You still haven't said if you'll be my best man. Guess that means yes, huh?" Ross said happily.

What did he think? That he was the biggest fool ever to come out of the state of Pennsylvania. "It sounds like you've got things under control. Who else would you get for your best man?" It wasn't a yes or a flat no. It would give him time to think of a way out of this web. He gulped at his second glass of wine, grateful Ross hadn't noticed his vague response.

"Our friendship won't change when I get married, will it, Woo?" Ross asked anxiously. "I mean, you like Jory and she likes you. I don't want to have to worry about that, but I do need to know."

This can't be happening to me, Woo thought. Somebody else is sitting here in my body going through this. This isn't me. Why don't I just tell him what I feel and leave? He chose his words carefully. "I don't think your wife will want you hanging around a single guy too much. As a single guy, I won't want to hang out with a newly married couple. What will you do Ross, if Jory says no?"

"She won't. I can see it in her face, in the way she talks. We're going to find you some sweet young thing who will love you to death and give you a dozen children. From this point on I'm going on the lookout for you. If I leave it up to you, you'll end up being a bachelor. I want you to be as happy as I am. You deserve the best, Woo, and I'm going to make sure you get the best."

"If it's all the same to you, Ross, I'd prefer to find my own wife," Woo said coolly.

"Well, sure, but just in case nothing comes along real soon, I'll be on the lookout. We have similar tastes in women, so I know what you like."

"You make it sound like I'm looking for a brood mare. I'm in no hurry to marry. I have a couple of years of . . . of being like this before I can think about a particular girl or marriage. Where is it written that I have to get married?"

Ross snorted. "It's not written anywhere. You said, and this is a direct quote, 'I can't wait to fall in love, get married, and have ten kids.' You said that to me on a hundred different occasions."

"I was a kid then, what the hell did I know about life and responsibility? And wasn't it you, Ross, who told me over and over that I'm a dumb shit and homely as a mud fence," Woo said, then added bitterly, "and crippled in the bargain."

"I never meant it the way you're saying it, and you fucking well know it, Woo. I don't want to hear you talk like that."

"Maybe if you'd only said it once, I'd believe you. For some reason now, it seems like you did mean it."

Ross's vision blurred. He felt his throat tighten. "Woo, I love you like you were my brother. I wish you were my brother. There is nothing in the whole fucking world I wouldn't do for you. I never meant to hurt your feelings. I would never do that intentionally. It was like a game, you calling me a rich snob who needed a transfusion of real blood. I never got upset over that. It was a give-and-take thing. At least I thought so. Aren't you a little late taking me to task for it all? Jesus Christ, I owe you my life. We wouldn't be sitting here now if it wasn't for you. I don't know if this means anything to you or not, but I like to think I would have done the same thing for you."

"It means a lot, Ross, but then I already knew that. Listen, why don't we talk about something else?"

"Sure, what?" Ross said, a foolish grin on his face.

"For instance, today I called the office of *TIF*. Your mother sent on some folders of mine she said I left behind. She mailed them to the carriage house, and I got them when I got home last night so I called to thank her." "Clarence answered the phone and said Mrs. Landers stopped publishing *TIF* and left. The new tenant, Miss Ryan, would probably take over the offices tomorrow. Do you know anything about that?"

"It sounds like my mother and Jory struck up some kind of deal. Nah, Jory wouldn't do that. Mother probably moved to the warehouse."

"Listen, Ross, as much as I hate to admit this, my sister buys those . . . those awful magazines. I read them while I was home because there was nothing else to read. In the issue I read, your mother wrote a short letter on the editorial page saying that the magazine would soon cease publication, that there would be only two more issues. It wasn't important to me, and for all I knew, your mother might have used that as some kind of marketing ploy. I didn't think about it again until Clarence told me your mother left. If she was publishing somewhere else, she would have taken Clarence with her. At least I think she would have. She's your mother, Ross, I think you ought to check into it. Some of those high rollers she chewed up might be . . . gunning for her. It's a bit farfetched, but it is possible. She could be in trouble."

"Yeah, she is. She didn't pay Jory the rent for over a year. She doesn't think things through. It would be just like her to stop publishing to get out of paying the rent."

"Your mother is not that stupid, Ross. It's none of my business. I just thought I should mention it."

"I'm certainly not going to worry about it. Here's my father. Tell him what you just told me and see if he's worried."

"Tell me what?" Jasper said, accepting a glass of wine from Ross. Woo repeated what he'd just told Ross.

Jasper shrugged. "Justine is a law unto herself. I suppose, if any of us are interested, we could call Jory and ask her what she knows, if anything. Speaking for myself, I'm not interested enough to call. What about you, Ross?"

"I'm not either. Woo?"

"It's none of my business," Woo said.

"And on that note, I think we should order," Ross said, motioning to the waiter.

Later, over Ross's and Jasper's protests, Woo climbed into his van to drive back to Chestnut Hill, saying he was fine and he needed fresh clothes for the morning.

It was a lie, he would never be fine again.

Today was probably the worst day of her life, Jory thought as she slammed the load of books in her arms onto the kitchen table. She'd barely slept during the night, and when she did doze, she dreamed about Ross and Woo. When she finally crawled from bed at six o'clock, her nose was stuffy and her throat scratchy. Why shouldn't she get a cold, everyone else seemed to have one, and it was the flu season?

She'd spent the better part of the day at the West Chester University library and different bookstores, trying to find out everything she could about magazine publishing. When she returned home, it was to a ringing phone and Woo's note in the mailbox. She was reading the short note, her heart pounding in her chest when she heard Justine's voice on the other end of the line.

"I called to say good-bye," Justine said.

"Are you sure you're doing the right thing, Justine?" Jory asked in her scratchy voice.

"For me it's the right thing. Everything is waiting for you, Marjory. Don't be afraid to ask for help. Clarence is a wealth of information. He was my right hand for many, many years. He was much more than a janitor; that was a title he gave himself. He did everything. He's loyal and dependable. Hire good people and let them lead you out of the maze of newness. Watch and listen to them. I left my journals for you."

"I feel like I'm starting something from a mail order course. I don't know if I can do this, Justine," Jory said fretfully.

"You won't know unless you try," Justine said briskly. "Everything's been set in motion for you. Follow through. You'll be hearing from my New York attorney in a day or so. Advertise for good help or do as we discussed, recruit from the colleges in the area. I have to go now, I just called to say good-bye and to wish you luck. Please keep your promise to me, Marjory."

"I will, Justine. Happy New Year."

"The same to you, and thank you for Christmas. I'll always remember that. Another minute and I'll be making a fool of myself and be slobbering all over my nice new traveling suit."

"It's alright to have feelings, Justine. You kept yours bottled up too long. I did that too. Sometimes you have to yowl and scream and bay at the moon. I punch my pillow a lot. Try it sometimes," Jory said softly.

"I'll remember that if things get . . . sticky. Good-bye, Marjory."

" 'Bye, Justine."

Jory looked at the clock. Five-thirty. Time to make the dogs their dinner, fix some soup for herself, and then walk the dogs. She had plenty of time to do some serious thinking before Woo arrived at seven o'clock, plenty of time to make her decisions.

Jory worked automatically, her routine pat. She didn't finish her soup because it hurt her throat to swallow. Her ears were starting to feel achy. She swallowed three aspirin before she bundled up to walk the dogs. On her return she made a pot of tea and laced it heavily with plum brandy. She drank it at the table, her eyes on the kitchen clock. At a quarter to eight she finished the tea. She smoked until eight-thirty, one cigarette after the other, her ears tuned toward the window for the sound of Woo's van. At nine-thirty she turned out the light on the porch and the one in the kitchen. At ten o'clock she took a hot, steaming shower, hoping it would ease her throbbing headache and unclog her nose. At ten-thirty she rubbed Vicks salve on her chest and under her nose. She put both hot water bottles in the middle of the bed before she looked out the window to see if Woo had returned while she was in the shower. The driveway was empty.

"You can just go to hell, Pete Woojalesky," Jory muttered.

Jory settled herself between the covers, her head high on three plump pillows. In the stillness of the night she heard Woo's return a half hour later, heard the door close, heard his footsteps on the concrete and the tap of his cane, heard the door to the carriage house open and close. She almost jumped out of her skin when the phone next to the bed rang a moment later. The dogs growled softly as they shifted position on the heavy comforter next to her. The phone continued to ring. Jory buried her head in the pillow.

The door to the carriage house opened and closed. Footsteps again, the tap of the cane, and then the furious sound of heavy knocks on the back door. Jory rolled over, trying to remember if she'd locked the door. She had. She'd also attached the chain guard. "Stay out there till you freeze, Pete Woojalesky," she said. "See if I care."

She did care, that was the problem. She started to cry then, sobbing into the mound of pillows. "I hate men," she sobbed.

The whirlwind was intense, the four dogs burrowing and scurrying in the covers to lick her face, to paw her shoulders and arms. She gathered them close when the phone rang again. Suddenly her arm shot out. She picked up the phone and yelled, "What do you want? Do you know what time it is? You stood me up. Go to hell, Pete Woojalesky!" She slammed down the phone so hard the lamp moved two inches on the night table.

The dogs literally flew off the bed five minutes later when Woo banged again on the kitchen door. Jory pulled on her bathrobe and stomped her way to the kitchen, turning on lights as she went along.

"It's about time, I'm freezing my ass off," Woo said tightly.

"You should be so lucky," she said as she closed the door behind him. "You *said* you'd be here at seven. I waited. Obviously, you had something more important to do," Jory said pointedly.

"I tried calling you six or seven times today, but there was no answer. I even called the Landers Building, thinking you might be there. I didn't stand you up."

"Well, it doesn't matter now. It's late," Jory said, looking at her watch.

"I have something to say and I'm going to say it, then I'll leave," Woo said.

He looked tired, Jory thought. She could feel herself start to weaken. Today must have been torture for him, his first day back, and then the late hours and the drive back.

She was about to ask him if he wanted a cup of tea, when he said, "I'll be moving the first of February. I won't mind if you show the carriage house to prospective renters while I'm at work. I don't want you to lose money on my account. I'm sorry about this evening."

Jory clenched her hands into balled fists then jammed them into the pockets of her flannel robe. This wasn't what she expected. She felt sick when she said, "Why are you moving, do you mind telling me?"

"I had dinner with Ross and his father this evening, and—"

"You let me sit here and wait for you while you had dinner with *Ross*! Don't tell me, he told you you should move, and you always do what Ross says. Is that right?"

"No, that's not right, Jory, and you know it. It's been a long day for me, driving back and forth. It makes sense to move closer to where I work. Ross told me . . . he said you and he . . . well, what he said was, it didn't matter to him that you couldn't have children and he was going to marry you anyway. I'm sorry, I didn't mean it to come out like that, I really didn't," Woo said miserably.

"Ross told you that?" Jory whispered. "I see. What that means to me is because Ross said all this, you're going to step aside for your best friend in the whole world. By stepping aside, I mean, you're negating whatever it was that we had and going on about your business. Yes, that sounds right to me. Plus," she said, jamming her index finger under his nose, "you don't want to be saddled with someone who can't turn out babies every nine months. Yes, that sounds right too. Now, you turn around and get out of my house before I sic all four of these dogs on you and I take the frying pan to the back of your head. You know what, Pete, like Ross, you're too late. I'm not marrying Ross. I never gave him any encouragement at all. It's all in his head. You should have seen that. You are a dumb shit, just the way Ross said you are. I was falling in love with you. I would have told you before we . . . we . . . about not having children. Damn it, I would have told you! I don't want you to wait till February to move. I want you out of my carriage house tomorrow. I'll refund your rent and mail it to your office. Now, get out of here and don't ever come near me again. Give the same message to your friend. If I ever see either one of you on my property, I'll call the police. Out!"

"Jory—"

"Out! You have to pack. Don't call me either, and don't put notes in my mailbox. If you call me, I'll hang up. If you write me notes, I'll tear them up unread, so don't waste your time."

"Jory, please, let me—"

"I'll push you right out!" Jory said angrily, tears rolling down her cheeks. "Get out of here!"

"You don't understand—"

"Oh, that's where you're wrong. My mistake was in thinking you were different, that you were your own person. You aren't. You're just a goddamn extension of Ross."

Woo opened the door, and Jory slammed it so hard behind him that the glass rattled. She snapped the lock and slid the chain into the groove at the same moment she turned off the porch light. "Break your damn neck, see if I care." The kitchen light went off, as did the dining room light and then the hall light. She ran upstairs and flew into the bedroom, the four dogs on her heels.

"Don't cry. Don't cry," she said over and over as she fought to take deep breaths. "He's not worth it. You knew this was going to happen. That's why you drew back and waited. You did the right thing. Don't cry." The dogs nuzzled her, their furry bodies warm and comforting. She picked them up one at a time and lay them on the bed. She covered them with a light afghan she'd found in the attic. They were as close to children as she was going to get. She crooned to them, a silly little nursery rhyme she remembered hearing from somewhere. She stroked their heads until they were asleep.

Slowly and deliberately, Jory walked over to the night table and picked up the phone. She dialed Ross's number. He picked it up on the second ring. Jory identified herself and didn't bother to apologize for the call. "Ross, I want to tell you something and I want you to listen. When I'm finished, I'm going to ask you one question and you will give me an answer. Other than that I don't want you to say anything. I am not going to marry you. Not now, not sometime in the future. Not ever. I appreciate the fact that you would be willing to marry me *anyway*, even though I can't bear children. I do not want you to come to my home ever again. I do not want you to call me or write me letters. I am severing our . . . friendship. That's all it ever was, Ross, a friendship. Tomorrow I will mail you a check for the money I owe you. That makes the break clean. I plan to move on with my life, and that life does not include you, your father, or Pete. Pete, by the way, will be moving out of the carriage house tomorrow. Do you understand what I've just said, Ross? Just say yes or no."

"I heard what you said—"

Jory broke the connection, then laid the receiver on the floor.

"So there," she sniffled. "So there."

Chapter 19

Jory settled herself behind Justine Landers's desk. The moment she was comfortable, she raised her eyes and snapped off a smart salute in the direction of her benefactor's portrait. "It's been a hell of a year, Justine. I'm about as ready as I'll ever be." Her stomach lurched when she thought of the commitment she'd made to Justine and herself. God, what if she fell flat on her face? Her hand snaked out to draw the phone closer. She didn't hesitate, instead she cleared her throat and spoke briskly. "I want to place an overseas call." She rattled off the number from memory. While she waited for the call to go through, she stacked the mounds of paper on her desk into neat piles. Her fingers tapped on the glossy surface of the desk for another minute until she heard Justine's familiar voice. "I'm scared," she blurted out.

Justine chuckled. "That's good. Your adrenaline is flowing. That's just another way of saying you'll stay on your toes. You aren't making a mistake, Jory."

"It's just . . . what if women over forty aren't interested in this magazine? You're absolutely sure of this, Justine? I didn't do any market research. Instincts—yours, mine—God, what if they're wrong, Justine?"

"You have to be confident even when the ground is shaking underneath your feet, and for God's sake, never let them see you sweat, and by *them* I mean anyone who looks at you crossways. You have more going for you than I ever had. Today is scary because you're finally going to make this past year pay off. So what if you foul things up? You'll correct your mistakes and go on from there. How's it looking?"

Jory though about the question. "Good, Justine. Real good. It's the money thing that's scaring me. If this doesn't work, I'll be in debt to you for the rest of my life."

"You don't see me making demands, do you? Stop whining, Marjory, and get to work. Follow the plan I outlined for you, and do not ever, under any circumstance, even if you find yourself on your deathbed, relinquish editorial control. That was our only stipulation. Now, I suggest you straighten your seams and act like a publisher and the editor-in-chief that you are. Call me anytime."

Jory stared at the pinging phone. She slammed it back on the cradle. She slapped her hands palms down on the desk to stop them from shaking. The moment she felt in control, she looked over her shoulder to check the seams of her stockings. Satisfied, she saluted Justine again. "Yes, ma'am. I'm ready."

And she *was* ready. She'd risen at five o'clock and spent two hours looking for just the right outfit. Her Dartmouth-green suit wasn't just a suit, it was a creation, and it fitted as if it had been made especially for her. She felt comfortable as well as professional. Her lizard shoes had cost a fortune, twice as much as the matching briefcase. Justine had roared when Jory told her she'd dunked the elegant case in the bathtub and dried it in the oven to take away the newness. Two days ago she'd mastered the art of doing her hair into a French twist. This morning it had taken her only five minutes to twist and twirl her locks and expertly pin them into place. Her makeup was subdued, her jewelry in good taste. Even the dogs had new collars. Yes, she was ready.

There would probably be a few raised eyebrows when she walked into the conference room with all four of them. Too bad. This was who she was. Like it or lump it. This was her magazine, her building, she would be signing the checks, and if she wanted four dogs running up and down the halls, she would damn well have four dogs running up and down the halls.

She walked slowly, the dogs trotting alongside her. Patsy, her skinny secretary, fell into step with her, her notebook and pencil clasped to her thin chest.

"It's our first day, Miss Ryan," she gushed, "isn't it thrilling?"

"It certainly is. I just hope the world is ready for my magazine."

"Oh, it is, Miss Ryan. When I told my mother about it, she said it was about time someone recognized older women as real people. She's going to buy it, and so are all her friends. My mother has lots of friends."

"I needed that, Patsy. Thanks."

"Nervous?" Patsy asked.

"I feel like I got an itch in my git-along." Jory smiled at the blank look on Patsy's face. "It's just an expression. Here goes," she said, opening the door. Her itch intensified. *Never let them see you sweat.* God, what were they all thinking? She smiled before she took her seat, and motioned to the dogs to lie at her feet next to her brief-case. She smiled again as she greeted each person by name.

They were the best. Justine had said, "Pay them whatever they want and they're yours." What she'd done was pirate them from other magazines, and made no apologies for doing so. Money talks, she'd found out when Brian Andrews of *Time* jumped ship and signed on as her first editor. Morgana Sinclaire, a former high fash-ion editor, had been enticed from *Vogue* and appointed first Beauty and Fashion Director. It would be Morgana's job to find the *Seren-dipity* Woman. She'd jumped at the challenge to create the image of an attractive, sensuous, sexy woman. Morgana, in her mid-forties, said it was about time someone took the middle-aged and older woman seriously. Six section heads, three males and three females, lined one side of the long table, their pencils posed, their eyes ex-pectant. Flanking Morgana and Brian were two columnists snatched from the *New York Times*. With their salaries doubled, Jory had no reason to think that their monthly columns would be anything but power columns. The last man to be acknowledged was Roger Tyler, who would head up the advertising department. He had been recruited from Young and Rubicam at a salary that made Jory's head spin. They were the best, and they now worked for her.

"I have some ideas," Jory said brightly. As one, the department heads groaned. The dogs barked. The ice was broken.

Five hours later they were all on a first-name basis. Jory leaned back in her chair, the last of her lunch coffee in front of her. It was going to work, she could feel it. For someone who knew diddly about starting up a magazine, she felt she'd done well. Her insistence on a business-money-investment column as well as a political column was met with enthusiasm when she said it would generate advertisers. Tyler had smiled at her and nodded, as much as to say, So you do have a brain in that pretty head. Morgana had loudly approved when she said she planned to write a regular feature called "Serendipity," in which she would interview someone, male or female, with whom their readership would identify with. She'd clarified "someone" as an ordinary person. The staff approved.

"I see our typical woman as being in her mid-forties with a household income of, say, fifteen thousand dollars, whose home is probably worth, let's say, forty thousand dollars. I've worked up some figures here and would like to see what you all think. I believe, if we all do our jobs, that the growth of the magazine's target market would be from forty percent of the women who are over forty, this year, to forty-six percent in say 1960. I see a boom in advertising revenues as well as circulation increases. I predict our inaugural issue will fly off the stands. Now, this is what I want to see, what we're all here to work toward. Listen carefully. We sell out our first issue of three hundred thousand copies. I expect circulation to increase to a half-million copies over the year. As circulation increases from our guaranteed rate base of two hundred thousand to total circulation of half a million, advertising pages will follow right behind. I expect our advertising pages—and I think Roger will agree, will go to three hundred or three fifty." Tyler nodded. Jory felt giddy. These people *knew* what they were talking about. Justine had said don't be afraid to pay for the best. You won't fail if you surround yourself with people who know the business, and you'll learn at the same time.

The mood shifted then, grew intense as the staff began talking among themselves as though she wasn't there. Jory sat back, not knowing if she should be offended or not. Justine would have jumped in, refusing to be left out. Well, she wasn't Justine, but she damn well owned this project. She lit a cigarette, puffing smoke in every direction. Her eyes narrowed as she saw several editors frown. She blew more smoke as she listened.

"I'm not convinced older women will buy magazines . . . So what, being forty doesn't mean you're over the hill? . . . Hell, I don't even know if there are models out there over forty . . . You really think women are going to buy a magazine with an old broad's picture on the cover? . . . How many consultants are on our roster? . . . Who said we have unlimited money? . . . Budgets . . . Top names want top dollar . . . I'm game, but I think you're trying to target an illusory market . . . Who the hell is going to go out there and snatch all these top writers? . . . Goddamnit, you're putting the cart before the horse . . . Do we have a production advisor? Well, now would be a good time to tell us who he is . . . Do you really like the idea of a centerfold? . . . A show of hands here . . . Eight months isn't enough time . . . Did you say there's a printer and a printing schedule? . . . Bullshit . . . Do we have a fucking assignment editor? . . . Who's doing what? Who makes the final decision here? . . . Run that by me again . . . We *need* Madison Avenue and New York . . . Who in their right mind is going to pay to see before and after pictures of some woman's face-lift? . . . Who's fucking idea was that anyway?"

"It was my idea," Jory said quietly. "We're doing it, there's no room for discussion. Continue." She blew a perfect smoke ring and watched it float over the conference table. Blank stares greeted Jory's benign gaze. "This is good, we're talking. Or did you forget I was here?" This last was said so coolly, the women looked embarrassed, the men brazen.

"We're going to do our best, Jory, but it's my personal opinion this magazine is ahead of its time. I hope to God you can make believers out of all of us. I've always been one to go with my gut instincts, but starting a project this size on guts alone is bending my mind. I want that out in the open, right here and now," one of the men snapped.

"Then why did you sign on?" Jory asked quietly.

"For the money," another man said quietly.

"And that money will only continue if we are a success. I trust you will do your best, that all of you will do your best. We will not be an overnight success, but we will be a success. There is a market out there for this magazine, and we are going to tap it. If you all do your jobs right, we won't have any problems. You can come to me any time. My door will always be open to you. I promise to listen. I think we can adjourn this meeting now. We'll meet again tomorrow morning at seven o'clock here in the conference room. Breakfast will be catered. Don't be late. Gentlemen and ladies," Jory said, getting up from her chair. The dogs leaped to their feet at the same moment the others stood, confused looks on their faces.

In the hall, Jory turned the dogs over to Clarence. "A long walk would be nice, they've been cooped up too long."

"My pleasure, Miss Ryan," Clarence said happily.

"What do you think, Patsy?" Jory asked the moment both women were in her office with the door closed. "Did I do okay? Do you think those people in there are going to give me a hundred percent?"

"It's a man's world, Miss Ryan. I don't care what anyone says. My mom agrees. The ladies are behind you. I could see some doubt, but like you said, instincts are important, and they use theirs just the way you do. They're behind you. I don't know about the men. This is a job, and they're doing it for the money. At least they were honest about that. I don't think I'd let them make any *real* important decisions. If you have to fire someone, have somebody standing by just in case. Preferably a woman. That would be neat if you had all women working for you. I can't wait to tell my mom I sat in on the first meeting. Ohhh, this is going to be thrilling! When Mom hears about that face-lift, she's going to be so excited."

"Tomorrow morning I want you to call New York and find out if there are any plastic surgeons who will agree to an interview and if they have a patient who will agree to . . . you know, go public. It will be good press for the doctor, and we can even pay for the surgery. What do you think, Patsy?"

"My mom!" Patsy squealed. "My mom would do it. She hates the bags under her eyes and her double chin. Jeez, wait till I tell her!"

"Now that's a thought, Patsy. Tell her to come in tomorrow and we can talk. Around noon. You can go home if you want, Patsy. I'm going to stay on for a while. Since we don't have an assignment editor as yet, I'm going to see what I can come up with. I also want to call my old boss in Florida and ask him some questions. He might be able to get me some leads on top-notch professional writers willing to jump ship or at least free-lance."

"I'll stay," Patsy volunteered. "Mom keeps dinner warm for me. I can get a head start on transcribing all these notes I took."

"I'm scared, Patsy. What if I'm wrong, what if I have to go back to Mrs. Landers and tell her this is all a pipe dream and it won't work? She's counting on me. Why she has all this faith in me is something I'll never understand. I believe in what I'm trying to do, but what if it isn't enough?"

"Then," Patsy said, "you memorize that little ditty under the glass on your desk." Her dark eyes danced merrily as she pointed one long-tipped nail at the white square of paper Justine had left behind.

> In the end, vision, drive, energy, singleness of purpose, wise use of resources, and a commitment to a destiny worthy of his efforts become a character of a chieftain who excels.
> —Attila the Hun

Jory giggled as she read the words aloud. "Actually, Patsy, I think I like the one pasted on the door just as much as I like this one. Listen to this and give me your opinion: 'There is nothing more difficult to take in hand, more perilous to conduct, or more uncertain of its success than to take the lead in the introduction of a new order of things.' . . . Niccolo Machiavelli wrote that.

"Let's do this. Tomorrow I want you to take both of these . . . whatever they are, to a photo studio and have them blown up to the size of, say, Justine's picture, order one of each for every room in this building. I want them framed and hung side by side. If they were good enough for Justine to go by, then they're good enough for me."

Fresh out of Kathryn Gibbs, Patsy did her best to look and act professional, but sometimes, like now, Miss Ryan just made her want to giggle. Imagine hanging a quote from Attila the Hun in every room in the office. Miss Gibbs would surely faint if she ever saw such a thing.

Jory joined in the giggling and clapped her hands gleefully. "That should give them all something to think about. And wait until they find out whose picture is going on the first cover. No name, just the picture. I'm going to need a photographer who really knows his business to enlarge and reproduce a picture I have of Justine drying dishes in my kitchen."

"What if your staff disapproves?" Patsy asked.

Jory shrugged. "I'm in control. I owe it to Justine, and she's absolutely perfect for the first issue. People are still wondering where she is and why she folded *TIF*. I'm going to go ahead with it until someone can *convince* me it's a mistake."

"Oh, I'm really going to like working here," Patsy said, laughing.

"And I'm going to like having you. All those others . . . I saw the way they looked at me. Who am I? Where did I get all this money and the nerve, the gall, to think I can pull something like this off? Ha. They should all have known Justine Landers."

"Can I get you some coffee or a soft drink, Miss Ryan?"

She's nice, Jory thought as she congratulated herself on picking Patsy from the five interviewees the Gibbs school had sent a week ago. She'd been so anxious, afraid to stand straight because she was almost six feet tall in flat-heeled shoes. She was incredibly thin, with an eighteen-inch waist and legs like matchsticks. Jory had seen past the thinness, the awkwardness of the young woman's first job interview. Jory had liked the way she spoke of her family, of putting herself through the Gibbs school. She'd made the decision to hire her the moment Patsy confided that she'd heard the other girls talking in class, saying she'd be the last one to be placed because she was tall and gawky. She'd showed spunk when she said, "If you turn me down for this job, is it because I'm too tall or because I can't type or take dictation fast enough?" Jory had hired her on the spot.

"Where did you get those dimples?" Jory asked now, grinning.

"From the same place I got these chipmunk cheeks, my dad. My mom is thin like me, but my dad is kind of round. My brothers are built like him too. It's awful to be so tall. I probably wouldn't mind so much if I wasn't flat-chested. My mother builds up the . . . you know. I'll get right on this Miss Ryan," Patsy said, backing out the door.

"Olive Oyl," Jory muttered to herself when the door closed behind Patsy. "It's those damn sausage curls she wears." Maybe she could find a tactful way to get Patsy a new hairstyle more in keeping with the times. God, that was it, a make-over for an article. A good hair stylist. A cosmetician could do wonders for Patsy. Providing she was amenable to it.

Jory kicked off her shoes and fired up a cigarette. She blew a perfect smoke ring before she leaped up from her chair, her clenched fist shooting upward. *This is going to work!* Her sudden display of emotion made her weak in the knees. She sat down. Justine's words rang in her ears. *Publish a magazine for old broads like me, follow my plan and I'll put up the money. You'll have carte blanche. No one to answer to but yourself. Go on your instincts and you'll make as much money as I did with* TIF, *and at the same time you'll be filling a void out there for older women.*

God, she had so many ideas. The cigarette was a stub now. Jory put it out and lit a second one. A fast-paced article on the empty nest syndrome. All she had to do was find a woman whose youngest child left for college. The stay-at-home woman. *Housewife.* Gray hair, wrinkles. The list was endless. Ordinary people with a sprinkling of celebrity. Divorce . . . what it's like for the woman? Welfare mothers . . . What happens to a widow when her husband dies?

How does she manage? Can she manage her affairs?

Five minutes later she was speaking to her old boss in Florida. "The best, Sy, I need the best. Preferably women. Of course I have a pencil. Paper too. Yes, it will work, don't sell me short. I won the Irish Sweepstakes," she lied. "We're going with six issues the first year. Hopefully we can go monthly the second year. Okay, I'm ready." She scribbled furiously. Several minutes later she said, "Thanks, Sy. I'll airmail you a copy of our first issue. The cover? Oh, you bet I have one in mind. Does Macy's tell Gimbel's? Thanks again."

Jory clapped her hands gleefully. She took a deep breath before she placed her next call. Lillian Masters, feature writer for *Redbook*. The moment she finished identifying herself and explaining what she was about, Jory squelched the fear building in her stomach and said, "I'd like to put you on the payroll, not on a free-lance basis. You'll have an expense account. You don't write for anyone but *Serendipity*. Call me in the morning and give me your answer." She doodled as Lillian posed several questions. She answered them as she added and subtracted. Money was literally flying out the window. Another call to Justine was in order.

By evening's end she felt confident that Lillian Masters and Russell Clark would be added to her payroll. She signed on three free-lance writers at fifty cents a word. She knew it was an outrageous sum because the writers hadn't been able to stifle their gasps of surprise. *Don't be afraid to pay for the best.*

"It sounds like you're off and running, in the right direction," Justine said, chuckling from across the world. "Whatever it takes, you do. Marjory, it's in your blood now. Make me proud of you. No doubts now. One piece of advice, my dear. Don't become friendly with any of your people. Patsy and Clarence are different. You're the boss, don't ever let them forget it. You pull rank every single day. And for God's sake, don't worry about Russell Clark being a homosexual. He's a wonderful writer. He'll never let you down, and his style is unequaled. Now, if you can just get Bella Ingram, I think you'll have your ducks in a row. There isn't anything she doesn't know about banking and investments. I approached her once to talk about my own investments. She didn't like my brand of publishing, but as two older woman, we hit it off. She's the reason I was able to make the move. There isn't anything she doesn't know about investments, trusts, etcetera. She's one of the very few who've made it in this man's world. Call her and set up an appointment. Don't bring my name into it unless she balks. Pay her whatever she wants. She's worth it."

"Justine," Jory said uneasily, "the money is flowing out of here in a stream."

"That's my problem, Marjory. We agreed to all this before I left.

Finance is my problem. Look at it this way, if we have to, we'll mortgage the building. You can do that, you know. It's time for you to go home. Tomorrow is another day. Keep in touch."

"Don't worry about finances," Jory muttered to the dogs as she gathered up their leashes.

"Patsy! I thought you left an hour ago! Come on, cover your typewriter and I'll give you a ride home. It's eleven o'clock. I haven't had any dinner, and I know you haven't either. From now on if we work late, order dinner. We can't have this. First thing you know we'll get run-down and then we'll get sick. God, I'm tired. You must be exhausted. Now, Patsy!"

Jory described herself to Justine and Patsy in the weeks and months to come as an accident waiting to happen. There was no doubt in the staff's mind as to who was in control, and Jory exercised that control to the limit. Her blue pencil came to be known as a weapon and was aimed at anyone who didn't do things her way.

On a blustery winter day in November, Jory entered the offices to see a homemade sign that read, RYAN IS A DICTATOR. "It was here when I got here," Patsy bleated. "I was going to take it down, but decided you better see it. Someone is unhappy."

"Really," Jory said through clenched teeth. "It's probably the same person who sicced the *Times* on me." She tossed a copy of the paper onto Patsy's desk. "It's on the first page of the second section. Read it and weep. Is the coffee on?"

"I'll bring it in, Miss Ryan. You have several messages. I left them on your desk. It's not eight o'clock, and the phone's been ringing off the hook. Now, I know why," she said, her eyes raking the *Times* article.

"Close the door, Patsy. Who took this picture of me and the dogs? Do you know?" Patsy shook her head. "Who do you *think* told this *Times* reporter all this . . . garbage?"

"I don't know, Miss Ryan. Everyone has been grumbling and complaining about you. I'm sorry. They say you're running amuck, that you're out of control. They say you're going to ruin this endeavor before it gets off the ground. The worst thing they say is that you're like . . . they said it must be the building or something, you know . . . a bitch like Mrs. Landers."

"They said *that*? For God's sake, why?" Jory gulped at her coffee. "See if everyone is here, Patsy. If they are, go in the hall, blow that whistle we use for the dogs, and tell everyone to assemble in the conference room. So I don't know my ass from my elbow, huh?"

"Oh, I know who said that, Miss Ryan. It was Brian Andrews. He says that almost every day." Her hand flew to her mouth. "Jeez, I'm sorry, Miss Ryan. I kind of thought it was one of those inside office jokes and you knew about it. I guess that means we know who gave the information to the *Times*, huh?"

Jory looked down at the dogs, her eyes misty with tears. "I guess this is how Justine must have felt when everyone turned against her. I wasn't wrong. I know what I want, what Justine wants, and what they've been giving me isn't it. All I did was make it better. Dictator my foot. This is *my* magazine. I have creative control and editorial control. They all knew that from the beginning. Now, when we're ready to go with the prototype, they pull this. My God, what they must be saying behind my back. Well, gentlemen," she said to the dogs, "I don't care what they're saying. I can finish this myself if I have to. But by God, I'm not giving up without a fight. And I'm not calling Justine either."

The dogs watched her with unblinking intensity, their tails swishing furiously. The moment the whistle blew, they ran for the door.

"Everyone is in the conference room, Miss Ryan. Clarence is serving coffee. I'm ready if you are," Patsy said coolly.

"There won't be time for coffee, Patsy," Jory said, falling into step, the *Times* under her arm.

How innocent they look, Jory thought. But then betrayal always looked innocent in the beginning. The dogs barked as they raced up and down the room chasing one another, something they'd never done before. She issued a sharp command. The dogs quieted immediately.

Her heart thumping madly, Jory took her time looking at each member of her staff before she spoke. "Ladies and gentlemen, I want to show you all something." She pushed her chair back against the wall, turning slightly. She raised her skirt and pulled down her panties. "This, ladies and gentlemen, is my ass." She turned again and pushed up the sleeve of her blouse. "This is my elbow. You're all fired with the exception of Russell Clark. You can pick up your checks at the close of business today. You have exactly ten minutes to gather your things and clear the premises."

Back in her office, Jory collapsed into her chair. There was an angry knot in her throat. She would not cry. Her heart was beating so fast she thought it would leap into her throat, fight with the knot and strangle her. She looked up to see Clarence, Russell, and Patsy. Clarence held up a bottle of brandy. Russell made a low sweeping bow, and Patsy giggled.

"Mrs. Landers would have loved that performance," Clarence said, pouring brandy into three water glasses.

Jory snorted. "She would have, wouldn't she? I can't believe I did that!"

Russell chuckled. "They couldn't believe it either. Why did you single me out?" he asked curiously.

"Because you love words the way I do. You're the only one who really understands what it is I'm trying to do here. If I told them once I told them a hundred times, I didn't want them to use the words 'mature' or 'older woman.' One of them used the word 'ripe.' Now I ask you! You and Bella are the only ones who are staying. Provided you want to stay. Do you, Russell?"

"Hell yes! I like it here. I feel like I've found a home. I like what you're trying to do, and I think you're going to pull it off. So count me in."

Patsy giggled. "Me too."

"I'm here for the long haul," Clarence said, filling the three glasses again.

It was a miserable, wet, gray day in February when Jory, Patsy and Clarence at her side, entered the printer's offices to view the prototype for the first time.

"Ohhh. I love this smell," Jory said in a shaky voice that matched the shaking in her legs. "God, I can't wait to see it! I have to see it, Herb, I can't wait another minute. Did it come out okay? Is it first-class? Does it shout at you? Will women back up, take a second look and buy it? Oh God, oh God. You look at it first, Patsy. . . . Well?" she said hoarsely.

"Oh, my goodness, it's . . . it's . . ."

"Stupendous," Clarence said gruffly.

"You got a first-rate magazine here, Miss Ryan," Herb said blandly.

"Oh, *my God*!" Jory said, holding the magazine up in front of her. "This is . . . this is . . . about as perfect as you can get. Doesn't Mrs. Landers look . . . normal? Look at those wrinkles. That's my dish towel and plate she's holding. Oh God, oh God, and it's mine. I did it. I really did it. I think I'm going to faint. . . ."

"My mother is gonna love this," Patsy shouted, to be heard over Jory's and Clarence's jabbering.

"Clarence, stick this first copy off the press into an envelope and take it to the airport. Make arrangements to have it hand delivered to Justine the moment the plane lands. Take the money out of petty cash in my desk. She's going to . . . to like it, won't she, Clarence?" Jory said anxiously.

"I think you'll hear her all the way over here," Clarence said, tongue-in-cheek. "Sometime I want you to tell me how you managed to keep it a secret from her."

"I just told her Patsy's mother was going on the cover. She thought it was a good idea. I figure she'll be rip-snortin' mad for about five minutes, then she'll laugh her head off. My God, it's gorgeous. Now all we have to do is sell it."

"It's gonna sell, Miss Ryan. Trust me." Patsy grinned. "I'm buying three copies myself."

Jory giggled. "I'm buying a dozen."

Clarence chuckled. "Put me down for three."

"See, we're in business," Jory said, picking up a stack of magazines to take back to the office.

On the long walk back, Jory said to Patsy, "I didn't think we'd do it. When I fired the staff, I thought for sure I would go down the drain. By God, it was the best thing I ever did. Who needs those . . . those . . . what are they, Patsy?"

"Nonbelievers," Patsy volunteered.

"Right, nonbelievers. Our new staff is working out well. I think we should throw some kind of party to show our appreciation. Let's do it two weeks from Saturday. Make up a list, Patsy, all those nonbelievers from the *Times* and every other magazine that took potshots at me. The magazine will be out, the reviews will be in, and we'll know if we're selling. Engraved invitations. Call Herb. We'll cover the affair and do an article in the next issue. Comments and all.

"Justine was right, Patsy, this is in my blood. I feel it. I found my niche. I'm happy, Patsy, really happy. I don't ever want to do anything else. Thanks to Justine."

"Mrs. Landers must be a very fine lady."

"A very misunderstood lady, Patsy. I am so blessed."

"You'd be more blessed if you'd find a nice husband," Patsy said sourly.

"Now, that's where you're wrong. I can see the handwriting on the wall. This magazine is going to be my life. If I had a husband, he'd divorce me in a minute. I don't think you can have a successful career and keep a husband happy. Of course, I've never tried it, but knowing me, I wouldn't be able to give either one a hundred percent, and that wouldn't be fair to a husband or the magazine. I'm not unhappy, Patsy."

"I know you're not, and that worries me. You need friends, you need to get out more. Sex," she said, turning rosy pink.

"You don't have to get married to have sex, Patsy. When I have time and my life is under control, I might think about it." She thought about Woo then and wondered what he was doing.

"By the time you get around to thinking about it, you'll be old with wrinkles of your own," Patsy said. "Life will pass you by."

"Life is full of choices, Patsy, and don't ever forget it. For now, this is my choice. Mine. I know now I can do whatever I set my mind to doing. This is my choice for now."

"Alright, Miss Ryan, if you say so," Patsy grumbled as she held the door for her boss.

Jory smiled. "I say so."

Chapter 20

Clarence Henderson stood in the doorway to Jory's office and watched his boss stare out the window. For the past seven years he'd always, somehow, managed to catch Miss Ryan staring out the window. Particularly at this time of year. It also seemed, to his experienced eye, that she grew sadder each year. He looked at the Christmas issue of *Serendipity*. It had been Miss Ryan's idea to forego the traditional Christmas tree cover and go with Grandma Moses's 1953 painting of rural America, *Joy Ride*, on the cover; to honor the 101-year-old artist, Miss Ryan had said at the September cover conference. Sadder now since the artist passed away.

"Penny for your thoughts, Miss Ryan," he said, knocking on the open door. "Here it is, first copy off the press. It's a beauty. I brought the mail. I think you have a letter from Mrs. Landers."

Jory smiled. "And we both know what's in it. Lord, it's beautiful," she said, holding up the slick magazine. "We did okay this year. I think we might be in the black for the second year in a row. It's been a long hard road, Clarence. I truly believe I would have quit after the first year if it wasn't for you and Justine. Okay, let's see what our benefactor has to say," Jory said, ripping open the air mail packet. "Ah, here it is. It says Clarence Henderson on the envelope. And there's one for me."

Clarence accepted the square white card. "Everything's ready for the party, Miss Ryan," he said. "I went over to the hotel myself to check on things about an hour ago. It promises to be a very festive evening."

Jory nodded, her thoughts on her own white envelope. "Clarence, please close the door on your way out."

"Yes, ma'am."

Jory ripped at the envelope, not bothering with the letter opener. It wasn't a long letter, shorter than the usual ones Justine wrote from time to time. She leaned back on the pearl-gray swivel chair and lit a cigarette.

Dear Marjory,

It looks like another year is about to draw to a close. For you it's been a good year. The magazine is absolutely stupendous. I knew you could do it. I learned if you don't have faith in yourself, no one else will. Breaking even three years in a row and two in the black should make you delirious.

There were times during this past year when I wanted to come back, but my doctor felt it wasn't wise. I'm coping.

I'm looking forward to your visit. I can't promise to entertain you personally, but I've met this handsome Swiss banker who will make your blood sing. I talk about you a lot to him. He's a kind, gentle man, and so good-looking he could be a film star. He reads your magazine and has seen your picture. He says you are unbelievably gorgeous. Right up front I told him you can't have children. None of my business, eh? You're right, but I did it anyway. He loves dogs and has three of his own. If you two don't hit it off, I have four other possibilities on my list. I believe this is the man for you, Marjory, and yes, I have a heart. His name is Griffin Ballon. He lives here, but his mother was American, which means he has dual citizenship. I think he was born in Chicago. Alas, there won't be time for you to request more details before your trip.

I look forward to seeing you. I promise you a wonderful holiday. I know you will enjoy your first overseas trip.

Affectionately,
Justine

Jory sat back in her chair, her eyes closed. Seven years were a long time not to have seen someone.

All the details of her trip had been taken care of. She had her brand-new passport, her airline tickets, and Clarence and Tillie were going to stay in the house in Chestnut Hill and take care of the dogs. She had two suitcases full of new clothes and a fashionable new haircut the beautician said took five years off her age.

Because it was the holiday season, she thought about Ross and Woo, which wasn't to say she didn't think of them at other times of the year; she did. She tried not to think of them, but somehow they invaded her life almost on a daily basis. Her eyes snapped open. Perhaps it was the picture on her desk, a bifold: the left picture of the four dogs sitting like little soldiers, with the Gucci collars Justine had sent the first year she went to Geneva; the picture on the right was of her, Woo, and Ross standing by the door to the carriage house. Many people had asked her who the two men in the photograph were, and she always said the same thing: "They're someone I used to know." It didn't matter that the sentence didn't make sense. Each of them was a someone. Someone she'd loved for a little while.

Both Woo and Ross were doing well, so well they'd opened two other offices, one in Brewster and one in Germantown. Woo walked with only one cane these days. She knew that because she'd seen him in Wanamaker's one Saturday afternoon a year ago when she was Christmas shopping. She'd seen him in time to dart out of sight. She'd felt silly and foolish, but she'd done it anyway. A more sophisticated person would probably have gone up to him, stretched out her hand, bussed him on the cheek and trilled some kind of greeting. She remembered the way her heart took on extra beats and the way her eyes burned. An hour or so later, when she was paying for a pair of gloves, she heard Ross's voice and then Woo's response. And then she'd heard two female voices joining in the conversation. They were behind her, waiting in line. She used up five seconds of precious time thinking about how she looked before she forced a smile to her face and turned. Both Woo and Ross looked stunned; the young women, both pretty, wore equally surprised expressions. She'd said something appropriate, like, "How nice to see you," or something like that. Everyone said how well everyone else looked. Introductions were made. Hands were shaken, and she would have had to be blind not to see the diamonds on the young women's left hands winking under the overhead store lights.

Somehow she'd gotten out of the store to the parking lot, where she collapsed in a heap behind the steering wheel. She still didn't know how she managed to get home without causing an accident, because her attention was on everything but the road in front of her.

She'd finally seen Lena Davis up close. And the young woman with Woo was pretty and wholesome-looking. Her name was Ann Marie something. She'd read their engagement announcements. She'd gotten drunk that night and slept on the floor in front of the fire. Both Woo and Ross would be married in two weeks, New Year's Day. A double wedding. How like the two of them to have a double wedding.

And that, she thought, leaning over her desk, was the reason she finally decided to make this trip. She needed to put as much distance between herself and Philadelphia as possible when the double wedding took place.

She told herself over and over she didn't love either Ross or Woo. How could you love someone who said they would marry you anyway, even if you couldn't have children? How could you love someone who put his friend ahead of you and was willing to walk away from you so as not to hurt that same friend? Did Woo know Ross didn't care about him in the same way? Of course, it wasn't fair of her to think such a thing. If Woo didn't tell Ross his feelings for her, how could Ross know? She always got a headache when she came to this point in her thoughts. She felt one coming on now.

"Time to go home," she muttered. She whistled for the dogs, who came on the run, their leashes dragging behind them. Bringing the dogs to the office was one of the fringe benefits of owning the business. Everyone took turns walking them and feeding them. They were as much a part of *Serendipity* as she was. Hanging on her wall was a blown-up version of her first anniversary cover, with her and the dogs posing in front of the office Christmas tree they'd put up in July for the cover shoot. She always smiled when she looked at it.

Where would the two friends live? Jory wondered. No doubt next to one another or in close proximity. Both Ross's and Jasper's houses in Society Hill had been sold. She'd seen a record of the sale in the *Democrat*. Maybe Jasper, Ross, and Woo would live on the same street. She giggled at that thought. She wondered what a psychiatrist would make of that.

She'd gone to a psychiatrist the year she started up *Serendipity* because her emotions kept getting in the way of her work. Dr. Seymour Ravitch was a kindly, elderly man who looked at her intently, a deep frown on his face. When she finished blurting out what she thought was wrong, he'd said, in his heavily accented voice, "But what is *the problem*?" And she'd repeated everything she'd said previously. "Go home," he'd said. "There's nothing wrong with you, your pride has been injured and your heart is bruised. Save the fifty dollars an hour I charge and buy yourself a new dress. Each time you feel this way, buy a new dress or a new hat. Now, because I have to charge you for this hour, let's have a cup of my famous coffee and chat." In the last thirty minutes of the visit she'd told him more about her life than she thought possible. He'd patted her shoulder when she was about to leave, saying, "Anytime you feel troubled, stop in for coffee and we'll chat." They had a *long* chat and *two* cups of coffee after the Wanamaker encounter and the engagement notice in the *Democrat*.

It was Seymour's idea for her to make the trip to Geneva. "I think," he'd said, "you need to see your benefactor and to be away from here when the double wedding takes place. You need to do something for this lady, show her some kindness. I could be wrong, and if I am, *you* will send *me* a bill."

"I'm leaving, Clarence," Jory called now from the doorway, the dogs' leashes in her hands. "Take care of things for me."

"I will, Miss Ryan."

It was hard to believe, Jory thought, that these were the same offices she'd walked into years ago. All the old decor was gone, replaced with low, comfortable, modern furniture, busy green plants, and colorful, modern art on the walls. The ankle-deep carpets were a shade darker than the dove-gray furniture. The draperies were the same in all the offices, but streaked with a waffle-weave pattern of burgundy or pewter-blue. The glass and chrome gleamed and sparkled in the subdued lighting. Restful, comforting colors, but still vibrant enough to keep the employees moving at an even pace, herself included.

Outside, the wind whipped at her skirts, flattening the dogs, ears against their heads as they walked into the swirling snow.

"We're going home, guys," Jory said, starting her usual dialogue with the dogs, dialogue that continued until they pulled into the driveway.

This year she hadn't decorated the house inside or outside. Christmas of late seemed like a chore. After Woo moved, she'd struggled with a tree that grew smaller each year, until it was nothing more than a piney stem with little branches she could pick up with one hand. All the joy seemed to be gone. For years now she did nothing but work late hours, travel home, feed the dogs, shower, and go to bed.

The price of success. By her own choice.

"It's not that I don't want to be successful, I do," she said to the dogs. "But it's a hollow success. There's no one to share it with. You guys don't care as long as you have your chicken gizzards and you get walked five times a day. I need more. I need a life outside *Serendipity*. Now that we're a success and in the black, I'm going to have less of a life because I'm going to have to work harder, stay later, to make sure I keep pace with the competition. I want time to play, to get out there and spread my wings." She made a funny sound in her throat. "It takes energy and gusto to have a career and a personal life, and mine has been seriously depleted. Relationships take a lot of work and time. My own fault. Your lot in life," she said over her shoulder to the dogs on the backseat, "is to listen to me moan and groan. We're home!" The dogs leaped over the seat to land in a pile on her lap.

"Looks like Harriet is home and has her Christmas lights up." Harriet Mendelson, who rented the carriage house, taught junior high at Chestnut Hills High School and was an old maid by her own admission. She was cranky, belligerent, and she disliked animals. She paid her rent on time, but didn't believe in fraternizing with her landlord, which was alright with Jory because Harriet depressed her. The reason she depressed her was she could see herself turning into a Harriet Mendelson in the years to come.

Jory unlocked the kitchen door. This was the part she hated the most, coming home to a cold, dark house.

Jory clapped her hands. "Dinner for you, a drink for me, and maybe a sandwich later on. We don't want to mess up things for Clarence and Tillie. A fire would be nice. We haven't had one in a long time." She was talking just to hear her own voice. Talking and getting through the hours until it was time to board the plane for Geneva.

The hours ticked by until it was time to carry her bags down to the front door. Time for the limousine to pick her up for the drive to Kennedy Airport in New York.

Clarence and Tillie arrived at seven o'clock in the morning complete with a Christmas tree in the trunk of their car and a backseat full of luggage and brightly wrapped presents.

"You enjoy yourself, Miss Ryan," Clarence said. "Don't you go worrying about anything here. Tillie and I will take good care of the dogs. I'll check in at the office once a day. Wish Mrs. Landers a happy holiday and . . . and . . ."

"Give her a big hug and kiss. I always warm the dogs' food for them."

"I know that, Miss Ryan."

"They need their sweaters on in this weather. Clancy pees on his, so you have to wash it more often."

"I know that too, Miss Ryan."

"I bought you a turkey and all the . . . stuff you'll need for dinner."

"Yes, Miss Ryan."

"The Christmas tree stand is in the garage."

"You told me that."

"Miss Mendelson doesn't like the dogs, so make sure you keep them out of her way. For some strange reason they like her. I don't understand that. She doesn't like them, but they like her."

"We'll keep them out of her way."

"I bought her a fruitcake and wrapped it up. Give it to her when she comes to pay the rent the first of January."

"Get in the damn limo, Miss Ryan," Clarence said, nudging her forward.

"Have a wonderful holiday, Clarence."

"I'd like to get started on it, but I can't if you're going to keep me standing here in the cold," Clarence grumbled.

"I'm going. 'Bye."

She was on her way. She was really going to Switzerland. Her first real vacation, ever. Four-day trips to Florida didn't fall into the same category as this vacation.

Eleven hours later Jory stepped into a second waiting limousine, this one hired by Justine Landers to take her on the last leg of her journey.

It was dusk, and all she could see was snow and more snow. She wanted to ask the driver questions, but she was too tired. Exhausted would be a better word, she thought as she leaned back in the warm comfort of the limousine. "How far is it?" she asked the driver.

"A two-hour ride, miss," the driver said.

Jory closed her eyes and was instantly asleep. She woke when she felt the car glide to a stop. The second thing she felt was a cold *swhoosh* of air when the driver opened the back door. Jory stepped down onto hard-packed snow, the cold swirling about her ankles. She shivered, her teeth chattering.

"The door's open, miss, I'll bring your bags in. It's warm inside and there will be hot cocoa waiting." Jory ran, her steps loud as gunshots as she sped across the frozen snow.

"Madam is waiting for you, miss," the tall, regal housekeeper said briskly. "Try not to tire her. She's not supposed to be down-stairs, but she insisted on welcoming you properly."

Jory jammed her hands into the pockets of her wool skirt. To-morrow she would look at the furniture, the paintings, and the rest of the decor. Now, she only had eyes for the wizened creature propped up on the sofa in a mound of blankets and pillows. This couldn't be Justine. Not the Justine she knew. How ill she looked, how wasted. She fought the tears that were about to puddle in her eyes.

"I'm here! I cannot believe it! You live in *nowhere*! It's good to see you, Justine," Jory said, bending over to kiss Justine's wrinkled cheek.

"Just don't say I look well. The last time I looked in the mirror I scared myself, so I had them all taken out. Stand back, let me look at you."

Jory dropped to her knees and reached for Justine's hand. "You should have told me. I would have come sooner," she said huskily.

"What could you have done? Nothing. I don't want or need pity. I have friends for the first time in my life, a kind, caring staff. I even have a cat."

"But no family," Jory said sadly. "Do Ross and Jasper know?"

"Of course not. They wouldn't care."

"Justine, you don't know that."

"I know that for a fact. When you get to the end of your life, Marjory, you look at things a bit differently. I was not legally married to Jasper. Oh, we went through a ceremony the same way you and Ross did, in front of a magistrate. Justine Connors married Jasper Landers and Justine Connors signed the marriage certificate. But there is no Justine Connors Landers. Not legally. My real name is Ethel Pullet. My birth certificate and passport say so. I consulted three different attorneys, and they all told me the same thing. There was no need to file for divorce, because legally I was never married. That sort of makes Ross illegitimate, and he would not like to know that. Jasper would take all kinds of hissy fits. No, they wouldn't care. I'm in my acceptance mode, as I call it."

"I can't accept that," Jory said stubbornly.

"Which part?" Justine said testily.

"The whole thing. If they knew you were ill, they'd come here. I'm certain of it."

"Not ill, dying, Marjory. Do you think I want them to see me looking like this? It bothers me that you're seeing me, but you and I became friends. We are, aren't we?" she asked.

"Of course we are. I'm here, that should prove something to you."

"I guess I wanted to hear you say it out loud. You are my only tie to the past. As much as we dying people say we don't care about things past, we do. We all lie. I need a bit of rest now. You talk to me, tell me all about Ross and his father, but first pour me a double shot of whiskey. No ice."

"Are you allowed to have it?"

"No, but don't let that stop you from pouring it."

Jory worked a smile onto her face. She poured generously, adding the same amount of whiskey to her own glass. She grinned. "I see us getting tanked here, Justine."

"When I can manage it, I usually have three of these. Knocks me right out. Now talk. Wait, do you have any cigarettes?"

Jory opened her purse. "You aren't allowed to have these either, are you?"

"No, but don't let that stop you from lighting it for me. Give me the whole pack and the ashtray." Jory shook her head, but handed over the cigarettes and ashtray. "Now, start," Justine ordered.

Jory threw her hands in the air. "There's not that much to tell, Justine. Ross and Woo have three offices now, in Brewster, Paoli, and Germantown. Jasper still works for them. I sent you the article that was in the paper extolling their virtues and low rates. Jasper moved to Paoli. He sold your house in Society Hill, and Ross sold his. I really don't know where they live now."

Justine puffed at the cigarette, coughed, then sputtered as she gulped at her whiskey. "How did he take your dust-off?"

"Well, he wrote me one letter, and I sent it back unopened. For a long time I thought I loved him. I wanted . . . I guess what I was trying to do was recapture the past, trying to see if I could turn the clock back and make things work the right way. It was foolish on my part. I cared for him. I have this friend who is a psychiatrist, whom I talk to and have coffee with when things trouble me. He helped me see that even though I said I didn't blame Ross for my inability to have children, I was blaming him. What it boiled down to Justine was, I was a green, inexperienced kid who knew diddly about sex and things like protection. Ross, a young man of twenty-five, should have known to use a condom. I had no prenatal care. When Ross came back into my life, I took everything he offered and was punishing him. Not marrying him, not giving in, was my way of digging in the knife. Payback time, Justine. You should understand that it's not nice, but I did it. I probably would have buckled if I didn't have my revenge. I know that's wrong, I knew it all along, but it was something I had to do for me. It was wrong of him too, Justine. I can't have children. I wanted children so bad. A woman isn't a woman unless she has a child. Seymour says that isn't true, but it's true for me. I'm not whole. I want to be whole. I need to be whole and I can't be. Not ever.

"Ross said he'd marry me anyway. The key word here is *anyway*. I got that secondhand from Pete. I believe in my heart that Ross knew Woo and I had . . . something. He picked just the right moment to tell Woo he was going to marry me. Pete was vulnerable, grateful to Ross for all he'd done for him. It was the first day Pete returned to work. In fact he stood me up to have dinner with Ross. Ross didn't care about his and Pete's friendship, but Pete cared. He didn't tell Ross about us, and chose Ross over me. I could have loved Pete, Justine. For a long time I told myself he broke my heart. I threw myself into the magazine and worked twenty hours a day just so I wouldn't have time to think about either Ross or Pete. I'll say one thing, though, Justine, Pete was great in the sack."

Justine whooped with delight. "Tell me!"

Jory told her. Both women giggled like schoolgirls.

Justine held out her glass. Jory filled it. They fired up cigarettes. "Tell me about Griffin Ballon," Jory said.

"Ah. Now, there's a man." Justine sighed. "He's an international banker who just happens to be an attorney. He's thirty-seven and a widower with three children. His wife died five years ago giving birth to his youngest son. He's been handling my affairs, and we became good friends. He's sinfully rich and sinfully handsome. He travels all over the world. He was supposed to be here for your arrival, but he was called to Hong Kong three days ago. We always spend the holidays together. The children think of me as their grandmother. He's going to try and make it back before you leave. He's taken the children with him. I'm going to miss them this year. But you're here so it won't be too lonely." She crooked her finger for Jory to lean closer. "This man is your destiny, Marjory. I feel it here," Justine said, thumping her fragile chest.

Jory flushed. "We don't even know one another, Justine."

"I've told him every single thing I know about you. I've shared your letters with him. He knows about Ross and Pete. *Everything*, Marjory. I didn't spare myself either when I was telling tales. He's warm, compassionate, and understanding. He's a wonderful father, and I would imagine he was a wonderful husband. He loved his wife dearly. He wasn't born to wealth, he's earned what he has. He reads *Serendipity* from cover to cover. I caught him staring at your picture, the one inside where it says you're the publisher. He said, after thirty or so minutes of careful study, that your face was full of character, vulnerability, and life. Then he said, and this is a direct quote: 'I think this young woman is someone I want to meet and get to know.' Well, I jumped right on that statement and proceeded to tell him all about you. Every time he calls or comes out here, he asks for the latest information on you. He's already in love with you, even if he doesn't know it."

"I don't suppose you have a picture of him around, do you?"

"They're all over the place. I wanted to make sure you saw them," Justine said. "The best one is on the mantel, with his children."

Jory carried the framed photograph back to the chair she'd been sitting in. "Oooh, he's handsome. You weren't kidding, Justine. The children are beautiful. My destiny, eh? You're sure of that, Justine?"

"Just as sure as I know I'm going to die. I said that deliberately, Marjory, to make you believe me. By the time you leave here I think you're going to feel the same way he does. He travels to America every six weeks or so. Sometimes he leaves the little one with me. The two oldest are in school and have a nanny. Now, I think it's time you went into my drawing room to see my Christmas tree. I want your opinion on it. I'm sure it's all lit up. Run along, through the double doors and down the corridor to the first door on the left. I expect you to be effusive in your compliments."

Jory opened the door of the drawing room and gaped at the most magnificent Christmas tree she'd ever seen in her life. It was so fragrant she swayed dizzily. She tried to take it in all at once as something about the room teased at her memory. She walked around the room staring at the fireplace, at the comfortable chairs and sofa. The lighting seemed to be the same, the desk in the same place, the wicker basket holding the logs. It was her living room in Chestnut Hill.

Piles and piles of presents were everywhere, on the tables, on the mantel, in the corners and along the walls. The space under the tree was piled high, right up to the branches. She walked over to the tree to examine the fine ornaments she knew must have cost a fortune. She saw it then, right in front of the tree and hanging on a piece of green yarn. Her hand flew to her mouth to stifle the sound she thought might carry out to Justine in the parlor. Ross's wreath, the one he'd made that year so long ago. She carefully untied the string and carried it back to the parlor. She dangled it in front of Justine. "Where did you get this?"

"Where do you think? I had Clarence go to your house and steal it. He didn't want to do it, but he did because he knew it was important to me."

"Shouldn't I be saying, too much, too little, too late?" Jory cried, blinking away her tears.

"Probably."

"You're a phony, a fake, Justine," Jory said, wiping at her tears.

"That too," Justine said, blowing her nose.

"Ross is getting married on New Year's Day."

Justine struggled to a sitting position. "No!"

"Don't give me that, Justine. You probably knew before I did. He's marrying Lena Davis."

"So she finally got him. I didn't know, Jory, I swear I didn't."

"Maybe you should call him and wish him well."

"Maybe I should do a lot of things. Right now I have to concentrate on dying," Justine said sourly.

"Damn you, Justine, you're making me cry," Jory blubbered.

"In that case it's time for bed. You've had a long trip. I'll have the cook bring you up some hot cocoa and a nice sandwich. We'll talk again in the morning," Justine said wearily. "My houseman will see you to your room and then carry me to my chair. I have one of those fancy rail things that carries me to the second floor. Griffin insisted I have it installed. Such a wonderful man," Justine said, her head rolling in fatigue.

In her room, Jory found herself gasping in delight. It was obvious a lot of time and effort had gone into making the room comfortable for her. She was tempted, but only for a moment, to take a running leap onto the four-poster bed that required a step stool to get into it. Instead she stepped on the stool and boosted her rear end until she was sitting on the side. "Ahhhh," she murmured, "this will guarantee a good night's sleep." She flopped backward only to slide off the bed a moment later.

This room was no accident. She knew in her gut it had been decorated just for her. She could smell the newness in the window hangings, and some of the packing creases were still in the sheer curtains beneath the champagne-colored satin draperies. Somewhere, someplace, she'd seen a room almost identical to this one. And then she remembered a back issue of *Serendipity*, from which she had copied the bedroom right down to the wheat-colored carpet and burnt-orange throw pillows. She sat down in a light oak rocking chair that was so comfortable she knew she could fall asleep in it. She got up immediately to walk around the cozy room. The fire burned brightly in a huge fireplace whose hearth contained a wicker basket of logs and a poinsettia plant so large it looked like a tree.

Christmas in Switzerland.

Was this what the Swiss called a chalet? Tomorrow she would have to ask Justine. Tomorrow she was going to talk to Justine about a lot of things, providing her ex-mother-in-law was up to it.

Jory looked around for her bags and was stunned to see them in the corner, her clothes in the closets and dresser drawers, which were slightly ajar. She fished out a warm flannel nightgown and stripped off her clothes in front of the fire. The elegant champagne coverlet had been turned down earlier, the Swiss lace trailing down the sides of the bed. The sheets and pillow slips had the same exquisite lace as the coverlet. The fluffy pillows beckoned her.

Jory walked past the fireplace and would have had to be blind not to see the four pictures of Griffin Ballon on the mantel. She smiled and saluted the unknown banker as she made her way into a bathroom that left her speechless. Everything was marble and gold-plated. It was also carpeted and as big as her bedroom in

Chestnut Hill. The tub was huge, capable of holding at least three people, and sunken. A shower and a bidet took up one corner next to a matching commode. Huge, thick, bright orange towels were stacked on marble shelves and hanging on what looked like gold towel racks. A stereo system was built into one of the marble walls along with a recessed phone unit. An intercom was next to the phone. The marble vanity was long, taking up one entire wall with three basins. In each corner there were luscious poinsettias, and underneath each of the Christmas plants were pictures of Griffin Ballon. Jory hooted with laughter. She was still laughing when she finished brushing her teeth. "I'm intrigued, Griffin Ballon," she said, swiping at one of the pictures with her toothbrush. "Definitely intrigued."

Jory turned off the light and eyed the four-poster from her position in the bathroom doorway. She dug her toes into the swirl of carpet as she prepared to do what she'd wanted to do since entering the bedroom—leap on the bed. She flexed her knees, took a deep breath, ran across the room and, her arms outstretched for leverage, leaped on the bed. "I did it," she giggled as she snuggled down beneath the fragrant, scented sheets. She was asleep in minutes, her feet curled around the two hot-water bottles the houseman had placed under her covers earlier.

Jory woke to muted sounds in her room. She cracked one eye open to see one of the maids replenishing the fire. She snuggled deeper into the covers. "What time is it?" she called to the maid.

"Nine o'clock, miss. Would you like me to draw your bath?"

"No, I'll take a shower. Is Mrs. Lan—Miss Pullet awake yet?"

"No, miss, she doesn't come down till noon. Would you like breakfast served here in your room or in the dining room?"

"Downstairs will be fine," Jory said. "How is Miss Pullet this morning?"

"She's resting. She rises quite early, has her coffee, and reads the newspaper. She does seem to be in better spirits today than she was yesterday. Miss, this really isn't my place to be telling you, but Miss Pullet was very concerned about this bedroom. She had decorators come all the way out here almost every day, making sure this room was just like a picture she had cut from a book. She had the bathroom redone too. Do you like it?"

"It's beautiful. I'll be sure to tell her how gorgeous it is, and I won't say you said anything. It must have cost a fortune."

"Yes, miss, it did. I heard the decorator talking prices, and Miss Pullet said she didn't care how much it cost. She said the person—meaning you, miss—who was to sleep here, was very special."

"She said that?" Jory exclaimed.

"Yes, miss, she did. Miss Pullet talks about you all the time. The staff has been anxiously waiting for your visit. Miss Pullet thinks the world of you, miss. When she received your letter saying you were coming, she got herself so worked up we had to call the doctor to quiet her down. She told Justin—that's the houseman—that she regards you as a daughter. It's such a pity she never had any children. She does love Mr. Ballon's young ones. A proper granny she is to those children. Will there be anything else, miss?"

"Ah, yes, one little thing." Jory crooked her finger for the maid to come closer to her bed. "Is Mr. Ballon everything Jus—Miss Pullet says he is?"

The maid smiled. "And more. Miss Pullet has it in her mind that you two are a perfect match. That's all they talk about when he comes for dinner. You couldn't do better than Mr. Ballon, miss," the maid said, winking at her. "He's rich, but he's nice too. He always has a kind word for the staff, and he tips us to give extra attention to Miss Pullet. We fuss about her anyway, and none of us want to take his tips, but he insists. It's a pleasure to work here. Miss Pullet is very good and kind to everyone, and she does adore Mr. Ballon's children. Will there be anything else, miss?" the maid said, nervously looking at her watch.

"No, no, I'll get up now and be down for breakfast in a bit."

In the bathroom, Jory turned Griffin Ballon's pictures facedown before she stripped off her nightgown. Her body felt flushed when she stepped into the shower. She tried not to think about Griffon Ballon and all the wonderful things she'd heard about him. Instead she fixed her thoughts on Justine and the things the maid had said. Tears mingled with the dripping water from the shower.

How had all this happened, all the wonderful things that happened during the past seven years?

Justine was her benefactor, a surrogate mother of sorts, and her friend. She'd come to depend on Justine, calling her at all hours of the day and night for advice, writing her long letters, confiding in her, and now, just as she was making a success of things, Justine was dying and there wasn't anything she could do about it.

Justine referred to herself as a tough old broad, by which, Jory supposed, she meant to say she could handle anything, even death. Damn it, she liked Justine. More than liked her. Liking her had nothing to do with the help Justine had given over the years. She damn well genuinely liked the older woman, and she would grieve when she passed on.

Jory stepped from the shower to wrap one of the huge orange towels about her body. The room was full of steam, warm and cozy. She looked at the foggy mirror. Her index finger traced a heart and then the name Jory. She added an arrow and a giant question mark. She smiled ruefully, wondering if she would go through life alone or with someone who would love her unconditionally.

In her room she dressed quickly in warm, wool slacks and a bright cherry-colored sweater with reindeer prancing across the neckline and shoulders. She felt cheerful as she marched down the steps to the first floor, where she consumed an enormous breakfast of griddle cakes, scrambled eggs, and succulent pink ham. While she sipped at her third cup of coffee and smoked her second cigarette, she took the time to look around the dining room. The furniture was warm, rich, and comfortable. The paintings on the wall were American. Over the buffet a scene of Philadelphia in the early twenties. On the two small walls were pictures of the Cricket Club and the main street in Chestnut Hill. On the largest wall was a very small drawing that stood out starkly. Jory stared at it, certain one of Griffin Ballon's children had done it and Justine had hung it out of respect to her banker friend.

It was a crude drawing, but handsomely matted and framed. Jory walked over to stare at the small picture. In pleasing script the word "Home" was centered over the picture. In the bottom right-hand corner were the initials E.P. E.P.? Ethel Pullet, of course. One didn't need to be a Philadelphia lawyer to figure out what *this* was. Justine's home when she was a child. Jory's eyes burned as she stared at the rundown shanty with rags stuck in the broken window, with strips of wood nailed in between the slats. The front door wasn't a front door at all, but more like a slab of wood. Jory found herself biting down on her knuckles to prevent herself from crying. She continued to stare at the shack through a misty haze, at a plume of smoke curling upward, at the arthritic tree in the middle of a scraggly yard full of old tires, rusty wheels, and empty wooden boxes. In small letters the word "toys" was printed. Jory bit down harder on her knuckles when she concentrated on a stick figure dressed in baggy clothes, walking in a crab crouch, a long-necked bottle in his hands, up the crooked, cracked walkway to the door that wasn't a door. Justine's father, a whiskey bottle in his hand.

Jory ran from the room, down the corridor to the room that held the Christmas tree, taking long, gasping breaths. She sat down, her legs trembling and threatening to go out from under her, on a sofa that was like her own at home and just as comfortable. She lit a cigarette with shaking hands, blowing a gusty plume of smoke toward the Christmas tree.

"I suppose you want an explanation of that picture," Justine said fretfully as the houseman carefully lowered her into a deep, comfortable armchair with an attached ottoman.

"No, no, not at all," Jory said quietly. "Justine, you don't owe me any explanations about anything. How are you this morning? The maid said you didn't come downstairs till noon. Are you up to this? I have this feeling my visit is going to tax your strength. I don't want that, Justine. I can just as easily come upstairs and talk to you in your room."

"I want to be here. I had the tree put up early so I could spend my time in this room just staring at it. My time is . . . uncertain, and I guess I want to soak up as much as I can before I . . . go to that other place."

Jory was off the sofa faster than a shot and on her knees next to Justine's chair. She was crying, openly, making no effort to staunch her flow of tears. "It's not right. You should have many more years ahead of you. You . . . what will I do without you? You were always there for me . . . you were my support, my cushion. These past seven years were only possible because of you," Jory wailed.

"I knew you were going to bawl. Now stop it before I start. I'm just going . . . somewhere else. I'll be watching over you, and so will Griffin if you give him half a chance. Just because I'm . . . not here physically, doesn't mean you're going to fold up." Justine's voice weakened and then grew stronger when she asked for a cigarette. "When this is finished, light me another one," Justine grumbled. "While I smoke them, tell me about the magazine. How'd you like your room?"

"Justine, it's beautiful. It's from the July issue two years ago, right?" Justine nodded proudly. "Should I be calling you Ethel or Mrs. Pullet?"

"Hell no," Justine sputtered around the smoke coming out her mouth.

Jory hugged her knees, her eyes on Justine's thin face. How bright her eyes were, how very curious. "Well, here goes. The first two years were a living nightmare. I screwed up things so badly I wanted to quit, but Clarence wouldn't let me. I wasted money, dumped magazines, hired a few wrong people, believed other people when I shouldn't have, got taken to court by several of our advertisers. Whatever could go wrong, went wrong. I didn't really get my feet wet until the third year. Out of that year I put out four really good issues. I hired this all-female marketing firm to help me, and Justine, this group of gals was on the money. They were worth every penny I paid them.

"I couldn't get credit, as you know. A woman asking for vast sums of money made me a joke in the bankers' eyes. If you hadn't kept pouring money into the magazine, I could never have stuck it out."

"I set it all up for you, why did you even bother trying it on your own? I told you what would happen. I wanted to spare you the humiliation, the unfairness from all those damn, stuffy, holier-than-thou bankers," Justine said in her fragile, raspy voice.

Jory shrugged. "I had to try it on my own, Justine. I tried to view it as a challenge, and it was, believe me."

"What you did, Marjory, was to integrate pragmatism with inspiration, worldly toughness, hopefully garnered from me, and mixed it all with intellectual creativity. Then you took off the training wheels and went it alone. I wish I could say these are my words, but they aren't. It's Griffin's summary of your progress. As I told you, he's watched your career very carefully. Many times he itched to call you and tell you what you were doing wrong, but of course he couldn't do that. Instead, he listened and believed me when I told him you'd correct your mistake in the next issue, and by God, I was right. For a while there I think both of us viewed ourselves as the ultimate in fairy godparents. I wish you could have seen Griffin's face when he finally realized you had it all under control. We toasted you, Marjory, with the finest wine. Griffin said you'd reached a significant new level of personal advancement, where you can, possibly for the first time, set your own terms for your own life. We were so proud as we watched you seize that one moment and move boldly into new directions, directions that are important to you. He said you'd never rest on your laurels, and he was right."

A tear slipped from Justine's eye. "I feel like your accomplishments are mine. I know that's silly, but in many ways you're like me. The only difference is, you did things right, whereas I did it all wrong. I've lived with that, but I don't want you to have to do that."

"Justine, why me? Everytime I asked you why you've been so good to me, you poo-pooed away my questions. You didn't know me. Not really. During Ross's and my brief marriage, I think we spoke at the most, three times. Why?"

Justine puffed on her cigarette. "I hated what Ross did to you. Absolutely hated it. I saw Jasper in him all over again. What you did took guts, real guts. You went off on your own and you made a life for yourself, something I didn't have the nerve to do. You didn't whine and you didn't cry. I admire that. In your own way, you were tougher than all of us. I knew you loved Ross, just the way I once loved Jasper, but it was all one-sided. Do you know, Marjory, the day I gave birth to Ross, Jasper had a golf date. I begged him to stay with me because I was scared out of my wits, but he said he couldn't let his partners down. Ross was born at ten-thirty in the morning. Jasper showed up at the hospital, the one his parents endowed, at nine o'clock that night. He didn't go to the nursery to see Ross. He said, and this is a direct quote, 'It's good you delivered a boy, Justine, otherwise I wouldn't be able to hold up my head at the club.' I was in the hospital for ten days. They kept you a long time in those days. He never came back, and none of his friends, supposedly our friends, came to see me. No one gave me a baby gift. I took Ross home in a taxi. In a *taxi*, Marjory. When it was time for him to be christened, I had to *pay* the gardener and cook to be godparents. There was no celebration or anything like that. We went to the church and came home. I was so . . . ashamed. I don't think I ever got over that."

"Where was Jasper then?" Jory whispered.

"He said he was playing golf in some club tournament. I moved out of the bedroom, and that was the end of our marriage."

"Justine, that's so sad," Jory said with a catch in her voice.

"Yes, at that time it was. I was your age, possibly a year older, with no one to talk to, no one to help me over the hurdles. Light me another cigarette, Marjory."

"This is your third one, Justine," Jory said, sticking the cigarette between her lips. "I bet . . . Griffin doesn't do this for you."

"Oh yes he does!" Justine sputtered. "Of course he gives me the same lectures about it not being good for me." She snorted. "I'm at the end of the road, so it doesn't matter what I do now. My damn fool doctor even lights them for me. Why are we talking about this? We should be talking about Griffin and sugar plums and stuff like that."

"That's fine with me, but before we do that, let's talk about that picture in the dining room."

"It was just like that. Maybe worse. When the realtor brought me out here to show me this property, I fell in love with it and bought it on the spot. For all the wrong reasons of course, but that was when I first got here. The lawn was as green as money. I liked that. The sky at night was speckled with stars that reminded me of diamonds. The trees shading the front and back of the house reminded me of canopies. Compared to that stick of a tree at the shanty, this was like paradise. The house is stone, no place to stuff rags or boards. The windows will last hundreds of years. This house was . . . is the end of the road for me. Of course I didn't know that at the time. Gradually I came to view it differently, but not until I sketched that awful picture in the dining room. Grass wouldn't grow back there by the shanty. When it snows here, it's beautiful. Back there it was ugly and so very cold. I did my best to try and make it right before I left, but I was probably too late. I tell myself I tried and that's the important thing. Would you like me to call Griffin so you can talk to him?"

"No!" The single word exploded from Jory's mouth.

Justine smiled. "Talk to me about Pete and Ross," she said, "but first ring for the cook and ask for tea. When she brings it, lace it with brandy."

Jory did as ordered. When Justine was sipping at the tea and puffing on her fourth cigarette, Jory cleared her throat. "I rather thought . . . expected that Ross and Pete would fight over me. I wanted to . . . oh, hell, I don't know what I wanted. They just accepted my decision. Both of them. Of course, with Pete . . . it was different, he rejected me to retain his friendship with Ross. I cried buckets over that. I didn't care about his handicap, but he did, and that's understandable. I met them in Wanamaker's when I was doing some Christmas shopping. I turned around and there they were with their fiancées. They reminded me of two sets of Bobbsey twins. Everyone was embarrassed. Ross more or less looked through me, if that's possible. Pete . . . Pete just stared at me. I thought I saw a spark of something, but then maybe that was just my imagination. I had this crazy urge to hug Pete and to berate Ross at the same time. I didn't do it, but now I wish I had. I guess I had to go through all that to get to this place in time. The past is past and there's no going back. It just seems so . . . untidy, like there are loose ends that will never be cut off or tied up."

"If you had settled for one or the other of them, you wouldn't be happy, Marjory. You need someone who will accept you for who and what you are, and what you can be down the road. You would have stagnated with Ross or Pete. You would have become a lawyer's wife doing all the things that little circle of wives do. Charity work, ceramics classes, and making dinner parties and crap like that. That's not to say there's anything wrong with charity work and ceramics, but there's more to life. Each of us needs to be his or her own person. Both Pete and Ross, in the end, would have made you extensions of themselves, and I think in your heart you knew that. It's done, Marjory, don't look back."

"The wedding—"

"Their wedding. It has nothing to do with you. You're half a world away. Let's view it as phase three of your life. Hmmm, this tea is good. Makes me feel warm all over. That's what I hate the most, not being able to keep warm. I don't have much time, Marjory."

Jory set her cup on the end table. "How much time, Justine?" she whispered.

"I wish I could say months, but I can't. Days, hours . . . whenever He decides He wants me. Why He wants me at all is beyond me. I . . . I thought . . . actually, I'm kind of ready, but there are . . . I guess I'm afraid. No one knows what it's like up there or . . . *down* there. I remember my Sunday school teacher telling all us little children about Hellfire and brimstone. I'm so afraid, Marjory. If there was someone to hold my hand, to take me *there* . . . What do you think it's like?"

Jory reached for Justine's hand, and clasped it tightly in her own. Her mind raced as she tried to remember an article she'd wanted to publish, but hadn't because the editorial board said it was just too bizarre.

A young woman had walked into the office one day and had asked for her personally. She'd said she was in a car crash where three other people died. She herself had been taken to the hospital and operated on immediately. She swore she left her body, had hovered overhead watching the operating procedures, heard the doctors and the nurses say she was dead. She said she floated overhead for several seconds, felt hands all around her, and saw a beautiful white light with voices telling her it wasn't time for her to come to *them.* Then the woman heard one of the doctors say, "She has a pulse. We aren't losing her." The next thing she knew, she was back in her body, but she could still see beautiful white light and all these gentle faces who were smiling, including her grandparents and a very dear aunt and uncle.

Jory chose her words carefully. "I believe there is a place we all go after death. I like to think of it as a paradise with beautiful gardens, warm sunshine. It's a place that's free of pain, hatred, and greed. It's a place that's peaceful, where all those who've gone before wait to welcome you. I . . . When you cross over to that place, your mother and father will be waiting for you, their hands outstretched to bring you forward. Think about how nice it will be when you finally get to see your parents again. Hold on to that thought, Justine. Imagine you can hear your mother calling your name, imagine her arms outstretched to take you in her arms. Imagine how warm and wonderful you're going to feel. And then . . ."

"Yes, yes, then what?" Justine fretted.

"Then you begin your new life and prepare to . . . to welcome the rest of us when it's our time. If you happen to . . . to see my mother, will you tell her you stepped in and, you know, kind of made things easier for me? Tell her I wouldn't have screwed up my life if she was around. If you see Daddy, tell him I'm living in the house, and about the dogs and . . . everything. Oh Justine, I can't . . . I don't want you to . . ." She cried, her head against Justine's thin chest. She felt herself being cradled and cuddled the way her mother must have held her when she was little.

Both women cried for the would haves, the could haves, the should haves.

A long time later Justine said, "What if I go to Hell, then what?"

She sounded so serious, Jory raised her head to blow her nose lustily into a wad of tissue. "Then you're on your own, because I don't know anything about Hell. Furthermore I don't think there is such a place. I believe Hell is right here on earth, and we're living in it until the day we die. God loves us, why would He send us to a place like Hell? God forgives, Justine."

Justine sighed. "I feel better now that we've had this little talk. I think it's time to move out of this smoke-filled room so the housekeeper can air it out. I think you should bundle up and go for a walk while I take a nap. This is Christmas Eve, Marjory.

Maybe Griffin will call to wish us both a Merry Christmas." She rang the bell for the houseman.

Jory leaned down to kiss Justine on the cheek. Justine reached for her. "I'm so very fond of you, Marjory. I feel like you're my daughter in many ways. My only regret is I didn't stand in for your mother sooner. Run along, child, and get some color in your cheeks. And if it's all the same to you, Marjory, I'd like to forego that discussion on Ethel Pullet. Do you mind? I think you have it all anyway." Jory nodded.

Jory waited until Justine was settled in front of the fire in the large parlor before she dressed for the walk outdoors.

It was a winter wonderland, the evergreens graceful and feathery, with their tips crusted with sparkly white snow. Shoveled paths were everywhere, to the four-car garage, to the potting shed, to the utility shed, and a path that meandered into the field and beyond. She chose to follow it, careful of her footing. There was old snow and new snow piled along both sides of the path. The light snow that had fallen during the night had been swept to the side. She wondered why.

How clear the air was, how fresh and sharp. So sharp she felt like a knife was going down her throat every time she took a deep breath. She covered her mouth with her gloved hand and walked with her head bent. When she saw it, she knew what it was immediately. Justine's final resting place. If she'd had any doubts, the gravestone comfirmed that this indeed was a grave, a rectangle devoid of snow, the frozen earth piled on the side. Panic rushed through her as she backed up a step and then another, her eyes on the simple stone. ETHEL PULLET. There were no dates and no other chiseled markings.

If there was such a thing as a perfect final resting place, then this plot beneath the aged tree was it. In the spring when the old tree was dressed in its finery, the huge limbs would cast just enough shade, just enough dappled sunshine. How like Justine to prepare this place. Who would make the final procession out here? The servants, Griffin Ballon and perhaps his children. Herself, if she was notified in time. Perhaps Clarence and his wife Tillie.

She cried, great, heartrending sobs that echoed in the cold, freezing air.

Days, not months, was what Justine said. She wondered where the coffin was. In the garage, the potting shed, the basement? Or would they have to bring it out from town? Justine had once said that she didn't want to be embalmed. "I just want to go into the ground the way I am, no services, no mourning, no *nothing*." Did she make her wishes known to her staff, to Griffin Ballon? Who would see to it?

The walk back to the house was torture. It seemed to Jory that she would snap in two, that's how cold and brittle she felt. Her eyes were half closed with frozen tears on her lashes. She tried to run but she couldn't, so she trudged on, her heart thumping in her chest, not from exertion, but from sorrow.

Upstairs in her room she sat down on the hearth, her arms stretched toward the fire. Tears trickled down her cheeks. From time to time she wiped at them with the sleeve of her sweater.

The moment Jory felt warm enough to stir herself, she reached for the phone, dialed the operator, and placed a call to the States. Clarence picked up the phone on the third ring. She started to cry the moment she heard his voice. Between her sobs, she told the old man Justine's condition and about the grave under the tree.

"There's a time to live and a time to die, Miss Jory, and this is Mrs. Landers's time. She's ready, she told me so in her last letter. Death is hardest on those left behind. Be sure to wish her a Merry Christmas from Tillie and me."

"I did that already, Clarence. This place is beautiful. She must have been very happy here until she got sick. Why didn't you tell me you stole Ross's Christmas decoration?"

"She told me not to tell you. I'm sorry about that, Miss Ryan. Are you upset with me?"

"Of course not. If you'd asked me, I would have given it to you."

The old man chuckled. "I know that and you know that, but Mrs. Landers wanted me to *steal* it. I guess it was important to her. I couldn't say no."

"Of course you couldn't. How are the dogs, Clarence?"

"Fine. They sleep on the pile of laundry you left on the floor in your room. Tillie says they feel closer to you if they're around your things. They're in the kitchen with her now. She's making the stuffing for the turkey. Mr. Ross called here last night asking for you, Miss Ryan."

"Ross called! What did he want?"

"He didn't say. I told him you went away for the holidays and wouldn't be back till after New Year's. I told him I'd leave a message for you." A sour note crept into Clarence's voice. "Maybe he's getting prenuptial jitters."

"Maybe he wanted Justine's address, although it's a little late to invite her to his wedding. Do you think I should call him, Clarence?"

"Whatever it was, it didn't sound important. Wouldn't he have said it was important and he needed to get in touch with you if it was? All he said was to say he called. That means no, I don't think you should call him, leastways, not from Mrs. Landers's house."

"You're right, Clarence. Did anyone else call? Did anything come in the mail?"

Clarence made a funny sound in his throat. "You haven't been gone that long, Miss Ryan. The mail hasn't come yet today, and no one else called. You told everyone you were going away, so who would call?"

"The Pope, Gary Cooper." Jory laughed. "Have a wonderful holiday and hug the dogs for me."

"The same to you, Miss Ryan."

Jory replaced the phone on the little table by the chaise longue. She curled up and was asleep the moment her eyes closed.

The days following Christmas passed quietly and uneventfully. It seemed to Jory that Justine grew weaker with each passing day. Justine slept more, dozed as she read to her, often sleeping through her meals, other times barely touching the delectable food.

On New Year's Eve as the houseman was carrying Justine to her room she turned and in a voice that was hardly audible said, "Would you mind staying with me until I fall asleep? If I try, we might be able to see in the new year together."

Jory was reading from a popular novel at ten o'clock when Justine opened her eyes and said, "Hold my hand, Jory."

Jory laid aside the book, her eyes filled with fear. She reached for Justine's hands, holding them tight.

"I see them, Jory, just like you said. Ohhh, it looks so pretty. I never saw a light like this. Let go. Mama, it's me, Ethel. Mama, do you forgive me? I'm coming, Mama. Let me go, let me go. Mama, wait for me. I'm coming, I'm coming."

Jory let go of Justine's hands. She bit down on her lower lip so hard she tasted her own blood.

Justine Landers was buried beneath the huge tree amid a flurry of light snow on New Year's Day. The staff, the doctor who treated Justine, and Jory were the only ones in attendance. There was no minister, no prayer.

They walked single file back to the house, where a light lunch was served for the doctor's benefit. He left immediately afterward.

Upstairs, Jory packed her bags for the return trip home. Twice she tried to reach Griffin Ballon from the different numbers in Justine's address book, but was unsuccessful. Finally, in desperation, she sat down and wrote him a note, explaining as best she could what had happened. She signed her name, slid the letter into an envelope, and handed it to the housekeeper. "When Mr. Ballon arrives, please see that he gets this letter."

Jory arrived home the following day. Together, she and Clarence cried in each other's arms until there were no tears left in either of them.

"She wouldn't want this," Clarence said.

"No, she wouldn't. She made me promise not to tell Ross or Jasper."

"Are you going to keep that promise?"

"Yes. Oh, Clarence, I don't know if I can do it alone. Knowing she was in the wings ready to help made me feel confident. What if I flub up?"

"You won't. I think she hung on until she knew you were flying on your own. That's just my opinion."

Jory's shoulders straightened. "We'll do our best, and if that isn't good enough, then we'll try harder. How does that sound?"

"Sounds good, Miss Ryan."

"It does, doesn't it?" Jory smiled.

Three months later, on a balmy day in March, Jory leaned back in her chair and took a deep breath. April's issue had just been put to bed, and she was looking at articles for May. She'd been working around the clock and was exhausted. She could hardly wait to go home, shower, and crash on the sofa with a nice glass of wine. Her reward for another issue well done.

The phone on her desk buzzed to life. For a moment she was tempted to ignore it, but she didn't. "Yes?"

"Miss Ryan, there's a gentleman here to see you." Her secretary's voice dropped several octaves. She whispered, "This is one *very* handsome man. Put on your lipstick. I told him you'd be right out."

"Who is it?" Jory said, reaching in her drawer for her compact and lipstick. She was slipping her feet into her shoes at the same time.

"He won't say. A mystery man I guess. Hurry up, Miss Ryan, before he leaves."

She hurried, her heart fluttering in her chest. She walked across her office, opened the door and stared.

"Miss Ryan, I'm Griffin Ballon, and these are my children. We, ah, we were wondering if you'd care to have dinner with us."

He's your destiny, Marjory. "I'd like that very much, Mr. Ballon."

"Yippee," the littlest Ballon said.

"Great," the middle Ballon said.

"Super," the oldest Ballon child said with a wicked grin.

"Destiny," the senior Ballon said with a crinkly smile that warmed the entire room.

Thank you, Justine, thankyouthankyouthankyou.

Epilogue

It was the middle of May before Jory made the trip to Paoli with the box Griffin Ballon had turned over to her. "Justine said you'll know what to do with it." The only problem was, she didn't know what to do with it. For days she'd stared at the contents of the box, taking them out, putting them back till she thought she would wear them out. No matter where she put the box, no matter how she tried to avoid it, it was always there. Now, today, it was sitting on the front seat of the car with her.

She had no appointment with Ross, but felt he would see her. If necessary she was prepared to wait all day until the close of business hours to hand it over. Even now, at this, the eleventh hour, she didn't know if she was doing the right thing or not.

Jory opened the door, the box under her arm. Her head high, she walked up to the receptionist and announced herself. "I can wait if Mr. Landers is busy."

"He just came in from court. Have a seat and I'm sure he'll be with you in a minute." Jory sat down primly, the box on her lap. The receptionist was as good as her word. Ross came out of his office, his arms outstretched.

"Jory! What a wonderful surprise! It's good to see you! What brings you to Paoli? Let's go into my office. Can I get you something, coffee, a soft drink?"

"No thanks, Ross. I brought something for you. But before I give it to you, I'm not sure . . . what I mean is . . . I don't know what I mean," she said, thrusting the box at him. She sat down and folded her hands primly in her lap.

"What is it?" Ross asked suspiciously.

"Open it," Jory said.

Ross opened the box. One by one he lifted out the articles, a strange look on his face. "I don't understand."

"What is it you don't understand, Ross?" Jory asked quietly.

"Who does this belong to? I know the wreath is the one we made a long time ago, but what's this other stuff?"

"This other *stuff,* as you call it, is yours. They're your things kept by the woman you said didn't care about you. That same woman had Clarence steal the wreath from my attic so she could hang it on her Christmas tree. The little white outfit is your christening outfit. The blue blanket is the one your mother carried you home from the hospital in. *In a taxi.* That little silver tinkly thing is your first rattle. Those are your first shoes, bronzed and all. Of course, you recognize all those pictures. They're you at every stage of your life. The only thing missing is your wedding picture. Well, I've taken up enough of your time. I have to get back to town," Jory said, getting up.

"Wait just a damn minute. Not so fast, Miss Ryan. Where did you get these?"

"A man gave them to me. Since they don't belong to me, I brought them here where they do belong."

"My mother gave these to a man who gave them to you. Why?"

"I don't know, Ross."

"What the hell am I supposed to do with this . . . *junk?*"

If she'd been standing anywhere but where she was, she might not have done it, but the temptation was so great, Jory's balled fist shot out, landing dead center on Ross's left eye. He toppled backward to land in his swivel chair. Dramatically, Jory dusted her hands to show what she thought of her impulsive action. "You damn well deserved that, Ross."

"Jesus Christ, Jory!" Ross howled.

Jasper and Woo took that moment to stick their respective heads out of a doorway, their mouths agape.

"Jasper, Pete," Jory said curtly.

"Jory, it's nice to see you again," Jasper said happily.

"Maybe *you* can tell your son what all those things in the box are. He called them junk. Are they junk, Jasper?"

Jasper came into the outer office and pawed through the contents, a look of revulsion on his face. Jory clenched her teeth and then her fists. She looked at Woo. "Well, Pete, it's your call, do you want to go for two?"

Woo held up both hands. "Whoa. Do you mind telling me what's going on here?"

"Let them tell you. I just came here to deliver a package. I'm relocating to the other side of the world."

"Huh?"

"I'm selling the magazine. I've just had the offer of a lifetime. I'd be a fool to turn it down. A very dear, dear friend made it all possible, so I'm in the process of relocating."

"Huh?" Woo said again.

"It's called destiny, gentlemen. Mine."